Patterson's sleeping habits were those of the hunter. His rifle was always placed so that the stock and buttplate lay against his stomach with the lock between his legs and the barrel protruding toward his feet. Placed thus, the gun could be brought into action at a moment's notice. Also, if the rifle were ever touched by anyone other than himself, he would be instantly aware of it.

Such was the case at predawn, the following morning, when Patterson felt the ever so slight movement of the weapon as it inched down his body. His eyes slitted open. An Indian was kneeling at his feet, working the gun slowly from between Patterson's drawn knees. Patterson kicked the man in the face with such force that he felt the toes of his foot snap as if they were broken. The Indian thrashed in the dust, holding his throat and gasping. Patterson was on him instantly, his knife flashing in the early morning light. Before the blade could fall, however, strong arms pinioned the woodsman from all sides.

Susan's eyes flashed open and her hand reached for her musket—it was gone. An Indian grinned into her astonished face, caressing the gun lovingly.

Ivy, lying across the clearing, began inching quietly toward the honeysuckle barrier nearby, but a strong hand wound itself in her hair and lifted her to her feet.

Judith looked wildly about; the entire camp was encircled by grinning Indians.

DON WRIGHT

TOR

A TOM DOHERTY ASSOCIATES BOOK

THE WOODSMAN

Copyright © 1984 by Donald K. Wright

Reprinted by arrangement with Jameson Books/Greenhill Publishers—Ottawa, Illinois

First TOR printing: May 1986

A TOR Book

Published by Tom Doherty Associates
49 West 24 Street
New York, N.Y. 10010

Cover art by David Wright

ISBN: 0-812-58989-0
CAN. ED.: 0-812-58990-4

Printed in the United States

0   9   8   7   6   5   4   3   2   1

Prologue

Joseph Patterson stepped off the Scottish tub that the captain of the vessel proudly referred to as a sailing ship. At seventeen Joseph was a lad with a dream.

He stood straight and tall as he surveyed the dirty little seaport town of New York. He did not like what he saw. After wading through the muddy streets from one end of the town to the other, studying the crude log structures, he took a room in a small, unkempt inn and spent the early part of the evening cleaning and reassembling his wheellock musket. The gun was ancient even then, the year of our Lord, 1714.

He ran his hand lovingly over the smooth, polished wood and read again with pride the worn but legible letters engraved along the top facet of the octagon-to-round barrel: "W. P. Patterson, 1578."

Raising the gun to his shoulder, he smiled fleetingly, for it fit him perfectly, as if custom-made to his specifications. But it wasn't. It had been built by his great-grandfather, who presented it to his son, and his son after him, until finally it had passed into Joseph's eager hands. He carefully laid the gun aside and dragged his heavy leather pack across the rough flooring of the room he was sharing with four others from his ship.

Methodically, he began spreading the contents of the pack proudly before him: forty small mirrors, ten hand axes, twenty butcher knives, an assortment of cheap silver armbands and bracelets, and a large canvas bag filled with packets of beads.

The wheellock and the few trade goods that adorned the rough pine planks were all that he owned in the world. They looked small, indeed, as he surveyed them in the light of the flickering candle. But they represented a beginning, and that was all he asked, a chance for freedom—freedom to succeed or fail by his own merit.

He breakfasted the next morning, seated alone. He ate hurriedly while watching the shaft of daylight that carved its way gently through the paneless window and cut through the gloomy interior of the room like a knife.

As the brightening shaft inched its way across the floor, Joseph wolfed down the food, eyeing the light as if he were in a race against time.

In truth that was exactly how he felt. In his youthful and ambitious hurry to plunge headlong into life, he felt that with each idle moment, the world was moving on without him, and he resented anything that delayed his progress toward that beautiful, brilliant rainbow of adventure that had prompted his coming to America.

He struck out toward the distant hills, golden in the morning sunlight The wheellock felt light in his grip and the leather pack rode well, strapped high on his shoulders.

People shouted warnings as he passed, warnings about the unknown forests and the even more frightening unknown savages who lurked there.

He ignored them. He was a lad with a dream.

They watched him go and shook their heads in sadness, for they were sure he would never return.

He did return, loaded heavily with peltry of beaver, otter, martin, and mink, and when those same folk questioned him about the great unknown wilderness, he ignored them.

He sold the furs in England. The profit was modest, yet sufficient to outfit him with several times the inventory of his initial investment and still leave a few coins for saving.

When he left New York the second time, those same folk watched the silent boy march past and swore that his bones would be scattered by wild beasts and left to rot in the dampness of those unexplored forests of primeval grandeur. Again he fooled them, showing up one day with several naked savages trailing behind, bent at the waist from the weight of huge bundles of furs.

Part of his dream was coming true.

Four years the New York folk watched him grow more prosperous. They talked about how they too would venture into the vast wilderness had they no others but themselves to consider.

On the fifth trip, however, he returned with no furs, and no wheellock. But cradled tenderly in his arms was a girl child, three years old.

They questioned him about her, but he ignored them. They persisted: Why had he traded everything he owned for a three-year-old baby? He evaded the question, for in truth he did not know. Yet when he had stood in the Indian village and looked down at the white child lying amid a pile of dirty bug-infested furs, and she had stared back at him with large trusting blue eyes, he knew he could not leave her to the savages.

He had inquired about her, but the Indians had become evasive and tried to hide the bloody human-finger necklaces hanging at their throats.

All they would say (and it was all that he would ever know of her background) was that she had come from a distant place.

He bartered for the child: the Indians' eyes narrowed, and they grew sly and crafty when they realized how badly he wanted the infant.

He stacked his plunder, a piece at a time, in a large circle by the fire while the Indians stood cross-armed and stared straight ahead. When there was nothing left, he rose to his feet, showing them the palms of his empty hands. But they had shaken their heads and pointed to the wheellock, refusing to meet his eyes, for fear he would see the scorn that showed plainly in their faces and realize he was being very foolish. A girl child was a useless thing, not worth a packet of brightly colored beads. After he laid the wheellock alongside the other goods, they had wished him and the child gone, for they sickened at the sight of him, such was their contempt.

After he was gone, and after the lead and powder were gone, the wheellock was traded to a trapper for a copper kettle. Eventually the gun passed to a settler just outside Albany Township in New York Province; it would be many years before another Patterson would see the ancient gun, and then, only briefly.

In Liverpool Joseph withdrew a large amount of gold from his account and placed it in the hands of his banker. "See that she is well reared," were his only instructions.

The man followed him from the building. "Who are her parents, Joseph? Who is she? What are her bloodlines? For God's sake, man, is she a Christian?"

Joseph ignored him.

He did not return to New York that year, but went instead to Philadelphia, and from there into the unexplored regions of the Ohio Valley. He carried an English musket, not half so fine as the antique wheellock, but he was satisfied.

He spent two long years in the wilderness, trading with the Shawnee before returning to England. Yet when he presented himself at the home of his Liverpool banker, he was met at the door by a five-year-old girl who hugged his knees and refused to let go.

The banker's wife was astounded that the child remembered him. He learned from the woman that the girl, since named Victoria, was withdrawn and shy, but that she was a good child and minded well. The woman had looked at him with a sadness about her eyes and mouth. "You are the only person she fully trusts."

The woman touched his arm. "Why is that, Joseph? What happened to her before you found her?"

"I do not know," was all he said.

He visited the child every year, or sometimes every other year, depending on transportation from America to England. He was always met at the door by Victoria, arms outstretched, as if she had spent the entire time that he was away watching for his return.

When she was ten, she astounded him by saying quietly that when she grew up she intended to marry him. He had laughed heartily, which she had never seen him do, and she cried because he had made fun of her. But when he left, she made him promise to wait for her, and not to wed until she was grown.

At the age of fourteen she was a mature woman, possessed with an elegance and dignity that were almost regal. She was one of those few persons who are, by nature, refined and intelligent, which proved beyond a shadow of a doubt to her benefactor that the exquisite young woman was most certainly of noble birth.

That she was shy, to the point of being considered arrogant by those who did not know her, did not bother Joseph at all, for he looked to the warm and tender heart that was the essence of her being, and he was pleased. (Those very qualities that did not bother Joseph at all, and her inability to compromise a love that was, to her, unconditionally complete, would finally prove her downfall.)

When he was thirty-seven and Victoria sixteen, Joseph married her. Only then did he fully realize how deeply devoted her love for him was, and it humbled him. Her maturity, compassion, and tenderness belied her youthful age, which caused a sadness in him, for he was still—and always would be—a woodsman.

He suggested leaving her in England for safety's sake, but she had quietly but firmly insisted that they build their life together in the New World. He had kissed her then, held her close, and told her that he loved her, and she was happy because she knew she had pleased him.

He built a mansion for her in Schenectady Township, in New York Province, and at night when they held each other close, Joseph would kiss her tenderly and talk of the westward expansion of the colonies; the opening of the wilderness; of forming a landholding company. And she would lie in his arms and gaze into his eyes, gently stroking his temple, and, in time, whisper that they would soon have a son named Morgan and that he would travel with his father and share in his great dreams.

"He will be a woodsrunner, like his father before him," pledged Joseph grandly, kissing her eyes, her nose, her lips.

"Nay!" said Victoria, drawing away, her voice ringing with pride. "He will be the greatest of woodsrunners...he will be *the woodsman!*"

Then they made love, united not only physically and emotionally, but more importantly, by each other's dreams as well.

1

Lieutenant Southhampton, aide to Gen. Edward Braddock, moved impatiently, yet carefully, among the tents of the Virginia Militia. His movements were those of a man impressed with himself; as indeed, the twenty-year-old lieutenant had a right to be. After all, he was the aide to the most important man of arms in America.

He stepped gingerly around scores of men lounging in the late sun, careful not to brush his elegant attire against the lower-caste Virginians. He detested their presence on this expedition to wrest Fort Duquesne from the French, but Governor Dinwiddie, along with Benjamin Franklin, had been quite firm, insisting that the militia accompany Braddock's thirteen hundred regular British troops. Braddock had argued that "these savages may, indeed, be a formidable enemy to your raw American militia, but upon the king's regular and disciplined troops, sir, it is impossible that they should make any impression." Dinwiddie had been unimpressed by Braddock's cynical statement, and the British had, with vocal reservations, accepted the fact that the local rabble would follow along, like a one-armed beggar, hoping to rush in and snatch a portion of the glory after the British regulars had paved the way by quelling any French and Indian resistance and securing the Ohio Valley.

Southhampton's penetrating gaze swept over the camp, taking in the tents, lean-tos, and makeshift shelters that housed the two hundred militiamen. He was disgusted with the disorder and lack of military etiquette that the camp flaunted. He paused beside a man doing a less than satisfactory job of mending a rent in his deerskin hunting frock and, in a high-pitched nasal whine, which seemed to afflict most British officers, he asked the whereabouts of Morgan Patterson.

"Why, I don't know, governor," said the man, squinting at Southhampton. "He's not in this outfit." The man bit off a piece of thread and spat it out. "I'm not sure but what you'll find him over near the sutler's camp. They's a game of chance goin' on over there."

Through slitted eyes the Virginian watched the lieutenant walk away. Then he mimicked Southhampton's nasal whine: "Why, thank you, gov'nor. Glad I could be of service...." His voice modulated into its soft Virginia drawl: "You highbrow popinjay arse. 'Tis officers like you that's gonna get us all killed before this venture is over."

He squinted a moment longer at Southhampton's retreating form, then turned his attention again to the hunting shirt. The words of his final sentence, *get us all killed*, hung heavy in the hot July air, causing his hand to tremble so violently that he pricked himself with the needle. An omen?

Vernon Kemp rolled the dice...and lost. He got slowly to his feet, standing tall above the men still on their hands and knees watching the dice tumble across the small cleared spot of hard-packed earth that served as a game board.

"'Tis a week's rations of grog I've lost this past quarter hour," he roared belligerently. Some looked up in surprise, which quickly turned to fear, for Vernon Kemp had a reputation, gained honestly, of being the meanest fighting man among the North Carolina teamsters. He had cracked several heads on this expedition, and rendered men unfit for duty, causing them to return to Fort Cumberland, whence they came, in disgrace, having seen neither action nor enemy. Yet, when word of that action reached Cumberland, those same men would bless their lucky stars for Vernon Kemp; he had probably saved their lives.

The prospect of doing without rum for a week weighed heavily on Kemp's mind, causing his face to mottle with anger, not at himself, who was actually to blame for the loss, but at the dice, the mere instruments of his misfortune. With an oath he stepped into the cleared spot and ground the dice into the earth under his highbuckle shoe.

He stood there, fists on hips, glowering at the men still on their hands and knees, daring them to say something—anything. Men began to shuffle backward on all fours, not bothering to stand erect for fear their intentions would be misunderstood. They were not cowards, nor were they fools. To avoid trouble with Vernon Kemp was just good sense.

With a sigh for the inevitable, Morgan Patterson rose to his full height. Even barefoot he stood just over six feet. Yet he was forced to look up through his brows in order to lock eyes with the North Carolinian. He slipped his shot pouch and powderhorn off his shoulder and dropped them silently to the ground.

"Patterson," said Kemp, taking a deep breath and letting it out noisily, "you're a good man with a rifle gun, and I wouldn't want to be breaking your arms, but I will if it's fightin' you got on your mind."

Vernon Kemp was not afraid of the woodsman. He was not afraid of any man alive. But he respected Patterson, for he knew him to be a quiet, dangerous man, and with a battle scheduled for the very near future he had no desire to maim the man who was said to be the finest rifleman in the whole company.

He watched with mixed feelings as Patterson unbuckled the three-inch-wide leather belt that held his knife and hatchet (tomahawk, the Indians called it) and dropped it on the shot pouch.

"Now, Patterson," said Kemp, hitching up his breeches and planting his feet firmly on the ground, "I done told you how it is. I'd be willing to let you off because we need your rifle, but don't push me, boy, or I'll stomp a mudhole in your arse."

Kemp's eyes narrowed as he calculated his adversary's strength, paying particular attention to the twenty-one-year-old's confident movements and quiet certainty.

"You can't whip me, boy." It was a soft-spoken warning that caused the spectators to glance uneasily at Patterson, who smiled slowly, eyeing the man in amused silence.

"I've never been whipped in my life, Morgan," cautioned Kemp. "And they ain't no hunerd-an-eighty-pound woodsrunner goin' to do it now."

3

Patterson began slipping his buckskin hunting shirt over his head: it was the mistake Kemp had been waiting for. Bunching his shoulders, he charged with the ferocity of an angry bull, catching Patterson off guard and flinging him through the air like a rag doll. Patterson struck the hard-packed earth so heavily that the men who witnessed it swore later that the ground shook a full five minutes. He was on his feet instantly, slinging his hunting frock aside and taking several deep breaths to try and stop the lancing pain in his chest caused by the wind being knocked from him. Clad only in breechcloth and leggin's, Patterson balled his fists and moved cautiously toward the bigger man.

Southhampton arrived in time to witness it all. He stood in open-mouthed wonder that the young man was able to regain his feet, much less that he intended to continue such a one-sided contest.

Before coming to the colonies, the lieutenant had never seen a display of fisticuffs, and he took a perverse pleasure in watching one human maim another. That he had neither the courage nor the stamina to engage in such pastimes was beside the point, and had it been brought to his attention that he reeked of cowardice he would have donned the same cloak others used: that a gentleman was above such base actions.

He studied Patterson's face for indications of fear, but neither the bronzed aquiline features nor the cold blue eyes showed any emotion. Southhampton was disappointed. He had expected to find terror there.

Kemp dropped his head and charged again, but Patterson was prepared. He sprang forward and kicked the man in the forehead. The impact of Patterson's bare foot dropped Kemp to his knees, bringing a roar of approval from the bystanders.

"I'll kill you for that, Patterson." It was barely a whisper, but it sounded loud in the hushed stillness that fell over the militiamen.

Patterson smiled, showing a row of even, white teeth.

Kemp charged again, arms windmilling with the force of sledgehammers, but Patterson stepped aside and hit the big man behind the ear, dropping him to the ground with such force that dust boiled up around him. The crowd shouted and jeered at the fallen man, delighted to see him groveling in the same dirt where he had left many a man lying in times past.

4

Southhampton's eyes narrowed as he considered Patterson again, noting the broad shoulders and well-muscled arms and chest. Perhaps he had underestimated the man. The thought shocked and angered him that a young man his own age should have the boldness of spirit that he so obviously lacked, and he hated Patterson for it. He screamed for Kemp to get up and thrash Patterson soundly, an effort that won him the hoots and jeers of the onlookers. Patterson's ice-blue eyes bore into Southhampton, forcing the lieutenant to take a quick step backward, such was their fierceness. He was saved any further discomfort, however, by a voice from the circle of spectators.

Susan Spencer pushed her way through the inner ring of men and stepped boldly toward Southhampton. "I said, lieutenant, I will wager two pounds on the woodsman."

Her dark brown eyes held a glint of mischief as she waited for his reply.

Southhampton eyed her from head to toe, taking in the coarse linsey-woolsey dress that hid, he was certain, a sensuous figure. Her heavy black hair hung loose and straight, and she carried a sunbonnet in her hand. Southhampton's eyes met hers. "I do not make wagers with camp followers."

His sarcasm caused her to laugh. "I am no camp follower, sir, and in truth, I but wondered . . . if your purse was as big as your mouth."

Southhampton's face shaded as the throng of men surrounding him guffawed and clapped one another soundly on the back. They knew the girl and appreciated her wit, and she knew them and felt at ease in their presence.

She was a hometown lass: Williamsburg had always allowed her liberties in speech and action that a strange woman neither could nor would attempt for fear of placing herself in an undesirable position. But Susan Spencer never gave it a thought. She was spoiled by the trust, respect, and love lavished upon her by the men from James City and York counties who had taken the field with Braddock.

To Southhampton, however, she was nothing more than a base-born slut who had made a fool of him in public. He eyed her with distaste as he drew his purse from a pocket within his tunic.

"I shall wager with you, my dear, but we shall make it worthwhile."

Susan raised her eyebrows in question.

"Ten pounds . . . sterling."

She sucked in her breath. "I've not got ten pounds, sir."

The crowd grew quiet. Vernon Kemp climbed slowly to his feet, his mouth agape, for ten pounds was a worldly sum to most of the men assembled there.

Southhampton smiled. "I thought not." He studied her closely, his eyes roving and probing her every curve until, in spite of herself, she glanced down to be sure she was fully clothed.

He pursed his lips and dropped his weight to one leg, giving the impression of nonchalance. "I shall make it light on you. Ten pounds . . . against a night with you, alone, in my tent."

Her mouth dropped open in surprise and disbelief. "I told you, sir, I am no camp follower."

Southhampton waved the ten-pound note under her nose. "As you Americans so vulgarly put it, either put up or shut up, my dear."

An onlooker spoke angrily: "You have no call to talk to the lass like she was trash, lieutenant. 'Twas naught but a friendly wager she offered in fun."

"She is no lady," sneered Southhampton, "and I will be damned, sir, if I shall treat her as such."

He looked hard at the men around him, noting their stormy faces. But such was his contempt for the Americans that he ignored the threat and turned again to Susan. "I know who she is. She is a common tavern wench, an indentured whore. Nevertheless, she is quite comely, and I shall enjoy sampling her charms before the night is over."

He turned arrogantly to the crowd, secure in his belief of English superiority; and in that respect he was correct. The assembled crowd was fearful of the British show of force and was cowed by the arrogance of the British regular army and its officers.

Southhampton laughed contemptuously. "Yes," he confirmed, "I shall enjoy her thoroughly—unless, of course, she has ten pounds sterling—which she doesn't."

"Call the wager off, Miss Susan," said one of the Virginians. The others nodded their agreement.

Kemp stiffarmed the man who had spoken, knocking him backward into the crowd. "Let the wench wager her arse if she's a mind to; 'tis none of your affair."

6

Susan knew a moment of panic as she glanced at her friends. Her eyes finally rested on Patterson, to see his reaction to the disgraceful insinuations concerning her virtue. But his face was cold and hard, with perhaps a hint of loathing deep within his eyes.

She turned, unbelievingly, to stare open-mouthed at Kemp, for never, not even in the tavern where she was employed, had she heard such common language voiced in her presence, and it mortified her. She realized with a certain amount of shame that she had inadvertently overstepped her boundaries.

Patterson spoke quietly: "I shall not fight under such a wager, lieutenant. But regardless of the lady's position...I do think sir, that you, as a gentleman and an officer, owe her an apology." Before Southhampton could reply, Patterson turned to Kemp. "Master Kemp, however, is another proposition entirely. Being neither officer nor gentleman, he is to be overlooked." Patterson paused, and the hint of a smile that had hovered at the corner of his mouth vanished, leaving his lips hard. "But should he insist upon abusing Virginia womanhood, I am quite sure someone will be more than glad to accommodate him on the field of honor."

Before the startled Kemp could voice his slow-minded response, Susan addressed Southhampton. "If it pleases you, lieutenant, I would prefer to be released from the wager. 'Twas intended to be fun only, but it has suddenly grown out of hand. I ask your pardon, sir."

Southhampton gently tugged a lace handkerchief from the cuff of his tunic and brushed a speck of dust from his tricorn. "The wager is ten pounds, my dear, and I dare say I shall enjoy collecting my winnings."

Patterson turned disgustedly toward the spot where he had dropped his gear.

"Do you forfeit, Mr. Patterson?" asked Southhampton, following Patterson with his eyes.

Patterson spun on his heel. "I'll not fight, sir, unless the wager is called off." It was then that Kemp hit him, a glancing blow that cut Patterson's cheek to the bone.

Patterson's head burst into an array of shooting stars. He thought he heard the girl cry out but there wasn't time to consider it, for he struck out blindly with his fists—more a reaction than a planned defense. He was pleased to feel his knuckles make contact with flesh and bone, and he knew, without seeing, that he had

7

knocked Kemp down. The momentary reprieve while the teamster climbed to his feet gave Patterson the opportunity to gather his wits.

When Kemp charged again, Patterson hit the man a tremendous blow to the heart that staggered Kemp backward and sent a shock of pain the entire length of Patterson's arm. Kemp bellowed with rage as he circled cautiously toward Patterson. Then, standing toe to toe, they battered one another until their faces were bloodied beyond recognition.

The crowd grew silent. Susan stood wide-eyed, frightened, her face grimacing each time Kemp's ponderous fists bludgeoned an unprotected portion of Patterson's face or body.

Southhampton was watching Kemp closely. It was obvious the man was tiring; his movements were becoming heavy and deliberate.

When a hard righthanded blow from Patterson crushed Kemp's nose and sent the man reeling, Southhampton moved quickly to his side and took a firm hold of his arm.

"Use your weight," he whispered through his teeth. "Get in close and crush the bloody bastard."

Kemp's eyes narrowed as he studied Patterson with new interest. He absently drew the back of his hand across the lower portion of his face, smearing the blood that flowed freely from his mangled nose and mouth into a grotesque pattern across his cheek.

Almost as an afterthought his eyes fell to the back of his bloody hand, and for the briefest moment, the men assembled there witnessed the slack-jawed expression of undisguised astonishment that filled Kemp's face.

His features were expressionless, however, when he jerked free of Southhampton and, with a speed that belied his bulking size, collided with Patterson.

Patterson attempted to twist free, but his movements were agonizingly slow and labored. Kemp lifted him off his feet and flung him amid the casks and barrels stored beside the sutler's tent. Then Kemp was on him, wedging him firmly between two casks. Slowly, methodically, with calculated intent, he began to pound Patterson to death.

The crowd surged closer, blocking Susan's view, and although she pushed and shoved and tried to force her way into the human mass that barricaded the storage area, she could find no opening.

The screams of pain, audible above the shouts of the crowd, caused her heart to beat uncontrollably. The shocking cries of human suffering continued, growing in volume until she thought her eardrums would explode.

She ran to Southhampton and clutched his hand. Something akin to horror had replaced the mischievous look in her eyes. "Stop the fight, sir," she pleaded. "He'll kill the woodsman sure!"

Southhampton disengaged her hand, and with a crooked smile of triumph marring his overly handsome features, he none too gently cupped her breast, feeling its firm full shape through the thin fabric of her dress. His mouth twisted. "You will present yourself at my tent precisely at midnight. Is that clear?"

Susan dropped her eyes to his kneading fingers, then quickly lifted them. Southhampton was pleased to see complete surrender in their depths.

"The wager was called off, lieutenant," she responded bitterly. "But I will come to you, if you stop the fight."

Southhampton cocked his head to one side and surveyed her bosom.

"I will think about it," he said slowly, as his hands possessively sought and found her nipples, "but I really do not care one whit whether Patterson lives or dies."

"Think about it!" cried the girl angrily. "While you think about it, keep your hands to yourself!" She twisted from his grasp, eyeing him hatefully.

He spun her about and forced his hand slowly down her body until it rested suggestively on her abdomen. "I will stop the fight when I decide to, my dear." His face was so close she could feel his lips move against her cheek. Then he told her precisely what gallantries he would require of her when the time came.

Susan stood dumbstruck. Never had she heard such words, many of which she did not even know the meaning. Nor could she imagine anyone saying such things, much less doing them.

Southhampton smiled contemptuously. American women were such cowards and gave in so easily. They were not even worth the effort of bragging about when one made a conquest. Judith, his fiancée, would have scratched his eyes out if he had whispered such filthy words in her ear. He arrogantly pushed Susan from him. "Midnight, my dear—not one minute later!"

9

She staggered away and leaned heavily against a wagon wheel. "Oh, Lord," she thought. "What have I done? I have never been with a man. I can't go through with it . . . I just can't." But she knew she would do as the lieutenant had instructed, because Patterson's life depended on it. Her head was spinning and she was sure she was going to be sick. She almost collapsed with fright when a Williamsburg man lifted her off her feet and swung her about. " 'Tis Kemp," he cried.

"Kemp?" she repeated dumbly.

"Aye!" he laughed, swinging her around again. "He has given up and is screaming for someone to get him aloose from Patterson." The man cackled joyfully at the look of disbelief that crossed Susan's face.

" 'Tis true! Patterson has Kemp's finger between his teeth, and I believe, by God, he's goin' to chew it off."

At that moment, Kemp pushed through the crowd and ran toward the surgeon's tent.

Susan blinked in wonder. The crowd parted, and amid much backslapping and congratulations, Patterson emerged.

Susan almost cried out, so battered was his face. His whole upper body was drenched with blood, sweat, and grime. One eye had already swelled shut and his lips were puffed and bleeding. The deep gash on his cheek was filled with dirt and bits of grass. He was a far cry from the handsome lad whom she had eyed more than once this past month, since the army had left Fort Cumberland. He walked directly to Southhampton, who stood with his mouth agape.

"You owe this woman ten pounds sterling—and an apology." The movement of his split lips caused new blood to trickle down his chin and drip onto his bare chest.

The onlookers circled the trio and waited. They were a surly bunch, unpredictable, filled with righteous indignation from the victory, even though they had nothing directly to do with it.

Still, they were waiting, as if each one had personally whipped Vernon Kemp and saved the lady's virtue, and they demanded the wager be paid in full.

Southhampton nervously withdrew his purse and fingered out the ten-pound note. He passed the money to Susan.

Patterson caught the lieutenant's wrist, the pressure of his grip shutting off the circulation to the officer's hand.

"Sterling, lieutenant," he demanded. "The wager, sir, was ten pounds sterling."

Southhampton winced and futilely tried to free his hand. Patterson gripped harder, and Southhampton cried out in pain.

"The note is acceptable, Mr. Patterson," said Susan quickly, her voice suddenly as dry as parchment. She was well aware of the severe penalty that would await Patterson should he willingly, or otherwise, harm an officer of the British regular army, and the mere thought of Morgan Patterson hanging from the gallows caused her eyes to widen in horror.

"The apology, sir," demanded Patterson coldly as he released the lieutenant's wrist.

Southhampton looked wildly about him; nowhere did he see a friendly face, or even one that was familiar. He was plainly frightened, alone as he was in an alien camp.

"I beg your pardon, mistress," he murmured as he bowed to Susan, who nodded her acceptance of the less than suitable apology. Patterson turned away disgusted with the whole affair and ran his fingers inside his mouth.

An onlooker laughed heartily and clapped Patterson on the back in a rough show of affection. "Knocked some teeth loose, did he, boy?"

The woodsman tried to grin, but winced instead.

"I got the leaders of Kemp's thumb stuck between my teeth," he mumbled through his probing fingers.

He withdrew his hand and flicked a long bluish-red piece of matter from his fingers. Southhampton's face turned white and for a moment he was sure he would vomit—and then he did.

Word filtered through the camp that the surgeon had to finish cutting off Kemp's thumb, and the roistering throng, with the exception of Southhampton, loosed a mighty huzzah for Patterson, who stood calmly fishing another piece of leader from between his teeth.

Southhampton delicately wiped his mouth, then gagged again on the vile taste. He approached Patterson cautiously, nervous because he had cast his lot with a loser and now stood alone among the triumphant. His hatred for Kemp, the defeated, was surpassed, however, by an even greater hatred for the victorious Patterson.

"Patterson," he snapped, "the general demands your presence immediately."

Patterson eyed the lieutenant stonily and considered backhanding the man. He did not like Southhampton, detested him actually. After a long moment, Patterson shrugged. "I'll be with you directly, lieutenant."

The crowd began wandering away, bantering about the fight, reliving the best parts.

Patterson soaked his head in an oaken bucket. After washing away the blood and grime, it was apparent that even though he had suffered a terrible beating, he wasn't hurt as badly as Susan first had thought.

He had just donned his hunting frock when Susan reappeared. She was holding a cup of rum and offered it to Patterson. The shy smile that extended even to her eyes died, however, when Patterson angrily brushed the cup aside, spilling its contents on her dress. Reeking of alcohol, she even smelled the part of the common camp whore that Southhampton had insisted she was.

"Sir," she said, stunned, confused by the young man's hostility, "I am sorry if I offended . . . I was merely offering . . ."

He shoved past her, toward the impatient lieutenant.

"I am well aware of what you were offering," he said over his shoulder, "and were I inclined, which I'm not, to purchase a woman's favors, it certainly would not be yours. Why, for ten pounds a man can buy all the whores in camp!"

She caught his arm and spun him toward her. "I wasn't offering you anything but a cup of rum, sir. I am not a . . . the kind of woman the lieutenant said I am." She searched his face, dismayed by his remarks about her virtue.

He pulled his arm free. "You put the price on your body, mistress, not I."

"But—but you fought for me," she whispered.

"I fought to keep from being beaten to death," he said simply, irritated because she had assumed he found her worth fighting for.

She observed him in shocked silence, then said, "I beg your pardon, Mr. Patterson; I have caused you great pain, and suffering—for that I apologize."

Patterson eyed her angrily as he again moved toward

Southhampton, "You're a fool, lady—there's not a white woman alive that's worth fighting for."

"You wished to see me, sir?" Patterson stood at attention just inside Braddock's marquee, and stared straight ahead.

The general sat with a field desk across his lap. He glanced up from the report he was writing. "I sent Lieutenant Southhampton after you an hour ago. Where have you been, Mr. Patterson?"

"I beg the general's pardon, sir, but I was detained," Patterson answered in his slow Virginia drawl.

Southhampton interrupted. "He picked a fight, sir, with a wagon driver and, I might add, sir, the army has one less man with which to engage the enemy."

Braddock smiled. "As long as it was a militiaman, we have lost nothing. However, had you chosen to insult a British regular, you would have been flogged. Is that clear, Mr. Patterson?"

Patterson continued staring straight ahead, still at attention.

Braddock's eyes bulged in anger. "Is that clear, sir?"

"Perfectly clear, general."

Braddock's eyes narrowed as he studied the woodsman. He felt that somehow he had been bested, but he could not put his finger on the reason for such a feeling. His eyes narrowed even more. *Respect*, he thought; *Patterson does not respect me*. The simplicity of the truth sobered Braddock momentarily. He studied Patterson's battered face, wondering what it was about America that prompted the colonials to have such faith in themselves. But he did not pursue the matter, finding it irritating and a waste of time, for, in truth, he really did not care one way or the other what caused the American attitude. They were a loathsome lot at best.

"Stand at ease, Mr. Patterson," said the general slowly, still intensely eyeing Patterson.

"Thank you, sir." Patterson leaned cross-armed on his rifle.

Southhampton sneered at the rustic's lack of military training, but to the lieutenant's regret, Braddock appeared not to notice.

Braddock continued, "Mr. Washington has advised me, sir, that you are the best free spy in the colonies."

Patterson shifted uncomfortably. "Begging the general's pardon, sir, but Christopher Gist is the best woodsman there is."

13

"Your modesty is touching," Southhampton sneered.

Patterson turned to Southhampton, gazing long and hard at the man before he spoke. "'Tis not modesty, lieutenant, 'Tis only the truth."

The general interrupted. "Very well, Mr. Patterson, be that as it may, but Mr. Gist is not present, so you will have to suffice."

Patterson reluctantly turned his attention to Braddock. "What would you have of me, sir?"

Patterson emerged from Braddock's tent and glanced toward the western horizon. The sun was nearly down.

George Washington, standing some thirty feet away, caught Patterson's attention by raising his clay pipe, and beckoned the woodsman to join him.

They moved toward the treeline, neither man entering into conversation. Washington pulled long on the pipe, then exhaled a spiraling puff of smoke toward the heavens.

"Horse kick you in the face, Morgan?"

Patterson smiled. "I got into a fight with Vernon Kemp."

Washington frowned as he drew again on the pipe. "'Tis a wonder he did not break your fool neck."

"I believe he did; and my back too."

"Did you kill him?"

Patterson winced as he shook his head. "'Twas a friendly fight, George."

Washington's frown deepened. "You should have killed him, Morgan." He studied the young man intently. "You must surely be getting soft to let scum like Kemp off with just a beating."

Patterson laughed. "Do I look like I won?"

Washington changed the subject. "What did Braddock want?"

"He has sent Gist off on some wild-goose chase and has ordered me to scout the four points of the compass a day's march in each direction. He intends for his engineers to lead the troops without the aid of guides. He has even put John Findley to driving a wagon. 'Tis hard to believe."

Washington drew long on the pipe. "Perhaps the general is unaware of Findley's qualifications as a woodsman."

"Findley is almost a legend in his own time, George. And you know as well as I that Braddock is aware of it!"

14

(Fourteen years distant, in 1769, John Findley would put his stamp on American history by leading Daniel Boone and four others through the Cumberland Gap for Boone's first view of Kentucky. But on the evening of July 5, 1755, as Washington and Patterson discussed Findley, their primary concern was with what history would record about the battle that would be fought within the week. And both men knew if the English were to prevail, every ounce of cunning, bravery, and knowledge of the wilderness would be needed by the forerunners of Braddock's army.)

"'Tis madness, George," Patterson continued. "The enemy will hit us somewhere out here so that, should it become necessary, they can fall back to Fort Duquesne. Findley, Gist, and I need to be spying out the trail between here and there, not running through the forest in every direction but the right one, or driving some fool supply wagon."

Washington nodded. "Braddock is a stubborn man." He passed the pipe to Patterson. "I fear it will prove our downfall, Morgan."

"I tried to explain the type of warfare he might expect from the French and Indians," said Patterson, tamping the pipe with the tip of a calloused finger, "but Southhampton made a joke of it." He took several deep draws before returning the pipe to Washington. "Before this foray is over, George, I shall probably do something very foolish where the lieutenant is concerned."

"And I shall play the violin when they hang you," returned Washington softly, not looking at Patterson, but observing a young woman approaching from the direction of the officers' quarters.

Patterson had noticed her too, and even in the twilight he was impressed by her beauty. Her hair had a silver glow about it that fascinated him, and he fought down the urge to reach out and touch it.

She would have passed without acknowledging their presence had Washington not called her name and bowed low, almost sweeping the ground with his cocked hat.

She hesitated, glancing at Braddock's tent, then at Washington. Indecision played across her classic features, and for an instant Patterson was sure she intended to ignore Washington's courtesy and continue on. But she fooled him; she curtsied beautifully and offered Washington her hand, which he kissed graciously.

"'Tis a pleasure seeing you again, Miss Cornwallace."

15

"Thank you, Mr. Washington." She forced a smile in return. It was obvious that she resented being detained and Patterson regretted Washington's insistence on passing pleasantries with her when she wished to be elsewhere.

"And may I present my good friend, Morgan Patterson," said Washington with a flourish.

Patterson bowed with difficulty, barely able to subdue a groan. The woman neither curtsied nor offered her hand, and Patterson's sun-darkened face flamed under the snub. He rose to his full height and stared at her.

She burst into laughter. "Really, sir, your pretentious attitude and mannerisms are quite comical. You neither look nor smell like a gentleman; 'tis obvious you are play-acting."

Patterson was silent for several thoughtful moments. Then he smiled and bowed again. "And you, mistress," he said softly, "neither look nor smell like a soldier, but I shall give you the benefit of the doubt, for I am quite sure a lady of quality would never enter General Braddock's quarters at this late hour...unchaperoned."

Her face flushed a crimson red that not even the deepening shadows could hide. "Whatever do you mean?" she whispered, breaking the awkward silence.

Patterson looked hard at her. "Only that appearances can be deceiving, mistress." He bowed again, then disappeared into the darkening forest.

She stood transfixed, not believing she had heard him correctly. She fumed, for it was the second time in less that many hours that she had been humiliated by an American. She thought again of the girl who had stood before her, barefoot, in a shabby homespun dress, and had offered to tutor her—Judith Cornwallace—in the art of manners.

Washington cleared his throat. "I assure you, mistress, Morgan meant no disrespect."

Judith turned angrily to Washington. "And I assure you, sir, his insinuations shall not be forgotten. My fiancé, Lieutenant Southhampton, is in General Braddock's tent, and I shall take great pleasure in seeing to it that he is made duly aware of the disrespect I have received this day. It should not surprise me, sir, if he called Mr. Patterson out."

"'Twould be a grave error, Miss Judith. I fear you have

misjudged Morgan Patterson. He is a gentleman, whom you have insulted, and he is an excellent shot with either handgun or rifle."

Judith shrugged. "Lieutenant Southhampton is familiar with firearms, sir."

Washington bowed. "As you wish, mistress."

"And," Judith added angrily, "I resent your implication that I am the cause of my mistreatment. Mr. Washington, I am a lady, the only real lady on this silly venture."

Washington smiled sadly. "I can assure you, mistress, this is not a silly venture, and ... being a beautiful lady does not excuse bad manners—"

"My manners are implicit sir," she said heatedly. " 'Tis your uneducated Americans posing as ladies and gentlemen that are in dire need of the proper education." She looked toward Braddock's tent. Southhampton had stepped through the flaps and was walking in her direction. She curtsied to Washington, then hurried to her fiancé.

Washington shook his head in disappointment as she engaged the lieutenant in animated conversation that became more heated with each passing moment. He was forced to suppress a laugh, however, when Judith, frustrated, stamped her small foot, creating a puff of dust that settled gently over the lieutenant's highly polished boots. But her tantrum fell on deaf ears, for James Southhampton entertained no romantic notions about Judith's wounded pride when it involved the possibility that he might be required to face Patterson on "the field of honor."

Judith stamped her foot again, and Southhampton, priggishly, pointed to the dust on his boots. Washington bit hard on his pipe stem to keep from chuckling when she snatched up a handful of the powdery dust and sprinkled it over his immaculate red coat. Then she turned on her heel and, eyes straight ahead, marched past Washington. He bowed to her. "Bravo, Miss Cornwallace."

She wheeled abruptly, eyes smoldering. "If I were a man, Mr. Washington, I would call your precious Morgan Patterson out— and I would shoot him! I would shoot him dead!"

"If you were a man, Miss Cornwallace," Washington drawled, "America could boast no beauty at all, for you are indeed lovely when you are angry."

17

"And you, Mr. Washington," she spat, arching her eyebrows, "may go straight to hell."

Washington inclined his head in a mock bow. "And to think," he chided with a smile, "you use that same mouth to pray with."

Judith tossed her head scornfully, the ringlets of her hair bouncing like springs of fine curled golden wire. "I pray with my heart, not with my mouth, Mr. Washington." As she stalked off, Washington's smile widened, exposing a row of badly discolored teeth.

He glanced again at Southhampton, who was delicately brushing his tunic, careful not to get any of Judith's dust on his white breeches. A mismatched and misplaced pair, those two, Washington decided, watching the lieutenant's effeminate movements. They have nothing in common, not with each other or with America. 'Tis a pity.

Washington's thoughts turned to Patterson. He had known the man for years; in fact, they had schooled together for two of those years. Yet he hardly knew him at all. He admired Patterson's loyalty and courage, and he respected the man's honesty and integrity, but Patterson had a side beyond the reach of even his closest associates. It set Patterson apart, and gained him the reputation of being antisocial, cold, and dangerous.

But if Patterson was aware that his curious behavior was responsible for the stories that shrouded him in mystery, his only outward acknowledgment was to draw further into himself.

Washington moved restlessly. He had pondered the question for months and was no closer to the answer now than before. The puzzle was maddening, and it irked him that Patterson, even in the strictest confidence, had never divulged the reasons for his obvious apathy toward white women; an apathy so profound, one might reason that Patterson didn't need women.

But Washington knew his friend better than that. On their sojourns into the frontier, which had been frequent these past two years, Patterson had astounded him time and again with his affable warmth toward Indian maidens.

Invariably, when he and Patterson would approach an Indian village, young women would appear, as if by magic, to stand with eyes downcast in respect as the woodsman rode past. Occasionally he would rein in to converse with a girl, and she would speak with

18

flashing eyes and a knowing smile. Washington would sit by his fire alone on those nights and wonder what it was that could pierce a man so deeply—and with such force—that he would shun his own kind to find solace in the arms of a savage.

During those times Washington felt distant from Patterson, because he had as little use for Indians as the woodsman did for white women. The irony was that Patterson's distaste for white women seemed to flame their curiosity and desire, whereas Washington's standoffishness toward Indians only kindled their resentment and distrust.

Washington shook his head as he stood there in the deepening shadows of dusk, and vowed that before he died he would learn the secret of Morgan Patterson.

Patterson threaded silently through the sparse undergrowth toward his camp, which stood in a secluded clearing well away from the noise and activity of the army encampment.

Although it was dark beneath the towering trees, the small clearing that housed his lean-to was still illuminated by a sun already set.

Patterson approached cautiously, from habit, and was rewarded for his stealth: a man and woman were struggling violently. It was evident the man had every intention of forcing her into the makeshift shelter, and equally evident she had no intention of entering. Patterson watched, undecided as to what his role should be. Men were constantly slipping into the brush with one camp whore or another, and although this rendezvous appeared to be unwanted by the woman, Patterson had no desire to interfere in a domestic quarrel. He would have turned away had the man not pulled the girl roughly to him and tried to press his mouth over hers. She squirmed from his embrace, which caused him to yank her more tightly against him. She kicked his shins, but that only enraged him further. Then, all else failing, she attempted to bite him, but that too was unsuccessful, and his mouth sought hers. At the last moment, she twisted her face aside, and his lips merely brushed her cheek. He slapped her, a hard, open-handed blow that caused her to recoil from him. Her eyes, even though they watered from the sting of the blow, were haunted, imploring, yet filled with pride and determination before closing tightly in anticipation of a second blow.

Patterson's mind snapped to another woman—a woman with dark hair, much like the girl in the clearing; a woman with the same courage and despair in her eyes as she too fought to retain her dignity and self-respect.

Instantly he was in the clearing, and dropped the man to the dust with a wicked kick to the groin. He then stomped him in the face, and into unconsciousness.

"Did you kill him, sir?"

Patterson heard the words through a red haze that engulfed him, and the vivid memory of a man sprawled in the absurd throes of death, his blood running through the cracks in a porch floor, filled his mind. Patterson formed the words on the tip of his tongue. "Aye, son, I did." But the haze cleared before the words were spoken, and he shook his head.

"He's alive."

Patterson's shoulders sagged, and weariness marked his every movement. The girl reached out timidly and touched Patterson's arm. He drew away, leaving her bewildered and embarrassed.

"I only meant to thank you, sir. It seems that you are my protector. It must be God's will."

Patterson's angry voice shattered her reflections. "I am nobody's protector, and certainly not yours. You are trouble, mistress. It follows you like a shroud." His eyes bore into hers. "Just leave me alone."

Her expression sagged into anguish as she studied his battered face, but she said nothing.

Patterson stepped over the unconscious man and entered his lean-to. He opened his haversack and angrily stuffed in several small buckskin sacks of food and his extra pair of moccasins. He put in a small skillet and a cup made of horn. Then he slung the haversack over his shoulder. He rolled his blanket and tied the ends together and slung the blanket over his other shoulder.

When he emerged the girl was gone. Patterson eyed the unconscious man, kicked him savagely in the stomach, then trotted toward the obscurity of the towering trees.

Susan Spencer, hidden by the same darkness into which Patterson was disappearing, watched him go. She wondered about him; he had, without a doubt, saved her virtue for the second time in one day, yet would accept not even her earnest thanks.

20

2

Patterson gripped the forestock of his rifle so tightly that his knuckles turned white. His other hand fingered the lock, the thumb tracing the outline of the hammer. He did not cock the weapon; instead, he used the barrel to ease aside the thick foliage that concealed him.

Two hours he had lain there, moving nothing but his eyes and occasionally the muzzle of the rifle. The battle raging in the valley below was unreal—ghastly—with British dead and wounded littering the trail in every direction, their scarlet coats plainly visible through the clouds of dense blue-gray smoke that hung low in the summer sun.

Patterson was not surprised by what he saw. Not exactly—he had expected the worst. Or rather, he had expected a pitched battle that would be costly to the British in men and equipment—but not anything like the tragedy now occurring.

The screams of the dying, pitched shrill above the continuous thump of the British drums, drowned out the fifes—if any were left. Drums—beating out a rhythm so the thirteen hundred high-stepping British regulars could push forward with fixed bayonets to engage an elusive, unseen foe.

Drums—sending wave after wave of scarlet-coated soldiers, marching proudly abreast, eyes straight ahead, to step over their fallen comrades, until, finally, there was no place to step but on British blood and guts. It was madness.

Patterson's hand froze on the rifle lock. A half-dozen Indians in battle paint, their naked bodies greased and glistening in the morning sun, rushed past him through the tall ferns, eager to join their French allies and war against the hated enemy, the English.

Only his eyes moved as he watched the nude torsos of the Indians drop over the hill and move downward toward the bloody cauldron. He was tempted to cry out to the savages; to tell them that there was little need to hurry, that they could stroll down the hill and kill British soldiers at their leisure without even breaking a sweat. Sweat—he stank of sweat, and he stank of something even more nauseating: the metallic odor of fear.

It was a scent alien to him; he had smelled it only on others, and he had secretly been contemptuous of them for their weakness. Yet now, that same awful stench burned his eyes and filled his nostrils until he was sure he would suffocate. He silently cursed the entire British army for its gross stupidity, and he cursed himself for reeking with the stink of cowardice.

What he witnessed, however, was enough to fill even the strongest heart with terror—over fifteen hundred Englishmen, including the militia, were pitted against a mere four hundred French and Indians, and they were being butchered like sheep driven to slaughter.

Fleetingly, he considered the women, the camp followers, but he quickly dismissed the thought; they were someone else's problem. He thought instead of the Virginia Militia; just where in bloody hell were they? He had yet to see a man in homespun, or buckskins, engaged in battle—it bothered him. His eyes involuntarily probed the length and breadth of the battlefield, straining to penetrate the groundcover of heavy acrid smoke in hope that the militia would appear. Instead he witnessed a devastating carnage. The king's regulars were in hopeless confusion. They were being fired upon from all sides, a type of warfare beyond their imagination. They had no foe to shoot, no battlefield to march across. They were nearing panic. Braddock couldn't be seen, but Washington was there, riding back and forth, using the flat of his sword to try and hold the men; to steady them into some semblance of order.

Washington's horse went down, kicking out with all four legs. It made no effort to rise. He abandoned the animal and caught another as it ran wild-eyed through the ranks of the terrified regulars. He vaulted into the saddle and was immediately back in the battle. (Washington would have four horses shot from beneath him before the battle ended.) Redcoats lay everywhere, some screaming, some crying, others beyond such human emotions. Pack animals milled loose, or tried to break free, adding to the mayhem. The regulars began floundering, lost without leadership. (Almost every officer and noncommissioned officer was killed in the first volley fired by the enemy.) And having not been trained to think for themselves, the British soldiers raised no defense at all. A few threw away their weapons and ran. Then more fled as panic spread through the milling ranks.

Patterson watched as the whole British army broke and ran. Washington, on yet another horse, was standing on the stirrups roaring insults and curses at the retreating soldiers. It was a wasted effort; the redcoats were routed and were sweeping Washington with them, leaving the dead and wounded to fare for themselves.

Patterson's stomach lurched as he saw hordes of Indians dart from the brush and hatchet the wounded soldiers as they tried to drag themselves after their fleeing comrades.

"Lord God," he whispered silently, raising his eyes to the heavens. "Do you turn your back on your own kind?"

As if in answer to his question, he saw several Indians driven backward, to fall in grotesque positions and lie still. Another Indian, engrossed in cutting off the head his victim, sat down heavily, clutched his chest, and crawled into the brush dragging his gruesome trophy behind. The others melted into the forest, as if they had never been.

Patterson grinned with pride. The Virginia Militia had finally broken through the panic-stricken regulars. Advancing toward the enemy, the militiamen took advantage of any cover available. They fired, reloaded, moved forward to another bit of cover, and fired again. The French and Indians began to withdraw. Patterson could see the flash of bronze bodies and white tunics as the enemy retreated toward Fort Duquesne.

The screeching and yelling of the savages dwindled to nothing. The day might yet be saved! The British were regrouping, and

23

Patterson thought that surely they would seize the advantage the militia had secured. Instead, they organized into formal firing order, the front ranks kneeling, the back ranks standing, and fired the only destructive volley of the battle—right into the backs of the militiamen.

Patterson was aghast. He lay there slack-jawed, incredulous. The British regular army had shot the Virginia Militia to pieces. Then something equally harrowing caught his attention. A large body of Indians was quietly congregating. Patterson estimated their number to be close to a hundred. Even though he could not hear what was being said, he had no trouble reading their gestures.

They were intending to slip around the meadow where the heat of the battle was in full pitch, and fall upon Halkett's command, which was at the rear of the column protecting the baggage and the women. Although not a military man, Patterson was familiar enough with tactics to understand that if Halkett's rear guard fell, the English were defeated. He refused to consider the plight of the women should the French and Indians triumph, because to his way of thinking, they had been a burden to the army since leaving Cumberland and their misfortune was no concern of his.

He frowned irritably, his eyes narrowing into a fixed squint, as he remembered the blackhaired girl saying, "It seems that you are my protector." He peered hard at a small patch of pale blue sky that pierced the heavy foliage above him.

"I am not her protector!" he cried silently, with uplifted eyes. "It is not your will—I am no white woman's protector."

His jaw set in a grim line. He watched the patch of blue as if he expected a sign. When nothing extraordinary occurred, he nodded his thanks and returned his gaze to the gathering warriors.

He would warn Halkett. The women were Halkett's problem. His hand moved to his powderhorn. He pulled the spout plug and poured a small quantity of the black grains into his palm. Then he spit into the powder and worked it into a thick paste, which he streaked across the deep tan of his face like warpaint. He cast his tricorn aside and shook his long hair free of the eel skin that held it in a queue. He hoped his ruse of posing as an Indian would allow him the freedom to dash through the forest unmolested and reach Halkett in time to avert total annihilation.

Glancing again at the assembling Indians to assure himself that

24

they hadn't gotten ahead of him, he bolted down the hillside—his hair flying in the breeze. He looped out and away from the fighting in the valley and made his way without incident to the rear of the column. He would slip into Halkett's lines from behind. As he broke from the brush that lined Braddock's makeshift road, he was startled to see a British officer scrambling toward him, his head turned, looking back upon what would later be called the Battle of the Wilderness.

The panicked officer spotted Patterson standing not twenty feet ahead. Crying out, he cast his pistol aside and dropped to his knees. "Please don't kill me," he whined, "I am worth much ransom money . . . my family will pay dearly for my safe return . . . please . . ."

Patterson eyed the man with furious contempt. "Pick up your pistol and stand on your feet like an officer of the British army, lieutenant!"

Southhampton sprang to his feet. He recognized Patterson's voice even if the painted savage before him was a stranger. The relief that accompanied the realization that he was, at least for the moment, in no immediate danger of being butchered, quickly turned to a coward's courage, and Southhampton angrily demanded to know why Patterson was posing as an Indian.

Patterson wasn't impressed by Southhampton's bluster; in truth, it disgusted him.

"My appearance is not important, lieutenant," he replied. "But your appearance is. Why are you not with Braddock?"

Southhampton walked to where the pistol lay.

"I asked you a question, lieutenant."

Southhampton retrieved the gun, whirled, and cocked it, his hand trembling. "You have no authority to question a British officer, Patterson, but since you persist, I am searching for my fiancée. She and her handmaiden are out here somewhere." He gestured vaguely to the surrounding timber.

Patterson moved to pass him. "Search if you will, lieutenant. I've tarried too long already. Indians are moving on Halkett at this very moment."

Southhampton caught Patterson's arm, his eyes widening in alarm. "Wait!" he pleaded. "I am no woodsman. I'll never find the women in this wilderness. . . ." He watched Patterson's face as he spoke, but all he saw on the painted features was contempt.

"Listen to me, Patterson," he begged urgently. "You know these forests. You could find the women ten times quicker than I." His grip tightened on Patterson's arm. "Let me warn Halkett—I know the way back to the column."

Patterson attempted to free himself of Southhampton's hand but the lieutenant squeezed more tightly.

"Would you let them die out there, man! You'll be the murderer of two innocent women! Do you hear?"

Patterson snatched his arm free. "If Halkett isn't warned, two innocent women's lives will be a drop in the bucket compared to the number of men that'll die here today, lieutenant!"

"I'll warn Halket, rest assured, but please search for my fiancée, please!"

"Damn it, man!" snapped Patterson in disgust. "Do you have any idea where she is?"

Southhampton pointed north. "I'm not sure exactly, but somewhere out there."

Patterson trotted off in the direction the lieutenant indicated.

Southhampton waited until the woodsman had vanished, then, with total disregard for British lives, male or female, he broke into a stumbling run toward the Monongahela River and the safety of its far bank.

Patterson crossed a swift-running tributary of the Mononga-hela and for thirty minutes worked his way into the dense woodland beyond. Search as he might, he could find no sign of the women. He had used all his woodsman's skill to try and locate them, having cast in a circle, run straight lines, even climbed tall trees to survey the direction Southhampton had indicated. But there was nothing.

Patterson cursed the whole business. The women could have returned to the column earlier, or have been captured and killed. Either way, he did not intend to waste another minute looking for them.

He turned and raced toward the sound of gunfire that was barely audible through the heavy foliage of the forest. It was when he was recrossing the creek, a good two miles from where Southhampton had said they would be, that he saw them. They were crouched on the far bank in a terrified embrace, their faces turned toward the distant sound of battle.

Patterson quietly slipped into the water and waded toward the women, unmindful of his savage appearance. Had he imagined the reaction his painted face and long shaggy hair would induce, he certainly would have called out to the ladies.

Silence, however, was part of his nature, so he was unprepared when he reached out with his rifle barrel and touched one of the women on the shoulder, and she responded with a seizure of hysterics.

The women sprang apart, one slumping to the ground in a swoon, the other a whirlwind of ferocity. She leaped at Patterson with the agility of a terrorized panther, holding a small pearl-handled dagger low to her side, the cutting edge up.

Patterson had lived with danger too long to be taken completely off guard, yet the speed, and unwavering intent of the woman caught him by surprise. She was on him instantly, bringing the knife in low, striking for the abdomen.

As the knife flicked up, Patterson hit the girl with his free hand. The blow left her mouth and nose a crimson smear.

She hesitated for the briefest instant before fear and determination sent her crashing into Patterson with an impact that nearly staggered him.

He slapped her hand down and twisted sideways in one fluid motion, but the momentum of the attack carried her on, and he felt the razor-edged steel of the blade grate off his thigh bone and drive through his leg. The shock of it ashened his face. First disbelief, then anger blazed in his eyes, causing the girl to notice their pale blue color. She released the knife, but before she could speak, Patterson spun away, instinctively cracking her across the jaw with the butt of his rifle. She went down in a crumpled heap.

"Damn her!" he cried, as he eased himself down on the rough stones of the creek bank.

"Thank God! Oh, thank God, you're English!" sighed the girl who had fainted. "I thought you were a savage. We were so afraid!"

Patterson snatched his belt free and wrapped it tightly around his bloody thigh. The pain was nearly unbearable and his teeth clenched tightly as his trembling hand grasped the knife handle. With both hands he pulled mightily. He gritted his teeth, and perspiration dripped from his chin in large beads. The flesh, attempting to seal itself, had virtually gripped the blade from all sides and would not yield.

"Woman," he gasped, "if you're through thanking God, I need your help worse than he does."

She scrambled over the unconscious form of her companion and peered into his face.

"You!" she gasped, recoiling onto her haunches in disbelief.

His eyes flicked up in equal surprise and Judith was shocked by the pain that was registered there. It was the first emotion she had seen him display and she scorned him for his weakness. That she had never experienced physical agony was neither here nor there, and she regarded his unmanly show of pain as something deserving reproof. She despised him for it.

He released his grip on the knife and showed her his bloody palm. "Lady, I'm bleeding to death," he said simply.

She took one look at the point of the blade protruding from the back of Patterson's leg, and fainted again. He glared at her and cursed violently, unable to understand how anyone could be overcome by the sight of blood. He had loosened the tourniquet and was in the process of retightening it when he heard them coming—two of them.

His head snapped up, attempting to place the exact location of the sound. But sitting at the edge of the water, he was unable to see over the three-foot-high cutbank, five feet away. He quickly sought his rifle—Judith had fallen on it; leave it.

Dragging his injured leg, and being careful of the embedded blade, he crawled to the bank and crouched against it. His breath came in short gasps, and his vision weaved drunkenly.

He could hear them plainly. The one in front was breathing hard; the one behind was laughing fiendishly. He eased to a crouch and peered through the ferns that grew along the bank. One glance told the story; a naked white woman, obviously a captive who had tried to escape, was fleeing an Indian who was, by his playful antics, enjoying the chase, sure of the outcome.

They were headed straight for Patterson. The woman's frantic flight didn't falter as she approached the cutbank. Patterson glimpsed a flash of pale white flesh as she jumped for the creek. He ignored her. It was the flash of red that he went for. As the Indian passed overhead, Patterson caught the man's ankle in both hands and let the momentum of the Indian, plus his own weight, slam the man face down on the graveled creekbed. Before the stunned Indian could push himself to his elbows and spit out his broken teeth, Patterson was on him.

He struck the Indian viciously with his tomahawk. The Indian jerked violently and rivulets of blood stained the fast-moving water a bright pink. Patterson sank the hatchet deep into the man's skull again. Take no chances: the first rule of Indian fighting.

Patterson raised his aching head, then slowly closed his eyes. He could not believe it. Standing midstream was Susan Spencer, her knuckled fist clenched against her mouth, her eyes huge with horror. He stared at her but an instant. "Damn you, Lord," he cried, "I am not her protector!" Then the world slowly turned upside down.

While Morgan Patterson lay unconscious with three terrified women trying their best to save his life, a whipped, bedraggled army trudged slowly toward Fort Cumberland, over the same road it had just hacked out of the wilderness with such splendid arrogance.

And once the tattered force was safely across the Monongahela River, sixty-year-old Gen. Edward Braddock roused himself from delirium and summoned George Washington to his side.

With red-rimmed, fever-ridden eyes, he looked up at the young Virginian. "We shall know better how to deal with them at another time."

Washington was dismayed by the haggard condition of the wounded man, and he gently took the general's shaking hand. "'Twas just a battle we lost, general," he said kindly, patting the officer's palsied fingers, "not the entire war. We will fight them again...and we will win, sir."

The general smiled and closed his eyes. But Edward Braddock, famous British soldier, officer, and gentleman, had fought his last battle. His men buried him in the middle of the makeshift road he had just built. Then the remnants of his magnificent army tramped across his grave until even they could not point with certainty and say, "Aye, that is the spot where Braddock lies."

The pain in Patterson's leg roused him. He clenched his teeth and moaned aloud. A cool gentle hand caressed his forehead.

29

"His fever is down; we can be thankful for that."

He lay there wondering where he was and who had spoken. He smelled the pungent aroma of earth and dried leaves, and the peculiar, heavy yet clean odor that is found only in the tall timber.

He tried to open his eyes, but the morning light blinded him, driving needles of pain through his head.

"Is the pain that bad?" asked Susan.

Patterson studied her through half-closed lashes.

She looked at him anxiously. "Do you understand what I say? Can you hear me?"

He painfully nodded.

"Good," she said with relief. "I was worried that you might still be out of your senses."

He shook his head, but before he could answer, the girl who had stabbed him kneeled by his side and looked imploringly into his eyes.

"I am so sorry, Mr. Patterson." Her voice was a soft, trembling whisper. "I did not mean to harm you. I—I thought you were an Indian." Then she cried, her shoulders shaking uncontrollably, her chin resting on her breast.

A more compassionate man would very likely have been moved by her regret, but Patterson was not. She had intended to kill him, and almost succeeded. That she had not was a remarkable mishap, achieved by Patterson's finely honed reflexes. He thought about that as he watched her cry and felt nothing for her tears.

"She is sorry, Mr. Patterson," said Judith, as she moved into his line of vision. "She has offered an apology." Judith hesitated, then spat at him, "Which, sir, you do not deserve, nor would you have gotten if I had but known what my servant had in mind." She looked hard at Ivy, who lowered her eyes under Judith's intimidating glare. "You deserve nothing from Ivy," she continued stonily, "nor shall she apologize again."

Patterson felt a twinge of pity for the servant girl, and involuntarily, yet with a curiosity not within his keeping, canvassed her.

She was not tall, as the two others were, and her hair was of an amber hue, falling about her head in tight ringlets that accented large, very gray, and very beautiful eyes. Her small nose was perhaps a trifle wide, as was her generous mouth, and Patterson guessed that

30

Negro blood ran in her veins. Ivy was truly beautiful in an exotic fashion.

"And furthermore, Mr. Patterson," persisted Judith, "you have delayed us quite long enough. Now that you are awake, we must be off. The army could be miles away by now, because of you."

Patterson looked hard at her and his lips compressed into a grim line. He had not enjoyed his first encounter with Judith or his second, and this one was equally disenchanting. As he studied her, he was aware, with no sense of guilt, that had he known it was Judith for whom Southhampton was searching, he would never have agreed to waste precious time on her. If she had fallen into enemy hands, all the better. However, and much to his bewilderment, he still desired to touch her hair, and his hand moved involuntarily in that direction. He had seen Indians reverently caress objects that were extremely rare or sought after, but he had never experienced that particular sensation until the first time he had seen Judith. He could not help staring at the silver glow of her golden hair, which was piled high on her head, causing her to appear even taller than the five-foot-four inches she was. Her eyes, shaped exactly like Ivy's, were a pale blue, but with a touch of cynicism that hardened her gaze.

But unlike Ivy's, her nose was thin and elegant. Her lips pursed into a persistent pout that men found provocative. To Patterson, she was haughty, aloof, self-assured, vain, and selfish.

"Sir," she spat, looking down her nose at him, "I have endured this—" she gestured with her hand, "this wilderness, quite long enough." Without waiting for his answer, she turned to Ivy.

"You may do my hair now, and we will leave this ghastly place—thank heaven."

"We are not going anywhere," retorted Susan softly, "until he is strong enough to travel."

"I beg your pardon," said Judith, as if she had not heard correctly.

Ivy intervened, hoping to soften Judith's anger. "Mistress Judith, he is so very frail, I fear..."

"I care not what you fear! Do you understand me?" Judith was furious and her blue eyes flashed in the morning sunlight.

Patterson watched her through lowered lids. "Damned be the man that ever takes that one to wife," he murmured softly.

"I heard that," snapped Judith. "And I will thank you, sir, to keep your stupid thoughts to yourself." She started to turn away but changed her mind. "Furthermore, you can rest assured, you will never take me as wife . . . or any other way. As far as you are concerned—I am already married."

She tossed her head angrily and walked away. He very likely might have called her back to apologize for his thoughtless words, but Susan quickly moved between Patterson and Judith.

She was perfectly aware that he should apologize; it was the gentlemanly thing to do. Yet it annoyed her that he should, or would, humble himself before Judith for speaking his mind.

And Susan was also aware that she was enjoying the mutual loathing she had witnessed. But admit it or not, she had acted on impulse, or perhaps her intuition, when she hurriedly stepped between the two. Either way, she had no regrets, for she had succeeded in capturing Patterson's attention. "Are you not going to look me over also?" she asked openly. "'Twould hurt my feelings if you did not."

He frowned, wishing she would go away. She lifted her arms and twirled slowly, that he might see all of her, front and back. His attention, however, was drawn to her dress. It was his hunting frock. It fit her like a tent, hanging limply off her shoulders with the sleeves rolled up several turns. The bottom of the frock, that hit him above the knees, fell to her midcalf. But it was the vee neck that caught his eye. The opening extended almost to her navel, exposing an expanse of creamy white throat and breast. She had attempted to draw the opening together using pieces of short fringe, but the effort was wasted.

She sensed his scrutiny and self-consciously her hands moved to cover the exposed area, succeeding to a degree. The very act caused her to blush, drawing his attention to her long black hair that was so thick it made her oval-shaped face appear small. Her eyes, almost as dark as her hair, were full of mischief. Her nose was small and straight and her lips full and wistful. She was more lovely than he remembered.

Patterson discreetly averted his eyes as she again fumbled nervously with the frock.

"I hope you do not mind," she said with obvious

embarrassment as she tied the fringe of the opening in small knots, "that I have made use of your hunting shirt."

He told her he did not mind, but he avoided her eyes, for he was lying; he did not like being unclothed, even though he was covered with a blanket. He instinctively drew it closer about his neck and shoulders, then blushed with the realization that one, or all, of the women had undressed him. It angered him that they had. Never before had a white woman seen his naked body.

Susan saw the anger in his eyes and hurt showed momentarily on her face. "Please, sir," she pleaded, presuming his resentment stemmed from her wearing his frock, "I did not intend to anger you. I—I have nothing else to wear."

"It is all right," sighed Patterson, closing his eyes. His leg was throbbing and he was tired. He wanted to sleep.

When he awoke again, it was afternoon. He listened to the birds sing and knew a moment of complete relaxation before opening his eyes.

Susan knelt by his side. "Do you feel like eating?"

He forced a smile. "Aye, I am hungry."

She was elated to see him smile and it showed in her eyes as she spoke. "I have kept the food hot. I'll be only a moment."

She was back in an instant, carrying his horn cup. " 'Tis all that is left, so eat slowly, Mr. Patterson."

Patterson eyed the contents skeptically. "What is this stuff?"

"It is parched corn and jerky that I boiled into soup. 'Tis all that is left of your meager stores."

Patterson looked again into the cup. He remained silent but could not help wondering how three women could have eaten so much corn and jerky. There was enough in his haversack to feed a regiment for a week. He shook his head.

Judith approached, glaring at him all the while. "Believe me, sir, had I but known that a morsel of that foul-tasting mess had not been eaten, you would have had none left." She directed her glare at Susan, who met her gaze steadily.

Then Susan's eyes became mischievous, and she stuck her tongue out at Judith. Judith recoiled. Although she itched to slap Susan's face, she took a deep breath, and with a great show of dignity sniffed, "I suppose I shall have to accept such rudeness from a common barmaid."

Susan's face blanched as she stared at Judith, whose eyes twinkled in triumph. The blonde girl glanced at Patterson, laughed lightly, and walked away.

Susan's first reaction was to defend her reputation, but she knew that to do so would only add dignity to Judith's half-truth. Instead, she studied Patterson closely to get his reaction to Judith's catty statement.

"Call her back," he said flatly. "I will share with her." Susan stood up and turned toward the trees where Judith had disappeared, but Ivy reached out timidly and stopped her.

"You are very kind, Mr. Patterson," she said softly, still holding tightly to Susan's arm, "but your strength is most important just now." She faltered and dropped her eyes. "To be honest, sir, my mistress and I have heavily used what little food you had." She raised her eyes to Susan. "'Tis Miss Susan that has done without, so that you might eat." Patterson saw the quick shake of Susan's head to signal Ivy to silence, and he looked long at the girl, grudgingly admiring her thoughtfulness.

"Share with me, Miss Susan," he said, extending the untouched cup to her. "I will have it no other way."

Susan smiled shyly, then curtsied. "Since you put it that way, sir, I will join you gladly, but honestly, I am not hungry." She hesitated, blushed, then laughed with embarrassment. "I am hungry, Mr. Patterson—I lied to you!"

Patterson smiled in spite of himself as she took the cup. He appreciated her honesty, was even impressed by it, but the smile died almost as quickly as it appeared.

Susan became self-conscious as his hand touched hers when she accepted the cup, and she wanted more than anything else to explain the circumstances of her employment as a tavern wench—but she didn't.

With Judith and Ivy watching as she and Patterson slowly ate the boiled corn and jerky, Susan related to Patterson what had transpired since his killing of the Indian. She made light of her and Ivy's plight, of trying to drag him off the dead man and get him to a suitable hiding place. Judith had not helped, for fear of staining her dress with his blood, so the two of them, she and Ivy, had half-dragged, half-carried him up the creek, walking in the edge of the stream to obliterate any tracks they might have left. (That had been her idea and she was pleased with her cleverness.)

They had covered him with brush and left him on the creek bank while they searched out a hiding place. The difficult part had been moving Patterson from the creek to the campsite. Did he know he was heavy? No? Well, he was. Then Susan told of returning to the Indian, dragging him into the water, and floating him downstream for a mile or more before releasing his body, to be carried by the fast-moving current to heaven knew where.

She surmised that should the Indians find the body downstream, they very possibly might devote their attention to that area and not bother to search upstream for them. Patterson was pleased with her resourcefulness.

She informed him that they had been in hiding for two days and had seen no one.

Patterson asked about his wounded leg. Susan swallowed the last bite of gruel and wiped her mouth with the sleeve of the hunting frock. Then she told him that they had been unable to pull the knife from his leg, so they drove it back through the flesh, using the flat of his hatchet.

She did not tell him that she and Ivy had been sick to their stomachs when finally, with Ivy pulling and she hammering, the knife had oozed free.

She did say, however, that they had cauterized the wound, both front and back, with gunpowder. That had been Ivy's idea. (Ivy was pleased with herself.)

She did not tell him that he had screamed until they, fearful his cry would attract the enemy, stuffed his mouth with his leggin'. But Judith did. (She was pleased with herself also.) Susan apologized for the amount of food they had consumed and Patterson felt a moment of shame, for the girls hadn't done badly for the length of time he had been unconscious.

Susan did not tell him that his fever had been so high that they had stripped him bare and that Ivy also had stripped, to use her dress as a cold compress, making trip after trip to the creek in an effort to keep his body from burning up.

She did tell him that Ivy had ripped her petticoat into strips to use for bandages, and he thanked Ivy.

Ivy summoned the courage to tell him that she had been so afraid she had killed him that she had prayed to every god she had ever heard of, even the "great spirit" of the heathen Indians. They all laughed. The girls continued talking, but the soft drone of their voices and the hot food he had eaten lulled Patterson into a state of relaxed oblivion and finally into a sound sleep.

Susan caught the attention of Judith and Ivy, and put her finger to her lips, indicating quiet. Then she gently covered Patterson's shoulders with the blanket. Ivy looked down at his sleeping form. "His face is still cut and bruised," she whispered. "Will he never get well?" Susan looked up at the girl and amusement danced in her eyes. The skin on Ivy's nose had almost healed, but her jawline still showed the vivid blue mark where Patterson's rifle had struck her. "It will be several days before either of you look like yourselves, again!" She smiled. The smile softened as she turned her attention again to Patterson. "He looks so peaceful and young when he is asleep," she said wistfully.

"Yes," agreed Ivy, "and he is handsome—if you look beyond the ruin of his face."

"Even the mighty lion looks gentle when his eyes are closed," jeered Judith. "You two make me sick! You can be taken in so easily."

"What ever do you mean, mistress?" said Ivy, wide-eyed.

"My fiancé," returned Judith, "says Patterson is a ruffian and a villain. He told me that he saw Patterson hurt a poor fellow badly—took advantage of the man, actually, while the poor lout was stuck between two barrels."

Then, with the air of one who knows a secret, she leaned close to the two upturned faces. "And, I will tell you something else! James said that Patterson hates white women, even little baby girls, so we had best be on our guard at all times. There is no telling what sort of vile, wretched things he is capable of."

Ivy hastily retreated from the sleeping form. "Do you really believe we are in danger, Mistress?" she asked fearfully.

"Well," said Judith with an air of importance, "James says . . ."

"It seems to me that *James*," Susan interrupted, "says quite a lot, and while I am not totally disputing his story, I have reason to believe he is mistaken."

"James does not lie!" defended Judith. "He is an officer and a gentleman, and—and, he loves me."

Susan wondered at the touch of uncertainty in Judith's voice. Could it be that Judith was unsure as to Southhampton's true feelings? She looked at Ivy to see if she had caught the tinge of doubt in Judith's words, but Ivy turned her head and busied herself with her fingernails.

Clouds had covered the moon, casting the woodland into a darkness that was frightening. But to Patterson, who had just awakened, it was home, the only one he felt perfectly comfortable in. He lay there, feeling the night breeze cool against his damp skin. He had been dreaming again, the same dream that had haunted him since childhood, and he was drenched with perspiration.

One of the girls, Judith he believed, cried out in her sleep. He was thankful for the distraction, for the dream had left him shaken, as it always did. Holding the blanket close, he climbed unsteadily to his feet, swaying drunkenly as spasms of pain seized the muscles of his injured leg, compelling him to clench his teeth.

Two small hands gripped his arms to support his teetering body. It was Ivy.

"Mr. Patterson," she whispered, "you should not be up." He ignored her; in fact, he resented her assistance, even if it was necessary. He turned toward the sound of running water and judged the creek to be fifty yards away.

Judith moaned again and Patterson looked in her direction. "Is your mistress not well?"

"She is . . . fine, Mr. Patterson," said Ivy. "'Tis just that she is . . . afraid."

"Afraid of what?"

Ivy looked at the moon as it briefly broke through the overcast. She spoke hesitantly: "I—I am not at liberty to discuss my mistress's private feelings, Mr. Patterson." He noted the undisguised fear in the girl's voice as she continued, "I truly hope, sir, that I have not angered you with my evasiveness."

Patterson could see the whites of her overlarge eyes in the darkness, and he leaned closer to get a better look at her face. She instinctively drew back, and he wondered at her strange attitude.

37

"No," he said, bewildered. "You have said nothing to anger me. On the contrary, I admire your loyalty."

He heard Ivy's sigh of relief and it struck a sympathetic chord in him. Then, with a touch of astonishment, he realized that it was he of whom the girls were afraid.

The thought angered him as being ridiculous, and he forced it from his mind, turning his attention again to the sound of the rushing stream. "If you would help me to yonder creek," he said with a tinge of bitterness, "I need some time to myself." He leaned heavily on her shoulder and staggered toward the running water.

It had taken a strenuous effort and several hesitant attempts by both before he was resting easy in the shallows at the water's edge. His damaged leg was supported by an exposed stone. It had been a tedious task to lower him into a sitting position without submerging his leg, but they had somehow managed.

After seeing to his comfort, Ivy had waded from the creek and discreetly disappeared. He shivered as the cold water swirled around him, then, reluctantly, he eased back onto his elbows, then onto his back. He lay there, soaking up the cool, refreshing moisture. He rinsed his mouth and drank sparingly. Other than the constant pain in his leg, he felt fine.

She called softly from the darkness. Yes, he was ready to return to camp. He got his good leg under him and pushed himself erect. The effort sapped his strength, and he thought for a moment he would collapse. Ankle deep in the fast-moving water, he stood unmoving, waiting for the weakness to pass.

Judith stood on the bank holding his blanket. She broke the silence. "If you are waiting for me to wade out there and help you, you shall have a long wait, Mr. Patterson. I have no intentions of getting wet."

Her attitude embarrassed him, and it angered him even more that he should need her assistance.

"Why are you here?" he asked cruelly. "Are the others dead?"

Judith laughed lightly, the sound mingling with the music of the stream.

"'Tis merely my allotted time to see to your well-being, Mr. Patterson. We take turns, you know. And I can assure you, sir, it is not of my choosing."

She pursed her lips musingly. He sensed the expression more than saw it, for the night was too dark to define any detail in her face. Her voice, however, confirmed his suspicions: "If you were to ask me properly, I might...help you."

"Go to hell," he said flatly.

She flung the blanket to the ground and faded into the darkness. He stood there, helpless, and he hated her for it; for his being dependent on her at all; for being dependent on any white woman.

His hands convulsed into fists as his anger increased. "God," he prayed softly, "you know my feelings about white women. Why have you delivered me into their hands? Have I angered you?"

Susan appeared on the bank, stifling a yawn; then, without hesitation, she waded into the water. "Judith woke me. She said you refused her help."

"Something like that," returned Patterson below his breath.

3

He awoke them as the sun broke the horizon. They yawned and stretched and wiped the sleep from their eyes. Susan and Ivy even managed to smile, but Judith ignored him. Susan stretched again, languidly yet gracefully. "I dreamed I was home at Rosemont," she said to no one in particular. "If I ever get back there, I never will leave again. I swear I won't."

Ivy laughed. "Would you consider having a permanent houseguest?"

Judith looked at them crossly. "Would you two—shut up!" Susan raised her eyebrows in mock wonder and laughed, but Ivy averted her eyes and said nothing.

Patterson broke the tension. "We have got to get a few things straight." He looked at each girl in turn, then continued. "We have been thrown together through no fault of our own—whether we like it or not."

"I do not like it," interrupted Judith, raising her delicate eyebrows in challenge.

"None of us like it, Judith, " said Susan. "Let Mr. Patterson speak, if you please."

Patterson ignored them both and pursued his thought. "I shall not lie to you. 'Tis a long, hard journey before us—and dangerous. We will have to pull together—as a team—if we are to get out of here alive."

Judith scoffed. "You are making too much of our predicament, Mr. Patterson. Undoubtedly, my fiancé is searching for us this very minute; 'tis only a matter of time before he locates us."

"I hope that is true," said Patterson, thinking of Southhampton and what could very likely have been his fate when he returned to warn Halket that the column was about to be attacked. But he kept the thought to himself and continued. "But we cannot sit here and wait, on the chance that he might find us. In fact, 'tis a wonder the Indians have not already found us."

Susan spoke up. "But we are well hidden here. Can we not just wait till it is safe to use Braddock's road?"

Patterson shook his head. "Indians will watch that road for weeks to come." He looked at Susan. "All the known trails will be too dangerous to use."

"How far are we from Fort Cumberland, Mr. Patterson?" asked Ivy.

His forehead wrinkled in thought. "Perhaps a hundred miles— maybe more."

"A hundred miles!"

"Aye," said Patterson slowly, "but by the route we shall be forced to use—it will be more like twice that distance."

"You intend for us to walk two hundred miles!" shouted Judith.

Patterson grimaced. "If you do not lower your voice, mistress, our bones will likely rot right here." He ignored Judith's indignation and cleared a spot on the ground, raking back the leaves and twigs, until he had an area some two feet in diameter. Then with a sharpened stick he scratched an X into the dirt. "This is our position," he said, looking up through his brow. Susan and Ivy were watching with rapt attention, but Judith was staring off into the forest. "Miss Cornwallace," he said through his teeth, "you might pay attention. Should we have to make a run for it, or should one of us become lost, you need to know where we are."

Irritation marred Judith's features, but she joined the group and pretended to memorize the crude map Patterson was scratching into the soft earth.

He dragged the stick through the dirt leaving a line that resembled a crude horseshoe.

"That's the loop of the Monongahela," he said, satisfied. "If you ladies remember, we crossed the river here, and again here." He drew a straight line that dissected the loop as he talked.

"It would be nice to be able to go back by the same route we came, but since that is impossible, we are forced to move to these hills to the left of the river." He made some wiggly lines in the cleared spot to the left of the horseshoe.

"Those are not hills over there," cried Judith; "they are mountains! Steep, high, awful-looking mountains."

Patterson looked up at the girl, studying her blue eyes. "Yes, they are mountains. They are rugged, and dangerous, and will tax your endurance and stamina to the breaking point. But they are the only chance we have to get out of here undetected . . . if that is possible."

"I am not climbing any mountains," seethed Judith. "And it is beastly of you even to suggest such a thing."

"What would you have us do, Judith?" asked Susan, gazing hard at the blonde girl.

"We should go in search of the army. They cannot be far from here—and we should go on Braddock's road."

Susan considered telling Judith what she had witnessed of the British army just before she was captured, but didn't. Instead she turned to Patterson.

"You are in no shape to climb such hills, or mountains, Mr. Patterson. Why, one slip on those high bluffs would mean certain death."

" 'Tis a chance we shall have to take."

"Will we stay in sight of the river, Mr. Patterson?" ventured Ivy.

"I'm afraid not, Ivy. This whole country will be swarming with Indians searching for deserters, wounded, and men that have become lost. We will be forced to move twenty, twenty-five miles inland."

"You speak as though the army was defeated!" said Judith defiantly.

Patterson ignored her and continued his crude map.

Finished, he looked up and a whisper of a smile touched his lips. " 'Tis a long way home, ladies, and it shan't be easy—but, we can make it."

"When do you intend to start?" asked Susan.

42

"The first thing to do is move camp," he said in his matter-of-fact way. "We have been at this location much too long."

"Do you intend to travel wrapped in a blanket?" sneered Judith.

"No," said Patterson easily. "I intend to wear my breechcloth and leggin's, but I will wear this blanket until my leg heals enough to stand the pressure. And," his voice held a touch of mockery as he watched her eyes, "should it shock your modesty to see me in such a state of undress, you can rest assured I shall be as embarrassed as you—probably more so." Judith blushed but remained silent.

They were relocated by ten o'clock, having struggled two miles up the creek. The trip had exhausted Patterson long before he finally pointed to a secluded glen where they would camp. Patterson ascribed much of his weakness to hunger, and he knew the women were feeling the pangs also, for they were fast becoming quarrelsome.

He pondered the situation: finding food would have been simple but for his wounded leg. As it was, however, the leg was all but useless, and would be for another few days.

Susan sat down beside him. "We need food badly." It was a statement, not a complaint. He wondered if she had been reading his mind. "It is said," she went on, "that you woodsmen carry everything necessary for survival when you make a long hunt."

"That's basically true," he interrupted. "However, I was not on a long hunt; I was merely on a three-day scout—"

"You need not defend yourself to me, sir. I was just curious as to the truthfulness of the statement."

"It's true up to a point," he said, frowning. "What are you driving at, mistress? I have the feeling this is not just idle conversation."

She turned to face him. "I merely wish to borrow your fishhooks." Her voice had a definite edge to it that caught Patterson's attention and caused him to wonder if she was irritated with herself or him. She pushed a lock of hair off her forehead and sighed. "Mr. Patterson, I have fished many times with my—with Mr. Rothchild." She could have explained that Rothchild was the father of a houseful of girls, and not having a son for companionship, he had substituted the girls. She could ride, use a fowling piece, hunt, and fish, as well as most of the young men around Williamsburg.

Nevertheless, she had put her tomboy days behind her—hence, her angry attitude. But as she sat there beside Patterson and expertly tied a length of linen thread to a small hand-forged fishhook, she silently thanked Mr. Rothchild for his foresight. He had told her many times in his fatherly way that one never knew when one might need useful skills. So for two days following their change of camp, they survived entirely on Susan's skill with the fishhook.

During that time, Patterson was not idle. He taught the girls to load his rifle, going over each step repeatedly; they learned to measure the charge, patch the ball, and seat it against the breech. By the end of the second day they could load and prime as well as many of the militiamen who had followed Braddock into battle.

Patterson was pleased with their progress, especially Judith's. He would have been amused had he known that her enthusiasm stemmed from the fact that she still entertained the idea of shooting him for his insult the day Washington had introduced them.

Patterson exhausted the women, making them practice over and over how to quick-sight and fire the long Pennsylvania gun. Although he did not chance the actual discharge of the weapon, he felt certain the girls were familiar enough with the procedure that, if necessary, they could do so.

On the morning of the third day, he discarded the blanket and, very carefully, donned his breechcloth and leggin's.

Judith and Ivy were aghast at his seminakedness, but Susan was elated that he was able to walk alone, even if he did lean on his rifle for support.

As for Judith's and Ivy's reaction, Susan found it both amusing and irritating. It was a ruse to impress upon Patterson the delicate sensitivity of their nature, which, in truth, was not delicate at all, for the three of them had satisfied their female curiosity of the male anatomy while Patterson lay unconscious from Ivy's knife wound, and there had not been a blush among them.

But as her eyes took in Patterson's broad chest and shoulders and traveled down to his flat stomach, she blushed in spite of herself, and she realized with a start that Judith and Ivy were responding to his near nakedness in some primeval way. Her pulse quickened and her breath caught in her throat, yet she could not tear her eyes from his body.

To see him standing there, tall and virile, with just a hint of danger about his mouth and eyes, and with his lean muscles rippling in the morning sun, was a sensation different from what she had felt when he was unconscious and sickly. Shame overwhelmed her and she dropped her head and prayed the Lord to forgive her for her rising desires.

Patterson was unaware of the tension his masculinity induced in the three women, and they, for reasons of their own, were glad of his ignorance.

The need for food other than fish finally prevailed. So Patterson, with the girls following, limped through the woods pointing out plants and bulbs that were edible. The girls gathered the food, sometimes remarking that a particular plant or bulb was known to be poisonous. Patterson didn't argue and they refrained from questioning his woodsmanship, working in silence, except for Judith, who complained endlessly. Patterson ignored her, but her continual bickering, quarreling, and complaining played heavily on his frayed nerves. She did not understand the need for silence, nor the fact that their very survival depended on the unstinting cooperation of each person.

When they happened upon a small natural pond filled with cattails, Patterson decided that Judith would be the one to wade into the murky water and pull the bulbs. She protested violently and flatly refused to have anything to do with the pond, cattails, or him. Susan and Ivy watched in silence to see if Patterson's authority would prevail. Ivy doubted it, and Susan found herself more than a little reluctant to bet on Patterson.

He eyed Judith wearily, and his face was almost sad as he laid his rifle aside. The very act of relinquishing his weapon should have warned Judith that something was amiss, but so engrossed was she in her tantrum that he surprised her. He seized her wrist, put his foot against her buttocks, and propelled her headlong into the stagnant water.

Ivy cried out and ran to the water's edge, while Susan laughed and clapped her hands. Judith was on her feet instantly, cursing between her teeth, while wiping mud and slime from her dress.

Patterson stood grim-faced as she advanced toward him, cursing with every breath. "You have a savage mouth on you," was all he said.

When she threw what was a fairly decent overhanded punch, Patterson caught her small fist in his hand and gripped hard. Their eyes locked in a battle of wills. He put more pressure on her closed fist. Her face drained of color, and she bit her lip to keep from crying out. He slowly exerted more pressure and her eyes filled with tears, one breaking loose to trickle down her cheek. They held that pose for what seemed to Susan an eternity before Judith, not taking her eyes from Patterson's, said quietly: "I will gather the cattails, Mr. Patterson."

He released her hand, and without a word walked slowly toward camp. She had shamed him with her dignity. She had won.

The cattail bulbs roasted in the coals of a small, smokeless fire while the other plants and shoots and such collectibles boiled in his small skillet.

A strained quiet soured the camp. Judith's jeering eyes followed him wherever he went, and even Ivy—easygoing Ivy—refused to meet his gaze. Susan stirred the contents of the skillet and whistled an unknown tune under her breath. She discreetly avoided looking at anyone.

They ate in silence, each preoccupied. Patterson wondered about the army. Had it survived the onslaught? Was Washington alive—or Gist, or Braddock, for that matter? If so, what would be the next move?

Judith's thoughts were of Southhampton. Where was he? And why had he not come for her? She absently flexed the fingers Patterson had crushed and a twinge of pain caused her breath to catch. She studied her swollen hand and tears of hate filled her eyes.

Ivy's eyes were on Patterson. She was torn between loyalty to her mistress and admiration for the woodsman, and the dilemma had her thoroughly confused. That he was justified in his belief that Judith should share in the work was understandable. That he should resort to physical violence, to the point of harming her mistress, was out of the question. Ivy shuddered, remembering in vivid detail how, when Patterson had crushed Judith's hand and caused her mistress's silent tears, she, Ivy, had eased the pearl-handled dagger from its hidden sheath and, with the deliberate intent of a female protecting her dependent, advanced, slowly, toward the unsuspecting Patterson.

46

That he had released Judith's hand at the precise moment she raised the knife was all that saved Patterson from being struck again with that deadly little blade and, perhaps, even saved his life. When Ivy realized the terrible mistake she had almost made, she had thrown the dagger into the pond. But even before the blade had cleared her fingertips, she regretted the childish impulse that had prompted her to throw away her most prized, her only, possession. Her eyes followed the knife and marked the spot where it splashed in the water.

She spent the next fifteen minutes feeling along the muddy bottom with her bare toes until she located the knife. She vowed then never again to blame her failure to act as a reasonable human being on an object that was nothing more than an instrument of her own weakness. (She was perhaps a bit hard on herself; protecting a loved one can hardly be considered either unreasonable or weak. Her protectiveness would prevail later in her life and have a definite bearing on Patterson's unnatural attitude toward white women.)

Susan stirred the skillet and contemplated the trip that lay before them. The dangers and hardships they would face made her realize with an elated sense of adventure that she was looking forward to the thrill of it all. Also, when all was said and done, it appeared to be the only means by which she might see Rosemont—her beloved Rosemont—again.

The food was delicious after two days of nothing but fish, and Judith grudgingly admitted to Susan and Ivy that the cattail bulbs, or potatoes, as Patterson called them, were well worth the effort required to retrieve them. To Patterson, though, she said nothing. And each time he happened to glance in her direction, her hate-filled eyes taunted him.

They finished the meal in silence and relaxed in the noonday sun. Even Judith became amiable in the heat of the late July day.

The tranquility was shattered by an unexpected shout from deep in the forest. In one fluid motion Patterson was on his feet, rifle cocked.

The women were almost as quick, disappearing into the shadows of the underbrush at the edge of camp. The voice hailed again, closer than before, but Patterson was gone.

"But, m'sieur," said the Frenchman, shrugging his shoulders expressively, "of course I knew you were here. Would I have hailed

47

the camp if I had meant mischief?" He watched Patterson closely as he talked. "I have known you were here for almost a week." Patterson's eyes narrowed and the Frenchman hastily added, "it is true, m'sieur, but we can discuss this after you put down the weapon." He eyed the rifle barrel that was pointed menacingly at his head. "Please m'sieur," he said softly, "they have a way of going off—unexpectedly."

Patterson lowered the hammer to half-cock as he studied the intruder. The man was almost as tall as Patterson. His long black hair, worn loose, accented a short full beard. A round fur-trimmed hat with an animal tail attached to the crown sat at a rakish angle just above the coal black eyes that were set in a skin as swarthy as an Indian's. A light brown linen hunting shirt bordered with blue fringe fell almost to his knees. His moccasins were of the Algonquian style. The man smiled disarmingly as Patterson eased the buttplate of his rifle to the ground.

"Thank you, m'sieur," he said with relief.

"What do you want?" asked Patterson coldly.

The Frenchman sighed. "You are so unfriendly. But, perhaps you have good reason." He smiled again. "Could we not talk more comfortably in your camp?"

"No, we will talk right here."

"But, m'sieur, I would enjoy seeing the mesdemoiselles."

The remark caught Patterson off guard and his face indicated as much, for the Frenchman laughed heartily. Patterson considered the situation a long moment before flicking his head in the direction of camp, indicating to the Frenchman to take the lead.

The women watched from the seclusion of the underbrush as the two men stepped into the small glade. Patterson gave a low whistle and they timidly ventured from concealment to stand by the woodsman's side.

The Frenchman bowed to each girl in turn. "Mesdemoiselles," he said, showing a fine row of white teeth, "I am Fontaine."

Susan curtsied, followed by Ivy, then Judith. Fontaine hesitated, searching for the right words. "I am coureur des bois." He saw bewilderment cross their faces and added hastily, "a—ah—longhunter; a brush loper—a woodsman, like your M'sieur Patterson." His teeth flashed as Patterson's eyes narrowed in speculation.

"Yes, I know you, m'sieur," he laughed. "You were with George Washington at Fort Le Boeuf...two years ago when he made a big talk of war." Patterson looked closely at the man, trying to place him.

Fontaine continued. "And last year, you were with Washington when he surprised our reconnaissance party and killed or captured all of them." He smiled even more grandly. "All but one, that is."

Patterson's eyes narrowed. "So, you're the one that got away."

"Oui. I have seven bullet holes in my *camus*, but not a scratch on my skin."

Patterson smiled, eyeing the patches in Fontaine's hunting frock. "Perhaps your luck has run out, sir," he said easily.

Fontaine laughed again. "I think not, monsieur. I will not die in battle...I will die by the hand of a lovely woman." He winked at Patterson and grinned at the girls, who blushed under his direct gaze. "And," he continued proudly, "I was the one to lead our forces on Fort Necessity the next day. You gave us one hell of a fight there—not like the stupid battle a week ago." Patterson's face turned bitter and Fontaine was quick to clarify his statement. "I do not mean to anger you, m'sieur, but Washington should have been leading your troops." He shrugged elegantly. "We would still have beaten you, but not so easily, I think." Patterson laughed in spite of himself, impressed by the man's candid attitude.

"Enough of war!" cried Fontaine with a grand flip of his hand. "I have come to see the ladies." With a wide grin, he strutted to Susan and moved completely around her. He brought his fingers to his lips and blew a kiss to the universe. "Magnifique," he said, dropping one eyelid to Patterson. He moved to Judith and repeated the performance.

It was Ivy who held his attention. He walked around her twice, studying her from all angles. Patterson saw Ivy's dusky skin flush as Fontaine scrutinized her.

"What nationalité?" It was an abrupt question that both startled and embarrassed the girl.

She looked at Patterson, her face a vivid red. It was obvious that Ivy did not want to answer, but Fontaine persisted, causing her to drop her eyes and whisper, "I am a nigger, sir."

"A *nigar*," he said loudly. "Ho! I never before in my life have seen a *nigar*." Ivy cringed under his gaze, refusing to meet his eyes—or Patterson's.

Fontaine walked around her again, appraising her from all sides. Then he grinned in appreciation and pinched her buttock. For a startled moment no one moved. Then Judith stepped quickly to Fontaine and slapped him hard across the mouth. He stood there, anger replacing the look of surprise that Judith's blow had achieved.

"Mademoiselle," he said dangerously, "why did you do that?"

"You think because she is black you can treat her like dirt!"

Fontaine threw his hands toward the heavens and let them fall heavily to his sides. "Black? Dirt?" Hurt showed plainly in his eyes. "No, ma chérie," he said, not smiling. "You do not understand." Judith started to protest, but he waved her to silence and turned his attention to Ivy. With a pathetic smile, he said softly, "She is the most beautiful woman I have ever seen. I do not care if she is black. She is lovely. That is why I pinch her bottom."

His sincerity was touching and Ivy burst out crying, throwing her arms around Susan, who bit her lip as tears formed in her eyes also. Judith, experiencing a moment of disarming feminine tenderness, and the need to be held, moved to Patterson, laid her head against his chest, and she too cried.

A dumbfounded Patterson looked at Fontaine, who raised his eyebrows in wonder. Patterson put his arm around Judith. He felt her snuggle even closer against him. Then, suddenly, she tore herself from his embrace.

"How dare you!" she blurted. "I am an engaged woman; do you take advantage of me, sir?" Patterson stared at her, his face revealing nothing. Then without a word he turned and limped toward the fire.

Fontaine joined him as he seated himself by the small flame. "Englishwomen are crazy—eh, woodsman?" Patterson didn't answer, but he silently agreed with the Frenchman.

While Patterson and Fontaine sat leisurely by the dying embers and talked, Fontaine withdrew a long hunting knife and casually began flipping it into the dirt at his feet. He noticed the women watching from across the clearing and, emboldened by their interest, rose to full height. He bowed to the ladies, straightened and flung the knife toward a tree some forty feet distant. The blade quivered and flashed in the sunlight as it sank into the trunk. Fontaine grinned at the women, who applauded and cheered.

Patterson smiled knowingly at Fontaine, who winked back at him. Both men knew that any frontiersman worth his salt could equal such a feat—blindfolded. But the women were impressed and Fontaine was enjoying the attention.

Patterson lay back and extended his wounded leg comfortably before him. Fontaine retrieved his knife and the women encouraged him to repeat the performance, which he did. Then they began badgering Patterson to prove his skill. He politely refused.

Fontaine retrieved his knife and stepped off another ten feet. The knife whipped into the tree. Judith moved to Patterson's side.

"Are you afraid of the competition, Mr. Patterson?"

Patterson ignored her.

She turned to Susan and Ivy. 'All Mr. Patterson is capable of throwing...is his weight around."

Patterson's eyes slowly raised to Susan. Her face was imploring, begging him to defend his reputation. Their eyes held for a long instant before Patterson climbed to his feet. Favoring his wounded leg, he moved to Fontaine's side, then stepped off ten more paces. Fontaine grinned openly, wagging his head from side to side.

"She is too great a distance, m'sieur. Not even I, the great Fontaine, can do the impossible."

Patterson gauged the distance through slitted eyes, then astounded the group by removing his hatchet instead of his knife. Fontaine's eyes widened in wonder: to throw a tomahawk some eighty feet accurately was impossible.

The women were silent, watching Patterson weigh the weapon in his hand as he studied the tree.

Then the hawk was spinning, end over end, and a shower of sparks, coupled with the sound of metal against metal, momentarily illuminated the dim shadows beneath the heavily foliated branches of the tree where Fontaine's blade was embedded.

All eyes except Susan's were riveted to the arcing handle and half-blade of Fontaine's knife as it struck the earth some twelve feet from the tree that held Patterson's tomahawk.

Susan had seen what the others had missed: Patterson's face had turned ashen and his hand had instantly clutched the wound in his leg, and she held her breath for fear he would fall. But he straightened immediately and limped toward the tree to retrieve his weapon.

51

Her eyes misted. "Oh, Morgan, I did not mean to hurt you. I just could not stand them laughing at you," she whispered.

Fontaine whistled through his teeth as he fell in beside Patterson. "Magnifique, m'sieur," he said in awe. "I will tell this story around many campfires—you will be famous."

"Just a stroke of luck," said Patterson simply.

Fontaine's eyes narrowed. "I think not, m'sieur." Then he grinned sheepishly and leaned close to Patterson's ear. "But did you have to break my very best knife?" Before Patterson could reply, Fontaine continued in a mock pout. "To shame me before the lovely mesdemoiselles is terrible...but to break my favorite blade!" Fontaine laughed heartily and slapped Patterson on the back causing his wounded leg almost to collapse. But the Frenchman was in such a fine humor, he didn't notice. "Ah, Monsieur Patterson," he cried, "it was worth the loss to see such skill."

Patterson and Fontaine sat in the slanting shadows of the evening sun and talked of hunting and trapping. The women were across the clearing whispering in animated conversation. Now and then they would glance toward the men and giggle or laugh outright.

Fontaine studied the women. "I am reluctant to spoil the good humor of the ladies," he began haltingly.

Patterson nodded. "'Tis a false security they are experiencing, Mr. Fontaine."

Fontaine traced a pattern in the leaves with the toe of his moccasin. "M'sieur," he said slowly, "there is this thing I must tell you." Patterson remained silent, so Fontaine went on. "Pontiac, chief of the Ottawas, was engaged in the battle last week."

Patterson nodded. "I have heard of Pontiac."

Fontaine spat into the leaves. "He is worse than you know. He captured ten British soldiers and burned them at the stake the night after the battle. They died slowly, m'sieur. They screamed for three days."

Patterson's face hardened. He had seen the remains of a man burned at the stake. The man had burned slowly until his flesh had cooked and burst open...Patterson forced the memory from his mind and turned his attention again to Fontaine, who was still talking.

"He hates the English with a passion that is inhuman, m'sieur." The Frenchman crossed himself solemnly. "You have probably heard that the Ottawas eat English babies?" He paused. "I know for a fact it is true."

Patterson's eyes held Fontaine's. "Why are you telling me this, Mr. Fontaine?"

The Frenchman glanced at the women and shook his head sadly. "I am not a soldier, Monsieur Patterson, nor do I make war against women and children—I have a family in Canada." He reached into the neck opening of his hunting shirt and withdrew a golden chain and locket the size of a small cameo. "My wife," he said proudly, holding the locket for Patterson to see. Patterson studied the beautifully painted porcelain miniature of a lovely blackhaired girl.

"Is she Indian?"

The Frenchman grinned. "She is part Chippewa—just enough to give her fire." He winked at Patterson, then let the locket slide back into his shirt. "I wear it over my heart for luck," he said, with the tenderness of the French.

"And besides," he added cheerfully, spreading his hands in a gesture of finality, "it is just a matter of time now, monsieur, before your King George surrenders. So why should I not be generous—eh?"

"You do not know the English very well, Mr. Fontaine," said Patterson soberly. "It will take more than that one defeat to conquer us."

Neither man spoke for several moments. Then Fontaine broke the silence. "Pontiac found the man you killed. His Indians have been searching downstream for you, but they will pass through here tomorrow."

Patterson rubbed his injured leg absently. "'Tis a wonder they have not found us before now."

Fontaine told him then of finding the trail the women had left when they moved Patterson from the creek to the first camp, and how he, after satisfying himself of their situation, had backtracked, obliterating the trail as he went. He told of leading the Indians downstream, where they had accidentally stumbled upon the dead warrior. He assured Patterson that the whole forest was red with painted savages and it would be a miracle if Patterson got the women safely to Fort Cumberland.

Patterson gazed into the gathering darkness, his thoughts contradicting Fontaine's words. No, he decided, the forest was not red with painted Indians; it was red with British blood, and he, by God, would get the ladies back to Fort Cumberland safely.

Fontaine glanced at the setting sun. "I must go." He climbed stiffly to his feet and stomped the circulation back into his numb legs. "I have spent too many winters wading the cold water for the furs," he apologized, nodding toward his legs.

Patterson stood also and the women gathered around the two men. Fontaine smiled broadly at them. "Ah, chéries! Alas, I must go, but there is this thing I must know." They looked at him curiously. "Why," he asked seriously, "do you shed tears when one pays you a compliment?" His eyebrows were askance.

Ivy stepped forward. "Monsieur," she said shyly, "I cried because, sir, no one has ever before told me that I am beautiful . . . and I thank you for it."

"And besides," said Susan, "since when does a woman need a reason to cry?"

"Ah!" cried Fontaine, "French, English, Indian, this is true."

Fontaine offered his hand to Patterson, who promptly laid his own hunting knife into the exposed palm. Fontaine looked at the fine Damascus blade in surprise. "M'sieur," he said almost reverently as he weighed the knife, feeling its balance, "I cannot accept this—it is one of your prized possessions."

"It is a token of my esteem, Mr. Fontaine. At another time, I believe we could have been friends, sir."

Fontaine grasped Patterson's shoulder and looked into his eyes. "But, if I see you tomorrow, my friend, I will kill you." Then he was gone.

Ivy approached Patterson with a worried look. "Did he mean that—about killing you?"

"He meant it," said Patterson, gazing after Fontaine.

"But, you are friends—'tis plain to see."

"He will not kill me," said Patterson slowly. Ivy exhaled a sigh of relief. "For I shall kill him first."

4

At sunrise on July 17, 1755, eight days after the Battle of the Wilderness, the weary foursome were six miles north and east of Braddock's battleground. Patterson was closely followed by Susan. Ivy was helping Judith, who seemed on the point of collapse.

Because the safety of the women depended on their being far from yesterday's camp come sunup, Patterson had marched them unmercifully throughout the night. Slowly and ponderously they had climbed hills so steep that, at times, they had to cling to saplings for balance and leverage.

And when Patterson would signal for a moment of rest, the women would sink to the ground, or slump against tree trunks and swear that they could stand no more.

Yet Patterson pushed them on, down boulder-strewn ravines, through thickets that whipped their faces and arms, over vines and logs that were all but invisible in the darkness, so that they fell sprawling, whimpering in pain and disgust, before pushing themselves erect, to stumble on in Patterson's wake.

Patterson closed his ears to their muffled cries, and Judith's increasing demands to stop and rest. He reminded himself, and them, that their only chance was to keep moving. His alarm was valid, but Patterson was slightly less than honest with himself. He was thoroughly annoyed because of the task he was facing. He had no false impressions as to the dangers and hardships he had undertaken in behalf of the three defenseless women, and he worked his frustrations off the same way man has for generations: through physical exercise. The trouble was, his strength—wounded leg considered—was far superior to that of the women. They had given their best, and they were exhausted.

He wheeled around angrily, pushing Susan aside, and faced Judith. "Miss Cornwallace, you've got to keep up!" Ivy urged Judith on, speaking softly, encouragingly, like a mother to a child. "Ivy," he snapped, "turn loose of the wench; she's got to learn to stand alone."

Ivy quickly released Judith, who abruptly sat down. Ivy dropped to her knees and held Judith tenderly to her bosom.

"The sickness is upon her, Mr. Patterson," the girl said softly as she smoothed back Judith's damp hair and blotted her perspiring forehead with the hem of her dress.

"What sickness?" said Patterson, his eyes narrowing threateningly. "She was all right yesterday."

"That was yesterday," snapped Ivy. "Today she is cramping."

As if to punctuate Ivy's sentence, Judith clutched her abdomen, and groaned aloud.

"The first few days are very hard on her," said Ivy tenderly as she patted Judith's brow again.

"The first few days!" said Patterson hotly. "How long does this sickness last?"

"About a week," returned Ivy cautiously, surveying Patterson's angry face.

"You mean she won't be able to travel for a week?"

"Oh, she'll be able to walk, sir, it just means...well, it means we will have to slow down a bit."

"If we slow down, we're *dead*," said Patterson staring hard at Judith.

"Then we will just have to be dead," shouted Judith. "I can't walk another step; I just can't." She grimaced. "And don't look at me that way. All of us get the sickness; it happens every month."

"You all get it?" He looked at Ivy and Susan, who nodded their confirmation.

He thought about that a moment, and reached a decision: "Then you will all have to be sick at the same time. We cannot waste three weeks out of a month with such foolishness."

"'Tis not foolishness," cried Judith, breaking into tears. "You are so stupid..."

Susan turned aside, whether disgusted with Patterson or Judith or both was hard to say, and started toward the brush that lined the trail. She was halted by Patterson's angry voice. "Miss Spencer, just where do you think you are going?"

She rose to her full height, lifting her small head majestically. Her voice was as soft as Patterson's, and as arrogant. "Nowhere, Mr. Patterson. Absolutely nowhere!" Her eyes held Patterson's as she raised her buckskins to her knees, squatted, and made water.

Patterson was speechless. Something akin to animal terror sent him crashing into the underbrush, his face a vivid scarlet. He had learned a thing or two about the intricacies of women—the hard way.

He was back within the hour, having put his flight to good use by scouting their back trail for a mile or more. He had seen no sign of pursuit.

The women chose to ignore him when he returned. In fact, they refused to acknowledge his presence at all. Judith lay on a mossy spot of earth beneath a giant maple tree. Her eyes were closed and Patterson wondered if she were asleep. He studied her eyelids, paying particular attention to the dark smudge of her long lashes and was rewarded with the briefest flicker of movement before they closed tightly. Irritated by her pretense, Patterson turned his attention to Susan, who was in the process of plaiting her long black hair.

He watched her nimble fingers as they twisted and overlapped the individual hanks into one long braid that fell to the middle of her back. He was fascinated with her swift, deft movements, and would have said as much had she but glanced in his direction. Instead, she spoke to Ivy. "My hair is so filthy it sticks together." Then she leaned closer to the girl so that Patterson wouldn't hear. "I swear I can feel things crawling on my scalp. It's just awful, Ivy."

Ivy, who had cut her dress off above the knees, exposing the lovely contour of her calf and ankle, and was in the process of wrapping the material around her lower legs to protect them from briars and thorns, looked up at Susan in wide-eyed surprise and apprehension.

"Lord have mercy, Susan. I hope you don't have vermin; 'twould be terrible! Why, Judith would never forgive you if she were to catch something from you. I fear she does not care overmuch for you as it is!"

"I fear you are right," said Susan mockingly. "Take a look, would you?" She bowed her head and Ivy painstakingly searched and re-searched her scalp.

"You have no lice that I can see. But I have located the trouble ... 'tis a tick you've been feeling ... there, I've got it!" She held her fingers up for Susan to inspect the small brown insect.

"What are we going to do with it, Susan? I've never before had a tick."

"We'll mash it between two rocks," returned Susan, unable to believe that Ivy had never killed a tick, it being so common during a colonial summer.

Ivy handed the tick to Susan. "You do it," she pleaded. "I've ... well, to be truthful, I've never killed anything in my whole life."

Patterson overheard her and his hand moved involuntarily to his injured leg. He studied Ivy with interest, remembering that somewhere, hidden in the folds of that short dress, was a vicious little pearl-handled dagger, and for a girl who had never killed anything, she certainly knew how to handle a knife.

They plodded on at a slower pace, traveling without incident for two days. On the third day they stopped at a small spring, lunching sparingly on what little food they had. Patterson instructed the girls to stay close to the spring, explaining his need to spy out the area ahead. He suggested they try to sleep, especially Judith. They agreed they would; he should have known better.

He worked out in a long loop, covering a considerable distance, missing nothing. Catching a groundhog sunning itself in a small clearing, he killed it with the flat of his tomahawk, then cut the hog down the middle, flung the entrails out, and tied the carcass to his belt. He smiled to himself; the women would be delighted to eat fresh meat. A short time later, he dogtrotted into camp. Instantly he became cautious, scanning the woods in every direction, paying attention to the smallest detail. The camp was deserted.

Patterson wasted no time picking up the trail. The girls had followed the small stream north for a quarter mile, stopping occasionally to pick berries. In a glade several acres long, they had found an unusually large patch of the fruit and had picked for a long interval. It was there that Patterson found the scattered berries. They were strewn over an area ten feet in length, many of them having been trampled into the earth, indicating a struggle had taken place.

He dropped to one knee, studying the broken weeds and scuffed earth, unraveling the mystery, easily putting the pieces together.

Satisfied, he stood up, thumbed the frizzen of the lock forward, and blew the priming powder out of the pan. He cleared the touchhole with his vent pick and carefully reprimed the weapon. He wanted no misfires.

As soon as they were alone, the women had taken advantage of the cool refreshing water, stripping immediately and scrubbing from head to toe. They lay on the mossy creek bank and relaxed while the filtering rays of sunlight dried their bodies. They tried to sleep as Patterson had suggested, but the icy water of the spring had awakened them to the point that their nerves fairly tingled.

Then Judith suggested sending Ivy to pick the berries growing along the bank of the small stream, but Susan vetoed the idea. Ivy intervened, by suggesting they all go, and Susan finally relented. They picked berries, eating more than they kept, laughed and chattered, throwing all caution to the wind. One would have thought they were on a Sabbath outing.

On reaching the small glade, they were excited by the abundance of fruit they found and decided to pluck their fill there and return to the spring. Susan and Ivy began picking industriously with Judith following along behind, her dress raised in front to create a receptacle for the accumulated fruit. A pair of grouse burst from the treeline at the far end of the meadow and sailed quietly over the heads of the unsuspecting women. An experienced woodsman would have recognized the danger sign immediately and wasted no time in putting distance between him and whatever had alarmed the birds. Susan did watch the woodline for several long moments, bothered by the birds' hasty flight, but relented and returned to her berry picking.

She should not have been startled when they rose from the brambles where she was picking—but she was. They were tall men, as tall as Patterson. Their heads were shaved except for a strip of hair that had grown long at the crown. The tuft of hair was wound tightly so that it stood up like tall grass gently waving in the breeze. Their eyes were piercing, unblinking, like those of a reptile. Her heart stopped, then hammered wildly.

The faces of the Indians had been blackened with a paste of charcoal and bear grease. Their bodies were splendidly muscled and devoid of clothing or shoes. One wore a quiver of arrows at his side, suspended from a thong across his shoulder. His long impressive bow was drawn taut, the arrow pointing directly at Susan.

The other wore a hunting pouch with a beautifully engraved English powderhorn hanging from it. He carried a Brown Bess musket, which he held stiffly before him at arm's length. It also was aimed directly at Susan. His head was thrown back as far from the musket as his neck would allow so that he appeared to be looking down his nose at her.

The surprise caused Susan to jerk upright, and she visibly fought to maintain her composure. She took a deep breath, not taking her eyes from the Indians. "Girls," she said between her teeth, "do not scream, do not run, do not do anything but turn around slowly. We have savages all around us." Although the Indians were only two in number, to the terrified girl they were a horde.

For once in her life Judith obeyed without question, turning slowly as Ivy was doing, to face the Indians. Susan heard them suck in their breath as they became aware of the Indians' nakedness.

She watched in soundless dismay, her heart crying out in pity for Judith and Ivy as the full realization of the savages' undoubted intentions sank into them all.

Her compassion for the others was absolute and unselfish. It did not occur to her to wonder if either of them was experiencing the same tender feelings for her. She wanted to say something reassuring, to ease their mental anguish, but was afraid to speak— afraid that if she did, she would begin to scream and not be able to stop.

The Indian with the bow began strutting back and forth in front of the terrified women, exhibiting his manhood in lewd fashion, his face a hideous grinning mask. Tiring of this, he grasped Susan by the face, flinging her effortlessly to the ground. She raised her head slowly, blinking back the tears that threatened to engulf her and almost succeeding. The imprints of the Indian's fingers were vivid splotches on the sunburned skin of her cheeks; a small trickle of blood appeared at the corner of her mouth where she had bitten her lip during her fall. The Indian laughed, obviously in fine fettle for having captured three young white women. He turned his attention to Judith and placed a well-aimed vicious kick to the unsuspecting girl's most intimate and sensitive spot. The blow scattered the berries in every direction. Judith bent at the waist, fighting for breath, then emitted a slow agonizing wail and sagged to her knees. The Indian howled with glee.

The second Indian said something in a low guttural tone, and both guffawed. The first Indian then resumed his strutting. The one with the musket stepped over Susan and seized Judith's dress, giving it several quick jerks. Judith struggled to her feet, fiercely clutching her abdomen, her face stricken with terror. The Indian grasped Judith's dress a second time and yanked harder. The girl's tear-filled eyes pleaded with the Indian in hopeless desperation.

"Take off the dress, Judith," Ivy said quickly. "Do not fight with him or he will kill us all."

Patterson had grown into manhood reading sign, following trails, tracking, and stalking. He had learned from the best—the Eastern Woodland Indian.

For eight long years he had lived with the Shawnee deep in the Ohio country. It had been a hard way to spend his youth. He had distinguished himself early with the natives, learning their language, customs, and religion, then using that knowledge in his everyday life as the red man did. They observed in stony silence as the lad progressed; they approved of his diligence.

By the time he was ten, Patterson was accompanying warriors into uncharted wilderness on trading missions that took weeks of minute preparation, not to mention the extended days of travel required to complete the journey.

When he was twelve, he helped paddle a thirty-foot birchbark canoe down the Ohio River to a land of tall cane. Game was so abundant that the Shawnee took their winter's supply of buffalo, elk, and deer and started back upriver almost before the water had dried on the paddles from the downstream trip.

He had been afraid that first time when they had beached their canoes on the banks of an island just above a great waterfall, and had slept not at all that night because of the mighty roar of hundreds of tons of water plummeting over the falls and into the churning boils below.

He felt better about his fear when he realized that the grown men were as uneasy about the eerie place as he was. They moved out before daylight the next morning and paddled to a point just above the falls and immediately set up their camp. Young Morgan volunteered to assist the first hunting party out—wishing to put distance between himself and that terrible roar.

He had accompanied a party of twelve proven hunters into the interior of Kentakey, proving to be almost their equal in woodsmen skills. They had taught him well.

He had read the sign instantly: two Indians had captured the girls and fled before assistance could arrive from some unexpected source. The Indians had, no doubt, assumed that three women would not be in the middle of the wilderness unless they were escorted by a large party of guardians. Had they known the only protector of the women was one injured woodsman, they very likely would have waited in ambush and tried for his scalp. As it was, they had roughly prodded the women into line and set off at a fast mile-eating trot in the direction of Fort Duquesne.

Like any truly wild animal, the eastern Indian was unpredictable, but knowing him as he did, Patterson wasn't overly concerned for the ladies' virtue. While on the warpath, Indians rarely, despite popular belief, raped their victims. The truth was that sex to a male Indian was secondary, even in peacetime. Patterson had known one young Shawnee who went two years without touching his wife while their son was of nursing age.

What did bother Patterson, however, was the fear that Judith would not be able to keep up the grinding pace set by her captors. They were moving quickly, and Patterson knew without a doubt that if one or all of the girls faltered or lagged, the Indians would either slit their throats or bash in their skulls. He fully expected with each advancing step to find the girls butchered and abandoned.

He would have raised his eyebrows in wonder had he known how badly he had misjudged Judith's strength and character, not to mention her willpower. Unhampered by the confinement of clothing and scared almost out of her wits, she was trotting vigorously, showing little sign of the burning pain in the pit of her stomach. Susan and Ivy were also keeping pace.

The trail the Indians had taken led up a valley several miles in length. Patterson remembered it from his early hunting days with the Shawnee and was aware that by dropping over the northern ridge into the hollow beyond he could follow that valley until it intersected with the one the Indians were traveling. And if he hurried, he might reach the intersection first.

He cut the groundhog loose and, not missing his stride, angled toward the crest of the ridge. He ran the elevated position for a few hundred yards hoping to catch a glimpse of the women. Failing to do so, he scrambled down the far side. He wasn't dogtrotting anymore; he was running like a deer.

His leg began to throb, and he clenched his teeth trying to diminish the pain. He vaulted a creek twelve feet wide, then immediately leaped over a log four feet in diameter. It was poetry in motion, the control Patterson had over his muscular body. He was aware that the wound had opened, and he glanced at his leggin'. It was turning a dingy red where the blood had seeped through the deerskin. He paid it no heed. However, he did slip the heavy blanket off his shoulder and let it fall noiselessly to the ground.

He hated to let the blanket go, knowing full well he could not attempt to retrieve it, for if an Indian should happen upon it, especially a young man who was scalp hungry, he would, in all likelihood, lie in wait for the owner to return.

A mature Indian, however, would take the blanket and cast for the owner's trail, which he would have ..o trouble picking up and following. So, either way, Patterson wasn't going back over that particular path whether he rescued the women or not.

He put the blanket out of his thoughts and continued to run, dodging deadfalls, jumping age-old partially rotted logs, and splashing through tributaries too wide to jump, until his muscles began constricting and breathing became labored. His wounded leg inflamed his whole body, yet he refused to slow his pace.

He ran on, swinging his head from side to side in an effort to get more air into his lungs. He groaned aloud, thinking of the women should he fail to reach the intersection first. Then he felt his muscles loosen; his breathing came easier. He had his second wind.

The sun had arched high into the west by the time Patterson reached the point where the valleys intersected. He dropped to his hands and knees and laid his head on his forearms. His breathing was labored and ragged. Sweat poured in rivulets down his face and chest.

He fought down a wave of nausea, then pushed himself erect. The world spun sickeningly, then righted itself. He laboriously checked for signs of their passing, but found none. If the Indians had not changed course, his race was partially won.

Patterson had high regard for the eastern Indian as a fighting man, so he wasn't foolish enough to engage two full-grown warriors in hand-to-hand combat unless there was no alternative. But he had too long been the hunter not to have a few tricks stored in the recesses of his mind. His experience with buffalo, elk, and deer had proved to him that big-game animals, whose immediate dangers were at ground level, seldom looked above them. Many times he had stood on a tree limb and quietly watched animals pass directly beneath without their being aware of his presence. The Indian, having coexisted with wild beasts for centuries, had much the same habits.

Patterson selected a large oak that would serve the purpose. Its overhanging limbs, dense with foliage, practically covered the faint trail. After several frustrating attempts, he managed to pull himself into the tree and carefully inch out on a large limb about twelve feet above the ground. With luck, it would be high enough.

He rested his rifle in the fork of a small limb about shoulder high and sighted down the barrel. Content with the sight pattern, he gingerly released his grip on the weapon. It remained wedged in the fork. Satisfied that the gun would not slip from the tree after being fired, he shouldered the rifle again and brought the lock to full cock. He faced down the trail, intending to let the lead Indian come under and get completely beyond the tree before he fired. After that, it would be in the hands of the Almighty. He waited.

He heard them—the soft patting of bare feet, the whisper of weeds being brushed aside, the rasping gasps of people who had run far. Patterson held his breath, refusing even to blink his eyes. His instincts were to turn and look; it was pure agony to stand with his back to them, waiting for the lead Indian to fill his sights.

Then came a topknot, swaying to the rhythm of the trot, and

after what seemed to Patterson an eternity the complete head filled his gunsight. He shot the man through the back of the neck, taking out spinal cord and throat.

Everything froze. Then the girls began to mill about, bewildered, confused, not knowing what had happened. But Patterson's eyes were on the second Indian directly below him. The Indian's feet never moved, yet his body was serpentine, bending, bobbing, weaving, looking for the telltale smoke of Patterson's rifle. Not once did he look up.

Leaving the rifle wedged in the fork, Patterson eased off the limb. Whether the man heard or sensed Patterson's movement one could not tell, but all the woodsman dropped on were the Indian's tracks. The only thing that saved Patterson's life was his injured leg. As he struck the ground his leg collapsed, throwing him heavily to one side. Had he not fallen, the vicious thrust of the Indian's knife would have ended the fight then and there.

As it happened, however, the momentum of the Indian as he sprang at Patterson carried him over the fallen man, sending him sprawling in the dirt. Both men were up immediately. Patterson tried his favorite trick of kicking the man in the groin, but the injured leg slowed his movements. The Indian easily sidestepped the thrust and whipped his knife up, intending to plunge it into Patterson's exposed chest. Patterson hit the Indian a crushing blow to the face; he felt the man's nose break upon impact. A lesser man would have gone down, but this one merely shook his head, grinning while blood gushed from his nose and dripped off his chin. Indians were known to love hand-to-hand combat, and the one Patterson faced was no exception. The greater the fight, the greater the victory, and the red man was pleased to have such a formidable adversary. He chanted it all to Patterson as they circled one another, each looking for an opening, a weakness. The Indian said he would feast on Patterson's heart before the sun was down, and had the woodsman understood the Sauk and Fox dialect, he would have acknowledged the compliment. To eat the heart of an enemy was a sign of great respect for the courage and cunning of the man. But Patterson, not understanding the language, was unimpressed.

He was impressed, however, with the Indian's strength. Patterson had learned to fight Shawnee style. He was fast and agile,

65

but he knew that he was no match for the man he now faced, and that knowledge caused a sinking sensation in the pit of his stomach. Furthermore, his leg was practically useless.

Patterson tried a roundhouse swing with his hatchet hoping to decapitate the Indian. The man lithely ducked under the blow, then closed with Patterson, bringing his knife up for the kill. Knowing a moment of pure fear, Patterson dropped the tomahawk and grasped the Indian's wrist with both hands. The Indian tried to shake Patterson free, to no avail. He tried to sling Patterson from him by spinning around in quick circles, but the woodsman held tight.

With a bellow of rage, the Indian fell upon Patterson, pinning him to the ground, forcing his knife closer and closer to Patterson's exposed midsection through his sheer brute strength.

Susan screamed in frustrated anger as the Indian forced the point of his blade into Patterson's skin. Snatching up the dead Indian's musket, she cocked it and ran to where the two men struggled in mortal combat. Her intentions were good; her reactions poor. The gun discharged prematurely and powder burned both men's faces but hit neither one. Patterson groaned; the Indian laughed.

On the brink of death it is said a man's mind becomes crystal-clear. True or not, Patterson was thinking again, remembering a small pearl-handled dagger hidden in the folds of a dress.

Patterson's face was scarlet and the muscles of his arms were quivering uncontrollably as he utilized every ounce of his waning strength in an effort to keep the knife from slipping deeper into his flesh.

With the cords in his neck standing out like knotted ropes and his teeth tightly clenched, he called to the girl, who stood transfixed, her eyes glazed over from fright.

"Ivy, use your knife!" No movement. Patterson became frantic as the point of the blade sank deeper into the muscle tissue of his abdomen.

"Ivy!" he screamed in rage. "Cut his head off, damn you!"

Ivy came alive then, and the dagger flashed in the sunlight. She threw herself on the Indian, seizing his scalplock and snapping his head back for the split second it took to set the blade before his mighty neck muscles brought his chin down to rest on his chest. The time had been sufficient; the dagger was lodged against his throat.

Ivy sawed back and forth. Gouting blood from the man's neck caused the knife to slip in her fingers. He turned his head slowly, his eyes rolling sideways to lock with hers. They were terrible eyes; accusing eyes. She panicked and sawed even harder. Then a great blast of warm air and a powerful gush of even warmer blood immersed her hand and forearm as she severed his windpipe.

Ivy was wild, sawing madly, knowing even then that the man was dead. Finally, she stopped. The silence was thunderous. She released his scalplock timidly; the Indian's head slid sideways into the dust. His glassy eyes stared at her with sightless hatred. She stood up quickly and turned her back on the ghastly sight.

The dagger slipped from her fingers and dropped soundlessly to the earth. She swayed for a moment to the music of a silent orchestra. Then, as if in slow motion, her eyes rolled back into her head and she leisurely collapsed.

Susan cast the empty musket aside and ran to the fallen girl. Dropping to her knees, she drew Ivy's unconscious form to her and hugged the girl tenderly.

Judith, with one hand on her dress that she had been attempting to wrench from the Indian Patterson had shot, covered her face with her free hand to blot out the hideous scene.

Patterson, covered from the chest up with blood, pushed the body of the Indian from him and sat up. "Is she all right?" he asked Susan.

"Yes," she replied softly. He opened his mouth to praise Ivy, but didn't. Instead, he slowly untied his leggin' and slipped it down, revealing the open wound.

He got the story from Susan as they moved through the twilight in search of a safe place where they might camp for the night. She, walking beside him with the Indian's musket thrown over her shoulder and the shot pouch hanging at her side, told him frankly what had happened. After forcing Judith to strip, the Indian had donned the dress himself, ripping out the sleeves and sides. That done, he had paraded back and forth in front of the other Indian for several minutes. Susan thought the second Indian intended to take Ivy's dress, but he had not. The first Indian had then struck the girls several times with his bow, and motioned for them to follow his companion down the path.

They had stopped only one time to catch their breath between the berry patch and the place where Patterson had surprised them. Ivy had stumbled once and the Indian had beaten her savagely with his bow. After that, nobody stumbled, but Susan knew she could not have ran much farther. No, the Indians had not molested them, but they had educated them—they were the first naked Indians the girls had ever seen. "They looked just like naked white men," she blurted. Both she and Patterson blushed profusely.

They camped that night beside a creek, in a hazelnut thicket, the bushes so tightly woven that even the moonbeams had trouble penetrating the darkness beneath.

During the night Judith called Ivy to her, who in turn waked Susan.

"Judith is dying, Susan," said Ivy quietly, trying hard to control her emotions.

"How do you know?" Susan was alarmed as she moved quickly toward Judith's rigid form, a mere silhouette in the darkness.

"She told me so," Ivy said with taut self-control.

"It is a result of that terrible kick she received. She's bleeding, Susan; she's bled all the way to her ankles. She says she feels like her insides are falling out."

Susan knelt beside Judith and timidly touched her fingers to the girl's exposed inner thigh. She brought her hand away and absently wiped it across her dress, leaving a streak of red stain on the buckskin.

"Mr. Patterson," she whispered, sure that he was awake. "We must have a small fire...and some water."

"What for?" he asked, raising to his elbows.

Susan ignored his question, voicing again her need for fire and water.

"What's wrong with Judith this time?" He climbed to his feet.

"I have no idea what is wrong with Judith," retorted Susan angrily as she took his arm and directed him away from Ivy and Judith, so they would not hear her conversation and become frantic. "And," she went on, sure now she could not be overheard, "out here in this damnable wilderness, we are not likely to find out! Unless, of course," she added testily, "you have knowledge of a woman's internal organs—which I very much doubt."

"No," said Patterson, drawing away from the angry girl, "I

know nothing about women. When Indian women become ill, they go to the women's longhouse and stay there until they get well or die. Men have no notion what goes on in there."

"I thought not," returned the girl stonily.

"There is one thing I have noticed that almost all the women took with them to the longhouse..."

His tone prompted Susan to ask wearily, half-interested, "And what is it that your Indian women took to the longhouse, Mr. Patterson?"

Patterson pushed her aside and strode angrily toward the creek. Susan realized, too late, that he had sincerely been trying to help.

She caught up with him. "I'm sorry, please finish what you were about to say...please."

He ignored her and hastened toward the stream.

Susan watched him go, then ran her hand wearily across her eyes. Would she never learn to keep her big mouth shut?

Patterson kindled a fire in minutes, and shortly after, water was heating in his small skillet.

Susan and Ivy bathed Judith's legs and thighs with one of the strips that Ivy had cut from her dress not three days before. The other strip was used as a cold compress for Judith's bruised abdomen.

Patterson beckoned Ivy to him and handed her his horn cup. "'Tis sassafras tea," he said, looking coldly at Susan. "The Indian women say that it is good for stomach pains and they always take it with them to the longhouse."

Ivy eyed the cup hesitantly. "Do you really think it will help, Mr. Patterson? Indian remedies might not be good for white women."

"It might kill her deader than hell, for all I know!" snapped Patterson, wishing he hadn't bothered to offer the tea. "But I can tell you this for sure: Indian women, after using Indian remedies, are a damn sight more healthy than you three!"

They roused Judith and offered her the drink. She refused, complaining that nothing would lie on her stomach. But Ivy and Susan were adamant, and Judith finally relented. And to the surprise of the three girls, the tea lay quietly. So much so that Judith drifted into a quiet slumber.

The next morning Judith appeared to be worse. The bleeding had almost stopped, but Judith's face was a deathly gray. She made

Ivy promise, for the hundredth time, to inform her mother and father in England as to how their daughter had died. Ivy assured her once again that she would. Then she and Judith cried.

Susan wondered why Judith did not leave a farewell message for Southhampton, but she did not voice the question.

Patterson kept busy digging sassafras roots for Ivy to boil into tea.

For a day and a half they continued their vigil in silence, expecting Judith to draw her last breath.

But on the evening of the second day the bleeding stopped, and Judith's face regained some of its former color. Judith, however, remained feeble, and it was with a very soft voice that she called Ivy to her and touched the servant girl's hand. "I have bled all the blood out of me, Ivy. There is no more left to give. It is just a matter of time now . . . just a matter of time."

"But you look so much stronger, mistress," cried Ivy, clutching Judith's hand tightly. "Your skin is not clammy as it was yesterday."

Judith smiled affectionately at the girl.

"'Tis the way one gets just before one dies."

Susan moved to Judith's other side and gently took her hand.

"I'm so sorry, Judith," she said with sincere anguish. "I've felt so helpless because of our ignorance in matters such as this."

"It is all right," whispered Judith magnanimously. "It is not our fault that we were cast into the eternal pits of hell, with a madman like Patterson for a savior." Judith lay back and closed her eyes. "I will carry no malice in my heart when I depart this world, so I shall forgive Morgan Patterson for what he has done . . ."

"But, Judith," said Susan, "he's as ignorant as—no, more ignorant of women problems than an eight-year-old boy. Surely you cannot blame him—"

"He led us into this terrible wilderness," interrupted Judith with what appeared to be the last of her waning strength, "and he let the savages catch us."

"No he didn't," said Susan firmly. "Braddock led us into the forest—and we, ourselves, paid Patterson's warning about not venturing from the spring no heed at all, remember!"

"'Tis still his fault," said Judith stubbornly.

"Stop it, Susan!" cried Ivy, pushing Susan away. "'Tis un-Christian to argue with—with someone who is dying."

70

Patterson, who had been observing the debate from a spot near the fire, strode to where the girl lay. Hands on hips, he glared into her pale upturned face.

"Why don't you go ahead and die, damn it. We would all be better off if you did!"

Judith's eyes flared wide and she glared at the man standing over her.

He went on angrily. "Why, you're not fit to live . . . you're not fit to call yourself a woman. In fact, you wouldn't make a goddamned beauty mark on a real woman's arse!"

Judith sprang to her feet, weak and shaking from pain and loss of blood. Her eyes were blazing with uncontrolled hatred.

"You miserable scum-sucking swine," she spat. "I'll kill you— God help me—someday I'll kill you!" Then her eyelids fluttered and she collapsed.

Patterson caught her as she fell and gently laid her on her makeshift pallet of leaves.

"She'll feel better when she comes to," he told Susan and Ivy as his hand moved to caress the hair that had fascinated him since the first time he had seen Judith.

He should have paid less heed to Judith's golden curls and more attention to Susan, for she had armed herself with a stout stave about four feet long which she planted soundly across Patterson's bare back.

He sprang erect, spinning at the same instant to face his unexpected assailant.

"What in bloody hell did you do that for?" he yelled angrily when he realized what Susan had done.

"Because you are just as Judith said you are—insensitive! Uncaring! Brutal!" All the while she was speaking she was bringing the stick up to strike him again.

He moved close, caught her wrist, and hauled her against him so that her face was only inches from his. He spoke through his teeth: "Why do white women assume such airs? Why? It is because they never—I repeat, *never*—listen, ask questions, or wait for explanations. They assume that they know every goddamned thing about everything!"

Susan attempted to break free, but Patterson yanked her even

71

closer until she was flush against his body. Her eyes flashed defiance, and every muscle in her body trembled against his flesh.

"Whether you are aware of it or not," he explained, "folk who appear to be improving physically, as Ivy seems to think Judith is, will sometimes die anyway—because they believe, in their minds, that they are supposed to die. They just give up their will to live, as Judith has done, and they *die*. Unless something, or somebody gives them reason to fight for life; to want to live—even if the reason is nothing more than the urge to kill someone."

"It must be true, Susan," cried Ivy excitedly from where she knelt by the sleeping Judith. "Her breathing is easier, and her color is almost back to normal."

Susan searched Patterson's eyes, which were so close their lashes almost touched. She had an overwhelming desire to kiss him. But as her slightly open lips moved closer to his, he pushed her away and turned toward the fire. It was then that she bashed him—splitting both the stave and Patterson's scalp.

She offered no apology. All she would ever say in her own defense was that she felt justified.

They traveled for three days, seeing no one. Their progress was tedious because of Judith's inability to move at a pace faster than a snail's. Except for her labored movements and the unsightly bruise that covered her thighs and the lower portion of her abdomen, Judith appeared to be fully recovered. But she confided to Ivy that the pain in her stomach was of small consequence compared to what she had discovered when she touched herself with her fingers to see if in fact her stomach had fallen out, as she was afraid it had.

"I am no longer a virgin," she told Ivy simply.

"But, Judith! That cannot be; you have never been with a man."

"I do not understand it, either," said Judith. "It must surely be the result of being kicked in such an unlikely spot—I actually thought I was going to die so intense was the pain." Then Judith smiled wistfully, her eyes far away. "'Tis certainly not the way I had planned to lose my prized maidenhead."

"Oh, Judith!" gasped Ivy, mortified by Judith's amused suggestiveness. "You should be ashamed of yourself for such thoughts. Nice young women do not dwell on the subject of . . . of losing their honor."

Judith's clear laughter echoed in the summer air.

"Well, I hate to shock your modesty, Ivy darling," she replied affectionately, "but I am not one bit ashamed of my thoughts—in fact, I rather like them. I was just thinking, or wishing, that I had not been so upstanding and proper concerning my virtue. I would have preferred that James be the one to enjoy that onetime sensation rather than have it kicked out of me by a damned, stinking savage. . . . But, either way, it's gone, and I'm glad. Now I will not have to worry about protecting something I haven't got."

Ivy, however, had been Judith's friend and companion too many years to be fooled by Judith's outward show of indifference. She sensed that Judith was bothered, a great deal more than she cared to admit, by the physical alteration of her body; a body she had unconditionally protected these past two years so that she might present it proudly to her husband on their wedding night.

As the day lengthened, Judith complained that her long dress was hampering her movements to the point of causing her to be continuously exhausted.

"All you need, Judith, is to keep moving. 'Tis the best remedy there is for sore muscles and bones," remarked Patterson sourly.

But Ivy wasn't at all certain that Patterson was correct in his diagnosis that Judith was weak merely from inactivity; that physical exertion would in time build her body back to its former endurance. She felt that Judith's loss of strength was a direct result of her losing so much blood, but, try as she might, she could not understand how that could be, for everyone knew that any surgeon, who understood the intricacies of medicine, believed in bleeding a patient immediately. It was considered a cure for most sicknesses.

Still, Ivy had that nagging suspicion that weakness and exhaustion were directly related to loss of blood, and that Judith's dress, although it did hamper movement to a degree, had very little to do with her mistress's frail condition. Judith, it seemed to Ivy, grew weak even if she were standing still.

Ivy timidly voiced her opinion. "Mistress, perhaps it is more than the confinement of the dress that hampers your movements. Perhaps we should stop and let you rest for a while."

"No," said Judith defensively, "there's nothing wrong with me—nothing! I tell you, it is the material of this long skirt—it gets in the way." She could have added that she would be damned if she would ask Patterson to slow their speed on her account. She would die first!

Judith borrowed the knife Patterson had taken from the dead Indian and followed Ivy's pattern in style by cutting off the bottom of her garment. She embarrassed Patterson by catching him in the act of studying the exposed portion of her legs. She was strangely flattered by his curious gaze. Susan's and Ivy's reactions were quite different: Susan was hurt; Ivy was—Ivy.

They traveled on, Patterson in the lead, followed by Susan, Ivy, and a very sick Judith, who would not admit that the cutting off of the dress had changed nothing; she was still as weak as a new-born. But the altering of the garment would, in time, come back to haunt them, for they had not gone a mile when Judith foolishly cast the material aside. She glanced back once, to see the strip hanging on a low-lying branch, fluttering in the breeze. She turned to go back for it, remembering Patterson's warning about leaving a trail. But as he and the girls disappeared over a slight rise, the forest seemed to close in, imprisoning her. She thought she would suffocate.

She looked wildly at the towering pillars with their leafy branches soaring toward the heavens, and she knew a moment of pure terror. Choking back a cry, she stumbled blindly toward the others, telling herself all the while that Patterson was being overly cautious—that there was no way an Indian could happen upon so small a piece of cloth hanging on a limb in the middle of thousands of miles of wilderness.

She was soon to learn, however, that carelessness could transform a vast wilderness into a small parcel of land.

Patterson jerked awake, listening. He heard again what his subconscious had heard, a bird call with just a hint of human texture. He nudged Judith, who was lying beside him, and her eyes flashed open. She didn't move. The girls had learned a great deal in the past two weeks. He laid his toes against Ivy, but she was already looking at him. He wondered how long she had been awake. He turned his head. Susan had her back to him, but she also was awake; he could tell by her breathing. He noticed, with satisfaction, that she was easing her musket slowly to the ready position. There it was again: the bird call that came from a human. He wondered how the Indians had found them so quickly. He had done everything possible to leave no trail.

Patterson's camp was situated atop a small wooded knoll, a perfect position for a defensive action. The trees on all sides were large and tall, creating an umbrella effect, and shutting out the sunlight so effectively that little underbrush had ever rooted or flourished.

Patterson crawled to the lip of the knoll and peered into the gloom of the hollow below. He forced his gaze to take in the whole hillside where it flattened out at the bottom. He was looking for movement, any movement that wasn't natural. He was rewarded shortly, seeing the Indian mimicking the bird call. The man had his hands cupped against his mouth, and the fluttering of his fingers as he imitated the call of the loon caught Patterson's attention. Once he had the Indian located, it was easy to put together a head, body, and legs. It amazed him how he could look straight at an Indian and not see the man until he moved.

He lay there observing while the Indians congregated, counting nine in all. He glanced toward the women, flipping up five fingers, then four. They nodded in unison. The faces of the girls were drawn and pinched, but there was no outward indication of hysteria. Patterson motioned that they join him, and wordlessly they took their respective positions.

The three women and Patterson had practiced this maneuver several times in the past few days. He and Judith lay side by side as did Susan and Ivy. When he raised himself to fire his weapon, Judith was to do the same, pointing the crude wooden rifle Patterson had hacked out with his tomahawk, and simulate firing it.

He hoped that the smoke from his rifle would fool the Indians into thinking two persons had fired. While he was reloading, Susan and Ivy were to repeat the farce. It would take a tribe of Indians to attack a hilltop with four guns facing them.

Indians' lives revolved around war; they loved it. But dying uselessly wasn't part of the game. Patterson's strategy depended on this.

The Indians began filtering through the trees, working their way up the hill. Patterson brought his rifle to full cock. He to Susan to shoot low. He did not wish to kill the Indians, knowing that if he shot one in the stomach, another would be needed to help the wounded one. That would take two out of the fight, or at least off their trail if they were forced to flee.

Turning her attention from the Indians, Susan studied Patterson's profile. "A wager, Mr. Patterson," she said, forcing herself to smile. Patterson looked toward her, his face a question mark. "I will wager a kiss," she continued boldly, "that I hit more Indians than you."

Patterson blinked slowly, considering her words. He was shocked to say the least, but at the same time he was fascinated with her boldness. He had no desire to kiss her, but if a little thing like a wager could help improve her shooting..."Done!" he whispered as he sighted down the barrel of his rifle. Women were so foolish. There was no way Susan could outshoot him, and he knew it. He congratulated himself on his intelligence.

"Miss Susan, you are a sly one," murmured Ivy. "You know you cannot lose, even if you lose." Susan squeezed Ivy's arm.

The Indians had worked halfway up the hill when Patterson asked Judith if she were ready. She replied that she was. They came up together, Patterson aiming at the lead Indian's navel, Judith with the stick thrust out before her. He fired and saw the Indian go down, then immediately jump up. A small blue hole was visible barely an inch above his navel. He ran his finger into the hole to stop the gut that was trying to burst free, and raced madly back down the hill.

A second Indian let out a bloodcurdling shriek and dashed straight at Patterson, who had dropped to the ground to reload. Susan aimed the Brown Bess at the Indian and squeezed the trigger. The bloodcurdling scream ceased abruptly. The Indian's scalplock, where it had been twisted tight with rawhide, was gone. Frantically he felt his head over, but all that remained was a small knot of the rawhide. He too turned and fled down the hillside, stumbling often, shrieking wildly, pitifully. The scalplock was the proud symbol of manhood, and by accidentally shooting the savage's scalplock off, Susan had castrated him as surely as if she had used a knife. It would have been a funny incident indeed, had it not been a life-and-death matter.

The remaining Indians appeared to have vanished right before

76

the eyes of the whites. For ten minutes not a sound was heard; not a bird called, not a squirrel chattered. It was nerve-racking. Patterson's eyes began to tire.

"White brother!" It was a harsh guttural sound. "White brother, why do you shoot your red brothers?" Although his usage of the king's English was broken and caustic, Patterson could make it out. "We come to you in peace, but you shoot us like animals."

Patterson said nothing.

"Are your ears open, white brother?"

"I hear you, red brother," shouted Patterson.

"Let us talk in peace, white brother."

"My ears are open," responded Patterson.

The Indian moved into view, waving a long thin piece of cloth tied to a stick. "We are Ottawa," he bragged. "I am Oh-phan-tee-yag!"

Patterson flinched. "Pontiac!" A sardonic grin creased his face. Pontiac—the hater of Englishmen; the killer of innocent women and children.

Patterson remembered Fontaine's words, "If you get the opportunity, kill the man as you would a serpent, for he is more deadly than the rattlesnake and meaner than the copperhead."

Patterson held his breath as he raised his rifle and sighted down the barrel at the partially concealed Indian. "Pontiac, you pierced-nosed son-of-a-bitch," he mouthed as he let his breath out slowly, "I'm fixin' to kill you."

Judith laid a restraining hand on his arm. "Is it your intention to shoot the man?"

Patterson took a finer bead. "Just watch that little white pendant that dangles from his nose."

She gripped his arm tighter, spoiling his aim. "Surely you jest; not even you would shoot a man protected by a flag of truce."

"That is no flag of truce," Patterson growled through his teeth. "'Tis the bottom of your dress that he is waving."

Judith dropped her eyes to her exposed knees, and she blanched as she remembered her thoughtless gesture of the day before. Then she put it out of her mind—dress or no dress, it was a flag of truce and should be honored as such. Patterson shook her hand free and quickly resighted the rifle.

"You cowardly bastard," she whispered, her eyes full of

she rolled onto her side, watching him as he fingered

Patterson's shoulders slumped and he lowered the weapon. "He's gone."

"Good," she said, satisfied that she had saved the Indian's life.

Patterson's bitterness startled her. "Good, you say! Do you have any idea who that was? It was Pontiac—the most savage, bloodthirsty, French-loving whore's son that ever bashed a baby's brains out, and you call me a coward for...damn you, Judith, you haven't got sense enough to...to pour piss out of a boot!"

"That will be quite enough, Mr. Patterson," she retorted smartly. "A flag of truce is to be respected."

Pontiac interrupted. "Did you hear my words, white brother?"

Patterson searched hard for the Indian but was unable to locate him. "Red brother," he yelled, "we will not talk with you now. We are eating our morning meal and wish not to be disturbed."

"When you are finished eating, return with me to Canada. Our French Father wishes to speak with you."

"We thank Pontiac for traveling such a long way from home to escort us back to Canada, but we have business here and insist that the Ottawa go on without us."

"Shame, shame," said the Indian. "We will tell the Great French Father you refuse to join him." He hesitated. "He will be very angry with you."

Pontiac stepped boldly into view and strode haughtily toward the bottom of the hill. Patterson raised his rifle and took deliberate aim.

Judith sucked in her breath, sure he would kill the Indian, and hating him for it.

Patterson sighted on Pontiac's back for a long moment. Then with a sigh he eased the butt of the gun to the ground. He lay there, looking at nothing, thinking of nothing—breathing slowly, as if he were exhausted.

Judith turned her head that he might not see her—and smiled triumphantly.

Had she and the girls fortifying that hilltop in the remote Pennsylvania forest that morning known what her act of human kindness would eventually cost the English in lives, misery, and suffering, not only throughout the French and Indian War, but for years thereafter, they would have begged Patterson to kill Pontiac any way he could.

"Are they leaving?" asked Susan incredulously.

"Aye," said Patterson, with a sigh of resignation, as the rest of Pontiac's band walked boldly down the hill.

"Why?" persisted Susan. "They are nine to our four."

Patterson watched the Indians until they vanished into the forest before turning to Susan. "They believe us to have four guns," he said. "We have crippled two of their number, leaving seven. The odds are too great against them."

"Will they come back?" asked Ivy.

"No. They will wait in ambush somewhere ahead." He could have added that Pontiac would not be so foolish as to try a frontal assault again; and, as a result, he would be ten times more dangerous than he had been that morning. Instead, he put the Indians out of his mind.

Susan stood facing him, expectation plainly visible in the depths of her dark eyes. He wondered at her strange expression, then remembered the wager. His face flushed.

"We both scored a hit, Miss Susan. So the wager is a tie."

Susan quickly turned her head to hide her disappointment. She wished she had missed.

But Judith wasn't hampered by any wager. She stepped into Patterson's arms, pulled his head down, and kissed him soundly on the mouth. Patterson looked at her, shocked.

Judith smiled. Ivy cooed. Susan kicked herself.

5

Patterson very likely would have stayed rooted to the hilltop indefinitely had not Providence intervened. It commenced sprinkling, then raining; finally, the heavens opened. The rain fell in heavy sheets throughout the day and night, and far into the next day before dwindling to a steady downpour.

Taking advantage of the concealing rainfall, Patterson put miles between his party and the Ottawas. The women were haggard, weariness evident in their every movement as they trudged along in the quagmire created by the storm. Traveling became treacherous. Creeks that had been only a trickle became raging streams to be crossed with the greatest of caution. Judith lost her shoes, leaving them stuck in the sucking mud as she waded waist deep in the fast-moving current of one such stream.

Lightning flashed, momentarily illuminating the dark interior of the rain-lashed forest, revealing to them how utterly feeble their efforts were against the arsenal of the Almighty. They trudged on, wading creeks and climbing mudbanks only to lose a handhold and slide back into the surging, cascading washout; then, wearily, to try again.

Patterson stood with Susan and Judith on the edge of one such incline above a particularly treacherous creek they had just crossed. Ivy was halfway up the muddy embankment when her hand slipped.

Patterson quickly extended his gunbarrel to her, stretching out and down as far as he could in an effort to reach her. But it was a futile try, and he watched in helpless despair as Ivy made one grand attempt to grasp the rifle barrel before sliding sideways into the roaring vortex. She bobbed up immediately, only to disappear almost as quickly. Susan and Judith stood transfixed as Ivy surfaced again, to be tossed and turned, then sucked under for a third time. Patterson, in a running limp, bounded along the bank in an attempt to stay even with the struggling girl.

It would have been an easy task had he not been injured, but the wound itself, inflicted by the very person who needed his assistance that moment, was his downfall. The leg gave way and Patterson fell hard. It knocked the breath from him, and he lay there soaked and muddy, writhing in pain.

Ivy bobbed up twenty yards downstream. She was fighting for life, trying to stay afloat. As she disappeared from view once more, Judith put her knuckles to her lips, her eyes wide with fear.

"Ivy," she whispered, "Oh, Ivy." Then she cried, her tears indistinguishable from the raindrops.

"Judith!" shouted Susan, trying to be heard above the roaring torrent. "We have got to do something. See if you can help Patterson. I'll try for Ivy."

She left Judith standing there, not realizing the frightened girl had heard nothing she said. She ran past the prostrate Patterson without sparing him a glance, secure in the belief that Judith would see to his condition. She raced, slipping, sliding, falling to one knee, then continuing on, watching for Ivy to surface again.

She tried desperately to wipe the water out of her eyes, only to have the driving rain almost blind her as she searched for the girl now lost in the turbulent waters.

Then she saw her. Ivy was clutching a small overhanging root, trying to hold on against the awesome pressure of the water as it surged over and around her.

Susan could see Ivy's small white-knuckled hands slipping, an inch at a time, as her waning strength threatened to give way completely and allow the angry current to claim the prize it had seized and was fighting to keep.

Susan dropped her musket, flung herself to her stomach and crawled toward Ivy, who was clutching the root desperately. She was shaking her head, telling Susan to go back, that it was too late for her. Then her hand slowly opened and the water boiled up over her head.

But Susan did not stop; she plunged her arm, head, and upper body completely under the sucking torrent. The powerful current dragged mightily and for a terrible instant she thought that she too would be drawn into its deadly depths. She pushed deeper, winding her fist into Ivy's hair. Then she began crabbing backward, little by little, inch by inch, until she had the girl's head above water. Ivy struggled, trying to help, aware of what Susan was proposing, but her attempts were futile; in fact, they hampered Susan, and prolonged the rescue.

But finally it was over, and both girls lay in the driving rain, now weeping, now laughing. Wearily, they climbed to their feet and stumbled unsteadily toward Patterson. He had managed to raise himself to a sitting position, his back resting against a small tree. Judith stood over him with her knuckles still pressed to her mouth. She was in shock.

As the two approached, Patterson looked up at them with a begrudging pride, but spoke harshly. "You two all right?"

They nodded, shocked by his angry attitude. Patterson attempted to regain his footing, shaking off their efforts of assistance, electing to pull himself erect by his own strength and the use of the tree as support. He retrieved his rifle from the muddy water and thumbed open the frizzen. The priming was gummy, a black watery paste.

He used the corner of his breechcloth to wipe the pan clean, then flipped the frizzen closed. In rain like this, his and Susan's guns were only dead weight.

Lightning flashed and was followed by a deafening clap of thunder. A giant tree limb snapped off and crashed to the earth with such impact that the ground trembled. Patterson decided to hole up until the storm blew itself out and said as much to the three women. They looked at him with gratitude as another bolt of lightning lighted the area. They all were haggard.

They had been exposed to the elements so long that their rain-soaked flesh was wrinkled and pinched, their lips puckered and blue. Ivy's eyes were bloodshot from her ordeal in the muddy water and Susan's weren't much better. They all looked ancient.

Patterson felt a surge of cheap satisfaction as he watched them, recalling Judith's elegant dress and pompous hairstyle that first time he had seen her. She was certainly less than elegant now. His eyes narrowed as he looked at Susan, remembering her bravery as she lay in the stream pulling Ivy to safety. She was a strange one. It was evident that she was as much a lady as Judith; then again she wasn't. She was bold and occasionally impudent, but at the same time quite naive. He barely cast a glance at Ivy, whom he viewed as nothing more than a shadow of Judith.

As if Susan were reading his mind, she smiled, showing her teeth, a stark white against the deep purple of her lips. "A pretty picture we make, do we not, Mr. Patterson?" Her hair was plastered to her small head and rain dripped off her nose. The muddy buckskins clung to her body like a second skin, revealing the svelte figure beneath.

Aye, Miss Susan, he thought, a pretty picture indeed. But he didn't bother to answer.

Judith dropped her clenched fist. Teeth prints showed clearly in her white knuckles where she had bitten into the flesh. "Mr. Patterson," she said, forcing herself to remain calm, "I do not think I like you at all."

Patterson raised his eyes and squinted at her in the driving rain. "Judith," he replied deliberately, "I don't really give a damn what you think."

The rain continued into the afternoon before slacking off to a cold drizzle. Patterson found a jutting overhang of rock about four feet off the ground; it created a small cave which receded five or six feet into the hill. He motioned the girls to the overhang and lent a helping hand to Ivy, who seemed on the brink of collapse, before crawling in after them. He was pleased to find it dry beneath the ceiling of stone.

But there was no rest for him. He emerged immediately, leaving his rifle and shot pouch with the women. Using his tomahawk, he chopped down several small cedars, making sure to cut them off at ground level and cover the stumps with leaves. The saplings were placed against the face of the overhang, creating a comfortable room underneath. He turned and surveyed the wilderness. Not a tree appeared to be missing; everything looked natural, including the overhang. Satisfied, he crawled into the burrow. Susan and Judith had pulled the charges of the weapons and were attempting to dry out the barrels by running wet patches down them. It was a wasted effort. Careful not to uncover a rattlesnake or copperhead, Patterson gathered a pile of dry twigs from within the recesses of the overhang. With flint, steel, and a remarkable patience, he got a small fire started. Stepping into the rain again, he disappeared into the wet stretches of forest, returning moments later with an armload of semidry wood which he laid in a pile near the flames. He added a piece or two to the fire before turning to the women. Their clothing had begun to steam and they reeked with an odor he was unfamiliar with. He wondered if his man smell was equally offensive to their delicate nostrils. Patterson advised them he was going to the top of the bluff to spy out the area, so that they might tend to their needs in privacy.

He disappeared through the opening between the rock and the cedar saplings, climbed to the top of the bluff and cast a careful eye over the forest spread out below him. Fog lay low in the valleys, diminishing his vision to some extent, and the mist completely shrouded the woodlands. The forest was clean and beautiful; not an ax mark, burn, or girdled tree could be seen.

Melancholy washed over him as he sat high on the bluff absorbing the spectacular view. He could not have explained his gloominess had he tried. But it had something to do with this pure undesecrated wilderness, he sensed, and the changes being wrought by the white man—progress they called it. If a great tree spread its branches where a cabin was desired, the tree fell, never to grow again. If a forest stood where a field was fancied, the forest disappeared along with whatever wildlife it had nourished and protected. If a river overflowed and flooded a natural valley, creating fertile bottomland, it was dammed or dredged, polluted, or ruined. Game was slaughtered with wanton abandon. Buffalo were killed by the hundreds, just for the hide (sometimes only the tongue); elk and deer for a quarter section.

A land of milk and honey—but progress was turning the milk sour and the honey bitter because the white man could not live harmoniously with any of God's creatures, not even with himself. Greed, arrogance, stupidity, and the idea of something for nothing prompted the English to push for control of the Ohio Valley. The greedy and arrogant used the stupid to acquire that something for nothing. But everything had a price that someone paid one way or another. In the final analysis, usually the stupid—in blood, toil, tears, or death. He thought of the hundreds of men who had already perished with Braddock, not knowing what they were fighting over or why.

Patterson did understand settlement—though he had little ability to put that understanding into words—and his reaction was a profound sadness for himself, the Indians, the wilderness, and, yes, the white man. So he purged his soul by drinking deep of the purity of the virgin wilderness, knowing that its days were numbered, and that he was but a cog in the wheel that counted time.

Even though he heard Susan approach long before she reached the outcrop of rock he was using as a sentinel post, he was again impressed with the ability of the three women to grasp the many lifesaving lessons he had taught them. Almost every day he had shown them or explained something necessary to survival in the wilderness; the girls had been interested and asked many questions. Perhaps they knew their life might depend on it.

Susan sensed his mood and said nothing as she sat down beside him, crossing her legs and drawing them beneath her. They sat in shared silence for a long while before she finally broke the quiet.

"'Tis beautiful, is it not, Mr. Patterson?" She reached out to take his hand, and he felt a moment's pity for her because her fingers were clammy.

"Aye," he said slowly, turning toward her. "It is that, Miss Susan. But do you not find the very vastness of it somewhat frightening?"

She continued to stare across the endless wilderness, then after several moments answered softly, "A few days ago, sir, I would have answered yes to the question, but now"—she hesitated to collect her thoughts, her brow knitting—"now I would have to say no. I have learned that the forest is as kind as it is cruel; beautiful as well as frightening; tender and savage." She hesitated again, then resumed. "If one accepts it, as you have done, Mr. Patterson, the wilderness will yield more than it demands, and if someone more intelligent than I should ever study on it, perhaps it would be found that all God's creations would be equally just, if humans would but learn to live with them." She laughed lightly, embarrassed at her simple

85

attempt at philosophy. "Forgive me, sir, I do ramble on, occasionally."

"I did not know women were capable of such understanding," said Patterson seriously.

Her fingers stiffened. She disengaged his hand and stood up. Perplexed, he grasped her arm and turned her toward him.

"Do you cry?" he asked incredulously.

"No," she replied, not looking at him. "'Tis the rain in my face."

He accepted that, and asked her to resume her seat, which she did. But the moment was lost and a strained silence followed.

He finally turned to her and studied her face for several moments. She wondered at his actions and was about to voice her inquiry when he spoke. "'Tis none of my business," he said slowly, watching her eyes, "but who was that man at my camp, the one who was mistreating you?"

Susan's eyes twinkled and she smiled as if it were a private joke. "He was my benefactor," she said, suppressing a laugh.

"Benefactor!" exclaimed Patterson in disbelief.

"Aye," she said. "Did you not know I am a bound girl?"

He shook his head. "I had no idea. I must be as stupid as Judith says I am."

She did laugh then, a light melody echoing in the evening mist, and the sound was so pure and clear that Patterson was forced to smile in return. They sat like that for several minutes, yoked by the simple act of each finding in the other the ability to laugh at oneself. It was a good feeling, a fleeting moment of rapture treasured by both after their grueling hardships.

She wished the moment would last forever, but even as she gazed into his eyes, she saw the light flicker and die and she regretted that the intimacy was gone. She sighed and gently touched his arm. "Thank you. I needed to laugh." She let her hand fall away. "It's been so long." She leaned forward then and hugged her knees to her breast.

Patterson lay back on one elbow and looked musingly at her. "You laughed the other day, when I booted Judith into the pond."

She smiled wistfully. "Aye, but that was different. I—I feel at peace just now . . . 'tis difficult to explain." She looked across the wide expanse of wilderness and was quiet.

Patterson watched her through half-closed eyes, waiting for her to continue.

"I would like very much to tell you about myself," she said almost hurriedly, perhaps a bit apprehensively. She peered deep into his eyes hoping to see a glimmer of interest there.

Patterson sensed in her the desire to talk. And although he wouldn't admit it, he was curious about the girl and wondered about her past. He took her hand again, feeling her small fingers intertwine with his, as a frightened child's might have done. It dawned on him that she was afraid he would not listen.

"'Tis a good time to talk," he said gently. "I should consider it an honor to share your story."

6

Susan Marie Spencer was born October 26, 1737, in Devonshire, England, to Jack and Rebecca Spencer. Her early childhood was spent on the fringe of luxury, for she was the daughter of a successful shipping merchant during a time of recession in England.

Jack Spencer doted on his daughter, lavishing upon her gifts and toys until she was understandably spoiled, but he loved her for that also. Her mother was a gentlewoman and although she thought the sun rose and set in her daughter's eyes, she tried in some measure to instill in the child a measure of values, both spiritual and material. When Susan was four years old, her father started her education, employing a tutor from London. Susan was a bright child and learned quickly, to the utmost pleasure of Master Pittman, her instructor.

For the next several years, Pittman took a personal, as well as academic, interest in Susan's education, teaching her science, history, and other subjects to which women were not normally exposed. Susan's keen mind and wit were a constant delight to Mr. Pittman, and he reveled in the child's ability to grasp and reason in subjects far beyond her years.

She began to take notice of the world outside her home, particularly the dreary lives of the children her age who lived in the miserable tenant buildings on her father's estate. She was eight years old when she made her father furious by giving away her toys to those same children who came daily to watch her play in the small courtyard behind her home. They had accepted her toys with tight, close-mouthed expressions, turning immediately to run from her for fear that she might ask for them back. She was hurt, as only a child can be hurt, but she learned a valuable lesson. Her father had scolded her at length and had broken her heart. She had cried until, taking her in his arms, he had explained how friendship was earned through respect and loyalty, but never purchased with trinkets and gifts.

He explained further that not only the person accepting gifts, but also the one extending them would eventually forfeit dignity and self-respect, for one would learn to hate the other because each would bring to surface the shallowness of the other. It was a lesson she never forgot.

Her home was a happy place where her parents entertained frequently. And although Susan was too young to join in the festivities, she did sneak many a peep at the musicians, dancing couples, and elegant men and women who attended. She learned the minuet by dancing with her shadow in the seclusion of her room, and became quite adept. Many times she had lain awake listening to the young ladies in the next room giggling about this boy or that man until, finally, she would fall asleep to dream of dancing to beautiful music in the arms of some princely young gentleman. She looked forward with breathless anticipation to her sixteenth birthday, six years hence, when she would be formally presented. Sadly, the young girl's fancy was destined never to be.

Prosperity in England continued to deteriorate, and Jack Spencer was experiencing the decline in the worst way—financially. For the poor, a depression meant nothing, for they had nothing; but for the well-to-do, it could mean catastrophe, and such was the case for the Spencers. Jack had borrowed heavily on his holdings, mortgaging his home and estate. He invested every penny he could raise in a shipping venture to the East Indies. A cargo of spices, silks, and exotic woods, brought back from the Indies at this particular time and sold on the world market, could end the Spencers' financial problems for a long, long while. The ship went down in a great storm. All was lost.

Jack called the family together to explain the circumstances. He was very reserved in his comments and ten-year-old Susan didn't fully understand the tragedy brought about by the lost ship. With a child's confidence, she had taken her father's hand and told him all would be well and not to worry. Mr. Jack Spencer's worries were over the following morning. He had taken the easy way out, using a small pocket pistol. Master Pittman, unemployed and with no prospects for future employment, bade Susan and her mother a tearful farewell.

Immediately after the funeral, Rebecca and Susan were apologetically, but firmly, ushered from the only home Susan had ever known and left destitute in the streets of Devonshire. The very children with whom Susan had shared her toys taunted her until Susan's mother rapped one a solid blow to the head, momentarily ending her ridicule.

Susan held her small head high as she and Rebecca marched down the hill away from their home, leaving behind them their world. A bleak future, indeed, loomed fearsomely before them. Living from hand to mouth, they slowly made their way to London where jobs were said to be available, if one was not afraid of hard work.

London was little improvement over Devonshire. Unemployment was rampant throughout all of England. Susan could not understand her mother's reluctance to accept one of the many invitations she received to visit with this gentleman or that merchant. They seemed such fine people. But Rebecca continued to refuse such propositions, offering instead her services as seamstress, cleaning woman, maid, or in any other legitimate enterprise that would put food into their mouths.

But work was not easy to find, and Rebecca cried for her daughter, who grew thinner each day, until even her stockings refused to stay up, falling instead in ripples around her tiny ankles. Finally, on the brink of starvation and desperation, Rebecca relented. She and Susan moved their pitiful belongings into the modest townhouse of Lord Winthrop Boelinger.

Boelinger was rude to Susan and worse to her mother, but they were eating well. It did not bother Susan that she and her mother occupied separate bedchambers. What did upset her was the thin wall that divided their rooms. It offered very little privacy for the occasions when Lord Boelinger visited her mother. For Susan could plainly hear her mother's soft weeping after he was gone.

After one such occurrence, Susan tiptoed into her mother's room and asked her why she cried. Rebecca gently took the girl into her arms and told her that someday she would explain.

Then, late one night, Lord Boelinger had appeared at Susan's bed. Drunkenly, he babbled lewdly about her mother... and then about her. Susan screamed as he tried to force himself upon her. Hearing her daughter's cry, Rebecca had gone insane. She unsheathed Boelinger's swordcane and plunged it deep into his body. He had not died, but fearing for his reputation should his wife find out that he had attempted to molest a ten-year-old girl, the peer of the realm had used his money and influence to have Susan and her mother thrown aboard a ship whose cargo consisted of idle women, whores, debtors, thieves, and beggars. It was one of the first of many boatloads of unwanted dregs that were forcibly shipped to the New World, against their will.

The voyage was wretched. What little food they were given was vile; the hold, where the miserable passengers were housed, was foul with the stench of urine, feces, and unwashed bodies. Many died, which was a blessing to the survivors. The additional food and space, with one mouth and body fewer, were deemed a godsend. The human cargo was treated little better than animals, and it was animals, indeed, that were without ceremony ushered from the stinking, dark hold to stand on the smooth well-scrubbed planking of the ship's deck, blinking painfully in the sunlight.

"Tomorrow," rasped the captain without preliminaries, "will be your last day aboard this vessel." He waited as shouts of joy from the passengers died away. "I want you to look your best," he barked, "instead of like the filthy beasts you've let yourselves become while on this voyage."

The crowd remained silent, afraid to protest the fact that they had had little choice in the matter. The captain went on, ignoring their angry glances. "You will undress and wash yourselves." He held up his hand as several of the women protested. "Fear not," he said with a smile. "The crew has been informed that should harm come to any one of you, the guilty man shall be keelhauled."

Several of the bolder women wasted no time shedding their garments and stepped into the tubs of sea water the crew had prepared. Rebecca held Susan to her and hid the child's face as the deckhands gathered around the tubs to make sordid jokes and bold propositions to the bathing women, who, in turn, quoted prices and made lewd gestures toward the men.

When Rebecca's turn came, she politely refused, which touched off a clamor among the deckhands who had prepared her tub. The captain strode angrily toward her. "Woman," he said, "you can either undress yourself and get into that tub, or my men will do it for you." He looked hard at her. "I'll have no foolishness about it. You will take a bath—one way or the other."

"I'm not refusing to take a bath, sir," answered Rebecca. "I would just...appreciate some privacy." She realized the mistake of her words even as she spoke them, and after they were spoken she wished she had said nothing. All she had succeeded in doing was to draw the attention of everyone aboard to herself. She regretted her blunder.

The captain looked at her with amusement. "Privacy you want, eh?"

"No, captain," she said quickly. "'Tis all right. Privacy shan't be necessary."

"Ah, but I think it is," he said, turning to his deckhands. "Gather round her, lads. That's it, make a circle so she'll be sure no prying eyes behold her womanly charms." The men guffawed as they made a loose circle around the frightened woman and stood waiting expectantly.

So Rebecca was forced to suffer the indignation of bathing naked before the eyes of the captain and the entire crew as they made bawdy remarks, pinched her nipples, and caressed her buttocks until she cried from shame and humiliation.

The only bright spot in the sordid affair, and Rebecca consoled herself with the knowledge, was that Susan bathed in relative safety, away from the prying eyes, rough language, and, rougher still, the pinching and probing hands of crew members, for they were all gathered around her.

When the ship dropped anchor in the mouth of the James River, at a town called Norfolk, Virginia, the year was 1749; Susan Spencer was eleven years old.

She and Rebecca, along with the other survivors of the voyage, were quickly ushered toward the town square, where a crowd of people from all walks of life had gathered. Susan noticed that very few of the assembled mob were as finely dressed as she had expected; most were wearing homespun, a few were in broadcloth, and several standing off by themselves wore leather garments of a fashion she had never seen before. She would later hear them called woodsmen or longhunters.

She clutched her mother's hand as she noticed a group of Indians squatting in the shade of a tree, their expressionless faces showing nothing, their black flashing eyes missing nothing.

"What are those things?" she asked Rebecca.

"What things, darling?"

"Those red things sitting under that tree." She pointed at them.

"Do not point, Susan. 'Tis not polite."

Susan dropped her hand. "But what are they?" she persisted.

A man walking beside them intervened. "They be bloody savages, is what they be, young lass. They creeps around in the bloody night and cuts off people's heads, they do."

Susan clutched her mother's hand tighter and stared wide-eyed at the Indians.

The city was a bustling place. Men were running here and there carrying bundles, rolling casks, or driving carts. To Susan it was all confusion and chaos, but after the weeks she had spent in the hold of the cramped ship, it was bliss.

She gleefully pointed out this and laughed at that while her mother smiled and apologized for her. Then they were standing before a large platform in the center of the square. A table and chair had been placed on the wooden structure. The captain of the ship stood off to one side conversing with several official-looking gentlemen. He turned and advanced to the table, rapping three times upon it with the butt of a long pistol.

"This sale is now open! The terms are cash on delivery and no refunds." He coughed into a handkerchief, then wiped his brow with it. He motioned for a young girl, perhaps twelve or thirteen, to step up onto the platform.

"This is a prime lass," he bellowed. "She is trained as a seamstress. Now what am I bid?" One look at the girl told the story; her wrists showed scars of manacles, and her belligerent glare showed scars of something that went a lot deeper.

Someone in the crowd jeered. "Seamstress's arse. She's probably got the bloody flux. Look how bowlegged she is." Everyone laughed, including the girl.

Susan turned to her mother. "Are they going to sell us, mother?"

"Yes, Susan," she answered softly. "We will be indentured servants. Someone will pay our ship's passage and we will work a number of years to repay the debt."

"How long will it take . . . to repay the debt?"

"I don't know, darling," Rebecca said wistfully. "We will have to wait and see."

Susan watched as several of the younger girls were sold. Then the mature women were brought forth. Hoots and catcalls could be heard across the square. Susan didn't understand the meaning of it, but her instincts told her it was base and degrading, and she felt her mother's embarrassment.

Then she and her mother were standing on the platform, Rebecca clutching Susan to her, staring wildly at the leering crowd that faced them. The captain was speaking again. "I tell you, this woman and child are gentle-bred and of fine family." He was drowned out by the laughter of the crowd.

"We know what kind of women you bring from England: whores, hussies, and such, and we know what that woman and her bastard is. Nay, you'll not fool us with that rot, captain!" Another wave of laughter covered the voices.

Susan looked up at Rebecca. "Mother, what is a whore?"

Rebecca kneeled and held Susan at arm's length. "'Tis a bad woman, Susan." She struggled to hold her composure. "And no matter what—remember, we are good people."

Susan broke away and ran to the edge of the podium. Before anyone could stop her, she cried out, "You lie, sir. My mother is a good and decent person."

The captain snatched the child away from the crowd and pushed her roughly against Rebecca. "You best teach her some manners, woman, or she'll get a hiding sure."

He turned a smiling face to the crowd and mopped his forehead again. "Now what am I bid?"

A voice in the crowd called out, "Separate them. I want the woman, but the devil can take the wench." The crowd laughed again. Rebecca clutched the child even tighter.

"Please, captain, please do not separate us, I beg of you, sir." Tears were streaming down her cheeks, as she looked imploringly at the captain.

He ignored her, turning again to the crowd. "I will split the pair and then regroup them. They will sell whichever way the money is best." Roughly he pushed Rebecca forward, restraining Susan.

"What am I bid for this woman? Now look her over, lads; a fine specimen, twenty and nine years of age. Does domestic chores." He paused, then laughed at his own sordid joke. "Come on now, lads, what am I bid?"

A man in the crowd called out five pounds.

"Five pounds, you say," cried the captain, aghast. "Why, sir, she would bring ten times that in New York."

"Then take her to New York," howled the man.

Vernon Rothchild stood in the crowd and witnessed the sale of the women. He had been in Norfolk for over a month attending sale after sale of indentured servants. Disgusted with the lot that had just crossed the podium, he gave up his quest to find one woman in that long line that adorned the auction block who could capture—and hold—his attention.

He was in the act of turning away when Susan challenged the crowd in her mother's behalf.

Rothchild studied Rebecca with fresh interest, watching carefully as the captain pushed Susan into her outstretched arms. He was not only surprised, but pleased to note the undisguised love and pride that shone gloriously on her face as she drew the child to her. He studied her face closely for a long moment as she held the girl tight, and he was overwhelmed with the transformation that took place right before his eyes. The woman and the child were...yes! They were beautiful.

He was startled by the sound of his own voice when, without thought or intent, he cried out a ten-pound bid.

"Eleven," said the first bidder angrily.

"Thirteen pounds," challenged Rothchild.

"Thirteen pounds," echoed the captain. "Do I hear fourteen, fourteen anywhere?" He paused, looking over the crowd. "Thirteen once, thirteen twice, thirteen three times." He paused again. "Sold for thirteen pounds to Mr. ———?" He raised his eyebrows in question.

"Rothchild. Vernon Rothchild, sir."

"All right, sir," answered the captain. "And now we will sell the child, but remember," he said, looking at Rothchild, "they shall be regrouped and sold again. Is that understood, sir?" Rothchild nodded.

"All right," cried the captain, looking out over the crowd angrily. "How much for the lass? She's a fine intelligent child, strong and willing to work. How much, I say?"

"Two pounds," came a voice from the crowd.

"Nay," cried the captain. "I'll keep her myself before I'll settle for two pounds."

"Two pounds, six pence," called another, unimpressed by the captain's threat.

The captain feigned hurt. "Come, come, ladies and gentlemen. This child is bound for a full term. Aye, seven years of labor, and I am bid only two pounds six?"

Susan looked at the crowd, trying to put a face to the voice of the bidder, but everyone looked the same to her and she gave up, turning her eyes instead to her mother. Rebecca's face had drained of color and her eyes brimmed with tears. Her fingers unconsciously worked the fabric of her dress.

"Do I hear another bid?" cried the captain. None was forthcoming.

"Sold to Master National Larkin for two pounds six," he said disgustedly. "What am I bid for the pair?"

"Seventeen pounds," came a quick reply from Larkin.

Susan picked him out of the crowd. He was a big man, almost

gross. He had a jolly round face, but his eyes were small and cold. She shivered involuntarily, remembering her harrowing experience with Lord Boelinger. And the look in Larkin's eyes was much the same as his; she nervously pushed herself against her mother's skirts.

"Seventeen, once," cried the captain, "seventeen, twice—"

"Twenty pounds," came the quiet voice of Rothchild.

"Twenty pounds, you say, sir?" returned the captain, unbelievingly.

"Aye, captain, twenty pounds silver," said Rothchild firmly.

"Then, twenty pounds it is. Do I hear another bid?... Twenty pounds once, twice, three times. Sold to Mr. Rothchild." He turned to Rebecca, "Lady, you and your daughter will sign these indenture papers or make your mark if you can't write." He indicated the papers on his desk and handed a quill to Rebecca.

She signed her name in a beautiful scrolled handwriting, then passed the pen to Susan, who dipped the quill in the inkwell and followed her mother's example.

The captain picked up the indenture papers and stared at them. Rebecca Spencer, he read, and for a moment wondered if she was related to Jack Spencer, the owner of the ship sitting at anchor in the Chesapeake Bay. He knew an instant of uneasiness as he looked from the paper to Rebecca, remembering a night during a storm when he decided that piracy was more profitable than captaining a vessel for some high and mighty gentleman in Devonshire.

So he had shifted course, sailed to the coast of Carolina, gone into drydock, and given Spencer's ship a facelift. The cargo had been sold in Wilmington. Then he had set sail for England to pick up a new cargo—indentured servants for the crown. Rebecca and Susan Spencer would never know the ship that had transported them to America as virtual slaves was the same ship that had left Rebecca a destitute widow. The captain dismissed the whole idea as too preposterous.

"Mr. Rothchild," he said, "you have made a fine purchase, indeed. If you please, sir, we will clear the podium for the next sale."

Rothchild paid the captain, turned and bowed to Rebecca and, in turn, to Susan. Both mother and daughter curtsied low, then allowed Rothchild to assist them from the platform.

"Madam," he said kindly, "my cart is this direction." He

offered Rebecca his arm, took Susan by the hand and the three of them, with heads held proudly, passed through the mass that surrounded the podium.

"Make way! Make way!" someone shouted. "Make way there for the gentleman and his lady." Oddly enough, there was no hint of sarcasm in the order.

Rebecca and Susan stood beside Rothchild and watched the oxen strain against their yoke. Rothchild explained their destination.

"Your new home," he said as the cart rattled into motion, "is a day's ride from Williamsburg, which is three days by cart from here. If the good Lord's willing, we should be there Thursday." Rebecca smiled but said nothing. Rothchild continued, "I am a planter, madam, and the work is hard, but we eat well. The house is small but comfortable. My children . . ."

Rebecca interrupted, "You have children, sir?"

"Why, yes, indeed, madam," he smiled. "I have six living and one dead."

Susan clapped her hands excitedly. "Six children to play with, mother. Isn't that fine?"

"Susan, restrain thyself," her mother cautioned. "We were indentured to work; you must remember that."

"Yes, mother, but surely we'll not work every day and night."

Rothchild threw back his head and laughed. "She has you there, madam."

Rebecca glanced at her daughter and pride glistened in her eyes.

They crossed the James River by ferry on a fine Wednesday evening at a small town called Surry. It was Susan's first ferryboat ride, and she was delighted, pointing out this and that until Rebecca, embarrassed by Susan's behavior, finally made her get back into the cart, which left the girl sullen and resentful for the remainder of the boat ride. Her high spirits returned, however, as they neared Williamsburg.

Just outside the small township, Rothchild stopped the cart at the Boar's Head Inn, asking Rebecca and Susan if they would care to freshen up. They gladly accepted the opportunity.

Rothchild watered the oxen, then drew a bucket for Rebecca and Susan to use while he stepped into the tavern. They had just finished drying their hands when Rothchild reappeared. It was then that Rebecca took her first real look at the man, as he talked to the proprietor of the inn. He was about five-foot-ten and of stocky build. Strength and character more than handsomeness marked his face. His clothing was of a coarse material but fit him well.

With tricorn locked under his arm, he turned toward Rebecca and smiled. Realizing she was the topic of Rothchild's conversation made her face flame. "I am shameless," she mused, "wishing to be impressive for Mr. Rothchild's sake, when I hardly know the man."

"Just be yourself, ma'am," Susan said maturely. "You are the prettiest lady in all Virginia."

Rebecca stood a little straighter. "Why, thank you, darling. That was very kind."

Actually, Susan's statement had a lot of merit, for Rebecca was a beautiful woman, notwithstanding the tiny stress lines around her eyes that had appeared there the past few months. And Susan was a miniature of her mother.

Rothchild approached Rebecca. "Mistress Spencer, Miss Susan, may I present Master Kincade, proprietor of the Boar's Head."

Rebecca and Susan curtsied, and Kincade bowed stiffly. He straightened and looked Rebecca over critically, then Susan.

"A comely pair," he said thoughtfully. "Would you care to turn a profit, Mr. Rothchild? I would purchase their papers, sir, if the price were right."

Rebecca felt a sinking sensation in the pit of her stomach. She had felt safe for the first time since Jack had died, but now...

Rothchild's mouth tightened in disgust. "Their papers are not for sale," he said dryly, "for any price."

"Nay, sir," said the innkeeper quickly, realizing his mistake. "I meant no offense, I assure you." He had no desire to anger Rothchild, known to be a quiet man who minded his own business and expected others to do the same.

"Then you will be more careful with your tongue in the future, sir," said Rothchild.

Rebecca visibly relaxed, looking again at Rothchild. Her instincts were to reach out and touch him, so overwhelmed was she with gratitude. Susan, less restrained by social custom, ran to Rothchild, flung her arms around his waist, and looked up into his face adoringly.

Rothchild drove the oxen through the night while Susan slept. Rebecca, unable to sleep because of the jarring of the cart as Rothchild navigated the rough road, finally worked up the courage to ask the question that had nagged her the past three days.

"Mr. Rothchild," she inquired, holding the sleeping Susan close, "if I may ask, sir, what—" She faltered, unsure of herself, unsure, even, if she wanted to know the answer. She took a deep breath and blundered on, "What of your wife, sir?"

Rothchild said nothing for a long while, and Rebecca had a moment of anxiety before he finally answered. "My wife died two years ago birthing my youngest daughter; we saved the child, Mistress Spencer." He hesitated, as if searching for the right words, then said slowly, "She was a fine woman, and I loved her deeply."

"I am sure she was, sir," said Rebecca sincerely.

"Aye," he continued, as if he hadn't heard, "we were just getting the farm on a paying basis and were beginning to enjoy life somewhat. She and the children had done without to help me build, plant, and mend." He took a deep breath and sighed. "Then she was gone." They rode in silence for several minutes before he added, "Our first child was stillborn."

"But you have six more, sir," said Rebecca kindly, trying to pull Rothchild from his painful memories.

"Aye, I have six and I must say, madam, they are fast becoming wild Indians." He looked at Rebecca and smiled. "They are Becky, age fourteen; Anna, she is twelve; and then there is Melissa, ten. Let's see," he mused, trying to get ages and names in the proper order. "Then Frankie, age nine—they came close that time," he laughed. "Then there is Bonnie, she's seven; and last, and I should say least, because she is, is Wanda." He added simply, "I need a woman. Not just any woman, but a woman who loves children, to help raise my girls."

Rebecca looked up at him, wide-eyed. "All girls?"

He looked into her upturned face and sighed. "Aye, all girls."

They stayed like that, looking into each other's eyes as the cart rattled on, and Rebecca sensed a great loneliness in him. She drew Susan's sleeping form tightly against her and laid her cheek against the child's brow. "We are going home," she said softly to the sleeping girl.

It was a beautiful morning when the oxcart topped the slight rise, with Rebecca and Susan standing on tiptoe, trying to get a glimpse of their new home. They were over the hill then, and Rothchild, who had abandoned the cart to walk beside the oxen, called, "Whoa there! Whoa!" The oxen shuffled to a halt.

"Madam," he said proudly, "we are home."

Rebecca's breath caught as she gazed at the panoramic view that stretched for hundreds of acres in all directions, but the house was what held her attention. It was small and of the same style that Williamsburg boasted, with the entrance door at the right side, and to the left, two large windows. At the left end of the house was the chimney. The cypress shake-shingled roof was steep-pitched with three dormer windows. Although plain, the house was beautiful for its simplicity.

"You have built well, Mr. Rothchild," she said shyly. "I notice you have designed your home so you could build on, if you should so desire."

"Indeed I have," exclaimed Rothchild, delighted by Rebecca's perception. "And, as it shall be one of your duties to keep them, madam, I hope you will enjoy the formal gardens. They are small," he apologized, "but you may enlarge them, should you elect to do so."

"I am sure I'll find them perfectly satisfactory, Mr. Rothchild," said Rebecca, noticing for the first time the lovely formal garden, the plowed fields, and the large well-built barn behind the house. Then her eyes turned again to the house that was to be their new home—she loved it.

Susan was beside herself at the excitement of meeting the six children. She could no longer restrain herself, for she could see, even at that distance, a flock of children gathering at the front gate and waving toward the cart.

"Please, Mr. Rothchild," she shouted gleefully, "may we proceed, sir?"

Rothchild laughed and bowed to Susan. "I'm at your service, milady." And the cart rumbled on at what seemed to Susan a snail's pace.

Rothchild's six children were waiting at the entrance gate to the front yard when the oxen plodded up and stopped. "Mind your manners, children," said Rothchild in a fatherly fashion. "This," he gestured toward Rebecca, with Susan gone quite shy, peeping out from behind her mother's skirt, "is Mistress Spencer, who will preside over the housework, and this," he laid his hand on Susan's shoulder, "is Miss Susan, her daughter."

One by one the children curtsied to Rebecca, then looked long at Susan, who held even tighter to her mother's skirts. An older lady, dressed in linsey-woolsey, came from the house, wiping her hands on her apron, and smiling.

"Well, Mr. Rothchild, I see you got what you went for."

Rebecca liked her instantly. She was a large woman of perhaps forty, with a pleasant round face and body to match. She had an air about her that spoke of good humor and vitality.

"Aye, I did that, Mrs. Adams, and may I present," he added quickly, "Mistress Spencer . . . lately from England."

"Aye," said Mrs. Adams, taking Rebecca's hand, "and it is a pleasure, ma'am, but come in, come in, and the little one also and make yourselves at home. 'Tis a long ol' ride from Norfolk to Williamsburg."

All ten advanced toward the house. Rebecca learned that Mrs. Adams had agreed to keep the children while Rothchild was in Norfolk; that her husband's farm adjoined Rothchild's on the west; and that she had been the salvation of the Rothchilds for the past two years.

After tea had been served to the adults and cool buttermilk to the children, Mrs. Adams laughed and said, "I fear I must be getting home, Mr. Rothchild. The old man thinks I have deserted him as it is." She turned to Rebecca. "When you get settled, Mistress Spencer, please come and visit. I would like to hear about England. I do not miss it, mind you, but I like to hear what news there is."

Rebecca smiled. "I'll surely do that, Mrs. Adams," then turning to Rothchild in embarrassment, "if Mr. Rothchild permits."

"Phooey on him," laughed Mrs. Adams, speaking as if Rothchild were not present. "We'll handle him." She climbed heavily to her feet and walked to the door.

Rothchild stood also. "Allow me to escort you home, Mrs. Adams."

"Oh, no, sir," said Mrs. Adams with a wave of her hand. "I can make it fine. I need the exercise, I can tell you." Then she was gone.

Rothchild glanced at Rebecca and smiled, then turned his attention to the children. "Take Susan down to the barn and show her the new pigs. She has never been on a farm before, so you girls shall have to teach her many things. You might as well start now." The children, glad for an excuse to get out of the house, ran for the door, taking a bewildered and slightly frightened Susan with them.

After they had gone, Rothchild turned a serious face to Rebecca. "Mistress Spencer," he said, "I presume you would like to know exactly what your position will be here at Rosemont—which, incidentally," he added, "is the name given to this farm."

Rebecca dropped her eyes, dreading to hear Rothchild's next words. "Yes, Mr. Rothchild," she said softly, "I would be pleased to know exactly what is to be expected of me."

Rothchild outlined Rebecca's duties, which were basically what any other farm woman would have to contend with— housekeeping, gardening, the milking, and such. Of course, the children would help with the chores. Rothchild paced the room with his hands locked behind his back while he talked. "And, mistress," he said, looking directly at Rebecca, "concerning our relationship..." He paused and Rebecca brought her chin up, trying to be brave, but her lips betrayed a slight tremor.

"You were saying, sir?"

Rothchild stopped pacing and turned to face her squarely. "You will have a bedchamber of your own, if you call having two young children share your bedroom being alone and," he added, blushing, "although it is not necessary, I can assure you I will install a bolt on the inside, madam."

Rebecca was relieved but, at the same time, honest enough with herself to admit a touch of disappointment. She was startled by the feeling.

The tall, lithe girl leaned on the wheat cradle she had been using since sunup. Absently, she tucked a strand of thick black hair under her sunbonnet. Her large black eyes surveyed the parched wheat crop, and she slowly shook her head. Another drought year.

Susan Spencer was fifteen years old and already beautiful. She had filled out the past few months. And lately, when Rothchild had

103

taken the girls to Williamsburg, it seemed a goodly number of young men (and some not so young) had found excuses to be in the vicinity of Susan. But she wasn't aware of this—had not even pondered it—because her mind had been on the drought and the effect it was having on the community. Everywhere it was the same: dry, burnt vegetation. There would be no crop to speak of this year, either, as there was none last.

Next year would have to be better or several plantations would find themselves in financial trouble, including Mr. Rothchild's.

Her thoughts, as she leaned on the cradle handle, were interrupted by the dinner bell. Anna Rothchild laid a freshly tied bundle of wheat aside and turned to Susan. "Dinner time, Sue. Lord, I'm hungry."

Susan wiped the perspiration off the bridge of her small nose and smiled. "Bet I can beat you back to the house," she said, dropping the handle of the wheat cradle to the ground.

"Bet you can't." And with that, Anna raised her skirts to her knees and broke into a run.

Susan cried out with glee and the race was on. Anna, shorter than Susan and considerably more plump, was a pretty girl but lacked Susan's quiet beauty. She laughed as Susan caught up with her and then they were in the yard, laughing and putting their arms around each other for support. Rebecca looked reprovingly at them from the doorway, and they immediately sobered, only to break into another fit of giggling.

"Wash up, dears," called Rebecca, noticing how healthy all the children were and how fine they were turning out. She had long since stopped thinking of the Rothchild children as being anything but her own, making no distinction at all between them and Susan, and they loved her for it. All seven were Rebecca's pride. Becky, eighteen, had married last summer and moved to Suffolk, and Rebecca missed her as if she had been of her own flesh and blood.

Susan and Anna splashed water over their faces, dried quickly, and burst into the kitchen. Susan was surprised to see Master Kincade, proprietor of the Boar's Head Inn, standing by the table. She looked quickly at her mother and noted the strained expression on her face.

A feeling of foreboding caused her to consider Kincade thoughtfully as she curtsied and acknowledged his presence.

Glancing through her lowered lashes, she observed that he had not changed greatly these past four years. He was a large man and powerfully built, although he showed a thickness through the stomach that spoke of too little exercise and too much food. His hair was thin, with the hairline itself receding, leaving an overly long forehead and heavy jowls. His clothing was travel-stained and dusty, and Susan guessed that he was naturally an unkempt person. A slight shudder ran through her. Kincade revolted her.

"Ah! Miss Susan," said Kincade with a smirk. "You have become a lovely lass indeed, if I may say so."

Susan dropped her eyes again and timidly murmured, "Thank you, sir. It is nice of you to say so."

Rebecca intervened as Kincade tried to pursue the conversation. "Susan," she instructed, "you and Anna set the table, please. And be sure to set an extra plate for Master Kincade."

"Yes, ma'am," said Susan, turning from Kincade and moving to the large cherry hutch. She could feel his eyes pursuing her every move as her bodice clung to her young bosom when she stretched to hand down the pewter mugs from the top shelf of the cabinet.

Rothchild, who had been standing beside Kincade, walked to the oaken bucket and dipped out a gourd of water. He drank deeply, studying Kincade's expression as the innkeeper watched Susan, then he hung the gourd on a peg above the bucket. "Master Kincade," he said, "would you care to step into the drawing room while the ladies finish dinner?"

Without waiting for an answer, Rothchild adjourned to the room that served as parlor and bedchamber for himself and two of the children. Kincade plodded along behind.

Susan set out the pewter plates, knives, and forks while Anna placed a large pewter goblet beside each plate. Anna excused herself, saying she would run to the springhouse and fetch a crock of buttermilk. Rebecca began filling bowls with beans, potatoes, and cabbage.

"Susan," she said, "would you call the other children, please? And be sure they wash their faces and hands."

"Yes, ma'am," said Susan, stepping through the back door just as Anna was returning from the springhouse.

"What do you think Master Kincade wants?" asked Anna in a hushed voice.

"I know not," returned Susan, looking quickly over her shoulder for fear Kincade might be within hearing, "but I wish he had not come. I feel all nervous inside, and I don't know why."

"I feel it, too," said Anna as she brushed past Susan to carry the milk inside.

Kincade ate like a glutton, smacking his lips, licking his fingers, and belching periodically, as was the custom. It was a quiet, strained meal for the Rothchilds, and Susan, finding herself without an appetite, wished it would end. She knew Kincade's visit had something to do with her, but she could not imagine what it might be. However, if Kincade's thoughts were on anything other than food, he did a fine job of hiding it.

"Pass the potatoes and the cornbread, Miss Susan," he commanded.

Susan's eyes flickered resentment at the tone of his voice, but she covered her feelings by busying herself with the passing of the food.

The younger children were eating outside on a small bench and Susan excused herself, saying she should see to their well-being, in the event their bowls should need replenishing. Rothchild and Rebecca let her go, knowing full well the children did not need looking after.

Susan kneeled beside the makeshift table and began talking quietly with the children. She felt a peculiar closeness to them at that moment, more so than at any other time in the past four years. She could not explain it. She reached out and ruffled their hair, and they laughed and jabbered, being too young to sense the strained atmosphere at Rosemont that Kincade's presence had aroused.

Rebecca stepped from the kitchen and instructed the children to resume their chores. She waited until they had darted around the corner of the house, then turned to Susan.

"Would you come inside, darling?" she said, dropping her eyes. "Mr. Rothchild has something of importance to discuss with you."

Susan reached for her mother's hand and brought it to her cheek. "Mother," she asked softly, "is Master Kincade going to take me away?"

Rebecca took Susan into her arms and held her close. "That is for you to decide, darling. Mr. Rothchild will leave the final decision in your hands."

Rothchild stood as Rebecca and Susan entered the house, but

Kincade remained seated. Rothchild moved quickly to Susan and took her small sun-browned fingers in his hands. With his eyes on Susan, he spoke to the innkeeper. "If Master Kincade will excuse us, I wish to speak with Miss Susan alone." Kincade got heavily to his feet, made his apologies, and shuffled from the room.

"Susan," Rothchild said slowly, slipping his arm around her waist and directing her toward Rebecca, who had taken a seat. "Susan, I want you to understand something, and I really do not know how to put it into words." Susan started to protest, but Rothchild stilled her. "Please, let me finish before you say anything." He smiled sadly at her, and his voice was soft as he continued. "Since your mother, and you, have been at Rosemont, you have brought great joy into my family and this community. Not once have either you or Mistress Spencer brought a shadow of grief upon this household." Susan raised her eyes and blinked back the tears that threatened her composure. She waited patiently while Rothchild cleared his throat.

"I am telling you this," he continued, "because I want you fully to understand my position where you are concerned." He took a turn around the table. "Susan, you are one of my family," he faltered, then leaned heavily on the table, supporting his weight on widespread fingers. "You are like my own flesh and blood, as are my other children, and what I am to ask of you is as a father to a daughter but," he hesitated again, studying her face, "but, the final decision is yours alone, and whatever that decision is, we will abide by it." He looked directly at her. "Is that understood?"

Susan nodded, afraid to speak and give way to the agony she was feeling.

"Susan," Rothchild continued painfully, "Master Kincade has approached me with a business proposition." He watched her closely but failed to notice her eyes dilate. Other than that, she appeared perfectly calm. Rothchild went on. He liked nothing of this business agreement with Kincade, but was honor-bound to broach the subject to Susan so she could decide her future.

"Master Kincade wishes to purchase the remainder of your servitude, which is approximately two years. He has badgered me into letting you make the decision and I have agreed, although I must be truthful and say I am against this proposition.

"The terms Master Kincade states are as follows: you will be handmaiden to his wife and keep books in his inn. He assures me you will not work as a common tavern wench, unless you should so desire, except when Mistress Kincade needs an occasional helping hand. Your services as a scribe will be helpful in his business, for many of his patrons can neither read nor write. Should you at any time decide to withdraw your services, the arrangement is to be considered null and void, and you are to return here."

Susan wondered exactly what the payment for her servitude would be, but it would have been unladylike to inquire, so she merely said, "The proposition, sir, is not ungracious."

Rothchild continued as though she hadn't spoken. "Master Kincade agrees in turn to supply enough wheat, corn, oats, and two additional oxen for next season's planting and a sum of ten pounds sterling, at five pounds per annum."

Susan caught her breath. "But, sir," she stammered, "my worth is not that great. It would be a poor bargain for Master Kincade."

"No," Rothchild said solemnly, "you belittle yourself, my dear. You would be a great asset to Master Kincade, I fear."

"Sir," she said in a small voice, "might I speak to my ma'am alone?"

"Of course," Rothchild said patiently. "I will wait with Master Kincade, but," Rothchild's unblinking eyes held Susan's, "let the decision be yours alone. Let neither this farm nor me influence you in any way." He paused. "Do you promise me that . . . Susan?"

She ran to Rothchild and flung her arms about his neck, laying her cheek against his. "Thank you, sir," she whispered.

After Rothchild had excused himself, Susan and her mother talked quietly. Susan knew the circumstances the family faced because of two years of drought. She also knew there was no money in the household. If she should decide to accept Kincade's proposal, it would possibly put Rosemont back on its feet. At the least, it would give Mr. Rothchild two more years to try. Susan knew she really had no choice in the matter. She would accept the proposition gladly, for it would be only two years that she would be gone, and then she could come home for good.

"Susan," her mother said softly, "Mr. Rothchild is against this venture wholeheartedly. Why, he even offered Anna's service instead of yours, but Master Kincade was firm."

"Mother, he didn't!" said Susan, wide-eyed.

Rebecca nodded. "Yes—yes, he did. He feels you have experienced enough heartbreak in one lifetime and would spare you this..." she hesitated, searching for the correct words, "as Mr. Rothchild puts it, this ordeal in a public tavern."

"But, mother," cried Susan, "I am fifteen years of age, and I can care for myself. Besides, it is a chance to do something for the family, and you know we need the seed and the money."

Rebecca raised her hand. "I knew what your decision would be, darling, but do not let any romantic notions enter your head. For, should you choose to accept the proposition, it will be a difficult two years before you, make no pretense about that. You will have to be on your guard at all times, do you understand?"

"Ma'am," said Susan, laying her head tenderly against her mother's breast, "I will return to you a maiden, as I am now. I promise you."

The trip to the Boar's Head was uneventful. Mistress Kincade turned out to be a small thin woman, old before her time. Her hair was pulled severely into a bun at the nape of her neck and the drab homespun dress she wore hung like a sack on her flat-chested body. Surprisingly, her voice was kind, and she seemed genuinely happy to see Susan.

"My dear," she said, as Kincade presented Susan, "you must be tired after that long ride. Come, I'll show you to your room."

Susan curtsied, then followed Mrs. Kincade to a small alcove above the tavern. The room had one dormer window, a small bed in the corner, a battered highboy, and a cracked porcelain pitcher with a mismatched bowl.

"'Tis not much, my dear," Mistress Kincade apologized.

Susan replied softly, taking in the drabness. "It will do just fine, ma'am." Then she gently eased the valise containing her personal belongings to the floor.

"My man tells me you are right educated for a girl," the lady said, looking at Susan with interest.

"I do not know, mistress," stammered Susan. "I have had some schooling—yes."

"Well," said the lady sternly, "I don't read, write, or do figures. I want you to know that. So don't try to get uppity with me because of my ignorance—you understand?"

"Oh, no, ma'am," Susan answered quickly, "I would not mistreat anyone. Please do not think that of me."

Mistress Kincade patted Susan's shoulder. "I can tell you're not that kind of child. We'll get along well, I'm thinking."

Susan, being young, energetic, and mannerly, won the heart of Mrs. Kincade immediately, which, without realizing it, was the smartest move she could have made, much to Master Kincade's regret.

She helped the woman with her housework, cooking, and washing, and, to the delight of the elderly lady, insisted on combing her waist-length hair each evening. Actually, Susan enjoyed Mistress Kincade, finding her interesting, amusing—if occasionally cranky—but always appreciative of the girl's accomplishments.

Kincade's business increased noticeably. Almost every day travelers were stopping at the Boar's Head, for word spread quickly that the new girl who worked there would write a letter, draw up a bill of sale, witness a deed, or do the thousand other things that fell in that particular category, and word also had it that she could be trusted not to divulge or spread idle gossip concerning what she had written.

Susan found herself more often than not called into the tavern proper for one reason or another. She was shocked at first by the roistering of the patrons, but Mistress Kincade tutored her on their behavior, and Susan found them for the most part to be a fine, hearty folk. She learned to evade and discourage intimacy without offending, and quickly became a favorite.

Many a lad ventured into the Boar's Head to try his luck with the untouchable dark-eyed Susan, only to find himself completely in love with her and glad to add his name to the long list of admirers. One overzealous boy named Bobby Green even wagered a pound he could steal a kiss, which he did, only to have his face roundly slapped as a reward.

Everyone, including Bobby Green, laughed heartily as Susan, hands on hips, put Bobby and his actions in their place. She finally relaxed, however, and joined in their laughter.

Bobby Green was a well-built handsome lad of eighteen, the kind of boy every father wants, every mother dotes on, and every girl dreams of—except Susan. She liked Bobby because she couldn't help liking him, but something inside her told her to wait, to be patient.

If Bobby Green was for her, she would know in due time. But it wasn't easy, for Bobby worshipped the ground she walked on. He wasn't at all backward about his feelings and continually proposed marriage, sometimes ingeniously.

One evening, finding the tavern overly crowded, Bobby jumped onto a table and shouted, "Marry me, Miss Susan, or I will kill myself."

Susan, carrying a tray of mugs above her head, slipped a long-barreled pistol from the belt of a patron and presented it to Bobby. The crowd roared and Bobby pulled the trigger. The pistol boomed and Bobby dropped on the table, then rolled to the floor, hitting flat on his back. Susan dropped the tray and flung herself to the floor. With Bobby's head cradled to her bosom, she sobbed uncontrollably.

Bobby opened one eye, and grinned slowly. "You do love me, don't you!"

Susan dropped his head to the planks with a resounding crack. The patrons howled and pounded each other on the back, for they loved a good sport more than life itself.

Susan almost wished she were in love with Bobby Green.

She was seventeen when she began to notice the distinct changes in Kincade. He seemed to invent reasons to be near her, although he never actually said or did anything to cause alarm. She, nevertheless, began to dread his presence. Susan wished she could confide in Mistress Kincade, but that was out of the question.

She pondered the situation while lying in her small bed at night, rising often, to stare out the tiny dormer window at the orchard behind the inn. She prayed for this last year to hurry and end.

Kincade continued to pursue her, touching her hand while passing a tray of mugs, or bumping against her as she negotiated the aisle behind the counter. Occasionally, he hung his arm over her shoulder, as he presented her to a customer requiring the services of a scribe. Little things—nothing.

He began partaking of his own ale and many was the night Susan and Mistress Kincade were obliged to help him to his room. Mistress Kincade began to fret over him, not understanding the problem, and Susan was in no position to shed light on it.

The situation had become unbearable when Kincade finally

made his move. He enticed Susan to the wine cellar on the pretense of inventorying the wine casks. Susan, carrying parchment and quill, reluctantly followed Kincade into the recesses below the inn. Kincade lighted a candle, dropped a small quantity of hot wax onto a cask, and stuck the candle in firmly. It gave off little light, and Susan felt closed in.

"Master Kincade," she said, growing frantic and gazing into the shadows that surrounded her, "we need more light, sir. I do not like this place."

"Light?" said Kincade. "Light, you say? We need no light at all." And with that he snuffed the candle, throwing the cellar into darkness, except for a small shaft of lighter darkness at the top of the stairs. Roughly, Kincade drew Susan against him and, before she could protest, ground his lips against hers.

Susan's mind was wild; her every instinct was to fight, to run, to get away, but she fought hard to steady herself. She gained some control over her panic, and finally managed an icy calm.

As Kincade started to kiss her again, she said softly, "Master Kincade, there is something you should know, before you proceed with whatever you intend."

"Aye?" asked Kincade harshly. "And what might that be?" Kincade was bothered more than he would care to admit by Susan's aloof attitude. This was not as he had planned; she should have been terrified into submission, yet she wasn't.

Susan, astounded at her own calm, said coolly, "My father, sir, will kill you for this."

Kincade flung her against a cask, knocking her to the floor. "Kill me for what?" he said, his agitation growing with each word. "For stealing a little kiss? That's all I had in mind." His voice was pleading. "Honest, it was, Miss Susan; you know it was." He helped her regain her footing and quickly moved toward the steps.

"But what of the inventory?" she asked innocently.

"Bah! I can inventory another time."

Susan brushed past him and ran up the steps.

In late April 1755 Susan returned to Rosemont to attend the funeral of Anna Rothchild. Anna had cut her foot with a grubbing hoe and developed the dreaded disease tetanus. She had wasted away until death had seemed a blessing. Anna was eighteen years old.

Long lines of men in homespun stood before the quarter-ster's tent to sign their name or make their mark so they could w their rations.

And off to one side, standing quietly under the towering nches of a great elm, were the free spies or scouts. They were a ed unto themselves: individuals—quiet men for the most part—o like Boone preferred their own company, or that of other odsmen, to the boisterous antics of the soldiers. Susan watched m with a feeling of kinship, for she too was a loner.

She recognized several of them: Christopher Gist, captain of the e spies; John Findley, tracker and explorer; and . . . her eyes fixed Morgan Patterson. He was leaning loosely on his long nsylvania gun, talking to a civilian she would later come to ow as George Washington.

At that moment, however, she knew none of the young men, d she gave Washington not a second glance. It was Patterson's y dominion over the world that held her attention, along with the t that he had displayed no evident interest in her even though ers openly admired her. She found that downright insulting.

She saw him several times after that, but if he ever looked at her, e was unaware of it. And then, as the army moved out, she was too sy to look for him, and she didn't see him again until the day of e ill-fated dice game.

Each evening when the army bivouacked Susan would set her ld desk across her lap and keep a record of all goods unloaded m Master Kincade's wagons. It was a time-consuming, thankless b, and she found herself wishing she could just disappear into the ght, as Boone had the habit of doing. The moment the team was -keted Boone would vanish to reappear only at sunup the next y. She wondered if he had a woman among the camp followers.

It was also Susan's responsibility to cook all the meals for ncade and herself, so immediately after tallying the cargo, she mmenced supper. When that was finished and all the other chores e completed, she would slip off to the women's latrine, then b wearily into her wagon, pull the tarpaulin over her, and fall a fitful sleep that was sometimes long in coming.

She wished that she could imitate Boone, whom she had

116

Susan stood with her mother as the men of the community covered the pine casket with Rosemont earth. Susan grieved. Anna had been her best friend and confidante. Susan had loved her like a sister.

Rothchild drew Susan to him. "I lose one daughter and gain another," he said, his voice breaking. "Everything happens for the best. We must remember that, Susan." She laid her head against Rothchild's shoulder and wept openly.

She spent two weeks at Rosemont, during which time Vernon Rothchild and Rebecca Spencer were wed. It was a solemn event and Susan wondered about it—was bothered by it.

Susan and Rebecca spent most of her free days trading confidences and dreams. Curiosity finally got the better of her, and she asked Rebecca quite frankly why she had consented to marry Mr. Rothchild. She was deeply embarrassed at having asked such a forward question, even of her mother.

"You mean so soon after Anna's death?" Rebecca asked carefully, bringing the real question to the surface.

"Well, yes. I just wondered..." Susan's voice trailed off.

"Susan," Rebecca said softly, taking her daughter's hands in her own, "I married Mr. Rothchild at this time because," she hesitated, looking deep into Susan's eyes, "because he needed the love and understanding and tenderness that only a wife can give. Do you understand what I am saying?"

"I—I think so, ma'am, but..." Susan dropped her eyes.

"But what, darling?" asked Rebecca earnestly.

Choosing her words carefully, Susan said, "You did not marry him because you pitied him, did you?" She raised her eyes to Rebecca.

"No, darling, not out of pity," Rebecca answered softly. "I...I think I started loving him when he purchased us so many years ago." Rebecca's eyes held a faraway expression as she remembered that day so long ago when Susan was eleven years old. "I love him, Susan," her mother said simply.

Rothchild escorted Susan back to the Boar's Head only to find that the usual jolly atmosphere had turned sour with talk of war. General Braddock, with thirteen hundred troops, was billeted in Williamsburg. Rumors flowed like wine. Susan evaluated each, finally concluding that Braddock and his British regular army, plus the Virginia Militia, were to take a French-held fort at the forks of

113

the Ohio River. It would be easy. Braddock himself had said it would take not over three or four days, at most.

For Susan Spencer, May and June 1755 were unreal. Everywhere men were preparing for war. Soldiers were marching. Camp followers were moving hither and yon. The militia began target practice, which raised the contempt of the British regulars.

Cattle were driven in on the hoof and butchered; sheep and goats met a similar fate. Wagons began to arrive with what foodstuffs could be purchased, stolen, or acquired through requisition. Braddock had the largest army ever to assemble on American soil—and it would be fed!

Late one evening in early June, Bobby Green took Susan walking in the orchard behind the inn. It was a moon-splashed night and the fragrance of blossoms was divine. Bobby was unusually quiet and serious as he looked into Susan's face.

"You are beautiful, Susan," he said. "I love you more than life itself." He looked deep into her eyes—searching.

Susan dropped her head, ashamed of herself for wanting to hear the words while knowing she was incapable of returning them.

"I am going with the army, Susan," he said, studying her face. Susan touched his hand but said nothing. "Will you be waiting for me when I return?" he asked.

Susan nodded her head in affirmation, but still did not meet his eyes.

"Aye, Bobby Green, I will be here."

"But," he asked anxiously, "will you be waiting for me and me alone? Will you, girl?" He took both her hands in his.

Susan looked into his eyes. "Nay, Bobby," she said honestly, begging him to understand. "I cannot let you go to war thinking that I love you. 'Twould not be treating you kindly, because I do not love you the way you should be loved." Her voice was quiet. "I love you as a great friend, Bobby Green, and I'll miss you terribly while you are gone, and I—I would die if you should be harmed, but . . . I do not love you as a woman should love her man."

Susan slipped into Bobby's arms and kissed him tenderly on his lips, but when he attempted to kiss her passionately, she withdrew and he apologized.

She did not again see Bobby before the day the army broke camp

and began the long march toward Fort Cumberland, the place for the army, militia, teamsters, and scouts. She w unable to relate to him the knowledge that she too w accompanying the army on its journey into enemy territo

Master Kincade had contracted to supply the entire ar rum and had decided to oversee eighteen cask-filled wagons Susan was expected to accompany Kincade as official record ensuring Kincade against the army cheating him.

So Susan Spencer found herself perched high on a wa beside a twenty-one-year-old teamster named Daniel Boo wagon, overloaded with barrels and casks, was pulled by a heavy draft horses that Boone controlled with an occasional haw. Sometimes Boone would unlimber his twenty-foot bla whip to flick a horsefly off the ear of a horse. The man k business.

Susan talked and joked with the quiet man a infrequently was rewarded with a bit of Daniel's dry humor, the most part he had very little to say.

Fort Cumberland, Maryland, a palisaded structure wit story log blockhouse at the four corners, was situated in a amphitheater, almost entirely surrounded by the peak Allegheny Mountains.

Susan shuddered as she looked beyond the tall pointed the palisade and studied the dark and mysterious wilder seemed to stretch endlessly in all directions. She had never rugged forbidding country.

The fort itself was a beehive of preparation for the a Duquesne. Men were arriving daily in twos and threes groups, their muskets or rifles slung lazily over their sl

Wagons rumbled in, men hanging from all sides, la waving their hats at the women tending cooking fir clothes, or walking leisurely in the early June sun.

The ring of the farriers' hammers as they shod th animals echoed clearly off the wooded peaks of the

Companies of British regulars were marchin splendid in their scarlet tunics and white breeches, off the polished steel of fixed bayonets.

observed sleeping while standing or leaning against a tree, or while driving the team. But that gift eluded her.

As the wagons creaked over the ridges and down the long valleys, Susan considered her situation. The farther the army got from Fort Cumberland, the bolder Kincade became. She dreaded the thought of another showdown with the man; she was afraid he was beyond listening to reason. She would watch herself closely for the remainder of the journey, taking pains not to be alone with him . . . if possible.

Susan needed a friend, another woman to talk with, to confide in, but she ruthlessly avoided the camp followers' area.

For several days she had been aware of two young women, about the same age as she, who were camped close to the officers' quarters, and she promptly made up her mind to finish early and visit them. It would be a pleasant change. She worked hard to complete her chores before nightfall. Then she searched out Kincade to ask his permission to go visiting.

Kincade was tipping the keg and had been since they had made camp; he was in an ugly mood. "Found yourself a man, have you? Well, go ahead, do as you please; you'd just slip off if I said no."

Susan didn't explain, or defend herself. She did the only intelligent thing she could do; she left.

It was while she was en route to Judith's tent that she happened upon the fight between Patterson and Kemp, and she was curious, to say the least, to see the young woodsman face the well-known bully so calmly.

She had seen a few of the men Kemp had whipped, and they had not been a pretty sight. She had heard them talk and knew that Kemp was a man to be feared. Yet, the young man removing his hunting frock appeared not to be the least bit afraid.

She moved closer and watched Kemp throw Patterson to the ground, and when Southhampton cried loudly in Kemp's support, Susan naturally, without thinking, yelled as lustily for her champion.

And after the fight, when she fetched the rum for him and wanted so badly to tend his cuts and bruises, he humiliated her by ignoring her kind gesture. So she poured the rum on the ground, forced herself to smile, and went in search of the two young women—but Morgan Patterson still weighed heavily on her mind.

117

She found the ladies relaxing among several young British officers. Disappointed, she turned to retrace her footsteps, but a lovely girl with amber hair and beautiful gray eyes quickly moved to her side.

"May I be of assistance, mistress?"

"Nay, but thank you, anyway," Susan said. "I had intended to pay a social call, but you are engaged with guests, and I dare not interrupt."

"'Tis only some friends," the girl said kindly. "You would be welcome, I am sure."

"What is it, Ivy?" asked the exquisite blonde woman, sitting elegantly among the young officers.

"'Tis a caller, Miss Judith."

Judith and her admirers scrutinized Susan from head to toe. One or two of the officers began to rise, but Judith waved them back.

"Tell the poor child to trot along, for I am busy at the moment. Perhaps," she said, stifling a yawn, "she can return on the morrow."

Then losing interest completely, she turned her attention again to the young officers. Several of the men snickered as Susan turned away, causing her to stop and stroll back to the crowd. She had their attention as she raised herself to her full height and looked each one in the eye. When her gaze fell on Judith, her eyes were unwavering.

"Mistress," she said softly, but with an inner strength that belied her age, "humility is no stranger to me, I assure you, so I will suffer your catty remark none at all, but should you, and your gentlemen friends, desire a lesson in manners, I shall be most happy to be your instructor." There was no snickering that time as she curtsied to Ivy and walked toward the wagons.

However, Susan did suffer, indirectly, from the abuse of Judith and her gallants. For, instead of returning to her wagon, she decided to walk into the forest to be alone. She was startled out of her meditation by the thump of footsteps in the darkness. Glancing fearfully over her shoulder, she almost cried out when Kincade loomed. "You have wandered far into the forest, Miss Susan. You are meeting someone. I knew it all the time." His hand caressed her cheek. "You play the innocent so well; you almost had me fooled." His breath nauseated her, he was so close. "Perhaps I will do until he arrives, eh?" He laughed as Susan attempted to step away from him.

Then, catching her around the waist, he yanked her into his soft paunch.

She was terrified, but refused to let him know it. Instead, she pummeled Kincade's chest and face with her small fists. He chortled again, confident of a conquest as he bent to kiss her.

She quickly turned her head, causing his lips to brush past her cheek. Infuriated beyond reason, he slapped her hard across the face.

There was a great ringing in her ears caused by Kincade's openhanded blow, but her mind was clear, and she recalled her oath to her mother two years before. "I will return to you a maiden as I am now, I promise you." A tear forced its way from her tightly closed eyes and trickled down her cheek. Then suddenly she was standing alone, no longer encircled by Kincade's powerful arms and pressed downward by his massive flesh.

"... And I was never so glad to see anyone in my whole life, as I was you, Mr. Patterson," she said brightly, smiling up at him. "I shudder to think what might have happened had you not shown up when you did. 'Tis one thing for certain," she paused, studying Patterson's face before continuing, "Master Kincade would have had his way with me, one way or the other."

She drew her knees more tightly against her breast and locked her arms around them, then leaned forward to a more comfortable position. Patterson chose to remain silent, so Susan resumed her story.

"I did not sleep a wink that night for fear Master Kincade would return and create a ghastly scene. Actually, I did not see him until late the next evening." She paused, then laughed, turning her gaze to Patterson. "And he could hardly walk." Her manner became grim, however, as she concluded her story.

"The army was attacked three days later, as you well know, and ... and the whole thing was a horrible nightmare." Patterson stole a covert glance at Susan, but her eyes were far away, reliving the battle Patterson had observed from the hilltop.

Her voice was low. "Master Kincade insisted that I ride the lead wagon that day and I walked for what seemed like an hour before I reached the beginning of the train. I walked past wagon after wagon, a hundred and fifty in all, and rode with a stranger who knew very little about handling a team. How I wish I had been riding with Boone."

She looked at Patterson. "When the first volley was fired, all I could think of was to get back to my own wagon. Boone has a way about him, much the same as you," she said, looking into his eyes, "that makes a person feel safe in his presence." She dropped her gaze and continued. "I started running down that long line of wagons. The teamsters were screaming at me to get out of their way. They were trying to turn the teams around and there wasn't room. They should have known there wasn't room to turn those big wagons around..." She faltered, then went on. "I was knocked down by a runaway team and the wagon overturned, almost pinning me beneath it. I thought I would die, the dust was so thick, and the horses—they almost mashed me, rearing and kicking, trying to break free of their harness.

"I managed to get to my feet and continued down the line. People were screaming at me, cursing me, pushing me aside. I almost fell once and caught a man's arm for support...he hit me."

Patterson's eyes were almost tender as he looked at her. "Men do shameful things when they are terrorized, Susan."

She nodded and wiped her sleeve across her eyes. "I had just come in sight of Boone's wagon when I saw him do what all the teamsters should have done; he jumped down, cut the harness loose, and disappeared back toward the river. He never did see me, and that was the last I saw of him.

"The camp followers were screaming and running in all directions; no one knew what to do." Susan was speaking very slowly, remembering in detail that tragic day.

"It was all confusion, the army routed, the teamsters cursing and abandoning their stock, women falling down to be trampled in the melee." She put her hands over her face, but Patterson reached out and gently took them in his and urged her to finish the story. She took a deep breath and went on. "Then the savages were all around us, screaming and killing and dancing—it was horrible. They killed anyone who could not stand and walk—men, women—it made no difference." She looked into Patterson's eyes and tears began streaming down her cheeks. "Our army was there, Mr. Patterson; why didn't they help us? They could see what was taking place."

Patterson shook his head. He had no answer to her simple question.

Susan dried her eyes on her shoulder and hurried on with her narrative. Patterson was impressed with the girl's courage, for it was evident the telling of this portion of her story was causing her great pain.

"Anyway," she said, pushing a lock of hair away from her face, "the Indians gathered all the women together, myself included, and marched us into the forest. They stopped us about a half mile from the battlefield and stripped us of all our clothing."

Patterson nodded, but said nothing.

"We were terrified," she continued, "afraid they were going to kill us...or...something worse. Then...then Bobby Green was there; he took me by the arm and flung me into the brush, screaming at me to run for my life. I—I glanced back, once. Oh, God! I wish I hadn't. The savages were all around him, hacking, cutting—it was awful." She bowed her head, her eyes tightly shut, remembering in detail how Bobby had died.

"One of the Indians pursued me and...well," she said without raising her head, "you know the rest."

Patterson nodded slowly and patted Susan's hand. "Aye, Miss Susan," he said earnestly, "how I wish you could have been spared such a bloody spectacle as you were forced to witness."

"Nay, Mr. Patterson," the girl said, raising her tear-streaked face. "I pray, sir, have no pity for me. I am still alive, so God must have some plan for me."

She looked deep into Patterson's eyes, remembering how he had saved her from the Indian that had pursued her to the creek. *You are always there when I need you, Morgan; it must surely be God's will,* she thought. But before she could put her thoughts into words, Patterson was speaking.

"Miss Susan," he said urgently, "did not Lieutenant Southhampton warn Halkett that he was about to be attacked?"

"Why no, there was so much confusion—" she returned, not understanding the consternation that drew his brows together in sudden thought. "No. I don't believe he was there."

"Did you not see him at all, before or during the battle?"

"No," she shook her head while watching him intently. "I didn't see him at all, Morgan. Why do you ask?"

"'Tis not important," he said, climbing to his feet and

121

stamping the circulation back into his numb legs. "But, come." He held out his hand to help her rise. "We had best be getting back, lest Judith and Ivy think we have abandoned them."

But, try as he might, as they climbed down the hillside, he could not shake the nagging suspicion that Southhampton had intentionally sent him in the wrong direction in search of Judith and Ivy. Even more disturbing was the thought, the terrible realization, that if it were true the lieutenant had not returned to warn the column, then he was directly responsible for the deaths of scores of soldiers, not to mention the defenseless women who followed Halkett.

7

A cool reception met Susan and Patterson when they returned to the makeshift cave. Ivy cast a feeble smile, then dropped her eyes and busied herself at the fire. Judith's gaze, however, was undisguised loathing.

"Well! I certainly hope you two enjoyed yourselves." She was looking at both Patterson and Susan, but Susan knew that Judith's words were for her alone.

"Aye," she said, returning Judith's gaze. "I thoroughly enjoyed Morgan."

"Morgan is it now?" retorted Judith.

"What is the matter with them two?" Patterson asked Ivy as he moved to kneel beside her by the fire.

"I would not know, sir!" Ivy snapped.

"Damn!" said Patterson, as he laid another log on the fire. "Fontaine was right, English women are crazy."

It took very little effort for Judith to convince herself and Ivy that Patterson was having his way with Susan. She was outraged. Actually, she was exasperated more with herself than with either Patterson or Susan, for she believed it beneath her dignity to feel envy or jealousy, and she felt both.

While her mind was telling her she had no right to interfere, her heart was tormenting her with fantasies she did not understand. Despising herself, she turned her fury on Susan. "We knew all along what kind of woman you are. Why, you're no better than a common tavern wench! No—you're worse."

Before Susan could reply, Ivy intervened. "Miss Judith! How dare you talk to Miss Susan that way! I am ashamed of you." Ivy's voice shrilled. "Ashamed—do you hear?" She turned and fled.

Judith stared at Susan. "That was all your fault!" Then she pursued Ivy into the rain-drenched forest.

Patterson glanced at Susan. "What was all that about?"

Susan looked at him, a touch of pity plainly visible in her eyes. "A woman's heart is an intricate web, indeed, Mr. Patterson."

Patterson's eyebrows knitted. "I fear, Miss Susan, I do not understand."

"Worry not overmuch, Morgan."

Patterson noticed again the use of his given name and was pleased.

"You will understand when the time is right."

Judith found Ivy staring off into the evening. She approached her cautiously. "Ivy. Ivy, I'm sorry."

"'Tis not me you should be apologizing to, mistress." Ivy fastened her eyes on a dead tree limb and continued her vigilance.

"Don't be angry with me, please," begged Judith. "You have never been angry with me before."

"I have been angry many times, mistress," Ivy said, turning to face Judith. "But the circumstances we are living under are bringing out the worst—and the best—in all of us. I will no longer stand by and be a party to the mistreatment of Miss Susan. She has done nothing to deserve your wrath. I might also remind you that you are to be married to your English officer, should we live through this nightmare and reach the fort safely."

"My English officer!" exclaimed Judith. "Ivy, you are beginning to sound like these Americans that we so detest."

Ivy stared long at Judith before replying. "I no longer detest these people. I did when we first arrived in America, but I have changed." She reached out to Judith, excitement building in her voice. "Can you not feel it, Judith, a sense of being alive, truly alive, for the first time in our lives, and...and I will tell you something else; the only thing I detest is not being either all black or all white..." She hesitated, then smiled. "If I were all white, I would

124

give Miss Susan a hard time of it where Mister Patterson is concerned."

"Why, Ivy," exclaimed Judith, "I do believe you are falling in love with him."

They traveled cautiously the following day, making little progress. Susan and Judith were apparently not on speaking terms, which upset Patterson, for problems between the women were a luxury neither he nor they could afford.

The following day, July 27, broke clear and bright as they painstakingly worked their way down the craggy bluffs of the Alleghenies toward the peaceful valleys stretched out below.

It was a treacherous journey. The slopes were precipitous and covered with heavy timber, brush, and thickets. And boulders the size of a house often sat above spine-tingling dropoffs, boulders that could easily, if one broke loose, leave a crushed body beneath.

"Why did we not take a safer route, Mr. Patterson?" asked Judith bitterly as she followed close behind him. "It seems to me that you are going out of your way to force hardships upon us." She pierced his back with a hate-filled stare. "I shan't mind a bit to tell Lieutenant Southhampton what a truly despicable person you are."

"Tell the lieutenant whatever you damn well please." Patterson bulled his way between two large boulders only to be brought up abruptly by a sheer dropoff fifty to sixty feet straight down.

Judith, caught up in her schemes to expose Patterson for the villain that he was and thus heedless of where she was going, ran headlong into Patterson, causing his weak leg to collapse and pitch him over the precipice.

He cast his rifle aside as he fell, and his hands clawed at the bare rock, dirt, and leaves that matted the cliff's edge, but it was to no avail and he dropped out of sight.

"Oh, God!" said Judith, slumping heavily against the boulder for support. "Oh, God, what have I done?" She pushed herself away from the rock and, without a glance toward where Patterson had disappeared over the edge of the cliff, she quickly scrambled back through the opening between the boulders to where Susan and Ivy were resting.

"I've killed him!" cried Judith.

"Killed who?" said Susan, frowning.

"I've killed Patterson! I pushed him over the edge of the cliff. My God, we've got to do something!"

"You killed him?" breathed Ivy aghast.

"It was an accident!" Judith buried her face in her hands.

"Pray to God you're wrong," said Susan brushing past Judith and clambering through the opening between the rocks.

She moved cautiously to the edge of the overhang and peered into the depths below. Fir trees, their thick, deep green tops reaching to within ten feet of where she stood, obscured Susan's vision of the rocky hillside below, blotting out any glimpse she might have got of Patterson's broken, twisted body.

"Can you see him?" It was Ivy as she fearfully crept up behind Susan, afraid to venture any closer to the lip of the overhang because, unknown to Susan, she was terrified of heights.

"No," said Susan hopelessly. "He fell through those trees. I can see nothing."

Then she steeled herself, shoved Ivy aside, and scrambled back through the defile to stand menacingly before Judith. "You pushed him off that cliff on purpose, didn't you."

"Oh, God, no!" cried Judith, aghast at Susan's stormy face. "How can you think such a thing?"

"You have hated Morgan Patterson from the beginning. You've never cared whether he lived or died. You've said so a hundred times!"

"Yes, I have said that!" shouted Judith with a vengeance born more of fear, hurt pride, and self-condemnation than of actual anger, for even though she refused to acknowledge the truth, she too wondered if it had truly been an accident. The very fact that Susan would openly accuse her of murder speared Judith's self-conceit and left it in a shambles.

So it was understandable that Judith would resort to that sordid refuge of the highborn—withering scorn.

"Yes, I hate him!" Her eyes were mere slits of feigned hatred that under normal circumstances would have reduced an underling to dust. But Susan only smiled bitterly at Judith's searing declaration, so Judith continued, growing more arrogant with each spoken word.

"I loathe everything Patterson represents . . . and I hate you as well for you are just like him." She was, in a perverse sense, enjoying her theatrics. "Neither of you," she continued, "knows your station in society—for you are trash, both of you, yet you refuse to admit it!" She smiled defiantly. "If Mr. Patterson is dead—I am sorry. But no tavern whore is going to stand to my face and look down her nose at me for something that was an accident!"

Susan blanched with an anger so profound that for the first time, ever, she swore.

"Damn you, Judith; damn your black heart to hell." The words were barely audible, and Judith knew, even before Susan struck her, that her taunts had driven Susan to rage.

In seconds, both women were rolling in the dirt, screaming insults, scratching, kicking, and pulling hair in a most scandalous and shameful manner.

The pent-up emotion of days and nights of struggle and hardships, frayed nerves, and self-contained fear exploded. And Ivy, ignorant as to what course of action she should take, stood by helplessly while the two highborn young ladies beat, kicked, and scratched each other senseless.

She was appalled by the shocking spectacle they made of themselves; their dresses were above their waists, and occasionally their breasts were exposed. Their bare buttocks flashed stark white in the glare of the sun, as they thrashed and rolled, locked in hostile struggle, like two female gladiators.

But they were beyond caring how ludicrous they appeared, so determined were they to punish each other.

The fight might have gone on indefinitely had Judith, in a passion of pain and fury, not sunk her teeth into the tender swell of Susan's bare breast, and Susan, with unbridled agony, snatched up a stone the size of her fist and struck Judith in the eye, causing the blonde girl to open her mouth and scream.

Susan cupped her breast tenderly and rocked to and fro. "Damn you, Judith—damn you!"

"Is that the only curse word you know?" shouted Judith as she held her head to protect the eye that was fast swelling shut.

"If you two could just see yourselves!" cried Ivy, glaring from one to the other.

"And what did you accomplish? Did you prove anything—did you?" Ivy eyed the girls angrily. They were disheveled, bruised, and bleeding—and totally exhausted.

She started to speak again but Judith cut her off. "Just shut up. We've learned our lesson . . . for the time being anyway." She glared at Susan. "Unless, of course, Susan hasn't had enough!"

Susan's eyes flashed and she sprang angrily toward Judith, but Ivy quickly stepped between the two and, in a voice quivering with fear and rage, threatened to clout them both with Susan's musket.

So ended, temporarily at least, an encounter that was not only pathetic—but inevitable.

It took over an hour for the women to work their way along the cliff until they found a suitable slope where they could descend to the level where Patterson lay.

They made their way toward him in silence, envisioning a broken, twisted body.

The sight that awaited was Patterson, stretched out beneath a tree, mending with awl and heavy waxed linen thread the strap to his hunting pouch. It had broken during his fall.

"You're not dead," cried Judith with genuine relief as she ran to where he lay.

"'Tis no fault of yours," retorted Patterson. "I fell halfway through that tree before I was able to catch a limb."

"Oh, Mr. Patterson," cried Ivy, kneeling beside him and gently touching the cuts and scratches that covered his arms and shoulders. "Are you badly hurt, sir?"

He ignored her, turning his attention to the hunting bag. He could have explained that his arms were aching from being jerked from their sockets when he caught the limb, and that his injured leg was hurting like a day-old toothache, and that every muscle in his back had been stretched beyond its limits, not to mention the burning sensation caused by the cuts, scrapes, and scratches he had received from broken limbs. But he didn't explain, or complain, as he would have called it. He ignored the question and left Ivy embarrassed at having displayed such obvious affection.

Judith's elation at finding Patterson alive had vanished the moment he ridiculed her, to be replaced by her normal, insolent attitude.

"I did not push you over the edge of the cliff on purpose, Mr. Patterson. But whether you believe it or not is of little concern."

Patterson raised his eyes and slowly studied her bruised and battered face with the black eye already swelled closed.

"Did I say I thought you did it on purpose?"

"Well...no."

"Then why don't we let the subject drop?"

"As you please," she said indifferently.

Susan leaned her musket against the tree and sagged wearily to the ground next to Patterson.

Patterson eyed her disheveled appearance and wondered what had taken place in his absence, but he was too much the gentleman to inquire. Instead he asked pointedly which of them had brought his rifle gun down?

"Your rifle gun?" inquired Susan, looking askance at Patterson, who studied each girl in turn before shaking his head in exasperation.

"None of you did, did you?"

Patterson climbed painfully to his feet and squinted up at the lip of the overhang so far above.

"We did not know your gun was there, truly we didn't, Mr. Patterson," said Ivy.

Patterson searched Judith's face, for he was sure that she knew he had cast the weapon aside when he fell.

Judith looked quickly away. "I knew the gun was there," she said, staring at the stone bluff, "but I forgot about it when Susan...I forgot...that is all I have to say, except that if you think I shall climb back up there to get it, you are badly mistaken."

"That rifle gun cost a year's wages, Judith...and you forgot and left it lying on a bluff?"

"I will retrieve it," said Ivy quickly. "'Tis plain to see that Mr. Patterson is in no shape to make such a strenuous trip."

She had hoped that her generous offer would ease the tension between Patterson and Judith, but it was a wasted effort, for they still stared coldly at each other.

"I will go with you to get the gun," suggested Susan wearily, as she too painfully gained her feet.

"Nay, you rest, Susan," was Ivy's kind reply. "I am the only one in this group that is in any kind of shape to make such a climb. I will go alone—but thank you for offering."

Susan didn't argue, but it bothered her, the girl going up the mountain alone.

Ivy backtracked around the hill to the place where they had descended. After a brief rest, she began the tedious chore of pulling herself up the rugged incline and was stunned at how difficult the climb was compared to the trip down.

When she finally reached the plateau she sought, she was exhausted to the point of nausea. Her dress clung to her sweat-drenched body like a second skin; her arms and legs shuddered from spasms. She lay there with her cheek pressed against the brown and gold carpet of age-old leaves and evergreen needles and closed her eyes. It felt wonderful, to lie there and smell the earthy, pungent odor of the forest and feel the crisp yet soft layer of leaves beneath her body. Her mind wandered and she easily might have drifted off to sleep had not a noise from somewhere higher up the mountainside roused her to full consciousness. She continued to lie perfectly still, except for her eyes; they were narrowed, scanning the terrain above her as far as her angle of vision would allow. On the summit, several hundred feet above, she saw three Indians slowly working their way toward her. When they disappeared into a dense section of laurel, she sprang to her feet and ran for the boulders where Patterson's rifle lay. Her heart beat wildly as she sprinted between the huge stones and squirmed into the crevice that led to the overhang. She had expected to hear warcries long before she reached the rocks, but none had come. Perhaps she had gone undetected.

She scrambled through the defile to the lip of the dropoff and peered wildly into the depths below. The awful realization of how high she was hit her like a kick in the stomach and she shrank against the wall of stone and hung there, afraid even to breathe. With a voice choked with terror, she did manage to shriek to those below one coherent word: *Indians.*

Patterson had long since finished the repair of the shot-pouch strap and was anxiously watching, as best he could through the thick foliage, the rim of the cliff above.

"'Tis taking Ivy a long while to fetch my gun. Do you suppose she has lost her way?" The question was directed at Judith, but Susan answered instead.

" 'Tis a hard climb to that bluff, Mr. Patterson—almost straight up. Ivy will be along presently; just be patient."

"There is one other thing . . ." said Judith hesitantly, refusing to meet Patterson's searching expression, and wishing she had mentioned the fact earlier, when Ivy had volunteered to retrieve the rifle. For it had crossed her mind at that time that Ivy was a poor choice to risk, if the endeavor involved climbing to any promontory. "Ivy is terrified of height."

"I wish you had spoken of it earlier," said Patterson, looking again at the cliff. Then, as if in afterthought, he said he would climb up the tree and see if he could determine whether Ivy had reached the gun.

He was almost to the top when Ivy cried out her warning.

Forgetting the aches and pains that had dogged his every movement thus far, he clambered the remaining few feet to the crest of the swaying tree.

He could see Ivy plastered against the wall of stone, her eyes wide with fright, and her fingers white and bloodless as they tried to dig into the granitelike surface.

"Ivy," he said as gently as he could so as not to startle her, "can you see me? Here, in the tree just below you!"

Ivy's eyes inched down.

"To your left," said Patterson. "Over here just a little more."

Ivy saw him and relief momentarily erased the horror in her eyes.

"Ivy, where are the Indians? Where are they, Ivy?"

"Up on the . . . mountains," she said as if dazed.

"Ivy, my rifle gun is lying just above me . . . at the edge of the bluff. Can you get it?" He watched her closely to see if she still possessed her sense of reasoning and understanding.

"Get my gun, Ivy," he repeated urgently.

"I can't, Mr. Patterson. I—if I move, I—I'll fall."

"Just ease down the wall and reach out with your left hand. Do it, Ivy."

Ivy closed her eyes, and for a long moment Patterson was sure she had given way to the terror she was experiencing. But then, ever so slightly, with her back pressed tightly against the wall, she began moving downward.

"I—I've got it, Mr. Patterson." She clutched the weapon to her, then pushed herself tightly against the wall.

"Pitch me the gun ... come on ... throw it to me."

"I can't! I'll fall if I let go of the wall."

"Yes you can," he said easily. "Just flip it out here. You can do it."

"I'll fall!" cried the girl, pressing even harder against the stone.

Patterson wrapped his leg around the tree trunk and leaned as far toward Ivy as he dared. "Pitch it to me, Ivy. See, I'm just a few feet below you ... you can almost touch me."

They heard the warwhoops. The Indians had started through the defile, secure in the knowledge that their quarry was trapped and awaiting the kill.

"The gun! Throw me the gun!" shouted Patterson above the bone-chilling cries of the savages. "Oh, God!" he moaned. "Don't let her die like this ... please."

The first Indian leaped through the opening. He raised his tomahawk just as Ivy flipped the gun to Patterson, who caught the weapon by the stock, thumbed back the hammer and fired.

The Indian was slammed against the stone wall. Then he pitched over the edge of the cliff and plunged heavily through the trees to crash sickeningly on the rocks below.

"Jump, Ivy!" cried Patterson. "Jump to me—I'll catch you—trust me!"

A second Indian leaped through the cleft in the boulders. A deafening roar from the tree next to Patterson shook the wilderness.

The Indian turned and fled back through the gap, his arm shattered above the elbow.

"Jump, Ivy! Jump, damn it!" shouted Patterson as he glanced quickly at the tree that held Susan and saw with satisfaction that she was already clambering down the ladderlike branches toward the ground.

He glanced at the ledge and saw a third Indian move cautiously through the defile, his eyes scanning the trees, searching for the marksmen who had already shot his brethren.

Patterson watched in angry defeat as the man spied Ivy cringing against the wall, wild-eyed, like a trapped animal that has been backed into a corner and awaits the finishing blow.

The Indian, holding Ivy spellbound with his lidless gaze,

carefully laid his bow aside and drew his scalping knife. He sensed in the girl the terrible fear that was paralyzing her, and he sneered triumphantly, tasting the kill.

As he cautiously advanced along the narrow ledge toward her, Ivy inched backward along the wall until she was standing on the very edge of the precipice.

She cowered against the wall as nearer he moved. The razor-edged blade of his knife flashed brightly in the sunlight. His teeth glistened in a painted face that grinned fiendishly. She was his.

But as his hand sought her wrist, Ivy took a deep breath, closed her eyes, and hurled herself into the void over the rocky hillside far below.

It seemed to Patterson, who had not missed a heartbeat of the drama on the ledge, that Ivy hung suspended forever in space before she plummeted toward the ground. It took every ounce of strength he could muster to keep from being wrenched from the tree as he leaned far out to draw the falling girl to him in a crushing embrace that very nearly snapped the limb he was standing on. Shock exploded through every bone in his body. He clenched his teeth to keep from crying out as the arm that was wrapped around the tree for leverage was sawed against the rough bark of the trunk, leaving skin and flesh open and bleeding, causing him momentarily to release his grip on his rifle so that it clattered through the branches for several feet before finally coming to rest in the thick foliage of a lower branch.

Ivy clung to Patterson, her arms wrapped tightly about his neck. She buried her face in the hollow of his shoulder, and pushed ever deeper against him like a terrified child awakened from a nightmare.

"Hold me," she whimpered, her lips pressed against his neck. "Please hold me."

Patterson wound his arm more tightly about her, and for a fraction of a moment, caught up as he was in tender compassion for the girl, he laid his cheek against her hair and touched his lips to the top of her head. His eyes, however, were watching the Indian's every move, for Patterson was painfully aware that he and Ivy were openly exposed to a hail of arrows. Then, without thought or reason, he moved his body to shield the lovely girl he held so close. The Indian retrieved his bow and notched an arrow. He drew it tight until the flinthead was touching his fingers and the turkey-feather fletchings rested next to his eyes, and the veins in his muscular arms stood out like ropes. Then he drove the arrow into the trunk of the tree, not six inches above Patterson's head.

His eyes held Patterson's. "One so courageous as she," he said, nodding toward Ivy, "does not deserve to die like an animal trapped in a tree." It was said in perfect English.

Patterson studied the man; he was younger than the woodsman had supposed, and definitely white, although one would have been hard pressed to guess the truth, had he not spoken the king's English so well.

Patterson surmised that the young man had been taken captive and raised as an Algonquin. It was not an uncommon practice. Nor was it uncommon for a captured white, in time, to become fully Indian, preferring the native ways to those of the white man.

The Indian continued. "She should be allowed to live; to give you many sons that we, the Huron, would find worthy in battle. We are sick of the redcoated fishbellies that have come against us." His eyes moved to Ivy, and Patterson was astounded by the admiration that was evident in their depths as he gazed at the girl, whom, only moments before, he had intended to dispatch with his scalping knife.

"Guard her well, woodsman," he continued. "I would kill many enemy to have a woman such as she—but it would do me no good..." He gazed longingly at Ivy. "She would kill herself before she would let me take her."

It took Patterson a long moment to realize that the young warrior had honored Ivy's courage. She had leaped from the ledge to what seemed sure death rather than be taken by the enemy, and for that he intended to spare her. Patterson nodded: "I will guard her life like my own—we thank you."

Susan, upon reaching the ground, had wasted no time reloading and was scampering back up the tree during the exchange. She had heard none of it so she could not be held directly responsible for what followed. She rested her musket across a limb for support. Letting her breath out slowly, she aimed the heavy gun carefully on a spot below the Indian's ribcage, and gently squeezed the trigger.

The ball took the man above the navel, traveled upward,

bursting his lungs and heart, and tore out his back just above his shoulder blades.

He stood absolutely still for the briefest moment before his knees, already lifeless, buckled and dropped him over the edge of the cliff. He felt nothing as he crashed to the rocks below, for he was already dead.

Susan was bewildered by Patterson's attitude. For, after he and Ivy had clambered down the tree, neither had spoken, or indeed even glanced in her direction. Patterson had immediately begun inspecting his rifle with the greatest of care to ascertain the damage, if any, to his gun. Susan observed him in silence as he lovingly caressed the weapon, running his hands along the stock and forearm, and down the long, tapered barrel. That the gun was Patterson's most prized possession, having fed him when he was hungry, clothed him when he was bare, and more than once saved his and others' lives, did not enter Susan's mind. All she saw, and understood, was that he touched the gun as if it were a woman—a desirable woman—and she was jealous.

Ivy raced to Judith, who took the trembling girl into her arms. Their actions would long remain an irksome mystery to Susan for neither Patterson nor Ivy ever told her that the Indian she killed had just granted them their lives. She told herself it really didn't matter, but inwardly she longed for Patterson to praise her aim and her courage.

He did finally turn to her, with a sad smile, and tell her in his soft way that she had done well. The words salved her injured feelings somewhat, and yet she had the nagging sensation that although he had spoken the truth, he had left something unsaid. She fretted about it as they trudged down the hill.

They camped that night in a canebrake at the bottom of the mountain. After Patterson had seen to their well-being, he told them he intended to scout the area. Ivy was not fooled. She approached him as he reprimed his rifle. "You are going up the mountain and bury that boy, aren't you?"

"Aye," he said, slipping his priming horn into his pouch. "It is something I have to do."

"I know," she whispered as he slipped away into the darkness. She felt close to him at that moment—almost the same tender and touching feeling she had experienced when he had held her so tightly in the tree. Strange feelings churned in her breast; feelings not at all displeasing.

Patterson worked his way slowly up the mountain. His whole body ached with fatigue and strain. His injured leg throbbed from the new insults it had endured, and filled him with a weakness that left him unstable.

Still he pushed on, strengthened by the determination to fulfill a self-imposed obligation, no matter the consequences.

He was surprised to see a fire burning brightly below the cliff. And even more surprised to see a solitary Indian, eerie in the flickering light, silently gathering stones in one hand and stacking them around the bodies of the two dead men.

Patterson knew the old man had heard him, yet he gave no indication of Patterson's presence, nor did he bother to look up from his grueling task when Patterson stepped into the firelight. Instead, he went on with his work, carefully gathering any stones that he could carry with one hand. His other arm dangled uselessly at his side, and when he bent to retrieve another stone, the arm flopped grotesquely, revealing the shattered bone that had been shot away by Susan's musket.

The man finally turned toward the woodsman. His face was lined and wrinkled, his mouth puckered and pinched from loss of teeth, and the skin above his eyelids fell in small folds, almost concealing the fierce black eyes that were still young despite the apparent old age of the man himself.

Patterson nodded to the Indian, then leaned his rifle against the nearest tree: a sign of friendship or truce. The old man remained immobile as Patterson approached the fire.

"Grandfather," said Patterson, kneeling beside the man, "Do you speak the Shawnee tongue?"

The old man blinked, surprised at hearing Indian dialect flow freely from the lips of a white man.

"I speak all the languages of the Algonquin nation," said the man with dignity.

"I am not so wise, or learned, grandfather," returned Patterson.

"I am versed only in the tongue of the Shawnee. Forgive my ignorance of the Huron dialect."

"You are young, my son," said the Indian, his glittering eyes holding Patterson's. "There will be many winters for you to study the ways of others, so do not fret."

He waited patiently for Patterson to make known the reason for his strange intervention.

"Grandfather," said Patterson, "I have come to keep the wolves and panthers from the bodies of the two men that died today. I would consider it an honor if you would permit me to bury them in a fashion that befitted Huron warriors."

The old man blinked again. "You know the customs of the Algonquin?"

Patterson nodded.

"Have you found such a place nearby?"

Again Patterson nodded.

"I would like for my son, and grandson, to be buried as warriors have been buried for generations when they fell in battle. It would be good for an old man to know they rested in peace."

"I would consider it an honor to carry their bodies and lay them to rest," offered Patterson quietly, sure that the old man would be agreeable since it was plainly evident that he was physically incapable of accomplishing such a feat one-handed.

Patterson moved to the body nearest him and lifted it to his shoulder. The corpse had already stiffened, making the job much easier, yet, even then it was a difficult chore because the shattered body was laced with splintered bones.

Patterson carried the dead men a short distance down the mountain to a large hollow chestnut log, and as gently as possible, he wedged the bodies into the opening. It was hard, desolate work, pushing the first man deep enough into the log to allow room for the second. But with the assistance of the elderly Indian, he finally managed. He took special pains with the boy, to be sure he lay perfectly at ease—he owed him that much.

Satisfied that he had done the best he could, he began stacking stones in the opening to seal the ready-made coffin. The old man stopped him. "My son," he said gravely, "would you respect an old man's request to cut this useless piece of flesh from my body"—he

137

nodded toward his shattered arm—"and bury it with the bodies of my son and grandson?" His eyes rested on Patterson, dark and unfathomable.

Patterson held the old man's gaze. It was common practice for an Indian to sever a finger at the first joint to show respect and heartbreak for the death of a loved one, but to relinquish one's arm, even an arm that was useless and would doubtless remain that way, was a poignantly heroic show of grief—for it was almost sure to prove fatal. "Grandfather," he said with sincere courtesy and admiration, "I would be honored to perform such a small service for one as great and noble as thee."

He left the old man sitting serenely beside the chestnut log. And when he was some distance away, he drove his knife into the ground several times to rid it of blood and bits of meat that clung to the blade. It had been no easy matter removing the arm, even though the bone was already shattered. Patterson looked at the old Indian, a mere shadow in the darkness, and his eyes were bleak with thoughtful pity; white men considered Indians to be savages, devoid of tenderness and sympathy, but Patterson knew without a doubt that the old Indian would sit by the burial log that held his two loved ones, and grieve himself to death, or bleed to death—whichever came first.

Ivy feigned sleep as she watched Patterson slip soundlessly into camp. She could only guess at his purposes as he eased himself down to sit cross-legged, Indian fashion, and assume the pose of one in deep meditation—as indeed he was. He was praying to Owaneeyo, the Algonquin god, to have mercy on the old man and let the end come quickly and peacefully.

But Ivy knew none of that. What she did know was that Southhampton was abysmally wrong when he told Judith that Patterson was a man without compassion or feelings—and Ivy's lovely gray eyes glistened in the moonlight just before she closed them and slept soundly for the first time since she had met the woodsman.

The scorching heat of the first day of August caught the four as they pushed their way up a long, broad valley that had once been a magnificent river but was now an impenetrable flat, covered with an awesome tangle of fallen trees; canebrakes higher than a man's head; thickets so dense as to be almost impregnable; vines, briars, and nettles that seemed to be evil spirits the way they gripped and tore at the small troop that braved its interior. Even the small creek, a puny remnant of a once mighty river, lagged sluggishly along its muddy banks as if, indeed, it too found traveling a worrisome toil as it wound its way down the barbarous, incontestable basin.

The earth beneath the thick foliage was steaming with the foul odor of decayed vegetation and stagnant dampness.

To add to their ordeal, the air of the lowlands, unlike that of the cool heights of the ridges, lay thick and heavy, burning their lungs like a hot mist.

Yet the obstacles that the terrain threw in their path were nothing compared to the insects that plagued the four beyond endurance. Gnats endlessly buzzed about their heads and infiltrated their eyes, nose, and mouth, causing them to cough and hack.

Deerflies bit and stung every exposed bit of flesh, bloodying it and raising welts. And the worst of the lot, the mosquitoes, stung everywhere, raising welts in intimate places beneath their loose clothing. It was maddening.

"Christ!" said Judith as she flailed at the clouds of insects that buzzed continuously about her swollen, discolored eye. "Why are we down here in this awful place? Why did we not stay on the mountain?"

The question was directed at Patterson.

"Indians are watching the ridges," he answered simply. "They won't think to look for us here."

"Why not, Mr. Patterson?" asked Susan.

"Because no Indian in his right mind would be caught dead in a place like this!" said Judith, staring bitterly at Patterson.

The woodsman remained silent for, in truth, Judith was quite right.

For hours, Patterson, with the women close behind, worked his way over the latticework of dangerous deadfalls, beneath vines, and around briars and thickets, coming at last to stand on the muddy bank of the small stream. He, like the women, was exhausted, irritable, and in no mood for foolishness.

"Ladies," he said, scooping up a handful of stinking, muddy

earth, and covering the exposed area of his face and neck, "you will find this disagreeable, but it will keep a few of these damned bugs off you."

The women watched in silence as he smoothed the vile-smelling mess over his chest and abdomen, then over his exposed thighs above his leggin's.

Susan immediately followed suit and in a matter of moments was completely covered. "Shoo-wee!" she said, wrinkling her mud-covered nose. "This smell will take some getting used to."

Ivy, not so quick as Susan to comply, daintily fingered up a small handful of the stinking mess and gingerly rubbed it on her forearms.

She studied her arms for a thoughtful minute. Indeed, the insects would light upon the mud, but wasted no time taking flight in search of easier prey. So, with the help of Susan, she hastily plastered the stinking gumbo everywhere.

Judith, with a touch of contemptuous amusement, remarked upon the "deplorable fashion of her three companions."

"I would rather brave the insults of these detestable insects," she announced, fanning her neck and throat with her hand, "than to debase myself with such pig filth as you seem bent on covering yourselves with."

She cast a jeering glance at Patterson.

"And you, sir," she spat, "are most certainly quite mad even to think that I would lower myself to your standards—or—to that of your full-bosomed whore." She raised her chin to indicate Susan.

In speechless, embarrassed shock, Susan's hand went automatically to her breast, where Judith's tooth marks would have shown plainly had they not been covered with a coating of heavy mud.

Patterson glared at Judith with mounting fury. He had offered her respite from the furious insects, and she had snubbed them all. His hand closed on the nape of her elegant neck, almost lifting her off her feet, and then he began slopping the slime on her face, neck, and arms. She fought him fanatically and then grew rigid as stone when his calloused hands unwittingly dipped low into her tattered dress, and smoothed the foul mud over her semiexposed breast.

"You son-of-a-bitch," she exploded with a vehemence rarely found in one so young. "Do you dare to touch my bosom? No man, not even my fiancé, has ever taken such liberties, yet you . . . fondle them . . . at will." She was so enraged her breath came in short gasps, and her eyes were enormous spheres of blue ice.

"You flatter yourself, mistress," he said gravely, "for, in truth, I was unaware that my hands had accidentally touched that portion of your body, and I assure you, had I but noticed the least bit of—" He flushed, searching for the correct word to indicate the rise of a breast, but could think of no suitable synonym. At a loss for words, he said the one thing that lanced Judith deeper than he could ever have guessed, or would have wished. "Actually, Miss Cornwallace," he said without emotion, "you are as flat-chested as I."

Susan, who had been raptly observing the encounter, was appalled by Judith's reaction, for she had expected no less than a volcanic eruption from the blonde girl.

But, as Patterson turned on his heel and strode haughtily down the creek, Judith's overlarge eyes dropped to her immature bosom and, moments later, great, silent tears fused with the mud on her face and fell in staining drops to the front of her dress.

Susan stood in silent pity, her fingers unconsciously caressing the tooth marks on her full, young breast.

"Go with Mr. Patterson, Susan," said Ivy with soft anguish. "My mistress needs to be alone for a few moments."

"What is it, Ivy?" asked Susan with true concern. "I'm afraid I do not understand what has happened."

"I will explain, someday . . . please go."

Ivy was close to tears as she gently pushed Susan toward the direction Patterson had taken.

Susan moved uncertainly toward Patterson, unaware that he had accidentally shattered Judith's self-esteem by alluding to the only imperfection of Judith's superb figure, an imperfection that so haunted Judith that she had wept into her pillow many a night.

They struggled on, climbing over and under ancient, twisted trees that had felt the wrath of some terrible tornado of a past era.

Their bodies perspired so freely that the mud coating dripped endlessly on their clothing, leaving rivulets that drew new hordes of insects to exposed skin.

Nerves frayed and tensions snapped like lightning in a summer storm.

Food was scarce, and they were starved. They weakened from the lack of it. Finally, Patterson killed a rattlesnake, which he immediately dressed and set to roasting over a small, smokeless fire.

Judith was famished, and even though her belly ached and growled, she refused to touch the flesh of the snake.

"I have eaten squirrels, rabbits, birds of all description, including the golden finch, freshwater mussels, and of late even those awful-tasting crawfish you bring us, but I will not partake of the flesh of a serpent, Mr. Patterson." She turned her back on the cooking snake and seated herself primly on a fallen log.

"Suit yourself," said Patterson as he turned the roasting meat.

"Our Bible teachings are in direct opposition to eating serpents, Mr. Patterson," said Ivy, attempting to explain Judith's reluctance to eat when it was evident that she was already badly undernourished. "But I am so hungry," she continued, studying the roasting reptile with a rapt expression, "that, I dare say, I would take a bite of Satan himself if he were roasting on our fire."

"My sentiments exactly!" cried Susan, laughing while she knelt beside Patterson to help with the cooking.

"Then eat and be damned," said Judith dully.

They ate in silence, except for an occasional slap at an insect that had found a thin spot in the mud that covered their bodies.

And Judith, true to her religious beliefs, went to sleep that night with her stomach filled with righteous indignation, which she considered sufficient food for her soul. But her stomach still gnawed and growled its angry protests at her saintly reasoning.

Patterson watched her from the corner of his eye the next morning, more than a little impressed with her fortitude and self-willed determination. For the first time since having met her, he found himself grudgingly admiring the one trait she had displayed the previous evening.

His charitableness, slight as it was, was shattered when Judith approached.

"Mr. Patterson," she began angrily, "you have just got to find me something to eat—something my delicate stomach can digest. And you must do it now, this very minute!"

"Mistress," said Patterson, reaching for his rifle and wishing he were somewhere else, somewhere far away from Judith, or for that

142

matter, far away from all three of the women, "you will eat what there is...or starve. It makes very little difference to me."

"You have made that plain at every opportunity, Mr. Patterson, and I am sick of hearing it, and I am sick of you!"

Patterson glanced sideways at the girl. "You'd best not throw up! What little food is left in your belly might be all that keeps you alive these next few days." Then he laughed.

His mocking sent Judith into a cold rage, which brought words between her teeth that almost singed the bark off the nearest tree.

Susan watched the blonde girl with open-mouthed wonder.

Indeed, she was so caught up in Judith's astonishing vocabulary that she leaned forward until she was standing on her tiptoes. "Good Lord!" she whispered to Ivy, who was donning her shoes (the only one in the company who could boast a pair). "Has Judith always talked like that?"

"Yes," said Ivy, not the least bit interested.

"I've never heard a lady say such things," said Susan. "In fact, I have only heard such words once in my entire life and that was when Lieutenant South——" Susan hushed abruptly, realizing she had nearly mentioned the name of Judith's betrothed.

"Who did you say?" asked Ivy frowning.

"I said I heard an army lieutenant use some of those same words on a...a silly girl that was at a place she shouldn't have been. But they certainly did not sound anything like the way they did when Judith said them."

She gazed admiringly at Judith, who was standing with hands on hips, looking up into Patterson's flushed face.

"They sounded almost beautiful, the way she said them," continued Susan in a confused voice.

"Aye," said Ivy laughing, "she has a special way of swearing that sounds almost like words of love. Why, I've seen men take a terrible cursing from Judith and walk away with the look of one who has just been seduced."

Susan was wide-eyed. "Ivy," she said, feeling most foolish but bound to ask, "what does someone look like just after they've been—seduced?"

Ivy dropped her head back and, looking much like Judith, laughed gleefully.

"I have no idea," she said finally. "All dreamy-eyed, I suppose." Then she sobered. "About Judith's language. All the grand ladies at the queen's court use such...indelicate words—in truth, all the modern ladies of London's social set use such grammar. But for most," she said, eyeing Susan warningly, "it sounds absolutely vulgar."

They moved on, and Patterson's advice to Judith proved well founded because food was nonexistent. They grew weaker with each new day and found themselves, more often than not, leaning upon each other for moral and physical support.

Susan began using her musket as a crutch, pushing the stock into the slimy earth until the gun became so fouled that it was useless. Judith wept incessantly, agonizing about her feet. But it wasn't until she began to limp so badly that she could only lurch a few steps before falling to the ground that Patterson became alarmed. He discovered that the entire layer of skin on the bottom of her feet had rotted away, and the sensitive pink underflesh was raw and bleeding. Patterson winced at the sight and felt a twinge of guilt, for he had ignored Judith's pleas for help, supposing them to be the wailing of a spoiled brat.

They rested at that spot for almost a week. Patterson scraped the mold from the bark of a black oak tree and prepared an ooze in which to soak Judith's tortured feet. He hunted afar, bagging small game and birds which the women devoured before they were half cooked, and sometimes before they were cooked at all. Patterson watched them rip and gnaw the flesh of the animals, smearing blood across their faces. He found himself more than a little alarmed by their animal greed.

Patterson finally told the girls that they had tarried long enough. Judith's feet were partially healed and further delay might prove fatal. He cut the bottom from Susan's hunting frock and tied the leather around Judith's ankles, creating a sacklike moccasin that would help protect her feet from briars, stones, and sharp objects, but not, he knew, from the never-ending muddy dampness beneath the putrid leaves and vines of the lowlands.

For twelve days they walked, limped, and sometimes crawled through the waist-high vegetation, mud, and stench of the swampy bottoms before they finally climbed wearily onto a long sparsely wooded plateau. It was like stepping through the gates of heaven. Relief was immediate, and they rejoiced by lying down in the good, sweet-smelling grass and sleeping peacefully.

While their feet healed and their bodies mended, Patterson kept their minds occupied by continuing their training in the ways of the wilderness, explaining such things as the fact that moss grew on the northwest side of straight trees, and that limbs would be larger and more numerous on the south side. The women were attentive and Patterson was pleased. They were fast becoming adept woodsmen.

He took advantage of idle moments, ranging far and wide in search of game that was much more plentiful in the timbered, woodland ridges than it had been in the sun-scorched bottoms.

With a charge in his rifle so light that it made a muffled *poof* instead of an echoing *boom*, he shot a twenty-pound gobbler from its roost in a tall pine.

After feasting until they could not hold another bite, the well-fed, contented girls, feeling playful for the first time in weeks, tied the tailfeathers of the bird into their greasy, matted hair and teased Patterson by insisting they were Indian princesses. He smiled tolerantly at these wood nymphs. Ivy's amber hair was so sun-bleached that it resembled the burnished rose gold he had seen on an ancient clock in Williamsburg. And Judith was indeed striking with the turkey feathers stuck upright in her blonde tresses, which accented her sun-browned skin and pale blue eyes. But it was Susan that he stared at. The feathers in her coal black hair hung gently down the side of her deeply tanned face, and her dark eyes glistened with laughter as she asked if the three of them were as beautiful as his Indian girls.

He didn't answer. Instead, he studied her minutely, thinking all the while that she could pass for a light-skinned Mohawk maiden. They were reputed to be the most beautiful Indian women on the continent. Susan blushed under his scrutiny and averted her eyes, and Patterson almost reached out to her, so much did she trigger certain feelings in him.

Judith observed all this with mixed feelings until, in mounting anger, she tore the feathers from her hair and flung them at Susan. "Have them all, you savage-looking slut!" she spat, snatching the feathers from Ivy's hair and flinging them at the surprised girl also.

"Damn," muttered Patterson. It was time they were moving.

It was near noon six days later when Patterson smelled smoke accompanied by the sickening sweet odor of the newly dead. He raised his head, sniffing as a wild animal might have done.

"Wait here," he said as he checked the priming of his rifle. "I may be awhile, so do not be alarmed if I do not return immediately."

The women nodded, watching intently as Patterson vanished silently into the woods. In ten minutes he was peering through the brush some thirty yards from a smoldering cabin. He surveyed the area keenly for several minutes, then stepped into the small clearing.

The blackened stone chimney was all that was left of the one-room log house. But it wasn't the chimney that held Patterson's attention. The remains of the inhabitants, all five of them, lay in the clearing before the cabin. They had been stripped of clothing and were severely mutilated. The man had been savagely tortured and Patterson, hardened to frontier life, cringed inwardly at the spectacle. Indians had caught the family unawares, for there was no sign of resistance. What followed was a nightmare.

They had cut a small hole in the man's stomach and extracted a portion of intestine, tying it to the neck of the dog. After the man's hands were severed at the wrists, the animal had been released. The terrified dog had run, stringing out the man's intestines with every jump. All the poor fellow could do was to run with the dog, trying to catch the animal using nothing but his bloody stubs, which very likely had brought a howl of laughter from the savages. After the man had died, either from loss of blood or from having his guts literally ripped out, the Indians had cut off his head and used it in a game of kick, supposedly for the entertainment of his wife and children. They had also cut off his feet and private parts, although they were not in evidence; they had probably thrown them into the blazing cabin.

The youngest child, a five-year-old girl, had been killed by a single blow to the head. She had died instantly, for even in death, her face retained a wild, startled look of surprise. A boy, perhaps eleven, had had his throat cut. He had been scalped.

Patterson dreaded turning his attention to the older girl and her mother, knowing what he would find. The girl had been inhumanly tortured. It was difficult to tell her age, but Patterson guessed thirteen years. Her legs were thin and her hips and breasts were those of an adolescent. She had been fiendishly raped, probably many times. Dried blood crusted her entire body. Her face was a hideous mask of pain and agony. And even the milky film over her open, sightless eyes did little to erase the insane stare of them. Patterson could only guess at the degrading torment—spiritually, mentally, and physically—the girl had experienced. He was in a cold rage when Judith startled him, asking with contempt, "I thought your beloved Indians did not rape white women?"

Patterson turned on her like a wild man and backhanded her across the mouth, staggering her into Susan and Ivy. Judith's eyes enlarged to the size of saucers, but not a sound was heard except Ivy catching her breath. All three stared at Patterson, waiting, wondering what would come next. He was a far different man from the one they knew, and they were frightened at what they saw in his eyes.

"I told you to wait, but no—you just had to see." He was breathing hard. "Well, take a good look, damn you." He flung his hand out in anger. "But bear this in mind: these women were killed by white men. Aye, white men—worse savages, by far, than their red accomplices." Patterson grasped Judith's arm and flung her forward, causing her to stumble.

"Go ahead and look," he commanded. "This is what I would have spared you, had you but paid attention." He turned to Ivy and Susan, who instinctively shrank back. "You two come out here," he indicated the spot where he stood, "and breathe the stench of human flesh, and get your fill of whatever it is that makes one human being wish to view another's indecencies. Go on. Get out here!" Ivy timidly came forward and edged past Patterson, then stopped abruptly, stifling a scream as she surveyed the bodies—her eyes fixed on the woman.

Like her daughter, she had been raped repeatedly. Held down in a spread-eagle fashion, she remained transfixed, suggesting death had overtaken her while she was being abused.

It was Judith, however, having edged beyond the woman to stand in shocked silence studying the daughter's body, who noticed the girl's wrists. One had been deeply slashed with a razor-edged knife, bringing death closer with each beat of her heart. "The child probably considered it a blessing," said Patterson, as he moved to Judith's side. But he wondered why one of the whites who were violating her body did her a kindness. It was a mystery to which he wished he knew the truth, but he refused to let his mind dwell on it for in all probability it would never be solved.

Susan was still standing where Patterson had left her and it angered him seeing her there. He stepped toward her. "I thought you wanted to see this," he raged.

"No," she said, dropping her eyes. "I have seen it before. My morbid curiosity was quenched years ago on board a ship bound for the New World."

Patterson spun on his heel and joined Judith and Ivy, who were peering wildly about. Judith appeared drawn to the rape victims as if by a magnet. In horrified fascination, she gazed first at the daughter, then at the woman. She stared at the mother's corpse so long that Patterson asked her what she was looking at.

"Mr. Patterson, why did they cut...her breast off?"

Still in a rage, Patterson answered without thinking: "Because some French son-of-a-bitch wanted a tobacco pouch, and they make them out of women's breasts. Now do not ask anymore goddamned questions of me." He turned and stalked off toward Susan.

"Why are you so angry, Mr. Patterson?" she asked as he drew near.

"Angry? I am not angry."

"Yes, you are, sir. You are angry, the same way a father is angry when a child has misbehaved and, as a result, placed itself in grave danger." Patterson made no reply, so she continued. "You blame us for the responsibility you have chosen to shoulder on our behalf."

"Aye, what choice did I have?" he asked harshly.

She dropped her eyes, afraid to look at him; afraid she might see something more than anger and hurt, knowing she could not bear to see hate in his eyes.

He continued, "Every time I look at that girl or that woman, I see you...and Judith...and Ivy. And all it will take, mistress, is one moment of unawareness—one unguarded minute on my part—and it could be you lying out there, do you understand?"

Before she could reply, Judith said in a calm voice, "Mr. Patterson, promise me one thing, sir."

"And what is that?" he asked, turning to face her.

"Promise me you will kill me before you let this happen."

Patterson studied her for a long moment. He knew her request was made in earnest, and he wondered if, should the time come to make the decision, he could bring himself to kill such a beautiful woman. He glanced at the two mutilated female bodies and decided that yes, he would kill her before he would let a pack of beasts use her body to pleasure themselves over and over until she was a screaming lunatic, or until they tired of her, at which point they would kill her anyway. He turned to Susan and asked more harshly than he intended, "And you, mistress? Do you wish for me to take your life also?"

Susan lifted her chin and looked Patterson in the eye. "No, Mr. Patterson," she said softly. "That will not be necessary. For, you see, sir," she paused, raising her eyebrows defiantly, "I will kill myself before I let them take me."

Patterson's eyes narrowed as he studied her; he knew she had spoken the truth, and he felt humbled at her courage. He dropped his gaze and turned to Ivy. She laughed shakily, trying to appear light and easy, but she fooled no one. "Why Mr. Patterson," she said, "I would just naturally die of fright and save you the trouble, sir."

Patterson's lips formed a crooked smile, because without his realizing it he, as a brave man, appreciated courage in others; and without a doubt, these ladies were blessed with an abundance of courage.

"All right," said Patterson, studying the hard-packed earth to be sure they had left no visible sign, "we'd best be gone from here. We've got a long way to travel."

"But, sir," clamored Judith, "what of these poor people? Surely, you intend to bury them in the proper Christian manner?"

"No," he said, stepping away, "I will not bury, or move, or touch one person, or one thing in this clearing, nor shall you."

Patterson could have explained that at that moment another war party might be in the vicinity, and should they find any sign—a grave, or covered naked bodies, or any other Christian act—they would know immediately that Englishmen were near and would search out their trail until they were located.

He could have made it plain that he was not without feeling, and if circumstances were different, he would gladly have done the decent thing for those scattered bodies—but he didn't explain. He would not be intimidated by Judith, or the other women, not when their lives depended on it.

Judith blanched, and pushing past Patterson, she bolted

blindly for the sanctuary of the forest. Ivy followed. Susan touched Patterson's arm. "As much as you would like for us to believe it, you are no animal, Mr. Patterson. You have a reason for leaving those folk as we found them. You could have explained."

Patterson merely grunted, then dogtrotted toward the darkness of the tall trees, leaving Susan to stare after him.

They traveled fast the remainder of the day, and nighttime found them far from the burned-out cabin. They had a cold camp that night, afraid to trust a fire, knowing a large party of French and Indians might still be in the area.

Patterson hollowed out a depression in the leaves and went immediately to sleep. It was one of those pitch black nights, the kind of darkness that hides one's hand not six inches before one's eyes.

He had no idea how long he had slept when he came suddenly awake with the sensation of warm, moist lips pressed hard against his. His eyes flew open. He could see nothing; then the lips were gone. He tried to pretend he was still asleep and the kiss had been a dream, but he knew better. He raised his fingers and gently touched his mouth. Dream or not, he had never in his life been kissed with so much tenderness and passion.

He lay there, lost in thought. He did not like games; did not understand them. If a woman wanted him, then why did she not say so? Why did she slip around to kiss him? Why did she kiss him in the first place? Then he pondered the most significant question: Who was it that had kissed him? He mentally tried to imagine what it would be like to kiss each girl individually, but he had so little experience at such things that he gave up in frustration. He would wait until morning; surely the guilty one would give herself away. Yes, he would watch them closely come morning.

Morning came and Patterson was more perplexed than ever. Not one of the girls looked as though she were hiding anything. That one had silently come to him in the night and kissed him long and passionately, then silently disappeared, was maddening. He was determined to know which one it was. He covertly observed the girls in turn. Each was performing her morning duties with the same efficient skills he had taught them weeks earlier. Patterson was irritated. He liked this foolishness not one bit.

Judith glanced in his direction, smiled, and beckoned him to her. *I might have known it was you*, thought Patterson, as he studied her face.

A slight frown knitted her eyebrows and she asked with concern: "Are you not well, sir?"

Patterson, taken completely off guard, said, "Why, yes, Judith. Perfectly fine. Why do you ask?"

She peered closely at his face. "I do not know, sir." She hesitated, searching for the correct words. "You look so...intent. I just wondered if you were ill."

Patterson was disappointed. "I feel fine. Is there anything else you would care to discuss?"

Judith's face flushed. "Why, yes, Mr. Patterson, there is something else. I wish to apologize for the way I have been acting lately. I will try to do better in the future." She studied him closely, suspiciously. "Are you sure you are feeling well, sir?"

"Aye, mistress," he said. "I am indeed well, thank you. As for the way you have been acting—well, we will just have to wait and see." He wondered what she meant by "do better in the future." He had never seen a skunk change its stripes.

Judith's intense gaze followed him as he moved away. *I do believe the man is ill*, she told herself, smiling with satisfaction, for she had seen that same look on several gentlemen's faces since she had turned eighteen.

8

Patterson put the mystery behind him as they made their way over the hills, across the streams, and down the valleys. The only noticeable difference in Judith was her eyes. They no longer held that jeering, contemptuous expression that made her seem so haughty. Instead, they were inquisitive and thoughtful—and the change bothered Patterson. He did not like, or understand, people who were unpredictable. He preferred her reliably obnoxious.

Food was a never-ending problem, especially meat, so Patterson showed the women how to set small-game snares and deadfalls. He also showed them how to twist a squirrel out of a hollow tree using a green briar. He cut a long length of briar and split one end. He threaded the split end into the hollow and rammed the briar up the inside of the tree. The hollow extended only six or eight feet, so he had no trouble reaching the end of the opening. He poked and punched several times, but the tree was empty. He shrugged, explaining that not all hollow trees had squirrels in them.

Had the hollow run beyond reach of a green briar, he explained, one could build a small fire in the opening and smoke the critter out. But, he cautioned, smoke could be smelled from afar, so he would not demonstrate. To the delight of the women, he did kill several quail, Indian fashion, when a covey rose. He whirled a five-foot stick at the birds and the rotating pole knocked down three birds. Of all the snares they had set, only one produced.

So, for supper that afternoon, the party had three quail and one rabbit. It wasn't much of a feast, but the girls were thrilled with their fare and Patterson was happy that they were so easily satisfied. They were learning.

Although he slept with one eye open, the night passed without incident. He was disappointed; the knowledge angered him.

The next afternoon, as they trudged cautiously down a sloping hill covered with briars, hazelnut thickets, sagegrass, and brush, Patterson froze in his tracks and motioned that the women do the same. His head moved slowly, eyes squinted to see better the advance of a column of redcoats that had just emerged from the distant forest and entered the long, grassy field below the hill.

Judith, who had also seen the unmistakable red tunics of the British army, sprang past Patterson and raced down the hillside.

Patterson was on her in a split second, dragging her to the ground and covering her thrashing body with his, in an effort to silence the excited girl.

"Let me go!" she cried, flinging her head from side to side as she struggled to gain her freedom. "'Tis our army," she laughed hysterically. "My fiancé has come for me—let me go!"

Patterson locked his arms around the squirming girl, pinioning her.

"Listen, Judith, listen to me!" He used his free hand to hold the girl's face immobile while he whispered. Her eyes flashed with loathing as she kicked and writhed under him.

"'Tis not the army," he continued harshly as if he were talking to someone demented. "It is Indians, Judith, wearing the coats of dead men. There are no white breeches. Do you understand? No white breeches—'tis not the army!"

"You lie! It is James—he has come for me as I knew he would... *let me go*—you don't want him to rescue me!"

She snatched her face free of his grasp and took a deep breath, intending to call out to her fiancé, but the only sound that escaped her slightly parted lips was a soft sigh when her head snapped back and was gently turned to the side as if she were in slumber. Patterson wasted no thought on what he had been forced to do. He had not wanted to hit Judith, but neither could he allow her to jeopardize the lives of innocent people because of her belief that he was against her being rescued.

153

He quickly gathered her into his arms and crawled up the hill to where Susan and Ivy waited in nervous alarm.

"I think they saw Judith, Morgan," said Susan, trying hard to conceal her fear.

"They're going to catch us—oh, God!" wailed Ivy.

"We're not caught yet," said Patterson as he ducked beneath the impenetrable foliage of a thicket of hazelnuts.

Susan caught Ivy's hand and forcefully pushed her into the thicket.

Ivy crawled to Judith's side and lay down next to her mistress, now beginning to show signs of consciousness. As Judith's eyelids fluttered open, Ivy gently put her hand over the girl's mouth to prevent the likelihood of even a soft moan.

Patterson observed the gesture with approval, and was even more relieved when Ivy bent low and quietly assured Judith that it was, indeed, Indians she had seen and not Lieutenant Southampton.

"They may have seen us, mistress," continued Ivy, "so we must be very quiet."

Judith nodded her understanding, her eyes sliding toward Patterson to search his face as if she were seeing him for the first time.

Ivy removed her hand and settled beside Judith to struggle with the nerve-racking knowledge that they may have been discovered and might be spending their last moments on this earth. She instinctively held Judith to her and kissed the girl's cheek. Judith, taken completely by surprise by Ivy's show of tender affection, recoiled.

Ivy dropped her eyes. "I'm sorry, mistress."

Judith's flight down the hillside, however brief, had not gone unobserved. The lead Indian had caught a flash of movement above the brambles and bushes far ahead. He studied the terrain methodically, his black eyes searching the hillside slowly. Nothing moved, nor did anything appear less tranquil than it should. Still, he was not satisfied. He checked the bushes and weedtops to be sure that the breeze had not rustled the leaves and caught his attention— but there was no breeze.

He motioned several others to him and together they moved

silently into the dense underbrush that covered the hillside. The remaining Indians emerged from the woodline and continued down the field that swept past the hill where the four fugitives were partially concealed.

Patterson could hear them: a hundred bare or moccasined feet treading softly, like a whispering wind, through the sun-burnt brittle grass of late summer. He was not aware of the handful of savages who had moved up the hill and were slowly working their way toward him not a hundred yards distant.

Immediate discovery would have been inevitable, had not successive events intervened. A buck deer, bedding not twenty feet from Patterson's hiding place, suddenly bounded up the hill away from the whites and the commotion of the advancing Indians. And, as Providence would have it, the animal flushed a flock of wild turkeys. The birds burst into flight, flapping off in every direction.

The Indians howled savagely and raced down the hillside in wild pursuit.

Patterson had heard the deer flee and the turkeys flap away, but until the nearby Indians made their presence known by racing after the turkeys, he had not been aware that detection and probable death were at hand. He wondered if the women were aware of their close encounter with capture, or the fact that they were spared a gruesome ordeal by the irresistible urge of redmen to chase after game.

Patterson and the women, peering through the foliage of the hazelnut bushes, had an almost unobstructed view of a long portion of the field below. They lay there hardly breathing as the main body of Indians sauntered down the grassy plain until they were directly below the frightened watchers. Even Patterson's scalp crawled. The Indians began milling about, talking and laughing, and gathering sticks and brush. They were preparing to settle down for the night, and they were also waiting for someone, or something.

The wait was not long. Not an hour had passed when several French soldiers and two officers emerged from the treeline. With them were three British prisoners. All three were dressed in the traditional woodsman garb. The first had his hands tied behind his back. A rawhide thong ran from his neck to the man behind him, who was tied in the same fashion, with the thong extending to the third man.

The French prodded the prisoners into the Indians' camp,

creating a flurry of excitement. The Indians danced and shouted and tormented the three captives by shaking hatchets in their faces, cutting off hanks of hair, and jabbing them with musket barrels. They would save the actual torture until the prisoners were secure in whatever village the Indians resided. Patterson guessed they were Hurons from Detroit, but he had no way of knowing for sure.

The Indians did, however, set up a gantlet, which the captives were forced to run. They cut the men free, commanded them to strip, then retied their hands. They formed a double line about eight feet apart, with the Frenchmen, except for the two white-coated officers, joining the lines. Each participant held a short stave about three feet long and perhaps an inch or two in diameter. They stood there, joking amongst themselves, eyeing the Englishmen with anticipation.

The first man was brought to the starting line by an Indian dressed only in a loincloth and bright-red tunic worn open down the front. The Indian's body was painted half black and half white. His face was completely black except for two white rings around his eyes. His colorful body only accented the paleness of the Englishmen.

The Indian said something to the Englishman, and the man visibly tensed. Then, without warning, he was clubbed viciously, causing him to stumble the first few steps as he started down the gantlet. Once he regained his footing, however, he astounded the Indians by his fleetness and was beyond the gantlet with hardly a blow touching him. The savages were outraged.

The three women almost shouted in triumph as they watched from their hiding place. They turned grim, however, as the second man ran down the line. The blows rained heavily upon his head, neck, and shoulders, but he somehow managed to keep his footing and finally passed beyond the reach of his tormentors. The Indians hooted and howled.

The third man was even less fortunate. He stumbled and fell face down in the small avenue, and before he could regain his footing, the Indians converged on him, beating him unmercifully. Their wrath satisfied, they cast their staves aside and strolled away. The man lay in a crumpled heap; whether alive or dead was anybody's guess.

Patterson sensed, more than saw, Susan's movement, and his

156

eyes flickered wide in alarm as she eased her musket into firing position. Cautiously he put his hand over hers and, as she turned to face him, put his lips against her ear. "I know how you feel, but there is nothing we can do but lie here and watch. We cannot help those poor fellows, and if the situation were reversed, they would not help us. If they knew we were here, they would understand and approve of our secrecy."

He did not explain to her the unwritten law of the frontier: self-preservation first. He had known of several occasions where a man's family or friends had been butchered or taken captive while the man in question watched from hiding. Frontier folk understood this and did not think less of a man for it. The wilderness was a hard place and it took even harder people to conquer it.

The Indians ignored the crumpled form lying on the ground as they went about the business of preparing their evening meal. A large buck deer was carried out of the forest and quickly quartered. Each quarter was spit over the coals of a low-burning fire. The smell of the roasting meat put Patterson's stomach into convulsions. He knew the women were starving, as was he, and to see and smell food cooking, had to be driving them mad. He studied the women from the corner of his eye. Their faces were riveted to the sizzling meat. Ivy was absently licking her lips. Susan rolled onto her back and closed her eyes. Judith turned her head and began silently wretching. Patterson was relieved when the vomiting subsided. She turned her tear-streaked face toward him, nodding her head, assuring him she was through. Then she vomited again.

Occasionally his stomach would growl so loudly he was sure the savages would hear it, but the long afternoon wore on and night fell, leaving the Indian camp in darkness as the fires died out.

The moon climbed above the trees, illuminating the hillside with its soft light. Patterson considered trying to slip the women away in the semidarkness but discarded the idea. It was too dangerous. Their best chance for survival, he decided, was to stay where they were—and pray that the Indians would overlook them.

The night passed slowly for Patterson . . . yet, even then, with a dreaded quickness, for daylight would be the most dangerous time. Scouts would be sent out and probably a hunting party or two before the remainder of the Indians broke camp.

As false dawn approached, Patterson concealed the women as

best he could. He could only hope that they were hidden well enough to evade detection. The women watched trustingly as he covered their bodies with brush and leaves. He started to reach out, to touch them reassuringly, but the gesture was alien to him and he moved his hand instead to some dry grass, which he distributed here and there over them. Satisfied that he had hidden the girls as best he could, he covered himself, shifting his rifle so the muzzle was only inches from the back of Judith's head. If discovery was inevitable, he would fulfill the promise made only days earlier. She would not be taken alive. He would also kill Ivy and Susan if time permitted. As for himself? He would not be taken under any circumstances. He had no false impressions as to what his fate would be at the hands of the savages. He would be skinned alive and burned slowly over an open fire. No—he would rather die fighting.

The Indians broke camp at daylight, taking the three prisoners with them. They had kicked the severely beaten man until he finally struggled to his feet and trudged into line, but Patterson was sure he was in no condition to travel far.

The procession snaked down the meadow, oblivious to the noise it was making, and Patterson thought again how much like other wild beasts Indians actually were. When completely sure of their safety, the deer, bear, or elk were just as noisy in their travels, breaking brush and limbs, or snapping twigs underfoot; but the moment danger threatened, animals—or Indians—could ghost through the forest without a sound.

Two broke away from the main party and trotted toward Patterson, who inched further back into his lair and waited. They stopped at the bottom of the hill and conversed in low tones, one pointing directly toward the hill, the other shaking his head and indicating the woodland to his left. Patterson relaxed: perhaps the Indians would change direction. They didn't. They slowly worked their way up the hillside toward the hidden women. Patterson cursed his luck and slipped his thumb over the hammer of his rifle. He was sweating, whether from fear or anxiety he was not sure.

The Indians moved quietly up the incline, stopping frequently, looking first this way, then that, taking in everything their keen eyes could observe. The suspense was unnerving and Patterson physically fought down the overwhelming impulse to bolt. "Lie easy," he repeated under his breath. "Just lie easy."

The Indians were so close Patterson could smell them—a mixture of bear grease and tallow, of smoke and unwashed bodies, of dried blood and sweat. All these odors and others mingled together to create the particular pungency of an Indian who trod the warrior's path.

They slipped past Patterson, the distance so minute he could have touched their moccasins. His breath locked in his throat as one Indian stopped abruptly. *This is it,* thought Patterson as he eased the hammer to full cock. The audible click of the sear locking into position was drowned out as the Indian pulled aside his breechcloth and watered the brush directly across from where the four were hidden. Then he moved uphill and disappeared into the forest. Patterson let out a sigh; only then did he realize he had been holding his breath. He slowly removed his finger from the trigger and wiped the perspiration from his forehead. It was then that he noticed Susan's eyes. They were riveted to his in tormented anguish. Tears were swimming under the long lashes. His gaze moved to her musket. The muzzle was pressed gently against Ivy's back and the hammer was in full cock. *She would have killed Ivy—just as quickly as I killed Judith.* The thought startled him and he looked again at Susan, but her eyes were closed and relief was evident on her tear-streaked face. *She would do to cross the river with,* he decided. A rare compliment indeed, coming from a hardened woodsman.

An hour after the Indians' departure, the girls and Patterson cautiously descended to the deserted campsite. The meat had been completely consumed and the cleanly picked bones cast aside. Patterson cracked the bones with his tomahawk and showed the women how to suck the marrow. It was not the ideal breakfast, but it did help satisfy their gnawing hunger.

Judith slipped to his side. "Mr. Patterson?" she asked with unusual softness, which caused the woodsman to glance up in question.

"Those coats—" she stammered, causing Patterson to note the haunted look in her dark-rimmed eyes. "There were so many Indians wearing the coats of our army. Was our whole—were there any survivors?"

Patterson looked long at the saddened girl before answering,

159

because, in truth, he did not know. He did not answer her question outright but said instead, "We are alive, are we not?"

Judith nodded. "Yes, we are alive—but there were so many redcoats."

"Not so many, Judith. Perhaps fifty, no more. It just appeared to be hundreds of them as they moved in single file down the field."

Judith accepted his evasive answer and turned to join Susan and Ivy who were still in the process of cracking deer bones and sucking the pungent marrow.

"Judith," said Patterson, "I am sorry if I hurt you when I hit you—I am sorry it happened."

"Forget it, Mr. Patterson," said the girl as she strode away. "It merely revived my belief that American men are cowards—for only a coward would strike a lady, no matter the circumstances."

Judith immediately regretted the statement, for she, in spite of her determination to hate Patterson, admired and respected his courage. She turned to retract the words but Patterson was already moving toward the darkened forest.

As the sun climbed above the treeline, they were again making their way northeastwardly, and although they traveled with extreme caution, they still made several miles before sundown.

At the women's insistence, they camped beside a small fast-running stream that evening, and while Patterson set his snares, the women bathed. When he returned to camp, he noticed that their dresses had been washed and were hanging on tree limbs to dry. He thought about that mysterious kiss, and the naked women bathing not a hundred yards away. Curiosity got the better of him. He had never seen a naked white girl, leastwise not one who was naked by choice instead of force.

Using his woodsman's stealth, he edged his way toward the stream. He eased through the brush more carefully than he ever had when stalking the game trail, knowing full well he would rather be captured by a band of howling savages than be caught spying on three naked white girls. His stealthiness paid off. He parted the foliage and was rewarded by a view of Ivy's bare back as she combed out her long amber hair. Her movements were feminine and graceful and very pleasing to the eye. Unconsciously, his thoughts drifted to a different time and place, long ago it was, when another white woman stood naked before a horde of people. He remembered them, gawking and staring, much as he had stared at Ivy, and he saw the terrible shame on the woman's face, as unwanted eyes appraised her most intimate parts. Suddenly he was shamed for invading Ivy's privacy; he slipped away as noiselessly as he had come.

Had he stopped and gone back, he very likely would have taken a keen willow switch to their bare bottoms for they had doubled over in laughter. Ivy, catching quick breaths between fits of laughter, exclaimed, "I knew he would come. I just knew it."

Judith sobered and, with a thoughtful expression on her sunken-cheeked face, said: "I think I knew he would come also . . . but I wasn't sure. He's so . . . strange at times."

"Well, at least," said Susan, still laughing, "we know he is a man, but 'twas a dirty trick." They all giggled and howled again.

"Tell me, Ivy," said Susan, "what is it like having a man see you nude?"

"Well," said Ivy slowly, contemplating her thoughts, "I was not as embarrassed as I thought I would be; at least, not with Morgan being the one doing the looking. It just seemed," she hesitated, then smiled at Susan, "it just seemed natural to have him look at me. I was proud—yes, proud." Then Ivy quickly looked around, as if to be sure no outsiders were close enough to hear what she said next. She leaned toward Susan and Judith stepped closer also. "I will tell you this," she whispered. "I had the strangest impulse to turn around and let him see all of me."

"Ivy!" exclaimed Judith.

Susan laughed and clapped her hands. "Ivy, I fear we have something in common."

"What is that, Susan?" asked Ivy breathlessly.

"Like you, I do not think I would die if Mr. Patterson saw me naked."

Judith said dryly, "He's already seen you naked, remember?"

"But that was different," said Susan quickly as she turned again to Ivy. "Have you ever . . . been with a man, Ivy—you know what I mean? Have you ever made love with one?"

Ivy's eyes grew large as she looked at Susan. "Heavens, no. But I have often wondered what it would be like. One hears all manner of talk from other servants and all, but I have never done it."

Both girls turned as one toward Judith, who blushed profusely.

"I may be betrothed," she stammered, "but upon my word, I have never allowed a man such liberties with my body. A kiss or a caress, but never that. I think it despicable of you even to discuss such a thing. What has come over you?"

"Nothing has come over us, Judith," said Susan, "except the need to talk and think of things other than Indians, and killings, and war."

Then Ivy joined in. "And do not let on that you never think such thoughts, Judith! I have seen you tease Mr. Patterson with your eyes, even the other day when you showed him your thigh as you cut your dress off. You might fool him, but you are not fooling us, so—" Ivy stopped abruptly. She had overstepped her status as a servant, and by law she could be beaten for it.

Judith looked at her for a long moment, before replying coolly, "'Tis the second time you have forgotten your station, Ivy. However," she added musingly, "I think I like you better as a person than as a servant—for the time being anyway." Then she laughed. "You are quite right, Ivy. I have teased Mr. Patterson and . . . I do believe he is in love with me." It was a statement made coolly, without a trace of doubt. Susan and Ivy refused to meet Judith's haughty gaze, for each was afraid she had spoken the truth.

Their high spirits returned, however, as they walked toward the camp, reliving once again Patterson's spying on Ivy. They remained nude, secure in their belief that Patterson would be out scouting, or checking his snares, or whatever he did to keep busy while they dressed. That was the way it had always been, so finding the camp deserted when they approached, they thought nothing of the fact that he was missing.

A rabbit roasting over a small fire was proof that Patterson had checked his snares. The meager fare did little to appease the girls' never-ending hunger, but they put the physical discomfort out of their minds, and turned their attention instead to the vain side of their nature: the art of combing the snarls from their damp hair while they awaited Patterson's return.

Twilight came and Patterson had not returned. The girls watched the edge of the clearing anxiously, but he did not appear. Susan put the fire out and covered the coals with loose dirt to avoid any chance that the live embers might flame into life during the night.

Judith broke the nervous silence: "He is an ignorant savage to leave us like this." She stared long into the darkening forest. "I hate this place. I hate it."

Susan sighed. "I think we would all rather be somewhere else, Judith."

"But where has he gone?" she cried, turning her frightened eyes to Susan. "He is so strange and unpredictable. He may have abandoned us here."

"I think not," said Susan. "I believe he likes us far better than he lets on."

"I care not whether he likes or detests us," said Judith. "He could treat us more decently."

"He is doing everything possible to rescue us, mistress," said Ivy flatly.

Judith dropped her face into her hands. "I hate him, I hate him." Then she cried.

Susan gazed at Judith, trying to interpret the girl's feelings. She sensed a deep inner struggle within Judith, but she couldn't fathom what it was. She did know one thing, however; regardless of what Judith said about hating Patterson, the girl was trying wholeheartedly to win his approval.

Ivy moved to Judith's side and slipped her arm around her. "You do not hate him, Jude," she said softly. " 'Twould not surprise me to find that you are falling in love with him instead."

Judith laughed bitterly. "Ivy, you have taken leave of your senses. I loathe him; he is an ignorant savage, and I do hate him."

Susan eased down in her bed of dried leaves, making herself as comfortable as possible. She thought about Patterson and what Judith had said. He was a strange person, but he most certainly was not an ignorant savage. Different from most men, yes, but not illiterate or mean. He appeared to be well educated and, at the right moment, could be very gentle. She wondered why she was so sure of that. She thought about it a moment longer before her mind moved on to what they had learned about him that day. He is aware of our femininity, she thought, but what good does the knowledge do us? Is there no justice? Once, just once, I would like for him to look upon me as a desirable woman.

She was not aware of falling asleep until Ivy gently shook her. "Wake up, Susan. Wake up."

"What is it?"

"Judith is gone. She has been gone for hours."

"How do you know?"

"I saw her walk into the forest. I thought nothing of it and went back to sleep, but when I awoke a few minutes ago and found she had not returned, I became frantic. I have searched everywhere."

"Has Mr. Patterson not returned?"

"No," replied Ivy nervously. "I am sick with fright, Susan, just sick to death."

"It will be all right," said Susan, with a lightness she certainly did not feel. Suppose Patterson did not return. Surely he had not abandoned them. No, he would not abandon them. She wished she knew that for sure. And if Judith was lost, or hurt, she and Ivy alone would never find her. She felt like crying, but she knew it would do no good. Instead, she questioned Ivy as to which way Judith went, precisely how long she had been gone, and everything else Ivy could recall concerning Judith's disappearance.

At that moment, a thoroughly terrified Judith was sitting on a log with her face cupped in her hands, crying. Worried and unable to sleep, she had decided to walk in the forest, intending to venture only a short distance. She had needed time to think and try to sort out in her mind her feelings on certain matters concerning the heart. In spite of herself, she knew she was changing, but she did not want to change. What she wanted was for Lieutenant Southhampton to come for her, as he should have done days and days ago, and take her back to the security and safety to which she was accustomed. Why had he not come? Had he perished during the battle? She thought not. Did he not love her enough to come for her? Of course he did. But in truth, she was not certain. She was confused and scared. And worse, she had done a most foolish thing; she had panicked upon finding herself lost.

Not only had she yielded to fear, but she had run blindly through the night, stumbling, falling, hurting herself until exhaustion had caused her to collapse beside the log she was now sitting on, and cry her heart out.

She hated the forest and she hated Morgan Patterson, and she was sure she would die alone in the endless wilderness. No one would ever know what became of her, unless someday, someone should find her bones and recognize the crest ring she wore. Self-pity welled up within her. Most of all, she decided, she hated James Southhampton for putting her into this terrible position. Had he not insisted she walk with him into the forest on that fateful day when Braddock was defeated, she would not be in this dilemma. He had even tried to send Ivy back to the main camp, so he could have her "alone for once," as he put it. And after Ivy refused to leave, he had tried to seduce her in Ivy's presence.

But Judith had refused to succumb to his kisses, caresses, and words of love, and he, enraged, had stalked off, leaving her and Ivy to return to the column alone. Moments later, the French and Indians had opened fire on the unsuspecting army. As Judith recalled those events that had thrown her into a way of life that she did not know even existed, she cried again.

Then rage began building in her, spreading through her like a fire. She came off the log with fists clenched. "Damn you," she cried to the tall, majestic trees. "You will not have my body. I would not give it to Southhampton, and I will not give it to you."

She raised her fists toward the leafy branches high above her head. She had quit crying, and her red-rimmed eyes flashed defiance. "You have whipped me, scratched me, cut me, but if you take me, it will be after you have killed me. Do you hear? I will not give up!"

The leaves of the trees began to shake and, for a terrible moment, Judith was sure the forest was having a silent laugh at her expense. After collecting her wits, however, she realized it was only the breeze that comes with daybreak.

Susan and Ivy were worried—really worried. The sun was up, yet Patterson had not returned and Judith was still missing. The girls were torn between waiting for Patterson or striking out in search of Judith. Ivy wept while Susan consoled her as best she could.

"Susan," wailed Ivy, "we have got to find her; she will surely die if we do not."

Susan patted Ivy's shoulder as she held her close. "There, there," she said softly, "Judith will be just fine, Ivy—I just know she will."

"But there are bears and wolves and snakes out there," the girl cried, flinging her arms toward the dark forest. "And she does not know how to cope with such things."

Susan laughed in spite of herself. "And I suppose you do?"

"Well—no," admitted Ivy, dabbing at her eyes, "but if I were lost, it would make no difference—no one cares for me."

Susan felt a great surge of sympathy for Ivy, for she knew the girl's statement was made not from self-pity, but from the truth as she saw it.

"Ivy, please," whispered Susan, choking back tears of her own. "Do not think no one would miss you—I would, terribly, and Mr. Patterson would, and no telling who else."

"I know you would, Susan," snuffed Ivy. "You are the only true friend I ever had—except for Judith." Susan wondered how Ivy could consider Judith a friend when Judith had mistreated her so.

"Ivy, how long have you and Judith been together?"

"Ever since we were born," the girl answered, wiping her nose with the back of her hand. "My mother was Judith's wet nurse. In fact, we were nursed at the same time, me on one breast and her on the other. You see, I am but two weeks older than Judith."

"Then you were born at the same place as Judith?"

"Why, yes," said Ivy, looking at Susan as if she thought it strange that the girl might have considered something different. "We were born in a fine manor house with more rooms than I could count. My mother was then, and still is, the housekeeper. She oversees nineteen maids."

Susan smiled at Ivy's obvious pride in her mother.

Unconsciously, Susan's thoughts drifted to her own mother, and she wondered if she were well. She doubted that word of Braddock's defeat had reached Rosemont. She hoped it had not, for she had no desire to worry Rebecca, and she knew without a doubt that should the news have reached there, her mother would be anxiously watching the road for her return. (Word had reached Rosemont, however; without Susan's being aware of it, the month of August was well along.)

Susan realized with a certain amount of shame that she had been paying no attention to Ivy's conversation. Ivy didn't seem to notice, so taken was she with her story, and Susan was greatly relieved. She certainly did not want Ivy to think she was uninterested. Ivy told Susan of her and Judith's childhood, a fairy tale compared to Susan's existence after her father had died. "Judith has never wanted for anything," said Ivy, and from what Judith acquired, Ivy had also profited. The two girls had been together constantly.

9

Judith spent her fourteenth and fifteenth years at a private finishing school for young ladies, accompanied by Ivy as her abigail. Eyebrows had been raised over such a young and attractive girl serving as Judith's chaperone, but once it was known that Ivy was black and possessed a certain air of dignity, the situation became acceptable. Ivy thought it amusing, for she felt neither black nor dignified.

Judith spent a miserable two years studying such subjects as music, poise, fine sewing, and the countless other disciplines a young lady of quality must know.

She loathed Miss Farmington's Boarding School for Young Ladies. Ivy, on the other hand, found it quite interesting, paying close attention to each subject Judith was required to study. Perhaps because she had not been born a lady and knew she would never be a lady, Ivy tried that much harder to absorb each and every lesson that Madam Farmington and her instructors taught.

To Judith the whole affair was boring and a monstrous waste of time. She paid little attention to her studies, and on the few occasions when Madam Farmington gave tests, Judith depended on Ivy to supply the answers.

There were other young ladies there, but Judith found the students as boring as the school and she quickly discouraged any friendships that might have developed by her haughty, better-than-thou attitude toward life in general, and her unparalleled ability to be nasty to Ivy, whom she enjoyed belittling in public.

Ivy was embarrassed by Judith's behavior, but she took it in stride and did not complain, for she knew that when she and Judith were alone, Judith was kind, generous, and very tender toward her. It was quite easy for Ivy to forgive Judith her conceits, for Ivy was one of those rare people who have no false impressions of themselves; she was perfectly satisfied to be just what she was— Judith's handmaiden.

As the days dragged into weeks and months, Judith became a lady in spite of herself. She could walk, talk, play the harpsichord, be the gracious hostess, sew a lace kerchief, and be as grand as any of the girls. But if the truth had been known, they all could have taken lessons from Ivy.

The girls were also growing otherwise than in spiritual and academic matters; they were blossoming into lovely young women. Judith was the first to notice the difference. She and Ivy were on a shopping spree in London proper when she noticed several young lads appraising her and Ivy from a distance.

"Whatever do you suppose they are staring at?" she asked, dropping her eyes modestly, as Madam Farmington had taught her.

Ivy turned to look. "Why I do believe they are gazing at us, Judith."

"I know they are gazing at us, you nitwit; anyone can see that."

"But I thought you asked—"

"I know what I asked," snapped Judith. "What are they doing now; the young men, I mean?"

"Well," said Ivy, looking directly at the boys, "they are grinning like dolts."

"Isn't this famously exciting, Ivy?" said Judith, sneaking a quick peep at the boys, then staring straight ahead as the chaise she and Ivy occupied rounded the corner.

"Wasn't it marvelous, the spectacle they made of themselves," she said breathlessly as the chaise sped down the cobblestone street. "I am becoming quite ravishing, aren't I?"

Ivy glanced at Judith to determine the depth of her sincerity and was shocked to find Judith's enchantment with herself quite real.

"Oh, Ivy, I cannot wait to be presented. The men will fall at my feet." Judith's eyes were sparkling.

That evening as Ivy undressed Judith and prepared her bath, Judith posed herself before the large bevel-edged dressing mirror, turning her body this way and that. "I am quite beautiful." A statement rather than a question. "Of course, these will have to grow some," she said, cupping her small breasts. "I haven't got a bosom yet and I must have cleavage."

"You are not yet sixteen, mistress. There is time for cleavage to form before you are presented."

"But you are only two weeks older than I and you have cleavage," argued Judith.

"Mayhap in two weeks you will have cleavage also," Ivy said, turning Judith toward the tub of hot soapy water, giving her a gentle push. "Please take your bath before the water cools."

"If it does get cold, you shall have to draw more from the kettle. I shall not bathe in cold water."

Ivy bathed Judith, dried her, and slipped a silk nightgown over her head, then combed out her luxurious blonde curls until they shone.

When she finally undressed and slipped into Judith's leftover bath, the water was tepid and she shivered as she soaped her neck, shoulders, and chest. She looked down at the cleavage formed by her small perfectly shaped breasts and smiled smugly to herself.

As the second year of schooling progressed, so did Judith's concern over cleavage. She worried about it, cried about it, even prayed about it, but as presentation day drew near and her breasts still refused to fill out, she began to resent Ivy's bustline. Judith's bitterness became evident each time Ivy undressed. Ivy would feel Judith's eyes following her every move, and though she had never felt the need to be modest in Judith's presence, she could not help blushing as the blonde girl scrutinized her form. Enraged by the beauty of Ivy's young body, Judith finally shouted at her, "I bet all niggers have big titties. I just bet they do." Then she burst out crying, the great uncontrollable sobs of a brokenhearted fifteen-year-old.

Ivy stopped her narrative and looked at Susan. "I was completely crushed, Susan, for Judith had never, in all our lives, called me a nigger. It hurt me worse than anything she had ever done."

"But, Ivy," replied Susan, "I have heard you call yourself a nigger many times, and it did not seem to bother you."

"Aye . . . but when you call yourself something it is not the same

170

as when someone you love calls you the same thing." Susan silently agreed with her, recalling the day she and Patterson sat on the bluff overlooking the valley, and he had made a remark about her being insensitive. She had called herself worse than that many times, but it hurt when Patterson said it. "Please continue, Ivy," she pleaded. "What happened to you and Judith? I must know."

Ivy smiled and reached out to touch Susan's hand, a silent gesture of gratitude for Susan's undisguised interest. Then she continued.

Judith had cried for a long while, but finally her sobs subsided and Ivy fetched her a kerchief to dry her eyes.

"Ivy, I'm sorry," snuffed Judith, "but you have such nice ones and your mother does too, and I bet," Judith's voice had a bitter edge to it as she looked into Ivy's soft gray eyes, "I bet my mother doesn't have any at all and that is why she would not nurse me."

"Your mother is a noblewoman, mistress," said Ivy, "and ladies of quality do not nurse their children." She smiled impudently, then said, "You may just be the exception to the rule, Judith."

"I shall not!" screamed Judith, her eyes venomous as she stared at Ivy. "I will have no snotty-nosed babies hanging at my nipples!" Judith blanched, her own words causing her to look again at her immature breasts with their even smaller nipples, not large enough for a baby comfortably to fasten his lips around. Then she cried again, only harder than the first time.

Ivy would have consoled her had there not come a heavy knock on Judith's door and Madam Farmington's stern voice demanding to be let in. Ivy rushed to the door and cracked it.

"What is going on in there?" demanded Madam Farmington. "Judith is screaming loud enough to wake the dead."

"Oh, madam," said Ivy, her eyes wide and innocent, "'tis the curse, madam. It came on her all of a sudden and her poor stomach is cramping something awful."

"Well, mayhap I should look to her," said Madam Farmington, worry erasing the consternation from her face.

"Oh, no, ma'am," said Ivy, "if you would be so kind as to bring some fresh water, it would be appreciated, but Miss Judith is much too modest to allow anyone but myself to administer to her needs."

Madam Farmington's eyes narrowed as she looked directly at Ivy. "Indeed!" she said suspiciously. Then she turned and directed one of the students, who had been drawn into the hall by the noise, to fetch a bucket of fresh water to Miss Judith's room.

Ivy thanked her, easing the door shut. Then she winked at Judith and they both burst out laughing.

Judith's sixteenth birthday drew near and she was ecstatic. A great party was planned by her mother, and all the best people of London were sent invitations on silk cloth.

The Cornwallace mansion was astir with preparations for Judith's coming out. Silver was cleaned, floors were polished, and guest bedrooms were prepared for those who had great distances to travel. Foodstuffs of every description were procured. Ivy's mother was in a hundred places at once, ordering, pleading, cajoling, and occasionally cursing the maids when they paused to catch their breath.

Ivy was proud of her mother's ability to bring the best out in the people working under her, for even though the house seemed in a continuous state of bedlam, things were being accomplished. The mansion shone.

Ivy, however, had very little time to spend in idle observation for Judith was running her ragged: get this, do that, check her dress—it must be perfect. Should she wear a wig? No. Did her shoes match the dress? Yes. Gloves? Yes. She must have gloves...

Ivy was as excited as Judith, but secretly she would be glad when the whole thing was over so she could just sit down and rest.

Judith was absolutely stunning as she descended the circular staircase that opened into the great ballroom. Every eye was on her, many in open admiration...and not a few with hidden envy. But more important, Judith knew she was beautiful, and the ease and grace with which she greeted and thanked the guests would have made Madam Farmington proud.

The young men flocked to her. Could they get her anything? Punch? Immediately. Would she care to sit? No. Very well. Judith was delighted with the sensation she created. Compliments flowed like wine and she absorbed each one as her just due.

She danced and danced. She sipped punch until she was sure she would be sick and she flirted with all the young men equally, causing each to feel confident that the golden-haired beauty favored him the most. She finally allowed herself to be singled out by a dashing young man, quite handsome really, whose father had just purchased the lad a commission in the Royal army. He was James Southhampton.

To the disappointment of the young men, and the relief of the young ladies, Lieutenant Southhampton monopolized Judith's dances for the next two sets, then suggested some fresh air—which she reluctantly accepted. She did not relish being out of the limelight even for a few minutes, but because the lieutenant appeared to be the man most adored by the eligible young ladies, Judith consented.

Ivy, who had been observing the ball from a secluded doorwell, turned to her mother and said breathlessly, "Oh, Mother, isn't Judith just the most beautiful girl in the whole world?" Not waiting for a reply, Ivy babbled on: " 'Tis the grandest party ever, and I am so happy for her. She has waited all her life for this moment." Ivy had watched dreamily as the handsome young lieutenant whirled Judith lightly across the ballroom. Then she too slowly twirled and waltzed to the music. "I could not be happier were it my own party," she said, smiling at her mother.

Ivy's mother knew a moment of great sorrow for her daughter, but the sorrow quickly changed to a deep-seated bitterness. She reached out, taking Ivy's hand. "It may be Judith's coming-out party, but it shall be yours as well. Come, darling," she commanded, leading her daughter away from the gaiety of the ballroom. "I believe this to be the right time for you to find out whence you come."

She led Ivy onto the back veranda, down the winding cut-stone steps, and into the garden. The night was warm and the air was scented with the perfume of lilacs in full bloom. Ivy's mother seated herself on a stone bench beneath a large wisteria bush and gently patted the seat, indicating for Ivy to join her. Ivy slipped onto the bench, turning a little so she could watch her mother's face. Never, since Ivy had been born, had her mother talked about herself or her ancestors. With eagerness she waited for her mother to begin.

Lieutenant Southhampton had expertly guided Judith across the ballroom and onto the side veranda. They stood there a moment breathing deeply of the fragrant night air, and then Judith slipped to the wrought-iron railing and gazed up at the stars. She felt the lieutenant's arm gently encircle her waist.

"The stars are lovely," he said, watching her closely in an effort to gauge the effect of his romantic compliment, "but they grow dim and flicker out when compared to your beauty."

Judith laughed lightly and slipped from his embrace. She took his arm and smiled sweetly. "Come, shall we walk in the garden?"

Southhampton bowed, irritated by her failure to succumb to his suave manipulation. "A fetching idea, Miss Judith," he agreed dispassionately, taking her hand and escorting her down the flight of steps that led to the lawn.

It was a long and passionate—and for Southhampton, totally unexpected—kiss that Ivy and her mother interrupted as they seated themselves on the bench, and had they glanced through the wisteria vines, they would have seen Judith and Southhampton quickly separate and slip a little farther into the darkness.

"Ivy," said her mother, leaning forward a little so she could see her daughter's face in the moonlight, "I have been intending to tell you of our past for some time now, and I believe you to be mature enough to accept and remember what I divulge. It shall be your duty to pass our heritage on to your children, as I pass it on to you." She looked keenly at her daughter and was satisfied with Ivy's rapt attention.

Southhampton took Judith's hand, intending to slip quietly away, but Judith flung his hand aside and put a finger to her lips, demanding silence. The young man frowned, not understanding Judith's desire to eavesdrop on her servants' conversation. Actually, Judith did not understand it either, but she was eager to learn Ivy's secret. So Southhampton and Judith stood quietly, listening like thieves in the night, as Ivy's mother poured out her heart.

"I shall start at the beginning," the woman said, "and tell it to you as my mother told it to me." Ivy took a deep breath, anticipating the story that would unfold. For several years she had wondered

174

about herself; now, finally, she would know what her bloodlines were. This would be a night to remember.

"In the year 1661," her mother continued, "Charles II was crowned king of England and at his marriage to Catherine of Braganza in the next year, he presented to his bride a gift from a faraway continent." She paused, momentarily confused. "My mother was not sure where this continent was, or what the name of it was, but I am sure it is called Africa. Although I have only talked to a few of the blacks enlisted as servants here in London, I have it that all of them came from a place called Africa."

Ivy sat perfectly still, trying to imagine a continent of black people. She could not, try as she might, envision even a town or city full of Negroes.

"Anyway," her mother went on, "the gift was a young, and very beautiful, black girl. She had been sent to England by her father, as a token of good faith, and was to serve the queen faithfully for the rest of her life. That girl, your great-great-grandmother, was eleven years old and a princess by her own right, for her father was a great chieftain in Africa."

Ivy exhaled a long dreamy sigh, then eagerly asked her mother to continue.

"Your great-great-grandmother was mostly a conversation piece, clothed in animal skins, and adorned with strings of pearls and precious jewels. She created quite a stir at the queen's court because blacks were almost unknown in England at that time. When she was fourteen, King Charles bedded her and your great-grandmother was conceived." Ivy clasped her hands together in astonishment. The story sounded like a fairy tale, but she believed every word.

"Oh, Mother," she cried, "we have the blood of kings running through our veins."

Her mother smiled. "Yes, both black and white." She looked sternly at Ivy. "Never forget who your great-great-grandmother's sire was. He also was a king—in Africa." Ivy sobered, then pleaded with her to go on.

"In 1685 James II took the throne and shortly after, seduced your great-grandmother, siring my mother." Ivy's pulse was now racing with anticipation. "William and Mary ascended the throne in 1689 and rebellion broke out in Ireland and Scotland. As a result

175

of that war, Sir Richard Cornwallace, for valor on the battlefield, was awarded your grandmother by Queen Mary." Ivy's mother looked long at her daughter, then said: "I was born right here in this house, 1715."

Ivy physically contained herself by digging her fingernails into the stone bench on which she sat. She wanted desperately to know who her father was, but all at once she was terrified almost to tears.

All her life she had wondered who had sired her, but now that she was about to be told, she was terribly afraid, lest he be a stablehand, or a house servant. "O Lord," she prayed silently, "please let him be a gentleman." It took all the courage she could summon to whisper, "And my father? Who is my father?"

Both Judith and Southhampton leaned forward in anticipation of the answer, for they too were caught up in the story.

Judith almost cried aloud for the woman to continue, so anxious was she to find out who had fathered Ivy.

She mentally ran through the list of servants, stablehands, and workmen whom her father employed, but not one looked the least bit like the lovely girl sitting just across the barrier of fragrant wisteria vines.

Ivy's mother smiled and touched Ivy's cheek. "You are Judith's half sister."

Ivy stood up, her hand going involuntarily to her throat. "You mean Judith's father and my father are the same?"

Ivy's mother nodded. "But you must never let her know."

"Oh, mother," cried Ivy, "I have always loved Judith like a sister and she is my sister! 'Tis wonderful."

Ivy's mother stood and took her daughter's hand. "You must always remember, Ivy, that no matter what, you are black. No matter whose blood, or how much of it runs in your veins, one drop of black blood makes you entirely black."

Ivy hugged her mother close. "I know, Mother, but it is wonderful anyway."

For a long moment after Ivy and her mother had left the garden, Judith stood transfixed. Southhampton became nervous and cleared his throat. "Miss Judith, are you quite all right?"

Judith whirled to face him. "She lied! I do not believe her. You cannot believe her. I hate them both. I will have them lashed. They

176

will be exiled." Then she wept. Southhampton tried to embrace her, but she turned her back to him and cried into her cupped hands.

"Do not be overwrought," he whispered. "'Twas a fairy tale . . . just a fairy tale." But if Judith could have seen the frown that crossed his face, she would have known that he was not at all certain. He tried again to console Judith, but she pushed him away and fled toward the house.

Judith had Ivy neither whipped nor exiled. Instead, she became so demanding and demeaning that her actions brinked on cruelty. For the knowledge that had brought such joy and happiness to Ivy had brought only shame and bitterness to Judith.

Lieutenant Southhampton began to pay court to Judith on a regular basis. The two would ride frequently into the country, and of course Ivy would chaperone, but the close comradeship between the girls was missing.

On one such occasion, while Judith and Southhampton were picnicking, with Ivy sitting alone some distance away, Southhampton remarked that many of the plantation owners in the colonies had sired "yard children" from colored slaves and that it was an accepted practice.

Judith became irate, as he knew she would, and the unladylike phrases that she used to describe her feelings toward Ivy caused Southhampton to smile slyly to himself, for a plan had formed in the dark recesses of his mind.

He had watched Judith closely in the previous days, to determine the true depth of her loathing of her half sister. And during that time, using her bitterness to his best advantage, he had skillfully sought to widen even further the emotional gulf between the two girls.

He was now certain that if he could discreetly dispose of Ivy's ever watchful eyes, and manipulate Judith's vulnerable emotions effectively, she would prove to be an easy conquest.

Excusing himself, he walked up the hill from the towering oak where he and Judith had spread their blanket, and while the unsuspecting girls watched in muted wonder, he removed a halfpenny from his purse and cast it with all his might down the far side of the hill.

With a crooked smile, he turned and commanded Ivy to retrieve the coin—and not to return until she did.

Ivy's face was one of disbelief as she turned to her mistress for confirmation of such an order.

"Do as your master instructed," ordered Judith coldly.

Ivy's chin came up and defiance showed plainly in her eyes. "He is not my master, Miss Judith, and his command is nothing but a ruse to—"

Judith slapped her. "You will do as he says, or I will have your insolent tongue!" Judith's handprint was plainly visible on Ivy's pale cheek.

Ivy stopped her memoir and looked into Susan's smoldering eyes.

"You are angry because Judith struck me," she said apologetically. "Do not be, for she was within her rights . . . I was insolent . . . and deserved a beating."

"No, Ivy!" cried Susan, "'tis obvious what Southhampton intended. You were only trying to protect your mistress."

"But she was unaware of that," said the girl softly.

Susan nodded and touched Ivy's hand. "Please go on with your story."

As Ivy passed Southhampton at the top of the hill, he caught her arm and spun her roughly toward him. "You are trash," he whispered nasally. "Arrogant nigger trash—and you will suffer for it—I promise you."

Ivy's fist doubled into a small firm ball and her every nerve screamed for her to strike Southhampton. She turned and fled down the hillside. Upon reaching the bottom of the incline, she turned and gazed long at the crest.

Southhampton had disappeared.

With an impudent smile, she reached beneath the folds of her apron to the small pocket she wore there and withdrew a copper halfpenny.

Southhampton was incredulous and then angry as Ivy topped the rise and advanced toward the blanket where he and Judith lay.

The moments between Ivy's departure and return had been sufficient only to allow Southhampton the luxury of one passionate kiss.

Jumping to his feet while smoothing his breeches, he shouted at Ivy, "I made it understood that you weren't to return until you found the coin!"

"But, sir!" said Ivy innocently as she extended her open palm, "I have the coin."

As with many weaklings who find themselves bested by intelligence and finesse, Southhampton turned cruel. He conceived another scheme that would, he was sure, guarantee his seduction of Judith while shattering Ivy's self-esteem and soiling her forever.

On the next outing, Southhampton's groom accompanied the three to their private picnic spot. Peter was, perhaps, eighteen or nineteen with curly blond hair. His teeth were bad, as was his complexion, but he seemed a jovial sort as he and Ivy followed Judith and Southhampton into the country.

Ivy was not fooled. Nor was she disappointed in her presumption, for no sooner had they dismounted and made Judith and Southhampton comfortable, than Peter insisted that Ivy accompany him walking. Ivy dutifully asked Judith's permission, which was granted, much to Ivy's regret.

She was scared. Never had she been alone with a man and she entertained no childish romantic notions about Peter. She knew why he was there. Her mind was racing when he roughly took her in his arms. She smiled at him and tried to make her voice light.

"Why be so violent, sir? Can you not see that I have been anticipating this moment since we first met?"

He was startled. Southhampton had told him that he might find her disagreeable; but it appeared she was going to be easy. He quickly released her and stood back, letting his eyes rove over her body. Ivy slowly unbuttoned her bodice.

Judith was faring little better. Southhampton had waited too long for a chance to be alone with her and now that Ivy was safely out of the way, he contemplated no problems with Judith. But he was wrong. Though Judith teased and flirted, her moral standards were quite high, and it was a thoroughly confused lieutenant who gingerly rubbed the handprint on his left cheek.

"Mistress," he stammered, "I beg your pardon; I assumed you loved me as much as I love you."

Judith fought to control her anger. "You speak of love. Yet you treat me like a trollop. Very well, sir, I shall have none of your love."

"But I do love you," he cried. "And I shall speak for your hand, as I said I would, but I cannot wait. I want you now and forever."

Judith was not impressed. "You may speak for my hand anytime you wish, but," she lowered her eyes and blushed, "you shall not have the rest till we are wed."

Southhampton jumped to his feet and turned his back to her. Judith raised her lovely head and smiled knowingly.

Peter stood agape as Ivy unbuttoned her bodice and edged it off her shoulders. Anticipation made his breathing irregular. Ivy was indeed lovely.

"I should not tell you this," she whispered, trying to feign a pouting expression and succeeding.

"Tell me what?"

"'Tis nothing," she said quickly, turning her face away.

"What is it?" he demanded, not liking the interruption at all.

"First, sir, you must promise you will not let it make any difference, for I truly wish to make love to you." She undid another button and dropped the bodice further off her shoulders.

"I promise," he cried, not caring what it was he committed himself to. "Nothing can stop me from having you . . . nothing." He stood transfixed, staring at her exposed shoulders as she fingered another button through the eyelet.

"'Twas just a thought I had," she said, "that you might not want me if you knew I had the sailor's disease. But I like you so much, I just had to tell you." She dropped her eyes to her bodice as it slipped slowly to her waist.

She didn't bother to raise her head as the sound of Peter's running footsteps passed from hearing. With trembling hands, she began to rebutton the garment and she made a solemn vow, while standing there alone on that English hillside, that she would never be caught again without a weapon. She would protect herself and her mistress.

"Ivy, forgive me, darling," cried her mother, drawing the girl close, after being told of the near rape. "To me, you are still my little girl, but I should have realized that you have become a desirable young woman, and being of the class that you are," her face was bitter with resignation, "you will find the word *disrespect* common in your vocabulary."

"'Twas the first time anything like this has ever happened," said Ivy, not understanding her mother's obvious hatred of their station.

"And we can be thankful for that," said her mother. "But you can rest assured, it will not be the last."

"Mother, I was really scared. Oh, if only I had a rapier!"

"But—yes, you do!" the woman cried excitedly. "I should have given it to you the night of the ball. Come, I will fetch it now."

They left Ivy's small bedchamber and a moment later entered her mother's suite. It was lavish, with a large four-poster canopy bed, satin drapes, and cherry and walnut furniture aglow with beeswax. Her mother's room was as beautiful as Judith's, and she realized with a touch of embarrassment that her mother's life was still spiced with romantic intrigue. The woman opened a drawer in a large marble-topped dresser and lifted out some nightgowns, laying them gently on the top. Then she took out a small leather sheath and turned to Ivy.

"Your great-great-grandmother brought this from Africa," she said proudly, "and it has passed from mother to daughter for generations. Now it is yours."

Ivy gingerly took the sheath and turned it over in her hands. Slowly she extracted a small pearl-handled dagger. It was beautiful, with a fully engraved, razor-edged blade, six inches in length. The knife was cold—had an almost lethal feel about it.

"I shall ask James the gardener to instruct you on the advantages of such a weapon," said her mother, as she watched Ivy lovingly caress the glinting steel.

Ivy learned quickly and became quite adept with the use of her knife, but she never again had need of the knowledge until her encounter with Patterson.

She accompanied Judith and Southhampton on several more outings, but Peter was discreetly absent and there were no further unpleasant occurrences, except that Southhampton's attitude toward her had become almost insufferable.

Southhampton's plea for Judith's hand was well received and their engagement created a stir in their London social circle.

Judith's seventeenth birthday was celebrated with a big, uneventful party, and she found herself quite bored. Thanks to her engagement, she was no longer the most sought-after young woman in London.

Although the men continued to laud her beauty, they kept their distance. And the more she flirted, the more respectful they became. By the time the guests had retired, Judith had provided London society with enough gossip to last several months. She could not have cared less.

The gossip was cut short, however. Lieutenant Southhampton was ordered to sail to the colonies on a British transport being provisioned in the harbor at that very moment. He looked dashing in his scarlet coat, white breeches, and black riding boots, as he held Judith's hand and explained about General Braddock's being transferred to America with the largest army the colonies had ever seen and probably would ever see again. He told her that it was the opportunity he had dreamed about. Promotions would flow like wine, and he would become a colonel, or maybe even a general in the short time it would take to quell the French and their savage allies. He laughed when Judith inquired into the dangers of such a quest. He assured her that General Braddock knew his business, and so did he, Lieutenant Southhampton. Why, he would come back a hero, surely.

Judith was infected with his enthusiasm. "Then I shall go with you," she said contritely, thinking how brave and in love she must be for suggesting she follow him halfway around the world just to be near him.

"But you mustn't," he cried. "There is not time before I sail for us to be wed."

"Then I shall sail with you anyway," she said firmly, leaning back in his arms and gazing up at him.

"Miss Judith," said Ivy, "your father would never allow—"

"I shall handle my father, and you shall accompany me to the New World. Now, say no more until you are spoken to."

Ivy dropped her eyes.

"I beg your pardon, mistress," she said dutifully.

Ivy could only guess at what Judith told her father to get him to agree to this wild extravagance, but, to her amazement, he seemed only too happy to put a word in the right ear and, no doubt, a full purse in the right hand to secure passage for Judith and herself aboard the ship carrying Southhampton.

Judith found the hustle and bustle of preparing for the adventure exciting, but after the initial thrill had subsided, she experienced second thoughts about the whole affair and attempted to withdraw, saying she had been mistaken. But her father, Lord Cornwallace, was most insistent that she go through with it, so Ivy figured that Judith's little white lie had backfired. She was sure Judith had told her father she was pregnant.

Judith was quickly fitted for a wedding gown, in hopes that it would be ready when the troop carrier embarked, and by working night and day, the seamstress completed it and the trousseau only hours before the ship sailed.

It was beautifully made, and Judith was delighted with it. She held the dress to her bosom and gazed admiringly into the full-length mirror in her bedchamber.

"I will make a beautiful bride, will I not, Ivy?" She smiled confidently, turning this way and that to get the full effect of the gown.

Ivy stopped packing the large camelbacked trunk and looked longingly at the dress. "'Tis truly lovely, mistress, but I declare, if we do not get a move on, we will be late arriving at the ship."

Judith looked again into the mirror and sighed. "'Tis such a long way to the New World; it will be weeks before I get to wear this dress. James wishes to be married on board ship and it does sound romantic, but I want a grand wedding with a reception and ball. I will have nothing less." She reluctantly laid the gown neatly across the trunk.

A cold drizzling rain fell on the two girls, and they clutched their cloaks more tightly about them as they stood on deck and waved farewell to Lord and Lady Cornwallace. She had kissed her mother goodbye at the manor house, but Ivy secretly wished that she also had been on the wharf. She felt quite alone standing there watching the English shoreline slowly vanish as the ship moved deeper into the gloomy mist and rain, and sensed she would never again see her mother or England. When they could no longer see the wharf, they made their way to the cabin that they shared with several other officers' wives and ladies and tried to make themselves comfortable.

Southhampton again suggested having the ship's captain perform the marriage ceremony, but Judith declined the idea, complaining of seasickness.

Finally, in February 1755, the creaking bark dropped anchor at Alexandria, Virginia.

The day was bitter cold as the girls made their way to the private residence whose owners had agreed to house them until other arrangements could be made. Actually, they were fortunate to find lodging so readily, for the troops were occupying most of the available quarters in Alexandria.

Although the colonial house was one of the city's finest, it little resembled the elegance to which Judith was accustomed and, as they were ushered to the fireplace and stood warming their hands while the maid poured hot tea, Judith wasted no time in making her feelings known.

"Are all the homes in the colonies this shabby?" she asked, as the maid tipped the highly polished pewter pot.

"Shabby, mistress?" the girl asked, bewildered.

"Are all the homes this ugly? With no wallpaper, or crystal, or chandeliers, or silver?" she sniffed, looking sourly at the whitewashed walls, the wood-grained chairrail and wainscoting. "No family portraits? No carpets? It is so drab."

The maid glanced at the room, seeing its cheerful fireplace and high wingchairs, and the tables of polished American black walnut. To her, the room was by far more elegant than what most Alexandria homes could boast.

"Mistress," the maid said coolly, "mayhap you would be more comfortable somewhere else?"

Judith was dumbstruck, and disbelief governed her reply: "You are an insolent person, and I shall speak to your mistress about you."

The maid smirked and proceeded to fill Ivy's cup. "Is your mistress always such a bitch?" she whispered.

Ivy was aghast, not believing she had heard right. "I beg your pardon, ma'am."

They were saved any further embarrassment, however, by the entrance of a portly gentleman and his wife, who introduced

184

themselves as the owners of the humble home where the girls were to reside. They sincerely hoped the young ladies would find their surroundings most comfortable. If there was anything they desired, they should not hesitate to ask. If they would be so kind as to follow, the maid would show them to their chamber.

Once the girls were alone in their bedchamber, Judith turned to Ivy, who was unpacking the camelbacks.

"These are barbaric people, Ivy. I can see that we shall not like the colonies at all."

Ivy continued to unpack.

Alexandria was not so barbaric as Judith had first thought. She attended several balls and was the center of attention. There were countless dinner parties given in her honor, for, after all, she was the daughter of one of England's peers. Afternoon teas bored her to tears, but she suffered them for appearance's sake.

Spring arrived, and the army prepared for the field, so Judith and Ivy saw little of Southhampton for several weeks. He walked in one afternoon in early May and informed Judith of General Braddock's decision to depart Alexandria within the week. Southhampton suggested that Judith stay in the city until the campaign was over, but Judith threw such a fit that he quickly relented, and agreed that it would be a great adventure for her to accompany the army into the field, and, indeed, she would be mistreated were she not present to witness the greatest British victory in the New World. Ivy made the necessary preparations for prolonged travel.

10

Ivy's story caught in her throat as Patterson limped into the clearing with a large doe slung across his shoulder. He dropped the deer to the ground without ceremony. Susan moved to his side, reaching out to steady him, but his attention was drawn to Ivy. She had begun to cry while trying to explain about Judith.

Patterson listened to Ivy's babbling, then turned to Susan. "I cannot understand a word she is saying, except that Judith is gone." Susan was shocked by Patterson's haggard appearance. "Tell me what has happened," he said tiredly.

"In a moment," she replied gently, taking his rifle and laying it aside, "but first let me see your leg. It is bothering you."

"'Tis nothing," he said, closing his eyes and running the back of his hand wearily across his forehead. "Just the extra weight of the deer I have carried for several miles." He gestured toward the carcass lying on the ground. "My leg is still a mite weak to be packing such a load."

Susan related all that she and Ivy knew concerning Judith's disappearance. Patterson listened attentively, but if he was worried he refused to show it. Indifferently, he asked the girls to skin the deer while he built a fire. Actually, he was worried, but he had been too long a frontiersman to rush pellmell into the forest when he had already spent himself to the limit. While the girls skinned the deer,

186

he built a small smokeless fire, stretched out beside it, and went immediately to sleep.

"He is really worn out," observed Susan, as she and Ivy worked with the deer. "I've never seen him look so exhausted."

"Oh, Susan, do you think he will go after Judith?"

"You know he will, Ivy," she said, as she slipped the knife expertly along the hide, separating it from the flesh. "He has not let us down yet." She tugged gently at the skin. "Nor do I think he ever would."

Ivy looked at Susan. "Do you love him?"

"I think he is in love with Judith," said Susan slowly, avoiding the question.

Ivy sighed unhappily. "I would die for him, Susan, if he would but notice me."

Susan grinned. "Well, he appears to hate white women, so you may have a chance."

Ivy laughed and looked lovingly at Patterson's sleeping form. "I must admit," she said tenderly, "I have thought the same thing at times."

Before Ivy could continue, Susan sliced off a large piece of venison and set it to roasting over the fire. "He will be hungry when he wakes," she said, turning her attention to the woodsman and gazing wistfully at him. "He must have traveled a long way to get that deer. He would not have chanced firing a shot within ten miles of this camp."

She studied his hawklike profile and unruly black hair, which had pulled loose from the queue he usually wore, and absently she thought about shaving his bristling jawline, for his sprouted beard was matted on one side with deer blood. She decided it could wait until after he had rescued Judith. She turned the stick and grease fell from the cooking meat, sizzling as it hit the fire. She sank into melancholy. "Oh, Morgan, what is wrong with you?" she whispered. " 'Tis a pitiful man, indeed, that has no feelings for his own kind."

She had thought several times of plainly asking him why he disliked white women, but was afraid she could not be able to live with his answer, and she would rather go on not knowing, and have a ray of hope, than to know the truth and possibly have nothing, for whatever his problem, it ran deep and appeared to govern his life.

Ivy finished skinning the deer, leaving the hide spread out neatly beneath the carcass. She began butchering the meat, taking each piece and laying it on the hide. When she completed the task, she took what was literally the skeleton of the animal and laid it aside. Then, she folded the hide neatly over the butchered meat; it would help keep the flies off for a while at least.

Susan gazed longingly at the deerskin. The August nights had become chilly. She envisioned moccasins and leggin's galore. But she knew there wasn't time to stretch the hide, scrape the bits of flesh and membrane away, and prepare the skin for tanning, even if she used the quick method—tanning the flesh side only, leaving the hair side intact.

She sighed deeply, and pushed the thought from her mind. She dragged the remainder of the carcass away and covered it with brush. They would have to break camp soon or the stench would be unbearable.

The girls trudged to the creek and washed the blood and bits of meat from their hands. When they returned, Patterson was eating a portion of the venison Susan had cooked.

He sliced off a slab for Ivy and handed it to her, then cut a piece for Susan. The meat was rare, but it tasted exquisite to the women. Susan absently wiped a trickle of grease from her chin with the back of her hand.

"When are you leaving?"

Patterson glanced at Ivy, who returned his gaze. "Which way did Judith go?"

"She went out that way, Morgan," said Ivy, indicating the direction with grease-covered fingers.

Patterson swallowed a large chunk of meat and retrieved his rifle. "Take that hide of meat and move camp—maybe two, three miles upstream. We'll find you there." Then he was gone.

Judith was moving quickly, but it was with a clear head that she surveyed her surroundings. She tried to recall what Patterson had taught her about survival, but having paid scant attention, she remembered little. She did remember that moss grew on the northwest side of straight trees, so she went in that direction. Actually, she had covered a far greater distance the night before than one might have imagined. So, lost as she was, northwest seemed to her as good a direction as any other.

Tired, scared, and hungry, she trudged on. She rested often, reserving her strength, and drank sparingly when she found fresh water. Patterson had taught her that—never fill yourself with water on an empty stomach. It could very well make you sick. Judith's stomach was so empty that even the small amount of water she drank sounded loud when she walked.

She decided she would almost be willing for the Indians to capture her if they would but give her a bite of food. Still, she employed every precaution Patterson had taught her as she moved through the woods.

The sun was directly overhead, its rays filtering through the dense foliage in long shafts, blessing the forest with an enchanted splendor, and Judith realized as she gazed at the grandeur of the primeval wilderness that, under the right circumstances, the forest that was such a menace to her now could be a sublime and peaceful place. Then she laughed. Aye, she was definitely changing. A day ago, she had detested this forest—and now she was finding beauty in it despite her desperation. *Yes*, she concluded, thoughtfully, as she picked her way between the vines and decayed logs. *We are all changing, for better or worse, and there is nothing we can do about it.* Ivy was becoming her own woman, Susan had grown quieter and more self-assured, and Patterson was almost human, considering the way he felt about white women. She laughed again, and the sound wasn't nearly as harsh as her first mocking laughter had been.

The knowledge that her life was out of her own hands and in Patterson's infuriated her, and she positively hated the thought that a woodsman, Patterson, could dictate her every move. It galled her to be dependent on such an unruly, arrogant, unsophisticated nobody as Morgan Patterson; nevertheless, she secretly wished he would appear right then, out of nowhere, as he had done so many times before, and carry her back to camp. She turned her head and studied the forest in every direction, but Patterson didn't materialize as she halfway expected he might. She was disappointed. But for the life of her, she didn't know why.

At that moment, Patterson was faced with a life-and-death decision. He had picked up Judith's trail and followed it far enough to determine that she was traveling in a large circle, as most people do when lost. If she continued in a circle, he could cut across country and intercept her, saving long hours of tracking, but if she veered off somewhere in between, he might miss her completely and that could prove fatal. He decided to follow her trail rather than take the chance. Any other decision he might have made would have meant sure death for Judith, because without his knowing it, she was roaming farther away with each step she took.

Her senses had been aware of it for some time before Judith realized she was following an odor. Smoke—campfire smoke. Her heart beat faster, and she ran a few steps, then halted. Patterson wouldn't rush headlong into a camp, she reasoned. He would scout it first. With that in mind, she steathily crept up to the clearing. At first, she could see nothing, but as her eyes adjusted to the brightness of the open sunshine, she saw a man squatting by a low-burning fire.

She stepped timidly into the opening and tiptoed toward the squatting figure. She began to suspect that all was not well when the man failed to move as she approached. She changed course, angling off to the side, to get a better look at his face. She wished she hadn't. She fell to her knees and retched up what little water was on her stomach. Then she sweated. She was wringing wet by the time the nausea had passed. It took all her courage to look again at what had once been a human being. She turned her eyes away and stared at the treeline for a long moment, but her mind's eye could still see the face, with the skin of the forehead sagging down over the eye sockets, and the skull, where they had cut away the hair and flesh, crawling with large green flies that glistened in the sun.

The man was without clothing, but his body was so completely covered with dried blood and dirt that it was difficult to tell he was naked. She noticed that he appeared to be squatting in a large pool of fresh, bright-red blood, and she thought it strange. Sidling closer, she screamed as his eyelids flickered and opened.

"You are alive?" she whispered, her hand jerking involuntarily toward him in a gesture of compassion.

His eyes blinked slowly, as though trying to focus. Judith looked at him more closely; fear and pity gorged up in her until she was sure she would choke. The Indians had tortured the man beyond human endurance. They had cut off a sapling abut two feet above the ground, sharpened it, and screwed him onto it, forcing the pointed staff up through his rectum. They had scalped him and cut off the five fingers of his right hand, and then had burned him until his flesh had cooked and burst. Yet he lived. He was trying to talk, so Judith forced herself closer that she might hear his words.

"Merciful God in heaven, please kill me." It was a hoarse, grating whisper, not human in sound. "I am dead anyway, but you can ease John Pettigrew his suffering if you but have the decency to kill me."

Judith was frightened half out of her wits. "How can I kill you?" she cried. "I have no weapon." She searched wildly about, in a state of panic, but found nothing that would serve the purpose.

"Push me down." His eyes closed, then slowly opened. "A little farther and I will die—please . . ." His voice trailed off, but his agonizing eyes held hers.

"I do not know if I have the strength," she cried. She tore her eyes away and began to weep. He screamed at her, his face a hideous mask of pain. Judith put her hands over her ears, and her lips drew back over her teeth in a terrible grimace, but she could still hear his cries, and she could still see his grisly face. In all her life, she had never felt so helpless. She wanted with all her heart to help this piece of human flesh that was suffering pain beyond anything she could imagine.

Patterson passed the log where Judith had rested, and he thanked the Lord that he had elected to follow her trail instead of cutting cross-country in hopes of heading her off. For, directly upon leaving the log, Judith had moved straight north by west, and had Patterson left the trail, to short-cut her, he would have missed her by miles. But he hadn't left the trail and was close enough to hear, very faintly, an inhuman scream that could have come from none other than a human.

He increased his pace and his vigilance. If an enemy lurked nearby, Patterson would not be caught off guard. As he trotted quietly through the woods, his eyes were constantly taking in his surroundings, watchful for any color or movement out of the ordinary. It was second nature with him. His mind was on that ghastly screaming, but he refused to throw caution to the wind. If he did that, he might run into something that could have been avoided. He could hear the screaming plainly as he scrambled silently through the underbrush, and he smelled the smoke of the campfire, so he veered off and began a wide circle that would bring him in downwind of the camp.

Judith wanted to flee but could not. She had to do something—anything—to free Pettigrew from his torment. And whatever she was to do, she must do quickly while she still had control of her senses. If she were forced to listen to his suffering another instant, she felt sure she would go mad. She moved quickly to him and put her hands on his shoulders. As she threw her weight upon him, her hands slipped on his bloody skin and her face slammed against his naked skullbone. His screams mounted hideously, but Judith didn't hear them. She had mercifully fainted.

Patterson parted the brush and peered into the clearing. He saw the squatting figure of John Pettigrew and the prone figure of Judith, and he raised his rifle, taking aim at Pettigrew's head. As Patterson's finger touched the trigger, the man screamed again, causing the woodsman to hesitate, uncertain, then to survey the scene a second time. Something was amiss. It took Patterson several moments before he realized that it was the crouching figure whose unholy shrieks had shaken the silent forest these past minutes. He pondered the situation, then dropped the hammer to half-cock and sprinted to Judith's side. He determined quickly that she was alive, then turned his attention to the man. At a glance Patterson understood what had happened. Knowing full well his obligation to the tortured woodsman, he ended Pettigrew's suffering with one hard blow of his hatchet.

He left Pettigrew as he had found him, squatting over a stake that had been forced just far enough into his bowels to ensure a slow agonizing death. The man looked peaceful squatting there with his head bowed. And, indeed, he was at peace.

Patterson gathered Judith into his arms, and even though unconscious, she put her arms trustingly about his neck and pushed her cheek tight against his shoulder. He smiled at her relaxed upturned face and trotted into the shadows of the tall trees. He ran until his injured leg felt as though it would buckle, and only then did he stop and ease Judith's unconscious body to the ground. He tried to be gentle, but he was so exhausted that he fairly well dropped her. He slumped down beside her and extended his aching leg before him. He cursed the leg for its weakness and himself for feeling obliged to help Judith at all. He lay back and gazed at the canopy of leaves high overhead. The shafts of sunlight penetrating the forest were falling at a definite angle, so Patterson guessed it to be late afternoon. He turned his attention to Judith. Her face was covered with dried blood, but he could find no cuts or scratches, and his brow puckered in wonder. He got wearily to his feet and went in search of water to bathe her face and hands, afraid that should she regain consciousness and see how bloody she was, she might become hysterical.

He could have saved himself the trouble; Judith's hysterical days were over. Patterson, however, was unaware of the terrible battle she had fought with her emotions the past twenty-four hours, or that she had emerged victorious. She had faced the problem of being utterly lost and alone in a wilderness that stretched endlessly in every direction by simply setting out in a straight line. It would, she sensibly reasoned, eventually take her to a river, the river to the sea, and thence to a city along the seacoast. So concluding, Judith had covered several miles in a fairly straight line when she had encountered Pettigrew. And there she had won another battle. She had tried her best to put the man out of his misery, even though her every fiber had screamed for her to flee that horrid sight and sound. But she had not run. Instead, she had forced herself beyond her limits until nature had taken a hand, and that age-old sedative, unconsciousness, eased her anguish. So, it was a far different Judith whose eyelids fluttered open as Patterson bathed her face.

"Hello," he said, as she looked into his eyes.

She smiled, and for a fleeting moment was blissfully secure. Then she bolted upright, looking wildly about. "Morgan, there is a man—he's in terrible pain—we must help him!" She tried to stand, but Patterson gently pushed her back.

"Just lie easy, mistress," he said. "You have had a bad time of it, and you'd best rest a little."

She lay back as he advised. "Is he dead?"

Patterson nodded.

She closed her eyes. "It was awful," she said.

"You best not think about it, miss." He dried her face with a small piece of cloth cut from her ragged dress.

She shuddered involuntarily. "I will probably think about it the rest of my life," she murmured, honestly, as she gazed up into his face.

The sun was low and the forest had already become hazy as Patterson helped Judith to her feet.

"We can make a goodly distance before full dark, if you feel up to it," he said, watching her closely, trying to judge her strength.

"Yes, let's do make as many miles as we can. Ivy and Susan will be terribly worried."

Patterson looked at her from the corner of his eye. Could it be that Judith was considering someone's feelings besides her own? Satisfied she was sincere, he picked up his rifle and struck off in his usual dogtrot.

He chose a campsite just minutes before full dark. It was a rock overhang high on the side of a bluff that afforded a good view of the surrounding area and, if need be, could be easily defended. Also, it was dry. He apologized to Judith for not being able to have a fire, but he did share with her the small piece of roasted venison which he had thoughtfully strung on his belt. She ate her portion slowly, savoring every bite. Nothing had ever tasted so good. Patterson was puzzled by her. She seemed different, and it worried him, for he had grown accustomed to a bitch, not the woman who sat beside him. He admired the courage and fortitude she had demonstrated this day; aye, he was even impressed by it, and that unsettled him.

The moon drifted up, huge and full, a great golden disc hanging gently above the trees. A whippoorwill called, and a hoot owl answered.

"Peaceful, is it not?" she said, gazing into the darkness.

Patterson didn't respond. He was bone tired, as tired as he had ever been in his life, and he knew Judith had to be exhausted also. He lay back with his hands locked behind his head and relaxed. His leg ached with a dull throb, just enough to let him know it wasn't completely healed.

Judith moved closer and stretched out beside him, lying on her stomach, elbows braced, chin cupped in her hands. She lay there a long while, looking intently at him. Patterson considered her silhouette in the moonlight; she was lovely.

"Morgan, I want to thank you for rescuing me today."

Patterson was startled. "Why—forget it, Judith; 'twas nothing."

"I think it was wonderful," she said frankly. "I think it was very heroic."

Patterson raised himself to one elbow and squinted at her. "I'm no hero, mistress, and you know it."

She contoured her body gently against his. "I thought I was going to die today, and I realized that if I did die, it would be such a tragedy for... " she hesitated, then continued nervously, "I would have died not knowing what it would be like to... to love a man." She looked deeply into his eyes. "I do not want to die like that, Morgan." She turned her head, embarrassed by her honesty.

He was confounded by her simple confession. He cared not one whit whether she died a virgin or not. His only interest in her, he told himself, was to see her safely back to Fort Cumberland.

"Mistress," he said, "you shan't die here in the wilderness, I promise you."

She pressed closer against him. "But we have no way of knowing that for sure; it could happen at any moment."

He was bothered by her nearness, and troubled by the turn the conversation was taking. "Mistress," he said flatly, "I am trying my dead-level best not to let anything happen to you."

"I know you are," she whispered as she pressed her abdomen suggestively against his, her eyes bright with anticipation.

He gazed into her upturned face and was honest enough to admit that, upon occasion, he had stared hungrily at Judith, but that his longing rose more from curiosity than from want or need. He felt no such emotion now; instead, his age-old revulsion of white women was welling up within him, and he resented her advances, no matter that they were almost childlike.

She inched closer, molding herself to him. Her awkward attempt at seduction infuriated him, and he laughed harshly as he pushed her away. "You ask me to compromise your body, yet you have no idea what it is about."

She drew back as if she had been struck. "I admit I am quite inexperienced at playing the aggressor, but I would do my best to...please you."

He laughed again. "Please me? There is nothing about you that I find pleasing. You are cruel, arrogant, and selfish."

She jumped to her feet, silhouetted against the golden disk of the full moon. "You have looked upon me with desire. I have seen you." Before he could answer, she slipped her dress over her head and dropped it to the ground. She stood there in the light of the moon: proud, angry, beautiful.

"Now, tell me you find nothing pleasing about me. Go on, you son-of-a-bitch, look at me and say it!"

He turned his face away, closing his eyes. "Put your dress on and forget this foolishness, Judith. I am weary of it. I am very tired."

She fell to her knees, driving her fingernails into his bare shoulders. "Tired! How much strength does it take to lift a lady's dresstail." Tears of rage ran down her cheeks. "Nay, you are not tired—you are nothing. Not a man at least." She tore her hands away, leaving bloody scratches where her nails had ripped the skin. Then she spat full into his face.

In the woodsman's world, spitting upon another was the ultimate insult.

Patterson took her brutally. Wanting to hurt her at first. Succeeding.

A great horned owl sat quietly in the branches of a towering oak. With unblinking eyes filled with mock wisdom, the creature beheld the copulating humans far below, and only he, of all the night beasts, heard the intense, anguished whisper of the female: "I love you...damn you...I love you."

11

Susan checked her snares and found them empty. She frowned. Either game was becoming scarce, or she was setting her traps wrong. She absently ran her fingers through her hair, pushing it off her forehead as she studied the forest for signs of game. She froze. Through the foliage there was a flash of movement. Her eyes narrowed, becoming a squint, for the sun was barely up and the light was poor in the dense underbrush. She audibly sucked in her breath as an Indian moved directly toward her, his eyes riveted to the trail he was following. Perhaps he would pass without looking in her direction. She knew better even as the thought crossed her mind, for an Indian very seldom passed by anything without noticing it. He saw her instantly and flipped up his bow, loosening an arrow that buried itself in the tree next to Susan's head. She darted aside, more startled than frightened, and disappeared into a nearby thicket, heading away from the campsite where Ivy lay sleeping.

She raced like a deer, darting between trees, jumping logs, and ducking under overhangs. She glanced over her shoulder; the Indian was running with her, about thirty yards off to one side. She dropped down a gulley, then up the other side, and broke directly away from her pursuer, gaining a little edge. She considered trying a shot at him but was afraid she would miss and then she would be at his mercy. She decided to run as far as she could, then shoot him as a last resort. He regained the ground he had lost and, to Susan's dismay, appeared to be closing the distance between them. Desperately, she ran harder. Her mind raced back to a similar contest when she pitted her speed and endurance against an Indian and lost. But Patterson had appeared, like magic, to save her. She laughed and the sound was bitter. Saved her for what? For this fool Indian to capture or kill? Better not to have escaped the first time if this was to be her destiny. The Indian was gaining; she could hear him breaking brush as he closed in.

Susan's breathing was coming in great gasps, and she knew that she was about finished. Ahead lay a huge chestnut tree that had blown over during the last storm. It must have measured, at least, one hundred fifty feet in length and seven feet in diameter. She ran to the upper side, putting the tree between her and the Indian. Large branches had broken off on the downhill side and the Indian lost ground dodging the obstacles with their needlelike burrs. As Susan raced around the end branches, she ran headlong into the largest, most ferocious she-bear her terror-filled eyes had ever beheld.

The bear reared to its hind legs and spun toward her. Two cubs squealed and hastened to their mother. Terror upon terror gave Susan the additional strength to push her beyond the embrace of the enraged beast. Before it could give chase, the unsuspecting Indian rounded the tree and ran full tilt into its mighty grasp. Susan heard a terrible roar mixed with a human scream, and glancing fearfully over her shoulder, she witnessed a great struggle ensuing between man and beast. The bear had the Indian in a bone-crushing embrace, and the Indian was repeatedly thrusting his knife into the bear's flesh. Susan didn't linger for the outcome; terror gave wings to her feet as she fled into the dark forest.

"Well, if nothing was in the snares," complained Ivy, "then what took you so long?"

Susan continued building a small smokeless fire. "Oh, I went for a walk in the woods. There's nothing like a brisk, early morning hike to improve one's well-being. You should try it sometime."

"Oh, Susan, you jest," laughed Ivy, as she skewered a roast of venison on a green willow stick and moved to the fire. Susan stepped back from the flames and, hands on hips, surveyed the camp. It was well hidden in a tiny hollow, completely surrounded by dense undergrowth. A person virtually had to crawl into the small clearing to find it and, in truth, it had been by sheer accident that she had stumbled upon it. She had been following a game trail, looking for a likely spot for her snares when she was forced to crawl on her hands and knees beneath a low-hanging canopy of honeysuckle and grapevines. When she was finally able to stand erect, she found herself in the hidden clearing, completely encircled by honeysuckle-covered underbrush that raised to a height of twenty feet or more. The only entrance or exit was the faint game trail she had entered upon. It was a perfect hideout.

She had immediately backtracked and moved Ivy to the new campsite, and Ivy was delighted with it. She confided to Susan that it was the first camp they'd had where she felt absolutely safe. Susan silently agreed. She wondered, however, as she viewed the secluded glen if perhaps it might be too well hidden. Patterson could have trouble locating them. She decided to venture out directly after eating and wait for him. With that in mind, she ate quickly, told Ivy not to worry, and slipped quietly into the brush-covered tunnel.

Patterson looked at the muddy creek bank for the tenth time and scratched his head. He had checked the old campsite and picked up Susan's and Ivy's trail without any trouble. But he had lost it at the water's edge and had not been able to find it again. He had backtracked a half-dozen times, to no avail. He was puzzled; two women couldn't vanish into thin air.

"Are they lost, or are we?" asked Judith, a perplexed frown knitting her brow.

Patterson grunted: "Well, we are here and they are not. We know where we are, so they must be the ones that are lost."

"I beg your pardon!" came a voice from the underbrush. "We know where we are, but you failed to find us, so that means you are lost." Susan stepped from her place of concealment as quietly as a seasoned hunter. She was pleased with herself for Patterson was an expert tracker, yet she had eluded him. Her elation was short-lived, however.

Judith smiled sweetly and slipped her arm through Patterson's. "I am sure, Susan, that Morgan would have found the trail long before now... " she looked up at Patterson with exaggerated adoration, "but he has had so much on his mind, worrying over me, and all."

Susan looked from one to the other, trying to understand Judith's implications. She was shocked by Patterson's expression. His face had gone from bronze to white and then to one of anger, and though she didn't know exactly what that signified, the innocent little smile on Judith's lips any woman could read. She fought down the overwhelming urge to turn and flee, knowing how foolish she would appear. Instead, she smiled acidly at Judith.

"Aye, Judith, 'tis plain he has worried all over you."

Judith laughed delightedly.

Patterson shook off Judith's hand. He started to deny it—to deny anything and everything—but Susan had already turned away.

Patterson frowned at her retreating form and considered going after her to explain. But what was there to say? What had happened the night before could not be retracted. It had happened, and that was that. As far as Judith's declaration of love was concerned, words spoken in the heat of passion did not impress him—meant less than nothing actually. He became angry. He owed neither of these women anything, much less an explanation of his actions. Why should Susan care anyway? He mouthed a rare obscenity at her retreating back as she disappeared into the thick foliage.

"Really! Mr. Patterson," teased Judith, "do you always use such language in the presence of a lady?"

"Go to hell, Judith," he said softly as he stalked off in the direction Susan had taken.

Judith's jeering laughter made mockery of his anger, but had he thought to look over his shoulder, he might well have been surprised at the pain that shone briefly in her eyes.

Ivy fled to Judith and embraced her, asking question after question, while Susan absently cut a slab of venison for Judith and another for Patterson. He thanked her curtly and began eating, wiping the grease on his leggin's. She watched in silence until he had finished, then she moved casually to his side and eased to a sitting position. "I don't know whether you will care or not, but I had a run-in with an Indian this morning," she said sharply.

Patterson didn't comment, so she continued, giving him an entire accounting of the incident.

"You suppose the bear killed him?" he asked, as he stuffed another piece of meat into his mouth.

Susan said she didn't know, but by the size of the animal, she should think the Indian would have been no match for it. Patterson suggested they have a look when she ran her snares that evening. She agreed.

They made their way cautiously around the fallen chestnut tree, keeping their weapons ready, their eyes and ears alert. When they reached the spot where the struggle had taken place, the forest was serene. They strained their eyes, searching the woods as far as they could see, but there was no body, man, or beast. Patterson kneeled and ran his fingers through the leaves. He peered at the red sticky substance on his fingertips. "Hell of a fight," he said to Susan as he rose.

Frowning, he walked several yards to a small knoll and scrutinized the area. Then he motioned for Susan to follow. When she topped the rise, she saw the bear. It was down, and the two cubs were nosing her lifeless teats trying to suckle. When they saw Patterson, they squealed, sounding more like piglets than bears, and scampered up the nearest tree to stare down at him in terror. Patterson paid them no mind as he gingerly walked around the bear. The huge beast had died of multiple knife wounds, and its thick black coat was covered with blood. Susan looked at the animal in awe. "I cannot believe a lone Indian could kill such a beast."

Patterson glanced at her skeptically but refrained from making a comment. The bear was dead, and the Indian was gone, so evidently the Indian was victorious. Whether the man would live long enough to tell his story was another matter.

He unsheathed his knife and laid back the skin from a hind quarter. After cutting off a sizable roast, he laid the skin back in place. He smiled at Susan. "The Lord provides."

Infuriated at his nonchalance, and still burning with resentment from Judith's hints of intimacy—which he had not denied—she fumed at him. "Do not mock the good Lord, Mr. Patterson, or that poor bear either. Have you no decency left at all?" She turned and stamped off in the direction of camp, leaving Patterson with his mouth agape.

Heedless of his surroundings, he fell in behind her as she stiff-legged it through the fallen leaves. He was shocked—he had allowed himself the luxury of depending on her to be the steadfast, quick-minded, strong-willed woman who did not let personal feelings mar her better judgment. Yet there she was, acting the part of a white woman. He was disappointed.

And while he was angrily occupying himself with Susan's womanly imperfections, he, for the first time in his life, tramped after her with never a thought for their safety, or the trail they were leaving, or the lean, red, muscular body, with its penetrating black eyes, that dropped soundlessly to the ground from a low limb and disappeared in the opposite direction.

Susan ate her venison with cool detachment while the others dined on bear steak. But to her way of thinking, the bear had saved her life and she wasn't about to eat any of it. She watched Patterson and Judith from lowered lids and tried to determine the depth of their relationship. Something had happened while he and Judith were away, and Susan wished that she knew exactly what it was. She felt as if she had been kicked in the stomach by an ox, but she would be damned to hell before she'd reveal it. She really should not have been surprised or hurt, she thought. After all, Judith was more beautiful and sophisticated and wealthy. Susan realized with a shock that she was feeling sorry for herself and, in spite of how miserable she felt, she laughed. Her three companions looked at her, uneasy about her sudden burst of cheerfulness.

She didn't try to explain. Let them think what they would; she didn't care. All she wanted at that moment was to be back at Rosemont basking in the security of family and friends. She thought of home; of the cows that probably needed to be milked, and of the garden that needed hoeing; of the children with their dirty hands and faces that needed washing. She thought of her mother and stepfather and how happy they had been when she had last seen them. Susan was homesick—and heartsick.

Patterson startled her by gently shaking her shoulder. She looked up. "Guess I was daydreaming," she said crossly.

He nodded and sat down beside her. "'Tis a good thing—daydreaming. Why, I suppose, it is the mother of invention."

The touch of his hand, and his obvious desire to speak with her, caused mixed emotions in Susan; she wanted his attention, yet she didn't. Finally relenting, she asked shortly, "Why is it the mother of invention, Mr. Patterson?"

"Well," he replied, ignoring her sarcasm, "you sit around and dream of an easier way to do something, or a better way to do something, or a faster way of getting somewhere, and before long you have it all figured out. Of course," he lay back on one elbow and grinned at her, "it usually winds up being just a dream because most folk don't want to work hard enough to make it a reality."

Susan looked into his eyes: "So you really think if a person works hard enough, what they dream will come true?"

"Sometimes. Do you wish to talk about your dreams?"

"I think not."

Patterson nodded and changed the subject. "I must compliment you on your choice of a campsite. I would never have found it." Susan's barrier crumpled and she smiled shyly, savoring the compliment, for it was almost like words of love, coming from Patterson.

They tarried in camp the rest of the day, catching up on some much needed rest. Patterson pulled the charge and cleaned his rifle, as did Susan. Ivy cut up meat and herbs, for the evening meal, while Judith dozed.

They ate in silence, then extinguished the fire. Patterson chose a soft spot and lay down, drawing his rifle against his body. Judith smoothed out the leaves next to his, and lay down beside him. Hurt was showing plainly on Ivy's face as she made her bed on the opposite side of the small glade. She turned her back on Patterson and stared into the gathering darkness. She almost hated Judith at that moment.

Susan recalled what Patterson had said about working hard to invent a way to get what you wanted, and as she hollowed out a place in the grass and made her bed, she wondered how she could invent a way to make him love her. She thoughtfully compared herself to Ivy and Judith: all three had deep feelings for the woodsman—but was that so difficult to undersand? Had he not saved her virtue and her life several times over? And Ivy—Patterson was probably the first man who ever treated her as an equal—and as a woman, plying her with the same respect and, in his own way, friendliness that he granted Judith and herself. She winced as she thought of Judith, for even though she had tried to convince herself that it wasn't true, she knew that the blonde girl had given herself to Patterson. She could cheerfully have strangled Patterson, but her feelings for Judith were just the opposite—she pitied Judith. She rolled onto her stomach, laid her head upon her forearm and went to sleep, knowing that if she won Patterson's heart, it would certainly be hard work. But sometimes hard work can be a labor of love.

Patterson's sleeping habits were those of the hunter. His rifle was always placed so that the stock and buttplate lay against his stomach with the lock between his legs and the barrel protruding toward his feet. Placed thus, the gun could be brought into action at a moment's notice. Also, the arrangement, with the lock between his thighs, kept the firing mechanism dry of dew or light rain—and if the rifle were ever touched by anyone other than himself, he would be instantly aware of it.

Such was the case at predawn, the following morning, when Patterson felt the ever so slight movement of the weapon as it inched down his body. His eyes slitted open. An Indian was kneeling at his feet, working the gun slowly from between Patterson's drawn knees. Patterson kicked the man in the face with such force that he felt the toes of his foot snap as if they were broken. The Indian thrashed in the dust, holding his throat and gasping. Patterson was on him instantly, his knife flashing in the early morning light. Before the blade could fall, however, strong arms pinioned the woodsman from all sides.

Susan's eyes flashed open and her hand reached for her musket—it was gone. An Indian grinned into her astonished face, caressing the gun lovingly.

Ivy, lying across the clearing, began inching quietly toward the honeysuckle barrier nearby, but a strong hand wound itself in her hair and lifted her to her feet.

Judith looked wildly about; the entire camp was encircled by grinning Indians.

An Indian of medium stature disengaged himself from the circle and strode to Patterson. "Well, Patterson," he said into the harsh upturned face, "we thought we had a great joke on you this time." He motioned for Patterson to be released. "But you are still as wily as you were years ago."

Patterson scrutinized the man in the dim light, noting the tall

204

roach that dissected his head from crown to neck; the high, prominent cheekbones; the wide, thin mouth that, at the moment, was turned up at the corners.

Almost as an afterthought, Patterson realized the warrior had spoken in Shawnee.

"Black Fish?" queried Patterson in Shawnee dialect.

"It is I," said the Indian. "If I were anyone else you would be dead now."

Patterson gained his feet and, to the amazement of the women, clasped hands with the Indian.

"What is it that brings the great leader of the Shawnees to stalk Patterson in the dark of night and try to steal his most precious rifle gun?"

"To see if my son had lost his Indian ways since he has become a white man!"

Patterson held the man's eyes. "I am Shawnee, my father," he replied steadily. "I have not changed—I am just older—and tired. We have been many days evading the French."

"But why, my son?" asked the Shawnee. "The French and Huron are our friends; we are at war with the British—and the colonists."

Patterson was aware that the women could be in grave trouble. He felt sure, as the adopted son of Black Fish, that his safety was absolute. The women, however, were another question entirely. His answer therefore was issued slowly and with deliberate harshness to hold the attention of the surrounding throng of red men.

"My father," he began, "I will not lie to you and say the English are not my friends. Nor will I vow allegiance to the great French father. I know naught of the Huron, except that they are Algonquins, as are we—but I do know that I have a great prize in the women I have captured. They will bring a grand ransom—when I return them to their families." Ransoming a captive was a common practice, not only for the Indian, but for the white man as well, and he knew he was believed.

The Indian studied the woodsman solemnly for a long moment before speaking.

"Do captives normally carry weapons, my son?" The question was delivered evenly, but Patterson was not fooled. He had lied himself into a tight situation that could spell disgrace for himself and doom for the women. He eyed the tight, inquisitive faces of the Indians as they awaited his answer.

"My father," he answered smoothly, wishing to appear at ease, "I have taken a woman to my blankets. She hunts by my side, and tends my fire, and cares for my needs—she, the one with the musket, is my wife."

The Shawnee frowned as he turned his attention to Susan, taking in her appearance from head to toe. And she, not understanding the language but knowing full well that she was being appraised, stood straight and proud before his engaging glance.

"My son," said the man sorrowfully, "have you so changed as to forget your past? Have you thrown aside your hatred and taken a white woman to wife...after all that has gone before?"

Patterson stiffened. "My father, I have not forgotten my past, nor my feelings toward white women." He turned and motioned Susan to join him. She unhesitantly moved to his side and faced the Indians with a hauteur born of sheer willpower; inside she was quaking.

Patterson took Susan's hand and raised it in a salute. "This is my woman—she is Mohawk! She was reared by whites, much as I was raised by the red man. She speaks only the English tongue, and thinks as the whites have taught her to think. But inside she is still Mohawk, and I will teach her the ways of our people."

Before his foster father had time to comment further, Patterson pushed Susan from him, saying in English, "Build up the fire, and have Judith and Ivy put every piece of meat we have to roasting. These men are hungry." He looked deep into her eyes. "Do not question or act surprised by anything you see or hear from me. Tell Ivy and Judith to do the same." Susan nodded and turned to the fire.

While the Shawnee warriors devoured the entire store of deer and bear meat that the women had laid by, Patterson listened to Black Fish's news. His band of Shawnee had not been present at Braddock's defeat, having arrived too late. They had, however, attacked several backwoods cabins and carried off scalps, plunder, horses, and captives, who were being held not five miles away at their main camp. He explained to Patterson that they were to meet a body of French and Hurons there and then proceed to Chillicothe to celebrate their good fortune and divide the plunder and captives.

The French, he said, had insisted on moving the captives straight to Montreal, but the Indians had closed their ears, electing instead to display the captured whites in the Indian villages along the Ohio River.

"How did you find us?" asked Patterson when Black Fish had finished. "We were well hidden and had taken precautions to hide our trail. I am surprised that you were able to locate us."

The Shawnee smiled and eyed Patterson merrily. He enjoyed counting coup on a friend, especially one with the woodsman's reputation, and he wished to prolong the glorious moment as long as possible. So, he studied the woodsman for several long minutes before answering. "Indeed, you were well hidden," he said cheerfully. "But you are becoming lazy since taking a wife. One of our young men, who has since died of wounds from a she-bear, told us of a lone woman who was roaming the forest. It was a simple matter, my son, to have the area watched—you should have known we would do that . . . but, from what our spies tell us, you paid not the least attention to the woods around you when you and your wife came to the bear and took food. If we had not recognized you, you and your captives—and your woman—would be but scalps hanging at our belts."

Patterson nodded.

"I am deeply embarrassed, my father, that I should be caught sleeping like a white child in a bedchamber."

The Indian laid his hand on Patterson's shoulder. "You are thin and underfed, Patterson, and you limp from a leg wound. Your eyes are sunken and bloodshot, and your body is filthy—you have traveled far, I would say, and you have done well to evade the French and the people who would have killed you on sight. Do not feel bad, my son; I am proud of you."

As the Shawnee, Patterson, and the women trotted through the woods toward the Indians' main camp, Patterson explained it all to the girls. He instructed them to be strong when they entered the camp and, no matter what happened, or what they saw, to say nothing, nor appear afraid. And, above all, to stay close to him at all times. They agreed that they would. He reluctantly, and with great embarrassment, told them what he had said to Black Fish about Susan, and about Judith and Ivy being hostages.

The girls were amused, but when Patterson was called to counsel with Black Fish, the laughter died, and each trotted on with thoughts of her own concerning Patterson's selection of a bride, even though each knew he had done it because Susan held the musket.

Susan was embarrassed. But the fact that Patterson had chosen her caused her pulse to quicken.

Ivy wondered why Patterson had chosen a white woman. That he had not chosen her shattered the dreams she harbored that she might eventually win his love because she was not white.

Judith's happiness was dashed. At first she had thought it funny and had even laughed. But after the initial shock had passed, bitterness set in. She had given herself to Patterson—had lain with him as a wife would have done—yet, he had spurned her for Susan. Oh, God! she thought. How could I have been so stupid. I hate him. And, as her bare feet slapped the ground in cadence to the rhythm set by the trotting Indians, she murmured quietly, "I hate him, I hate him, I hate him."

They reached the main encampment late that morning, and wasted no time with preliminaries. Patterson instructed Susan to have Judith and Ivy gather wood for a fire. Susan, he said, was to oversee the job but not to join in the labor, for she was to be the slave owner. Judith and Ivy, like it or not, were slaves until such time as Patterson could get them to freedom.

Susan did as she was told, taking Judith and Ivy into the forest in search of dead limbs while Patterson visited with old friends and acquaintances, and secretly made mental note of plunder, animals, and captives who were grouped around the campsite.

He was bothered by the great amount of personal items that lay about; clothing, bedding, cooking utensils, pieces of furniture small enough for one person to carry on his back; kegs and barrels; and much more. He was keenly aware that the goods he observed were what remained of the life's work of many a family. Many innocent folk have died these past weeks, he thought, and this is barely the beginning...the beginning!

His brow furrowed as he remembered the beginning of the Ohio Valley wars. Only two years had passed since George Washington had raced his blown and foaming mount through the streets of Williamsburg to the very entrance of the Wren Building of William and Mary College. There he disrupted the class Morgan was attending by clutching the young man's arm and forcefully dragging him to Christiana Campbell's Tavern. Over a tall mug of ale he explained that Governor Dinwiddie was dispatching himself and Patterson to a French fort called Le Boeuf in the upper Ohio Valley, some six hundred miles distant. The youthful Patterson was elated, and wasted no time returning to his room to cast aside his city clothing and slip into his buckskin frock, leggin's, and breechcloth.

When he joined Washington at the post office on Duke of Gloucester Street, he penned a hasty letter to his father explaining the urgency of his mission. His transformation to a woodsman caused no small commotion among his college friends, for it was purely evident that he was no stranger to either buckskin or the big-bore rifle he carried.

Two weeks later, as Joseph Patterson read Morgan's short note, he applauded his son's foresight. Like Morgan, he had no doubts about the seriousness of France's possession of the Ohio Valley; the newly acquired Patterson Land Holding Company would be ruined.

In October 1753 Washington, Patterson, and the experienced frontiersman and guide Christopher Gist left Fort Cumberland, Maryland, for the forks of the Ohio. A month later Patterson and Gist stood quietly while Major Washington delivered to the French the Virginia governor's warning that they, knowingly or otherwise, were trespassing on English soil. Gist, eschewing social custom, spat tobacco juice on the floor when the French commandant retorted that it was their absolute design to take possession of the Ohio and, by God, they would do it.

Patterson had taken out flint and steel and struck a shower of sparks that arced brightly toward the floor. In the silence that followed, he said quietly: "Gentlemen, you have just witnessed the first sparks of what I fear will be a long and querulous conflict."

Patterson was with Major Washington again on May 27, 1754, when the first volley was fired, opening the French and Indian War in earnest. With three hundred men, Washington had surprised a small French reconnaissance party, killing ten and capturing twenty-one. One escaped. His name was Fontaine.

Flushed with victory, Washington had clapped Patterson on his back, saying, "Ah, Morgan, the bullets whistle, but there is something charming in the sound." Patterson silently disagreed.

The victory was short-lived. The next day a Seneca chief named Half-King slipped in and warned Washington that a large body of French and Indians were assembling to advance against him. Thirty minutes later, Patterson wearily trotted in and confirmed Half-King's report. Washington hastily threw up a breastwork and called it Fort Necessity. For nine hours on July 3, 1754, enemy bullets peppered the English. To make matters worse, rain fell in torrents, soaking their gunpowder and supplies. Then, with over seventy-five of his men dead or wounded, Washington surrendered; and as a direct result of that relinquishing of arms, Braddock sailed from England with thirteen hundred British regulars to accomplish what Washington had failed to execute—the taking of Fort Duquesne.

And now, thanks to Braddock's misguided adventure, Morgan Patterson viewed the plunder strewn about the clearing. The items lay forlorn, in piles, with careless disregard for the sweat and hardships that had gone into their creation.

He absently spun the wheel of a beautifully constructed spinning wheel, and could not help wondering about the man who crafted the machine—or the woman who had used and cared for it. Dead, or captured—probably dead. Patterson shook his head, unhappily. I am thinking the thoughts of a white man, he mused, bitterly. Then, with a burst of uncontrolled fury directed toward himself, he placed his foot against the spinning wheel and sent it tumbling end over end into the brush at the clearing's edge.

"What will happen to us, Susan?" Ivy's question startled the girl out of a meditation so intense that to be jolted back to reality left her short-tempered. So engrossed was she with thoughts of the nights ahead and her role, fictitious or not, as Patterson's wife, that Ivy's intrusion irked her.

"How should I know, Ivy! I understand no more about what is happening than you."

Judith, who had gathered a bundle of sticks, raised to her full height and studied Susan closely. The anger in Susan's voice was uncommon, and Judith was troubled by it. Even though she continually bickered and quarreled with the girl and found fault with her every gesture, she inwardly respected Susan's ability for cool thought and self-control.

Judith's eyes narrowed. Perhaps Susan was taking this business of being their mistress too seriously. "You are not our mistress, Susan," she said, marching toward another pile of broken branches and snapping off the twigs and small ends for kindling, "so do not get headstrong from your temporary position—"

"I'm not! Do you realize what is happening? Do you?"

"I realize we have been captured by friends of Mr. Patterson's," said Judith as she studied the unbridled fear in Susan's eyes. "It would be easy for me to talk myself into believing that he allowed us to be taken—but I do not believe that. I think it was by merest chance that the Indians discovered—"

"Of course it was!" snapped Susan. "He would not deliver us into the hands of our enemies."

"Of course not," said Ivy. "But . . . why are you so upset? We have not been bothered, or mistreated . . . and we know," continued the girl impishly, "that you will be a fine and just mistress."

Susan smiled woefully. "Do not make fun of me, Ivy. I am in a real dilemma."

"What is it?" frowned Judith.

Susan's bronze face flushed a deep scarlet.

Judith read Susan's face and understood perfectly. She had felt much the same the night she had thrown all caution aside and seduced Patterson. A picture formed in her mind; a scene, vividly real, of Susan and Patterson locked in naked embrace. A cold numbness surged through her and left her aching with a pain that was unlike anything she had yet experienced.

"What is it that you are worried about?" she asked with her usual sarcasm. "The possibility that he will . . . or will not demand his rights as a husband?"

Susan's face flushed even deeper.

"Oh, Judith!" said Ivy, staring at Susan.

Judith laughed lightly and turned to resume her gathering of firewood. "We shall see," she said to the two wide-eyed women standing behind her.

They deposited the wood at the spot Patterson had designated for their camp. It was at the far edge of the small glade, well away from the other captives.

211

The few Indians who had stayed in camp while the remainder hunted watched the women through slitted eyes as they made preparations for a fire. The girls ignored them, absorbed by the flint and steel Susan was wielding with such skill. In seconds she had a small wisp of smoke. She blew lightly on the embers and the sparks burst into a tiny flame.

Judith added small twigs, and Ivy fanned the flame into a fire. The observing Shawnees grunted their approval.

Patterson appeared at dusk carrying a small deer.

"Have Judith and Ivy skin it and prepare the meat," he ordered Susan. "You cook it, but have them serve it."

"All of it? You want it all cooked?"

"Aye, we will have guests for supper. They are extremely aware of etiquette and manners, so caution Judith and Ivy to be careful how they act."

"But they are savages!" snarled Judith. "I'll not serve savages—I'll not!"

Patterson's face turned harsh. "Susan," he said softly, extending his hatchet to her, "go cut a stave four or five feet long, and if Judith refuses another order, *beat her*."

"But, Morgan," cried Susan as she hesitantly took the hatchet, "I cannot do that."

"Either you do it, or I will do it." He fixed Judith with his hard eyes. "It will be done, I assure you. I'll not let her foolish pride endanger our lives."

"Then *you* beat me, you overbearing—"

"Shut up, Judith," snapped Ivy as she pushed her mistress away. "Do not put him in the position of having to save face by whipping you! It is folly!"

"Damn folly!" cried Judith, attempting to bypass Ivy and return to Patterson who was moving with Susan toward the treeline in search of a stave.

"Damn him!" she fumed again, shaking with wrath. "Who does he think he is?"

"He's our master, now," said Ivy, looking in the same direction as Judith, "and, like it or not, we will serve him as he wishes."

Ivy studied Patterson intently, then spoke again. "I will enjoy serving Morgan. I would be happy to do it the rest of my life."

Judith's eyes narrowed maliciously. "I'll serve no man," she vowed, "and certainly not him."

Had Ivy been watching, she would have observed the hint of a blush suffuse Judith's lovely face, for Judith knew, without a doubt, that she had already served him.

The dinner was a success. Ivy and Judith performed perfectly as waitresses, and Susan's cordial attitude and polite mannerisms won appreciation from Black Fish and his warriors.

Patterson was proud of the women, but his stonelike face betrayed nothing.

After the guests had departed, the women ate. They were ravenous, having not eaten since before sunup. As they ate, they talked of Indians—how polite and well mannered they were, not at all the savage beasts they were supposed to be.

Patterson listened to the conversation and knew a moment of pity for the women; it was just a matter of time before they would see the terrible side of the bronze men's nature, the savage side that they had heard so much about. He hoped that they were strong enough to endure the brutal sights that lay before them. With that thought in mind, he drew his rifle to him and went immediately to sleep.

"Well," commented Judith, observing Patterson's sleeping form, "you are safe tonight, Susan." Then she laughed.

They were up before daylight, stoking the embers to life and fanning them into a flame. They reheated the venison left from the night before and ate in silence. No one complained of having to eat leftovers, the memory of hunger still painfully fresh in their minds.

As the rising sun illuminated the campsite, the girls took stock of their surroundings, paying particular attention to the captives, who were being ushered about the camp by their Indian abductors.

The majority of the prisoners were stripped of their clothing, their naked bodies a pale gray in the soft light. Ivy and Judith silently thanked the Lord that they had not been forced to give up their clothing. They should have thanked Patterson, for it was he who had politely, yet firmly, leaving no room for argument, refused to allow the two women to be stripped. Black Fish had finally yielded to Patterson's will. "My son," he said, looking deep into Patterson's eyes, searching his very soul, "it is our custom to disrobe our captives; it is our right as the victors." His hand moved in an arc that encompassed the campsight. "These are our prisoners, they now belong to us just as our dogs, and our horses belong to us. They own nothing . . . except what we wish to give them." His eyes moved from Patterson to the women, who had watched the exchange between father and adopted son in ignorance of the gist of the conversation. "If you wish for your own captives to keep their clothing, then so be it."

He had turned then and strode magnificently toward the throng of naked men and women who were being assembled for their morning chores.

But Judith and Ivy knew nothing of that: indeed, had not understood a word of it, or realized how dangerous was Patterson's refusal to follow the age-old custom of the red men; and, even more harrowing, his decision to chance the wrath of his adopted tribe.

Patterson again cursed himself for a white man, but try as he might, he could find no logical excuse for his actions except that he could not bear the thought of Judith and Ivy standing nude before the appraising eyes of a score of men.

The answer would come to him in an old, recurring dream that same night, a dream in which he was once again a young boy standing high on a cart seat, watching with wide, horrified eyes as the only woman he ever truly loved was stripped naked before the eyes of such a crowd. He had lived with the dream for a long time, but never before had the naked woman spoken directly to him as she did this night. Her eyes held his above the glare of the weaving torches. "Morgan," she said, looking softly at him, "what does it matter to you if Judith and Ivy are stripped of their clothing? There are several other women captives in the camp, yet you cast not a glance at their nakedness. Is it because you care for them?" Her eyes held the question so positively that the boy dropped his gaze. "I care naught for Judith or Ivy!" he cried. "I care only for you."

He was pulled from his dream by a soft, earnest voice and gentle hands on his shoulders as Susan pleaded for him to wake up.

"You were dreaming. I am sorry to have awakened you but . . . but you were crying."

He pushed her away with such force that she fell heavily to her side, to lie there and study him wonderingly.

"I never cry!" he whispered savagely. "I did not even cry when it happened . . ."

214

"When what happened?" she ventured, eyeing him expectantly, hoping beyond hope that he would at last talk about his ghosts.

"*Leave me alone,*" he thundered, rising to his feet and disappearing into the darkness.

She watched him go, and her heart cried out to him, wanting to share his awful pain and suffering. She longed to hold him to her breast.

She eased out of her sleeping place and raced after him into the night. The blackness of the forest was an eerie void; not even a star showed through the tangled branches high overhead. She stopped and peered into the gloom, but even though her eyes were accustomed to the darkness, she could make out nothing, not even a tree trunk.

"Morgan?" she called softly, turning her head to try and penetrate the choking blackness.

She shuddered violently, nerves tingling. Something, or someone, was near, looming closer with each wild beat of her heart. She turned to run, to flee that unseen danger, for whatever it was that crept toward her, she was certain it wasn't Morgan Patterson. Then it was on her. She tried to scream but a hard, calloused hand clamped tightly over her mouth and a heavy weight burst against her forehead, knocking her senseless. She didn't remember falling, but she must have, for she was snatched up unmercifully by the hair of her head until her toes barely touched the earth. Her head spun sickeningly, and for a moment she was sure she would swoon. As she tried her best to keep from fainting, she heard a familiar voice, harsh and urgent. She did not understand the words, nor would she ever understand them, or any of the Shawnee language. Then she did swoon.

Her hair was released as abruptly as it had been grasped, and a steady hand helped her to regain her balance.

"You little fool," said Patterson in her ear, "that was a night guard you stumbled upon. 'Tis a thousand wonders he didn't kill you—and he would have if I hadn't been close enough to hear you call. Damn it, woman, what are you doing out here?"

"I—I was looking for you."

"Why?"

"Because."

"Because why?" he demanded, and even though it was too dark to see, she knew he was angry.

"Just because!"

She felt his arm tighten about her.

"You will never come closer to dying than you did just now, Susan." His voice was a harsh whisper, and she was certain she detected a small fragment of underlying fear in the sound. But a moment later, he spun her around and pushed her toward the camp with orders not to follow him again—ever!

She moved quietly toward the clearing, feeling desolate. Then her head came up and she smiled. "He cares! He doesn't know it yet, but he cares!"

Judith and Ivy inquired about the ugly bruise on Susan's forehead while they breakfasted on three-day-old, slightly rank venison the next morning, but she ignored their questions, leaving them bewildered by her silence. Judith finally demanded: "Did Patterson do that to you? Are you still a virgin?"

"Judith!" cried Ivy, aghast. " 'Tis obviously none of our affair or Susan would have explained."

"It is all right, Ivy," said Susan. "No, Judith, Mr. Patterson did not . . . do either of what you ask. Are you satisfied?"

Judith grinned crookedly. "You wish he had, don't you?"

Susan studied Judith for a long thoughtful moment.

"I will not sleep with him, Judith . . . no matter what I wish."

"My Lord!" said Ivy. "Just listen to you two. I have not heard such bold talk since Judith and I attended the queen's court. All they discussed were their affairs, and they pretended to be such fine ladies."

"Are you insinuating that I am not a lady?"

"Nay, mistress," returned Ivy quickly. "But I did not then, nor do I now, think ladies should speak so openly about their relationships." She blushed and dropped her eyes. "Giving oneself to a man should be a beautiful and personal thing."

Judith jumped to her feet and glared at Ivy. "I have given myself to no one. I but wondered if Miss prim-and-proper Susan had succumbed to her husband's desires."

"He is not my husband."

Ivy sprang between the two young women.

"Enough! We've work to do. Come, Judith."

She caught the girl's hand and tugged her toward the treeline where the other captives were busy gathering wood.

Judith had gathered her sixth armload of dry branches and was walking toward the clearing when she was brought up short by Susan as she ran through the tall green ferns that grew in the everlasting shadows beneath the trees.

"Judith!" Susan called breathlessly. "Fetch Ivy and come quick!"

"What is it?" Judith cast her firewood aside and ran to meet Susan. Worry caused small lines to appear between her eyes.

"What is it, Susan?" she repeated.

"Where is Ivy?" Susan caught Judith's arm fearfully.

"I am here!" Ivy dropped her bundle of sticks and ran to join the two women.

"It's one of the captive women," cried Susan. "Morgan took me to her. She's having a baby—I need your help: the baby is coming backward." She caught Judith and Ivy's hands and hurried toward the clearing.

They were forced to work their way through the throng of Indians who had gathered around the screaming woman. Several of the red men were squatted, to see better the child that was on its way.

Others stood leaning on their muskets, their faces unreadable, their thoughts untouchable.

Susan kneeled and laid her hand across the woman's damp brow.

"She's burning up with fever. If we don't bring that baby soon, she will die."

Ivy dropped to her knees. "Tell me what to do, Susan. I've never seen a baby born."

The woman screamed, and her body arched high before it fell heavily to the grass. Her white-knuckled fingers spread wide, then slowly clenched into a fist, leaving thin furrows of torn grass as they dug into the hard earth.

An Indian slipped his hatchet from his belt and tested the razor-sharp edge with his tumb, but another caught his wrist and, with one quick shake of his head, signaled him to wait, to be patient.

Judith stood transfixed, her eyes flowing over the heaving, overlarge abdomen of the pregnant woman to rivet on the large, full breasts that glistened with perspiration so dense that a small puddle had formed in the cleft and trickled toward her extended stomach.

Susan quickly shifted her position until she was kneeling between the woman's legs. She slipped her hand beneath the infant's tiny buttock, then gently applied pressure to the woman's swollen belly with her free hand.

"Push hard, Sarah," she said. "Take a deep breath and push hard."

The woman thrashed her sweat-dampened head from side to side and cried out in a ragged scream.

Judith dropped to Susan's side and studied the infant. Everything had been born except the head. She breathed deeply several times.

"How long has she been like this?"

"Since before I came for you and Ivy. Everything went fine until the head—the head just won't come."

Patterson squatted and studied the scene. "Just take hold of the feet and pull it on out of there," he offered.

Susan glared at him.

"Well why not?" he asked, angered by her scorn.

"Because it would very probably break the baby's neck!"

"Well, damn it!" he returned. "The baby's going to die anyway—the way it's going."

"Not if we can help it." She turned her attention to Judith and Ivy. "Lift her to a squatting position and hold her steady. Can you do that?"

Judith nodded uncertainly and changed position so she could slip her arms under the woman's shoulders. Ivy did the same. Together they raised her to a crouch.

Sarah tried to lie back, squirming and thrashing, but the girls held fast and talked endlessly to her until she quieted and attempted to assist as she was instructed.

"Take a deep breath and push, Sarah," said Susan. "Try hard; that's it; again now."

The woman strained; her abdomen convulsed, and the veins in her temples stood rigid. Sweat streamed down her face and dripped over her chin to splash wetly on her swollen abdomen.

The Indians moved closer. This was entertainment.

"Good God!" cried Judith. "Can't you get these fiends away from here, Morgan?"

An Indian standing close to Judith kicked her savagely in the ribs, causing her to release her grip on the woman's shoulders. Sarah fell sideways, screamed, and clutched her stomach, but Judith had regained her balance and had steadied herself, giving support to the weakened woman again.

Patterson looked hard at her. "You will never learn to keep your mouth closed, will you Judith?"

"I did not think these savages understood English."

"They don't," he said, "but they damn well understand your attitude."

"Push, Sarah!" cried Susan. "Push! I've almost got her."

Susan eased her fingers deeper into the woman and gently worked them over and around the infant's head. The tiny chin and mouth were visible. Then, finally, the baby slipped free.

"I've got her," sighed Susan. "My Lord, we did it!"

Susan held the squirming child high for all to see. Then using two pieces of sinew, she tied off the umbilical cord, and cut it.

"Let me see her," breathed the mother raggedly as Judith and Ivy eased her back upon the sweat-stained earth.

Susan gently placed the child in the woman's waiting arms.

"She's the most beautiful thing I've ever seen," said Judith breathlessly, her eyes wide with wonder as she gazed at the wailing baby.

Patterson looked critically at the newborn. She was covered with blood and bits of afterbirth; her skin was red with a thousand wrinkles, giving her the appearance of an ancient monkey. How, he thought, can anyone call that beautiful?

Sarah gently placed the child against her breast. Immediately the small sucking lips found the nipple.

Judith's eyes became round with surprise. "Oh, Ivy! Look! Isn't it just marvelous!"

Ivy studied Judith thoughtfully.

Susan wiped her bloody hands on the grass and stood up.

"Where did you learn to do that?" asked Patterson, curiosity upon his hawklike face.

"I have helped deliver calves, and pigs, and once even a foal—but never a baby."

"You did fine, just fine," he said, impressed by the girl's ability. He might have said more had Ivy not intervened.

"Shall we wash the baby, Susan?"

"Nay" replied the tired girl, "after the blood has dried and she is stronger we will clean her." She knelt by the woman's side and caught the feeble hand that was offered her. "How do you feel, Sarah?"

"Very tired, mistress," came the weak reply. Then she smiled. "May the Lord bless you and your friends." She indicated Judith and Ivy. "I owe you my life, and my baby's."

"You owe us nothing. Please do not feel that way."

"I would have died . . ." Sarah squeezed Susan's hand, but her strength was such that Susan could barely feel the pressure.

"Rest now," she said gently, as she laid Sarah's hand upon the baby. "Just rest and get strong." But even as she said it, she was doubtful that the woman would ever recover, for there was a pool of bright-red blood beneath her hips that grew larger by the minute and Susan had no idea how to stop it.

The Indians dwindled away after the baby was born, losing interest in the matter.

"You'd best put the girls back to gathering wood, Susan," said Patterson, as he moved off to join the Indians.

Susan nodded.

"Let me stay!" Judith said quickly. "Allow me to tend Sarah and the baby—I will gather firewood this afternoon . . . I promise— please, Susan."

Susan was astonished by Judith's sincere plea. That the girl would beg, would say *please*, left her speechless.

Susan glanced at Patterson, who was also watching Judith wonderingly. "Well, Mr. Patterson, can she stay?"

Judith raised her face to Patterson: the soft, agonized, pleading in her eyes left him shaken. He had never seen Judith so vulnerable.

"Yes," he said. "She can stay."

12

The long-awaited French and Hurons arrived late that afternoon. A flurry of excitement swept the camp. Every Indian who was not hunting, or otherwise engaged, met the newcomers with solemn dignity.

Black Fish made them welcome. His elegance and manners, as he greeted the guests, impressed Susan, observing from afar.

He shook hands with the French officer and tipped his head to the Hurons, who stood as statues in the background.

Then Susan's heart jumped: Fontaine was approaching the chief. If he recognized Patterson, who stood beside Black Fish, he made no indication.

Susan was puzzled until she realized that it would, indeed, be difficult to explain such an acquaintance.

Ivy dropped the bundle of sticks she had gathered and slipped to Susan's side.

"Is that Fontaine?"

"Aye, and as magnificent as ever. But remember," cautioned Susan, "we do not know him."

Ivy nodded, and walked swiftly to Judith, still tending Sarah and the baby.

"Fontaine is here," she said as she approached. "But we cannot recognize him."

"I understand. I will be careful if he is near."

221

Then Judith laughed and held the infant up for Ivy to see. "Her name is Mary. Isn't it a nice name? For Sarah's mother she was named Mary."

Ivy took the child and rocked it gently. "What will she grow up to be, Judith? We will never get back to civilization—she will be a savage."

"Stop talking like that! We will get back . . . and Mary and Sarah will go with us."

Ivy handed the child back to Judith. "They are taking us to a village far away. Did you know that?"

Judith shook her head. "No, I did not know. Did Morgan tell you?"

"Yes, just before the French arrived."

"Then, 'tis but a bit farther we will have to travel to get back to Fort Cumberland, that is all." She eyed Ivy intently. "What is wrong, Ivy? You have always been the stouthearted one. You never once thought we would not get out of the wilderness alive. What's bothering you?"

Ivy looked deep into Judith's eyes. "Why do you love that baby so much? You've never cared about children; what is it that makes you care so much for this one, Judith?"

Ivy looked away quickly, afraid that Judith would see the real question in her eyes: Why have you never loved me?

Judith, however, was so obliviously happy with the child that she saw nothing of the hurt in the servant girl's eyes, or the white knuckles of Ivy's tightly clenched fists. She pressed the baby against her bosom and rocked it gently, smiling serenely to herself. Finally, she relinquished the child to the waiting arms of its mother and stood, smoothing her rumpled, threadbare dress.

"Come," she said, taking Ivy by the hand, "we'll fetch another load of wood. There'll be more fires to feed now that the French have arrived."

Once they were in the forest, out of sight and sound of the campsite, Judith began talking. Her words came quickly, as though she were afraid she and Ivy would be interrupted.

She told Ivy her innermost fear—barrenness. Because of the terrible kick she had received the day they were captured by the two Indians, she feared she would never bear a child.

"I want a baby of my very own, Ivy, but I am sure I shall never get pregnant. My insides are ruined—you remember how much I bled."

"Judith," said Ivy, stroking her half sister's cheek, "if it is as you say, and you are barren, then I shall have a child for you, several of them if you so wish, and they will be of your own flesh and...I mean," she stammered, quickly explaining, "they will be like your own flesh and blood."

Judith's face turned ashen. "You dare offer me a nigger to raise as my own! You dare insinuate that it would be of my own flesh and blood!"

Ivy stepped back as though she had been slapped. "Please, mistress, please don't..."

Judith pushed Ivy from her and angrily strode toward the clearing.

Ivy leaned heavily against the rough bark of a towering tree and burst into tears. She had no idea how long she had cried when a soft voice in her ear startled her back to reality.

"I thought the entire wilderness was weeping, so brokenhearted are your tears."

Ivy spun away from the tree.

"Mr. Fontaine! How dare you slip upon a lady who wishes to be alone—and stop that infernal grinning!"

Fontaine grinned broadly. "Ah, mademoiselle, you are even more beautiful than I remember."

His hand moved toward her buttock.

"Mr. Fontaine," she warned, "if you so much as lay a finger on my..."

"On your beautiful bottom?" he finished for her.

"Aye," she said, smiling in spite of herself. "I swear to you, I will..."

"You will slit my throat from here to here, eh?" He grinned, making a slashing motion from earlobe to earlobe.

"Exactly!" she cried, laughing.

Fontaine laughed with her, then indicated a mossy spot beneath the tree. "Would you sit and tell me what has happened? I have had no chance to talk with Patterson."

She eased gracefully to the ground and Fontaine sat also. She told Fontaine everything that had happened since he had seen them last. She poured her heart out to him, telling at last of Judith's obsession with Sarah's new baby.

Fontaine listened in silence as the girl talked, watching her eyes and her lips, and he found himself longing to hold her, to kiss her, to possess her. Never had he desired a woman as he did Ivy, but he fought those feelings, for he knew that to approach her would be to lose her. He would bide his time; the trip to Chillicothe was a long one; anything could happen.

Ivy finished, and felt much better for the telling of it. Fontaine grinned and climbed to his feet, helping Ivy to rise also.

"Mademoiselle, très bien; everything will work out. Fontaine will see to it."

Ivy touched his calloused hand. "I think you are right, and I thank you, sir."

It was all the Frenchman could do to keep from lifting the fragile, sweet-smiling girl into his arms and holding her. And for a second, he was sure that she would not protest. But the chance was gone as quickly as it appeared.

"You must return, mademoiselle," he said dryly. "The captives are to be inspected at sundown by the captain; you must be there."

Ivy took his hand in earnest. "Thank you, Fontaine, for listening. You are a true gentleman."

"Ah, chérie! Do not place upon my shoulders such a heavy burden. Merci! A gentleman!"

Ivy laughed and skipped happily down the path toward the clearing, leaving the Frenchman leaning languidly against the tree.

A most beautiful woman, he mused as she disappeared in the tangled thickness of the woods.

As the golden disk of the sun sank below the treeline, the captives were roughly pushed into line for inspection. Ivy and Judith were brought to the end of the line and instructed to say nothing unless spoken to. Judith carried the infant, for it too was a captive.

Although the prisoners were few, it was almost full dark before the French officers advanced to Ivy who stood quietly beside Judith.

The captain appraised Ivy briefly before moving to Judith. His eyes widened as he measured the blonde girl from head to toe.

224

"How old is your baby?" he asked in surprisingly good English.

"She is not mine, sir," stammered Judith, taken by surprise. "Her mother is too weak to stand, sir. The infant was just born today."

The captain nodded, eyeing Judith more closely, his gaze moving over her lithe body.

His expression remained unchanged. "Black Fish," he said in French, "why are these two captives not stripped like the others?"

Fontaine interpreted for the Shawnee.

The Indian's eyes briefly rested on Patterson, then moved to the captain.

"They are the daughters of an English nobleman; they are worth a great ransom... unharmed."

The captain smiled as Fontaine interpreted. "The daughter of a nobleman, eh?" he said, in English, appraising Judith again.

Judith nodded but said nothing, electing to follow Patterson's advice and remain silent.

The look in the captain's eyes had struck fear into her.

The captain remained smiling as he touched Judith's hair with his fingertips.

"Return the baby to its mother and come to my fire, mademoiselle. I, Captain DeBeaujue, have never known an English lady of quality. It shall be a new experience."

"No," said Patterson softly.

"No, monsieur?" DeBeaujue turned a quizzical eye toward Patterson and studied him intently for several seconds.

"You are English, are you not?"

"I am Shawnee, the son of Black Fish!" said Patterson.

The Frenchman bowed to Patterson. "And pray, sir, what are these ladies to you?"

"They are my captives, captain. And I will not endanger such a ransom as they will bring, by allowing them to be misused—by you, or any man."

"Monsieur," said the Frenchman, much amused, "you are under my jurisdiction. If I so desire, I shall have the lady."

"And if you so much as lay a hand on her," said Patterson dryly, "I'll kill you. Is it worth it, captain?"

The Frenchman pursed his lips in thought. Patterson knew the man was weighing his decision thoroughly, wondering how much

225

weight Patterson carried with the Shawnee. The woodsman had gambled that the Frenchman would not press the issue. He was correct.

"Monsieur," said the captain, "your threat does not bother me. Au contraire, I would welcome meeting you on the field of honor, but, alas, amour can wait until a more appropriate time. But I assure you, monsieur, I shall have the lady."

The captain turned to take his leave but Patterson's soft voice stopped him.

"And I shall kill you, sir. But it will not be on a field of honor."

The smile that hovered around Patterson's lips was as bone-chilling as his cold blue eyes.

"Monsieur," said DeBeaujue, "you are no gentleman." Then he laughed.

The were up and moving before daylight.

Even though Judith carried the baby, it was obvious to all when they stopped at noon that Sarah was bleeding to death.

Judith sank wearily to the ground beside the exhausted woman and carefully placed the child on her exposed breast. The baby suckled greedily, making small, smacking sounds of pleasure.

"'Tis a most beautiful sight, the feeding of a child," said Judith, eyeing the mother and daughter wistfully.

The woman took Judith's hand and brought it to her parched lips and kissed it.

"You've been so kind, mistress," she said, holding tightly to Judith's hand. Then her eyes filled with tears. "I've a favor, mistress," She searched Judith's face with troubled eyes before continuing. "If I should die, would you take Mary and raise her as your own?"

"You won't die, Sarah," assured Judith, stroking the woman's perspiring brow.

"Answer me, please," begged the woman.

"Why . . . of course I would take her. I—I love her."

Sarah closed her eyes and breathed a long shuddering sigh.

They rested for ten minutes before being ordered back into line. Judith took the baby and moved to the trail. Sarah tried to rise, but the effort was too great and she sank heavily to the ground.

"Come on, Sarah," coached Judith. "You can make it; just try again."

Sarah's captor moved to her side and kicked her savagely. Still she did not rise.

The Indian slipped his hatchet from his belt and weighed it momentarily before raising it above the woman's head.

Patterson, who had trotted down the line to find out what the delay was, spoke quickly to the man, halting the blow momentarily.

He knelt beside Sarah. "Ma'am, you have got to get up."

"I can't, Mr. Patterson, I've not got the strength." She raised her haunted eyes to him. "He's going to kill me, isn't he?"

Patterson nodded. It was inevitable; there was nothing he could do to stop it. He was humbled by the woman's courageous acceptance of her fate.

"Ask him if he will permit me a moment to pray."

Patterson spoke; the Indian nodded.

He helped her to a kneeling position. She bowed her head in silent prayer.

Patterson stood erect, not daring to look at Judith. He hated what was about to happen, but he was powerless to prevent it.

"Mr. Patterson," Sarah said. "I've made my peace with the Almighty—I'm ready now."

She bowed her head a second and last time.

Judith turned away as the hatchet fell. She placed her body between that of Sarah and the child, shielding from the child's sightless eyes the murder of its mother.

She heard the hatchet strike bone, and she heard the gust of breath that escaped Sarah's lips as her lungs collapsed.

She thought it was over, but when she turned, the Indian had placed his bare foot against Sarah's neck and was cutting a circle in the crown of her scalp.

Judith watched with horror as the scalp came free with a sickening, tearing noise.

The Indian shook his grisly trophy to rid it of excess blood, then tucked it into his belt. He motioned for the column to move on, and without a word they resumed their trek.

As the day grew long, the baby began to fret. Judith was overwhelmed with tenderness for the child as it nudged and searched her clothed breast for the nipple that it fully expected to find there.

227

"You poor thing," crooned Judith as the baby began to wail with hunger. The cries intensified with each passing moment.

Patterson appeared beside Judith, matching his stride with hers.

"Judith, you must quieten the baby."

"She's hungry, Morgan. What can I do?"

"I know not, but you had best do something."

Even as he spoke, the line came to a shuffling halt.

"Put your hand over her mouth," warned Patterson as a Shawnee warrior approached.

Judith immediately slipped her palm over the infant's lips, choking off the angry wail.

The Shawnee brushed past Patterson to stand before Judith, staring stonily.

The baby squirmed and thrashed and, even though Judith tried to keep her hand over its mouth, the child managed to break free. A loud wail shattered the evening stillness.

The Indian snatched the child from Judith and held her high above his head. Judith reached for the infant but the Indian knocked her hands aside.

"Morgan, make him give my baby back! She won't cry anymore, I promise you." Judith's eyes were pools of liquid fright.

Patterson turned his back and walked away. Judith's pleading voice followed. "Please, Morgan. Please!"

She was crying—tears of one who is terrified of what is to come, yet powerless to stop it.

But Patterson was powerless also. He had already intervened too many times for her. One more act of kindness, white-man kindness, could bring every bronze skin in the forest down on him and the women.

He continued walking.

The Shawnee pushed Judith aside, causing her to stumble and fall. She sprang to her feet, but even that short space of time had been sufficient.

The Indian caught the infant by the ankles, and with a powerful thrust, burst the child's head against the trunk of a tall pine.

Patterson heard the sound, like a ripe melon splitting. He spun on his heel. Anger engulfed him, and he lunged several steps toward the Indian before he was able to check himself.

Judith stood transfixed, a figurine of finely chiseled wax. Only her hair, as it rustled in the breeze, gave proof that she was alive.

The grinning Indian held the pulpy corpse of the child out to Judith as she took a slow, labored step toward him. The grin vanished, and astonished terror suffused his painted face. He stepped back, drawing his hatchet as Judith wobbled toward him. He said something to the girl, but Patterson was unable to catch the words. Then, to the added horror of all who watched, he nervously struck at Judith with the tomahawk.

Actually, he used the weapon only to push Judith away, not intending to harm her. The razor-edged blade, however, caught her in the forehead, opening a deep incision that arched from her hairline to her eyebrow.

Heedless of the gushing blood, Judith took the child from the warrior's trembling hand and held it to her bosom. As she kissed the mangled, tiny lips, blood from her forehead mixed with that of the battered infant. Then she threw back her head and laughed hysterically—until the moment she passed out.

Susan and Ivy sprang forward to catch her as she fell, but they were too late.

Patterson sprinted to the fallen girl and knelt, cradling her blood-soaked face in his rough hands.

Indians began to gather, mouthing fast unintelligible sentences and gesturing wildly.

The Shawnee who had slain the child pointed at the unconscious girl with a shaking hand and spoke rapidly to the assembled red men.

Almost as one, they retreated and studied her prostrate form with what appeared to be shocked reverence.

Susan, kneeling beside Patterson, stared at the excited warriors. "They act crazy, Morgan. They frighten me."

Patterson gently slapped Judith's cheek in an effort to awaken her. "They haven't gone crazy," he said, refusing to meet Susan's eyes. "But..."

"But what?" asked Ivy, forcing him to look at her. *"But what?"* she repeated, fear inching into her words.

"But I'm not at all sure about Judith," he said, as he continued to cuff the unconscious girl's face.

Ivy laughed nervously. "What do you mean?"

"I don't know—maybe nothing. You saw it, same as I did...I don't know!"

Judith's eyelids flickered and opened. Patterson breathed a sigh of relief, but it was short-lived. He turned his head, his lips compressing into a grim line. Judith's eyes were dull and clouded, the pupils unseeing. Her mind had slipped into a world beyond the reach of mortals.

Ivy went wild. She caught Judith's shoulders and shook her savagely, shouting her name. Judith's unblinking eyes stared straight ahead, showing not a hint of understanding.

"Oh, God!" cried Susan as full realization of Judith's madness penetrated her like a razor-edged knife.

Ivy drew Judith to her and rocked back and forth, whimpering softly, "No, Lord, please don't do this to her...not to her...please, Lord."

Patterson was inclined to agree with Ivy. Judith was too animated, too full of life to be struck mindless, to live in the void of the insane—it just wasn't fair, somehow.

Yet the French officer was quite correct when he looked into Judith's sightless eyes and crossed himself; she had entered a world within herself, a safe and beautiful world that left her face serene and peaceful like that of a contented child.

Patterson examined the wound on Judith's forehead. It was a clean cut that would heal nicely if it didn't get infected. She would be scarred for life, but what did it matter now? He tried to remove the mass of tiny flesh that she wildly clung to, but she cried so pitifully that he abandoned the effort.

The French captain, so eager to possess Judith the night before, looked into her bloody face and blank eyes.

"Monsieur Fontaine," he ordered in French, "have the savages kill her. She is worth nothing to us now."

"Capitaine," Fontaine replied, piercing the officer with a hard gaze. "No Indian that ever lived would harm a hair on this woman's head. They believe that crazy people have been touched by the hand of God. If you even looked as though you would hurt her, they would cut you into little pieces and feed you to the curs."

The captain blanched as he visualized Fontaine's description of his demise. He turned to Patterson. "Monsieur, can she travel?"

"I'll carry her if she can't," replied Patterson in a flat voice. "The lady will not slow us down."

"Very good, monsieur."

"Judith?" said Patterson, watching her eyes for recognition of her name, seeing none. He shook her gently to try and catch her attention.

"Judith, we must go."

Judith drew her legs beneath her and struggled to stand.

"Thank the Lord she understands when she is spoken to," breathed Susan.

They traveled at a rapid, but not bone-tiring pace. Judith was placed between Susan and Ivy in the long line of humans that weaved through primeval hardwood forest. The girls found the traveling much easier than that to which they were accustomed, for their flight with Patterson had been over the roughest terrain, where men normally did not go.

In less than a week of westward travel they had recrossed the mountains and were standing on the banks of the Allegheny River.

Black Fish approached Patterson, his face troubled.

"My son," he commenced after taking Patterson aside, "we have many canoes hidden close by; they will carry us to the big river...the Ohio."

Patterson watched the old warrior closely, aware that something important was being said.

"We have been a week on the trail," the Shawnee continued, "and the weather is hot."

Patterson nodded, wishing Black Fish would get to the point.

"My son, the woman with the golden hair must give up the child. The infant has too long been dead; the stench is overpowering, blowflies swarm, and the maggots crawl. We wish no further harm to the woman...but we cannot take the child downriver—it is not right."

Patterson studied the river a long moment. "My father has been more than patient," he said finally. "I will take the baby tonight when my slave sleeps. My father is right; the time is overdue."

Patterson told Susan and Ivy of Black Fish's request. They

agreed that something had to be done, but they were fearful of the consequences.

"She might die, Morgan," Ivy cautioned, running her hand over her face in a forlorn gesture.

"It is a chance we have to take."

Susan, quiet thus far, spoke: "Maybe not. I saw a doll among the plunder...it's not as big as the baby, but if we wrap it in a blanket..."

"'Tis worth a try," said Patterson, delighted by Susan's idea.

That night he searched out the Shawnee who owned the doll and explained why he needed it.

The Indian immediately ransacked his booty, finally locating the raggedy doll.

Patterson waited until midnight and cautiously approached Judith's slumbering form.

He studied her innocent face, and then slowly removed the putrefying infant from her side, replacing it with the doll.

The stench of the maggot-infested, rotting flesh gagged him. He bolted madly for the river and cast the small bundle into the fast-moving current. Then he bathed from head to toe, using harsh sand to scrub his skin.

They watched when Judith awoke the next morning. She kissed the doll, as she had the child every morning for the past week, and held it close against her bosom, crooning softly.

Fontaine strolled close to Patterson.

"The mam'selle, she is all right?" He nodded toward Judith.

"She's all right," replied Patterson as Fontaine moved on past him toward where Ivy stood staring at the river.

"I am sorry about Mam'selle Judith," he said to the girl.

"We are all upset because of it, Mr. Fontaine." She glanced at Judith's blank face. "It seems so senseless..."

"There is reason for everything, my Ivy, even the things that appear...senseless, eh?"

"I know, Mr. Fontaine. But knowing does not help very much—I am angry with the Lord just now."

"Ah! Do not say such a thing!" counseled the Frenchman, crossing himself and eyeing Ivy woefully.

"Well, I am!" cried the girl. "She has been through so much already; He did not have to do this to her."

Fontaine smiled sadly. "Ivy, you are, what? Naive? Oui, that is the word, naive. You make a man have the troubled thoughts. You are so much the child—yet, so much the woman, too." He took her hands tenderly in his and caressed her small fingers. "Judith, she has not been through anything that you have not been through, eh? No! She has been through even less. Yet you never complain. Ah, ma petite, to have a woman such as you..."

"Please, Mr. Fontaine," blushed Ivy, removing her hands. "Your words embarrass me. I—I find them exciting, I will admit, but I wish you would not say such things."

"I would say many more things, if I thought you would but listen."

Ivy shook her head, hiding her eyes that he might not see the turbulence his few intimate words had caused in her.

She longed for only one man, and in finding that Fontaine could arouse her emotionally, she condemned herself for being faithless.

"No, monsieur," she said quietly, "I would not listen."

Fontaine's face dropped, then brightened into a wide smile. "Someday—you will listen!"

Ivy smiled also, at ease again. "Perhaps, sir—perhaps."

Susan joined Patterson at the river. He was watching the Indians raise ten thirty-foot birchbark war canoes that had been scuttled in the shallows of the Allegheny.

"We bathed Judith," she said softly, not looking at him. "It was awful, Morgan. I hope I never smell that smell again." She shuddered, and turned her attention to the Indians.

"Where are they taking us, Morgan?"

"Does it matter?"

"I guess it doesn't—we have no choice, do we?"

"No."

"Are you angry, Morgan?"

"Yes, I am angry."

"At me...or Ivy...or Judith?"

"No," he said, lips forming a grim line. "I'm angry at me."

She took his hand and turned him toward her.

"What is it?"

He didn't answer her directly. All he said was: "I have made a hell of a mess of things, Susan."

Then he moved away, to join the Indians as they laid the lightweight crafts in the sun to dry.

No, Morgan, she thought, as she watched him walk away. *You have done everything possible to secure our safety.*

"Get Ivy and Judith, and be ready to shove off at a moment's notice," he called as the Indians laid the last canoe on the bank.

She nodded and ran off to locate Ivy and Judith.

Patterson watched her sprint down the edge of the river in search of her two companions. There was something about her...She was dependable—all the girls were—even Judith, in her own way. But that was before....He shook his head to clear his aching mind. He blamed himself for Judith's condition. If only he had tried to save the child—but he hadn't.

To ease his suffering, he joined the Indians and worked feverishly patching the seams of the canoes with pine tar and preparing them for travel. The men were excited, for it would not take long to run downstream to the Ohio and then to Chillicothe. They had been in no hurry before reaching the river, but now they were anxious. They wished to be home, to show off the plunder, scalps, and prisoners they had taken.

Patterson glanced at the captives huddled together on the riverbank. They were mostly women, listless, terrified, confused, desolate. Their eyes were those of trapped animals. He put them out of his mind; they were not his problem.

Patterson, Fontaine, and the three women were assigned a canoe that was loaded to the gunwales with plunder. Patterson guessed that none of the warriors wanted to ride with a madwoman, so he, Fontaine, and the girls were given a cargo craft. He wondered about Fontaine's presence. Perhaps he had been placed in the canoe to ensure that they did not wander away, or become lost.

Patterson doubted that Black Fish would consider such a thought, but the French officer had a suspicious mind and kept a watchful eye.

The two men bent their backs, their muscles rippling, as they paddled into the current. When they reached midstream, they backpaddled, as canoe after canoe passed. When half the flotilla was strung out ahead of them, they maneuvered their heavily loaded craft into line.

They made excellent time going downriver. The current was swift, and the lightweight canoes fairly skimmed the surface.

They did not slow their speed as they approached Fort Duquesne but pushed on into the waters of the broad Ohio.

Patterson gave a sigh of relief as they swept around a bend, and in moments were completely hidden from the watchful eyes of the Duquesne garrison.

He had been sure that they would be signaled in and questioned at length, but the flagman standing on the parapet had waved them past without ceremony.

"Ah, m'sieur," said Fontaine, "I was sure we would be called in to be examined, but, bien, we are lucky, are we not?"

Patterson dipped his paddle to match the rhythm of Fontaine's and ignored the question.

Fontaine shrugged, and smiled widely at Ivy. "He is so untrusting, eh!"

They traveled all day without a break, finally pointing the canoes toward shore just before dusk.

Susan, Ivy, and Judith were helped ashore by Fontaine, as Patterson stood waist-deep in the swirling water at the river's edge and held the canoe steady.

Susan and Ivy immediately went in search of wood for a fire. The two men beached the light craft and disappeared into the tall timber carrying their guns.

Judith stood on the riverbank holding the doll close, her eyes glassy. She did not respond when the French officer approached.

"Mam'selle," he said, watching her closely for a reaction, "it is such a shame that you are mindless. One so beautiful should be alive, to enjoy the world around her." He touched her shoulder where her torn dress revealed sun-browned skin. There was no reaction.

His eyes narrowed as he studied her and a flicker of interest shone in their depths.

He caressed her shoulder, moving his hand gently across her

neck, then toward her breast where the doll lay in gentle embrace. As his hand neared the swell of her bosom, she whimpered and drew away, clutching the doll tightly against her body.

He studied her closely as she hugged the bundle to her and rocked it gently. It struck him that she was not turning away from his touch; instead, she had withdrawn for fear he might harm the doll.

"I will not hurt your child," he breathed, watching her closely as he again laid his hand on her shoulder. "I wish merely to see the baby—it is so lovely."

Judith continued to hum softly to the doll, now and then laying her cheek against the top of its head and kissing it.

The Frenchman's fingers played across her shoulders and down her back. She did not move as his hand dallied at her small waist, nor did she acknowledge the fact that it dropped even lower and fondled her buttocks.

He smiled, pleased with his discovery. Then, to be sure he was correct in his suspicions, he moved his hand again toward the doll. Judith's reaction was identical to the first time.

"A man can do with you as he pleases," he said to her, "so long as he does nothing to endanger the doll. This could prove exciting, very exciting, indeed!"

He glanced toward the forest where Ivy and Susan were gathering wood. "I will see you again, my crazy one—you can depend on it."

He walked away, his laughter mingling with the sound of Judith's tuneless humming.

They camped on the banks of the Ohio that night. Their campfires stretched for several hundred yards; the reflections shimmered brightly with each ripple of the current.

Susan laid back on her elbows and watched the river. "It is so different from the tidewater country where I live," she said to Patterson.

"Do you like it? This country, I mean?" He gazed at the darkened forest that surrounded them.

Susan didn't answer for a long moment. "I think I could learn to like it," she said finally. "I think I could learn to love any place, so long as..." Her voice trailed off, leaving the crackling of the fire loud in the stillness.

236

"As what?" prompted Patterson.

"So long as it was as peaceful as this," she lied, wondering why he could not see the truth.

"She is peaceful, is she not!" cried Fontaine from across the embers. "But that is not what you were about to say, Mam'selle Susan. You were—"

"Mr. Fontaine!" protested Susan, rising quickly to a sitting position.

Fontaine waved her back. "Forgive me, mam'selle. My big mouth, she is like flannel, always flapping in the wind."

"You do seem to have a lot to say, sir," said Ivy coyly, for even she had understood Susan's meaning.

"Ah!" said Fontaine, his white teeth sparkling in the firelight. "But every word I say, she is true—no?"

"Hell, no," laughed Patterson, in his slow, easy drawl.

"Well, I'll be a bloody Englishman—eh!" breathed Fontaine in mock seriousness. "His face, she did not break when he laughs!"

Patterson's laughter dwindled, but a smile remained and perhaps even broadened as Ivy and Susan laughed aloud.

"I love it when you laugh, Morgan," said Susan after a moment's pause. "You should do it more often."

Patterson's face clouded, and before they could protest, he climbed to his feet and disappeared into the darkness.

Susan watched him go, then turned to stare into the fire. "I also have a big mouth, Mr. Fontaine," she said.

"Mam'selle," said the Frenchman, "do not give up. I believe you are good for him."

His sincerity touched her, causing her to look again into the darkness where Patterson had disappeared.

"Mr. Fontaine," she said, not turning, "everything I say is wrong."

"I do not think this is true, mam'selle. I think he needs you very, very much."

Ivy sucked in her breath, a small gasping sound in the darkness.

"Are you all right?" asked Fontaine, turning toward the servant girl.

"I must see to Judith," said Ivy, gaining her feet and moving quickly away from the glow of the campfire.

"Did I say the wrong thing?" inquired the Frenchman as he turned back to Susan.

"It depends on which of us you were addressing a moment ago, sir," returned Susan with a sad smile. She changed the subject before he could reply.

"Mr. Fontaine, how far is this place we are going...Chillicothe?"

Fontaine met Susan's eyes. "Almost five hundred miles, mam'selle."

"That far?" asked Susan with a sinking heart.

"Oui, mam'selle. But the river, she is swift.... If we bend our backs from dawn to dusk, we can make a hundred miles a day."

We'll never get back, thought Susan, comparing the short distance they had traveled prior to their capture.

"But the journey," continued the Frenchman, "she will be easy for you. It is the woodsman and I, Fontaine, who will build our muscles and break our backs to keep up with the ten paddlers in the other canoes."

"Can we help, Ivy and I?"

"Non, ma chérie." He smiled. "Alas, it would be nice to see the deerskin stretch tight across your chest..." He laughed heartily then, as Susan's hand flew to her bust. "But," he continued, "you would disrupt my rhythm, and Monsieur Patterson would not like it."

"Fontaine," said Susan, laughing also, "you are a rogue, sir."

"I am that!" said the Frenchman, throwing back his head and guffawing lustily.

13

Patterson raised up on his knees so he could see over Fontaine's head as the canoe they paddled came in sight of the Indian village far ahead on the banks of the Little Miami River. He studied the landscape, the dwellings, the sky beyond.

And without realizing it, his mind drew vivid pictures of the first trip that had brought him to the very same town he now approached by water.

It had been by horse that first time—riding double with his father. He remembered it well—and the reason behind it.

Joseph, with Morgan on the saddle behind him, calmly reloaded his pistol. The body of the preacher lay sprawled in the doorwell, twisted and bent in the last throes of death. Morgan looked steadily at the body.

"Did you kill him, father?"

"Aye, son, I did."

"Why?"

"For your mother, Morgan."

The boy laid his cheek against his father's broad back and cried for his dead mother. It would be the last time in his life he would shed a tear for a white woman. They had ridden from Schenectady, New York, then, passing several outlying farms and cabins as they progressed deeper into the frontier. Occasionally, they would stop at a cabin to rest the horse or barter for provisions, and after they had disappeared into the wilderness, likely as not the woman would turn to her man and say, "A strange lad, that 'un. Nigh wouldn't let me touch him." Then she would frown. "Seemed scared to death of me."

And indeed the child was. Recurring nightmares of howling fiendish women ripping away his mother's clothing terrified the boy.

They rode for days, sometimes on well-marked trails, sometimes on faint paths, but mostly where no trails were, where every tree looked like the next one, and every hill identical to the one they had just crossed. They swam the mighty Ohio River, he on his father's back, Joseph holding on to the horse's tail.

Finally they arrived at their destination, an Indian town on the banks of the Little Miami River, called Chillicothe. It was a large town even by English standards, with bark-covered wigwams laid out in an orderly pattern, and a wide-open stretch down the middle to serve as a street. The industry there was equal to that of most English cities.

Young Morgan surveyed the town through the enlarged eyes of a scared, yet interested, five-year-old. Not everything he saw was alien to him. He recognized a tobacco patch and, beyond that, the tasseled heads of cornstalks in neatly laid rows. Also, there were fields of pumpkin, beans, and squash, and unlike the white man who used a straw-filled scarecrow to discourage predators, the Shawnee had built a covered platform in which an elderly man sat and performed that slight yet necessary task. It was his job, his service to the community and he took it seriously because, although aged, he was still needed and he measured his worth by that need.

Sunflowers, with faces as large as a man's head, grew on the outer fringes of the fields. Never had Morgan seen such huge flowers. Racks of meats cut into thin strips were drying in the afternoon sun.

Women were tanning hides, scraping away the unwanted flesh with bone implements and staking them out to dry. Others were grinding corn with mortar and pestle while still others were hoeing or weeding the fields. Morgan noted the open-air temple with its ceremonial fire burning bright. But he neither knew nor cared that the red man took his religion just as seriously as his white brothers. He was soon to learn, however.

Noise attracted his attention to a passel of dogs and children scampering wildly down the dusty street toward them.

Leaving the wide-eyed boy astride the horse, Joseph dismounted and walked to a large arched wigwam and called out a greeting, using a language Morgan had never heard before. A moment later an Indian threw back the skin flap that served as a door and stepped into the sunlight. Others began to gather, curious about the intrusion. Joseph spoke to the man, indicating Morgan with a sweep of his arm. The red man looked long at the boy, then walked to the horse and gently lifted him down. A beautiful Indian woman emerged from the wigwam and, before Morgan could protest, lifted him high and hugged him tightly against her bare bosom. Then she gently set him down. Morgan ran to his father and locked himself to Joseph's leg. Everyone laughed.

Morgan peeped shyly at the people around him. They were strange indeed. The men had roached heads and wore nothing on their bodies except a small breechcloth. The long hair of the women fell the entire length of their naked backs; a wraparound skin skirt, resembling a kilt, halted just above their knees. Neither men nor women wore moccasins. The children wore nothing at all.

Upset at the nakedness he saw, Morgan brought it to his father's attention, and Joseph, ignorant of his boy's turmoil, told Morgan that only white folk believed exposure of the body to be a great sin. So, Morgan Patterson, at age five, had the notion embedded in his young mind that a white person should never expose his or her body to another white. That idea would follow him into manhood.

Joseph explained to Morgan that the Indians were his friends; that they were of the Shawnee tribe. Morgan looked again at the faces surrounding him. Nowhere did he encounter an unfriendly expression. The Indian woman who had hugged him knelt before him and opened her arms invitingly. He clung more tightly to his father's leg. The woman smiled understandingly, then stood up and spoke at length to Joseph, frowning and glancing at the boy every now and then. Joseph explained to the woman what had happened in Schenectady. The listening array of men, women, and children was astonished. The women's eyes grew large and they put their hands over their mouths in the Indian gesture of disbelief. The men crossed their arms, lips compressed into thin lines. Never, in all the years that Morgan would live with the Shawnee, was the tragedy mentioned again. Indians rarely, if ever, intruded on one's privacy.

That night Joseph explained to Morgan his intention. The boy was to live with the Shawnee as the adopted son of the young Black Fish (who would years later adopt another white man as a son—Daniel Boone) and his wife, Wawega ("Born in the Ferns"). The couple had readily agreed to raise Morgan as their own, for Indians loved children—any and all children. The boy protested, but Joseph was stern as he explained that Morgan was to stay with the Indians and learn the ways of the forest and of the people who inhabited the vast unknown regions where white men never ventured.

Joseph explained to Morgan that he had been visiting Chillicothe off and on since 1720. He told the boy about his trips up and down the Miami, Scioto, and Maumee rivers, and he confided to Morgan that future expansion of the British colonies would some-day encompass even the Ohio River and take in the mystic hunting grounds called *Kentakey*.

He did not tell Morgan that the red men had politely, yet firmly, refused to grant him permission to enter those "dark and bloody grounds."

It was his desire, he said, that Morgan, given the chance, might succeed where he had failed and visit the land of tall cane. He went on to paint a vivid picture of the dream he and Victoria had shared concerning their son: a picture of fame, fortune, and adventure.

"But now," he said, holding the boy tightly, "with your mother gone, fame is suddenly without meaning, for the only joy of being famous comes from the fact that you impress someone special. And there is no living soul, besides you, son, whom I wish to impress.

"As for fortune, we are already monetarily wealthy—but, remember always, we laid our greatest riches gently to rest in the Schenectady soil." Joseph looked deeply into the boy's pale eyes. "For her sake, son, we will conquer new horizons—the very essence of life itself—for that is what she would have wanted."

He talked the night away—of a nation marching westward; of civilization moving in its wake; and they, the Pattersons, leading the vanguard.

The boy listened but understood very little of what Joseph was saying. Morgan remembered enough, however, so that when he did accompany a hunting party of Shawnees into the Kentucky country—four years before the first documented account of a white man setting foot there, Dr. Thomas Walker in 1750—he made certain to memorize in detail the trails and landmarks of the trip, especially the trail through "quasiots," the gateway to the land of tall cane, which Walker would rename the Cumberland Gap.

But as Joseph took the five-year-old in his arms that morning and hugged him close, Kentucky was still a dream and there were realities that needed discussing, for time was running short.

He tried very patiently to explain to Morgan that he had pressing business in England which, very possibly, would keep him away a long while.

"How long?" inquired the boy awkwardly.

"For weeks and weeks," said Joseph tenderly. (Had he known that it would take almost five long years to plead his case before the British Board of Trade—five years away from his son—and nine additional years before the ratification of the actual charter granting a group of prominent Virginians, Joseph included, five hundred thousand acres in the upper Ohio Valley, he very likely would not have left Morgan at Chillicothe, but would have taken the boy to England where he could have guided his early training, and probably, changed the boy's views of human nature.)

The next morning Joseph rode away, and for the next five years Morgan lived as a Shawnee, the son of Black Fish and Wawega.

In time, Wawega won Morgan's confidence and affection, and Black Fish won his admiration and respect. The boy was happy living with the Indians. He learned quickly and, more important, remembered what he had been taught. As a result, he became a favorite of the town.

When Morgan was ten his father returned. Joseph recognized his son by his blue eyes only, for all else was Indian in every respect.

The tall lad wore his hair well below his shoulders, and his thin well-muscled frame, naked except for the traditional breechcloth, was as dark as the Shawnee. But even more disturbing was the fact that Morgan remembered very little of the English language. So, immediately after erecting a log cabin on the edge of town, Joseph set to reeducating his son in the ways of white men and the king's English.

"Son," Joseph had laughed, "you are a disgrace to your white blood; the savage you have become." His eyes had misted then and he said softly: "But you are a pride unto my eyes—come! Let us make amends."

Joseph proved to be a gifted taskmaster. Yet even then it was a remarkable feat, for Morgan's education was accomplished at six-month intervals, because circumstances demanded Joseph's presence, at least the equivalent to that amount of time, in the circles of the civilized business world to which he was committed.

So, during each of Joseph's six-month intervals at the cabin, Morgan would move his belongings there and spend a great portion of that time relating all he had seen and experienced in his treks through the wilderness with his Shawnee patrons. Joseph would listen closely to his son's descriptions of the distant country and draw maps and make notes of Morgan's sojourns, while at the same time teaching the lad to read and write, as well as the basics of mathematics. Then he would return to his Virginia residence and use the newly acquired information on the Ohio country to compile ledgers, concentrating on the particular area Morgan had covered that year.

When the boy turned thirteen his father broached the subject of returning to the east. Morgan was against it, stating firmly, "Father, I have no love for the British. They are a cruel and deceitful people." But Joseph was persistent and Morgan finally agreed, taking sorrowful leave of his foster parents.

They returned to Virginia, taking basically the same route of travel used on their journey to the Ohio country. Only this time, when they stopped to replenish supplies or perhaps to pass the time of day, the tall lad who stepped lightly from his horse and stood quietly resting his long gun in the crook of his arm brought a far different response from the inhabitants of cabins.

As the broad shoulders of father and son receded to the rhythm of their trotting horses, one woman who remembered the boy turned to her man, and said through pinched lips, "'Tis the same lad as passed here eight or ten years ago. But his eyes? Did you not see his awful eyes?"

The man, watching the departing horsemen, replied, "Nay, I did not notice his eyes, but he carried his gun well and moved easy as a red stick, and he was respectful to his father. 'Tis enough."

But it wasn't enough, and the woman shuddered, remembering the eyes, glad he was gone.

Only bits and snatches of his life with the Indians ever became public knowledge. A white hunter or two had chanced upon him in an Indian village where they were trading, and brought the story out when they returned to civilization. Otherwise, eight years of Morgan Patterson's life were lost in the wilderness of the Ohio Valley. Upon reaching Joseph's Virginia home, Morgan was immediately enrolled in school. There he continued till he was sixteen.

A year after Morgan had begun his studies, George Washington was enrolled. Both boys excelled in their subjects and became steadfast friends. Washington, however, won the favor of Lord Thomas Fairfax, who held enormous grants of land in Virginia beyond the Blue Ridge Mountains, and at the age of sixteen he quit school to enter Fairfax's employ as a land surveyor. Young Patterson continued his studies, but with less enthusiasm than he had formerly held for higher education.

Joseph, aware of his son's dwindling interest in scholarship, changed his tactics: he sent Morgan to the College of William and Mary in Williamsburg. "Learn to be a gentleman, son. The family needs at least one and I am too old to change my ways."

Morgan did indeed become a gentleman, and the more he learned about the ins and outs of aristocracy, the more he realized that Joseph Patterson was by far a greater gentleman than many of the prominent men who wore that exclusive title. Morgan smiled to himself, for it dawned upon him that his father had manipulated him for education's sake.

And I would probably still be at William and Mary if Washington hadn't dragged me back into buckskins, he thought, as he absently leaned on his canoe paddle.

"Can you not hear me, m'sieur? Are your ears not open?" shouted Fontaine from the bow of the canoe.

"Damn, m'sieur!" the Frenchman bellowed when he was certain that he had Patterson's attention.

"The canoe, she is drifting cockeyed!"

Patterson glanced about him. True, the light craft had drifted sideways to the current and was very close to capsizing.

Patterson dipped his paddle deep. The muscles of his arms and back stood rigid as he spun the canoe into the mainstream. He dipped the paddle again and the craft shot forward, once more headed toward the Indian town looming large before them.

Susan glanced over her shoulder. "Daydreaming, Mr. Patterson?" she grinned. "Do you wish to talk about your dreams?"

"I think not," he answered, breaking into a smile. Those were the words she had used when he had asked that question of her the day the bear had been killed.

Susan's grin broadened. "We will trade dreams, sometime," she said, but the words were lost in the confusion as he nosed the canoe toward the riverbank, where the entire population of the village gathered to welcome their returning warriors.

14

As the flotilla drew near the bank, Indians of all ages splashed into the shallows and laid hold of the canoes, guiding them to the shore and dragging them out of the water.

Susan and Ivy held tightly to the gunwales staring fearfully about them. There appeared to be thousands of Indians, shouting, dancing, laughing, and, yes, some of the elderly women were even crying—pandemonium prevailed.

Patterson bounded out of the canoe and, before Susan knew what was taking place, he gathered her into his arms and lifted her to the ground.

"Smile!" he whispered fiercely in her ear. "You are supposed to be the wife of a warrior—a Shawnee."

She and Patterson were happily ushered toward the town by Indians who knew and welcomed the woodsman.

Susan looked over her shoulder for Ivy and Judith, but the mass of red people had completely surrounded her and Patterson, cutting off her view. She tried to turn, to go back, but Patterson caught her elbow and propelled her forward with such force that only his iron grip kept her from stumbling.

She stole a glance at him. His face was stone, and it shocked her how much like an Indian he appeared. Warriors whom she recognized from the trip downstream were walking tall, faces

247

immobile, as they held high the scalps and trophies the raid had produced.

Susan felt sick seeing the hair of her countrymen displayed in such a fashion, but she steeled herself and worked hard to show no emotion.

The Indians escorted her and Patterson through the center of town toward a large open-sided structure. Food of every description was displayed under its elm bark roof.

"Did they know we were coming?" asked Susan, bewildered by the preparations that had evidently just been completed in honor of the returning warriors.

"Aye," said Patterson. "A runner was put ashore this morning. We had to go all the way to where the Little Miami meets with the Ohio, then back to here. We took the long way, the runner took the short route."

"I've never seen so much to eat!" Susan examined the food with the eyes of a person who had grown to hold nourishment almost in reverence.

"Remember this," cautioned Patterson. "The women eat after the men, no matter how hungry they are."

Susan smiled wryly. It didn't anger her. Whatever would keep her safe she would do.

Women brought even more wooden trays of food, and children were loaded down with firewood gathered from the nearby forest. Old men were dancing, and chanting, and shaking ancient scalplocks that told of younger days and honorable deeds in battle. Young men, not yet ready for the warrior's path, stood with arms folded in an attempt at dignity. But their faces were their downfall for they could not disguise their pride in the returning tribesmen.

Ivy's and Judith's treatment was entirely different from Susan's. They were snatched from the canoe and flung to the hard earth without ceremony. Ivy screamed at the people of Chillicothe to tell them that Judith did not understand their commands, but her words fell on deaf ears.

Fontaine watched from within the crowd, but he was in no position to help. The girls were captives. To show an interest in their well-being could very well be dangerous, not only to himself, but to them as well. So he observed the mistreatment of Judith and

Ivy in stony silence, knowing that he could not raise a finger in their defense.

They were dragged to their feet and pushed up the embankment on which the town sat. Indians blocked the path, giving way only when the women were thrust against them bodily by the throng that moved in their wake.

Ivy lost her balance and fell. She was kicked brutally several times before strong hands raised her to her feet. It was Fontaine. Then she was pushed ahead, knocked sideways, regained her balance only to be shoved again.

Judith was faring even worse. She was trying to keep her balance and protect the doll at the same time. She stumbled and fell.

The horde screamed triumphantly as they kicked and beat the girl.

She tried several times to regain her footing but each time she was again knocked to the ground.

Finally, from a desperation born of sheer self-preservation, she released her deathgrip on the doll. It was immediately snatched from her by a howling, naked child who quickly disappeared into the milling crowd.

Amid kicks and flailing arms that struck her body from all sides, Judith crawled to her feet. She stood there, swaying, searching for her lost child.

The crowd surged closer, screaming insults at her.

A knife flashed in the sunlight as an ancient squaw entwined her fingers in Judith's blonde curls. The old woman hacked at Judith's hair, then with a scream of triumph raised her gnarled hand high above her wrinkled face and proudly displayed her blonde trophy.

They swarmed around Judith like locusts, each trying to gain a prize before it was gone. And when they were finished, the girl stood there gazing sightlessly about her, understanding nothing that had happened. Her hair was ruined. In some places it might have measured three inches; in others it was cut to the scalp.

The Indians jeered and shouted, shaking hanks of blonde hair in Judith's uncomprehending face.

Then, one by one, the jeering ceased; the shouting slowed, then stopped.

The crowd fell silent, into an ominous silence—for Judith had bared her small breast to a bronze baby being held tightly in the arms of its mother, and as the terrified woman stumbled backward away from Judith, the girl's clouded blue eyes filled with great tears that overflowed and trickled down her cheeks.

Then Black Fish was there, raging, gesturing wildly, touching Judith's ravaged head with his large bronze hand, covering her naked breast.

The Indians drew back, staring at the girl. They made the sign of disbelief. And those who had cut away her hair moved cautiously forward and laid their blonde trophies at her feet.

Ivy, who was far ahead, wondered at the sudden change. The Indians had settled into a milling mass that spoke quietly and gestured toward the river. She wondered where Judith was.

She watched with dread curiosity as the throng parted to reveal Black Fish leading Judith by the hand up the embankment.

"Oh, dear God," breathed Ivy. "What have they done to her?"

She started toward Judith but a strong arm blocked her.

"Non, my Ivy," said Fontaine. "Black Fish will take care of her. He is furious that she has been mistreated."

"Her hair! My God, Fontaine, look what they've done!" cried Ivy as Judith approached. "They've scalped her; her hair is gone!"

"Non," reassured the Frenchman, "they have only taken locks as...mementos. They have not harmed her...perhaps a nick or a cut—"

"A nick, or a cut?" cried Ivy. "She has no hair! It's gone! Only scraggly tufts are left...give me your gun, Fontaine, give me your gun!"

Ivy attempted to snatch the Frenchman's musket from him, but Fontaine caught her around the waist and drew her to him.

"Stop it, Ivy!" he rumbled. "They will kill you if you try to go back. I swear to you on my mother's grave that no further harm will befall your mistress—look! The savages are already ashamed of what they do, eh?"

It was true. The Indians approached Judith as she passed, many of them gently touching her; others, with unmistakable shame visible on their dark faces, speaking softly to her. Nowhere was a hand or voice raised in anger.

Ivy leaned heavily against Fontaine as Black Fish led Judith past. The Frenchman tightened his arm about her reassuringly, then released her.

"Walk just behind Judith," he said, "close, but not too close. You will be safe there—hurry!"

Ivy did as she was told, moving quickly to her mistress and, as Fontaine had said, no one touched or abused her.

The remaining captives, however, were a different matter. They suffered the same punishment Judith and Ivy had endured, except their was no relief for them.

Ivy felt a twinge of guilt about her good fortune as the milling mass of savages turned their vengeance on those poor souls.

Susan clung to Patterson like a shadow, her wide inquisitive eyes taking in everything around her. There appeared to be hundreds of longhouses laid out in an orderly fashion. Cultivated fields stretched out beyond the town in the fertile river bottoms.

She was seeing basically the same sight Morgan Patterson had seen some fifteen years earlier, and she was just as awestruck as the five-year-old Patterson had been.

An Indian woman approached Patterson and caught his hand affectionately. He swept her into his arms and hugged her. She was not a pretty woman, for she had begun to wrinkle and grow heavy through the middle, as many an Indian woman did after reaching her midtwenties. Yet Susan could tell that she had once been a beauty.

"Wawega!" Patterson cried happily, as he held the woman at arm's length, surveying her from head to toe. "You are still as beautiful as you were when I left here eight long years ago!"

"Eight years ago I was a young woman, my son," she smiled, obviously pleased by the compliment.

Although Susan did not understand the Shawnee dialect, she did see the flush of pleasure that filled Wawega's round, bronze face. She is blushing, thought Susan, stunned, and in truth shocked by the display of open, honest emotion. She had always believed Indians to be nothing but savages, and she was unprepared for love and tenderness among them. "I had no idea Indian women blushed," she said without thinking.

"She blushes at compliments the same as you," replied Patterson shortly.

"I did not mean—I don't know what I meant," stammered the girl, obviously embarrassed, for she knew as she said it that Patterson was well aware of her white perceptions of Indians, and it left her feeling artless.

"I'm sorry, Morgan," she said, regretful of her thoughtless words. "I am ashamed of myself."

Wawega watched Patterson and Susan with interest. She did not understand the English words any more than Susan did the Shawnee language, but she knew Patterson was angry at something the young woman had said, and she knew the girl had apologized. She did not question Patterson about it, for it was none of her business, and the native dignity of an Indian forbade invading a husband and wife's privacy.

Patterson ignored Susan's attempt at making amends. Turning to Wawega he presented Susan as his bride, which the woman was already aware of, for word had traveled quickly that Patterson was bringing a wife to Chillicothe. The woman moved to Susan and embraced her, saying in Shawnee: "Welcome to Chillicothe, my daughter—wife of Patterson."

"Who is she, Morgan?" whispered Susan when Wawega released her. "And what did she say?"

"She is my adopted mother, the wife of Black Fish," said Patterson proudly. "She welcomed you, her daughter, to Chillicothe."

Susan smiled at the woman and hugged her close, then kissed her bronze cheek.

The Indian woman's hand flew to her face. She rubbed the spot the girl's lips had touched; wonder filled her large black eyes.

"Did I make another mistake, Morgan?" asked Susan.

"It is an English custom, mother," he quickly explained to the Indian; "a sign of affection and respect."

The woman's face lighted and she smiled shyly at Susan.

"Indians do not kiss, Susan," he said. "It is not their way—she did not understand."

Wawega took Susan's hand and motioned for her to follow. She told Patterson that she would take the girl to the cabin built by his white father, Joseph, and make her welcome.

Patterson thanked her. To Susan, he said: "My mother will take you to the cabin I grew up in. I hope you find it to your liking."

"I'm sure it will be fine, Morgan," said the girl from over her shoulder as Wawega whisked her away.

As the two women disappeared toward the outskirts of the town, Patterson headed back toward the river. He hadn't gone far when he stopped short, horrified. Then his face hardened again into its unreadable mask.

Black Fish was ushering Judith and Ivy toward a longhouse at the end of the street. Patterson could only stare as the girls walked past, taking in their badly used appearance.

Both girls were bruised and bleeding, their tattered dresses stained with dirt, mud, and grass where they had been knocked to the ground and beaten.

Ivy glanced into his face as she passed, but she quickly averted her eyes and stared at the ground. It embarrassed Patterson, that fleeting look she had given him, for somehow it had all but condemned him for neglecting her and Judith, and being directly responsible for their brutal treatment by the red people; as if he could have prevented it.

But it was the sight of Judith that tapped a long-forgotten emotion from deep within him—sympathy, a feeling that had been buried in the dark recesses of his mind since childhood. He very nearly reached out to her, so pitiful a sight was she as she trudged past him without recognition, her glazed eyes blank. The hatchet cut on her forehead was crusted with dried blood and dust, and her lower face was streaked where tears had channeled through the grime. Her free hand hung listlessly at her side, the fingers jerking occasionally from some mental tic caused by something known only to her. Then it hit him. The doll was gone. He glanced sadly at the deranged girl and wondered if it was the doll her fingers sought.

He watched until the women disappeared into the longhouse, and then he ventured toward the mass of jeering people who were tormenting the other captives.

He stood in the shadow of a longhouse and watched the Indians debase the captives, and, although he had been excited by the spectacle when he was a child, he found no intoxication in it now. He hated it.

I have changed, he decided as the crowd swept past with the white prisoners. I am white, no matter what I want to be. Torture sickens me as quickly as it does the weaklings I've so long held in

253

contempt. I am no better than they. Nay, I am worse, for I know what I am, while they do not know they are cowards.

He turned his eyes toward the building where Black Fish had taken the women. You would spit on me, my father, if you but knew my true feelings.

Little did the woodsman know, as he condemned himself for possessing compassion, that many of the eastern tribes had also sickened of the brutal ceremonies, especially the ritual of burning enemies at the stake, and had already abandoned the practice.

He turned and trudged wearily toward the cabin Joseph had built eleven years earlier.

Susan met him at the door. "Have you seen Judith and Ivy?" Patterson nodded.

"Are...are they all right?" She watched his face intently. Again he nodded.

"Will they be brought here, to live with us?"

"No," he said simply. "They will be housed with the other captives, except Judith. She will be allowed the freedom of the village, to come and go as she pleases."

"That's wonderful," retorted Susan sarcastically. "Do not the Indians know that she is not responsible for her actions, that she could hurt herself if she is not watched?"

"They know; they'll be watching her."

"I just wish she and Ivy were here with us," sighed the girl dispiritedly.

"Well they're not, so hush about it." He pushed past her and entered the room.

"Am I to be alone with you . . . in this cabin?" she asked, following him into the dark interior of the log house.

"No," he said heavily, "you will have a woman to help you with the chores. She will also sleep here."

"A slave?"

'Don't be so damned pious, Susan. No, she will not be a slave, but if she were, that would be all right too!"

The girl caught his arm and spun him toward her. "By whose standards would it be all right?" she asked angrily.

"By all that's holy!" said Patterson in disbelief. "Do you forget that half your Virginia planters own slaves? Do you further forget that you, as an indentured servant, are no more than a high-class slave?"

"I'll not sleep alone with you in this cabin," cried Susan.

"I told you, a woman will be here."

"A savage! Someone who lusts like a bitch in heat!" Susan's hand flew to her mouth in surprise. Her extraordinary outburst hung uncomfortably in the dark room, as if the words were misplaced and searched for their rightful owner.

"You've said all I wish to hear, Susan." Patterson turned toward the door. "You'll have your chaperone, but you can believe this—you shan't need her!" Then he was gone.

Susan stood alone, staring at the empty doorwell, full of fathomless regret. She was startled from her thoughts by a timid knock on the doorjamb. She had been so engrossed that she had not seen the woman standing just outside.

The woman spoke perfect English. "May I enter, or would it be better if I returned later?"

"No! Do enter. Please," said Susan quickly.

The woman dropped her eyes and curtsied, then entered the room. She was neither a young girl nor an old woman. She could have been from twenty to thirty, or more.

Susan gaped at the woman. She was naked from the waist up like all the Indian women. Her hair was brown and hung loosely down her back. Her gray eyes studied Susan with equal interest.

"Yes," she said at last to Susan's questioning look. "I am white. Does that bother the Mohawk princess?"

"Mohawk princess?" said Susan, forgetting momentarily who she pretended to be.

"Aye," returned the woman, "I have been given the honor of serving the wife of Patterson, the son of Black Fish. It is said you are a Mohawk princess."

Susan's mind raced. Should she tell the woman the truth, that she owned neither of those titles? Or should she play her role and see what developed? She decided upon the latter.

"What is your name?" she said with a lofty tone foreign to her nature.

"I am Blue Bird," answered the woman with such alarming timidness that Susan immediately regretted her pretentious mannerisms.

"What is your Christian name?" she said, smiling sweetly at the nervous woman.

"When I was taken by the Indians, over ten years ago, my name was Abigail, but I have not been called by that name for a long time."

"You have been here for ten years?"

"Aye," said the woman, "probably eleven, or twelve."

"Are you a slave, or a captive?"

"Oh, no!" said the woman, drawing proudly to her full height. "I am Blue Bird, the wife of a warrior."

"The wife of an Indian?" Susan was incredulous.

"Do you find that disgusting?" asked the woman. "You of all people should understand, for you are married to a white—is there a difference?"

"You are right," replied Susan hastily. "Are you happy, living with the Indians?"

"Oh, yes. I am well treated, and my husband is a good provider. What more could I ask?"

"Indeed!" said Susan, thinking how simple were the ways of Indian women: treat them kindly, keep them well fed, and they would be perfectly satisfied. "Love," she said softly. "There must be love somewhere in the scheme of life to make it perfect."

The woman nodded uncertainly, thinking that love mattered little when one was dying of famine because her husband was a poor hunter. She changed the subject.

"I have brought skins for you and your husband's bed, and I am to escort you to the feast tonight."

Susan blushed, and almost panicked as she realized that she would be forced to sleep under the same robes as Morgan. "The feast?" she asked, in an attempt to sidestep the issue. "What is it in honor of?"

"Why, the return of our warriors," said Abigail with mounting excitement, "and the scalps and plunder that have brought honor and wealth to our town."

"Lord," thought Susan, watching the woman intently, "she talks as white as I, but she thinks as red as any Indian."

She was glad that she had not told Abigail the truth. That she had even considered revealing the secret left her shaken.

15

The feast began at sundown with the entire populace of the village present. It was a festive occasion, with laughter, singing, and loud banter pitched back and forth across the open space that surrounded the sideless, roofed-over structure that housed the food.

It could be a holiday in any town in the colonies, thought Susan, as she and Abigail moved toward the crowd that was gathered in what the white people would have called the town square or village green.

She tried to locate Patterson among the milling, laughing people, but he was not to be seen. She also looked for Judith and Ivy, but she knew it was only wishful thinking—they were not present.

Abigail spoke to several women as she and Susan passed. The women spoke in return, and cast appraising glances that were not lost on Susan. She was being evaluated and sized up, just as if she were at a social event in Williamsburg. She almost laughed outright, so at home was she at that particular moment.

They entered the building and moved directly to the food. Susan was ravenous and wasted no time in helping herself, stuffing her mouth full as the other women were doing. She ate corn, beans, and squash with her fingers and thought nothing of it. As she chewed, her eyes searched nervously for Patterson.

Abigail finally declared that she was full. Susan readily agreed, saying that her eyes had been bigger than her stomach; she had eaten hardly anything, yet she too was full.

"It is the way with one who has eaten little for several days," said Abigail. "The stomach grows small. You are starved but you cannot eat."

Susan grinned at the woman. "You too have been hungry. I find that surprising."

"All of us go hungry in the winter," said the woman. "It is the way of the Indian. Eat and waste when there is plenty; go hungry the rest of the time."

"Do you not store grain and vegetables?" asked Susan.

"Yes, we have storage bins for corn and such. But they never seem to last all winter."

As Abigail talked, Susan glanced at the crowd that milled aimlessly in the building. But it wasn't Patterson whom she saw—it was Ivy.

The servant girl, along with several other captives, was weighted down so heavily with wooden trenchers of leftover food that she fairly staggered under the heavy burden.

Susan had to restrain herself to keep from running across the room and taking Ivy in her arms. It was obvious, even from where Susan stood, that Ivy had suffered cruelly.

Abigail, who had noticed Susan staring at the captives, explained: "It is just the slaves clearing the podium in preparation for the orators who will speak shortly. Pay them no mind; they are less than dogs."

Susan continued to watch as Ivy made her way slowly out of the building and staggered toward the wigwams that formed the town. Had she been able, Susan would have gladly taken a portion of the heavy load off Ivy's frail shoulders, but that was out of the question—even she knew better than to attempt anything so foolish. But it was well timed when Abigail took Susan's hand at that precise moment and drew the girl away, saying, "Come, it is time for the speeches to begin."

They hurried from the building and joined the women and children who formed loose semicircles around the structure. Then, as if a silent command had been given, the Indians seated themselves in that peculiar cross-legged way they seemed to prefer.

Again Susan searched for Patterson, her eyes roving over the crowd. Again she was disappointed. The men formed loose half circles between the women and the podium and seated themselves.

Susan spotted Patterson then; he and several Indians had just arrived from the longhouses. They quietly entered the open-sided building that Susan and Abigail had just vacated.

Patterson did not glance at her, and Susan found the rebuff painful. He is still angry because of our silly quarrel, she decided. Well, I don't care! But she did care; her guileless face revealed all.

Quiet was settling over the seated assemblage. The attention of each was drawn to the center of the structure, where several chiefs and the French officer were making their entry. Fontaine was there, standing quietly off to one side, and Patterson crossed the room to take a position beside him.

Black Fish walked to the center of the building and faced the audience. He raised his arm and a hush fell over the crowd.

Abigail interpreted for Susan.

"Shawnee," he said, his voice rich with emotion, "we are honored to have guests join in our feast for the return of our warriors. The French and Hurons have traveled a great distance to join in these festivities. They are our friends and allies, and will stay with us until such time as they see fit to return to New France with the prisoners we took while running the warrior's path."

He droned on and on, explaining the French mission to Chillicothe, the upcoming war with Britain, the raid he and his warriors had just completed, and the glorious future for the red man once the English were driven from the Ohio country.

Susan was impressed with the man's statesmanship and dignified mien.

Then, one by one, other Shawnee took the stand to speak of past wars, and honor, and great feats. Susan studied the men in awe as Abigail interpreted. These were an intelligent people, she realized.

"Are all of them chiefs?" whispered Susan to Abigail during a change of speakers.

"No," explained the woman. "They are orators from a particular clan, but because they speak well and appear to lead the people, the whites call them chiefs. We think it is very amusing."

Susan blushed. It embarrassed her to find that while the white man held the Indians in such fine contempt, the red man was laughing all the time.

Then the Hurons took the stand, and the speeches continued.

Susan began to ache from sitting in the same position for so long, but she gritted her teeth and endured.

When DeBeaujue finally addressed the audience, Susan forgot her discomfort, for as the officer made promises and pledges to the Shawnee, Fontaine interpreted for Patterson, who interpreted for the Shawnee.

Susan found herself watching Patterson with a pride that surprised her. His soft, rich voice captivated her as it drifted across the assembled Indians.

She glanced about her and saw that many of the young women were not paying the least attention to what was being said; they, like herself, were engrossed in watching the interpreter. Jealousy flashed through her and she wanted to cry out that he was her man, her husband. But in truth, he was neither.

When it was finally over, she could hardly rise to her feet. Her legs were cramped. She bit her lip to keep from crying out in pain as she stumbled after Abigail through the darkened village to the cabin on the outskirts.

Immediately upon entering the dwelling, Abigail shed her skin skirt and slipped under her robes. Susan, however, made a great show of smoothing out the animal skins before she lay down and drew them over her buckskin dress.

The woman raised to one elbow and eyed her curiously. "Do you sleep in your clothes?"

"Yes," said Susan, turning her back to discourage further questions. She lay there wide-eyed, waiting, wondering what she would do when Patterson came.

She must have drifted off, because when he did slip under the robes she was unaware of it until she felt his body next to hers. She was instantly wide awake. But any fears she might have harbored about her virtue were unfounded. Patterson was asleep the moment his head touched the rush mattress.

He was gone when she waked the next morning. She marveled that he had left without awaking her. Abigail was up also, and had a fire blazing just outside the door.

Susan stretched gracefully, then stepped outside. The town had a tranquil peacefulness about it as the early light filtered through the haze of hundreds of cookfires. There was a hush about the women who performed their morning chores, adding to the serenity of the large village.

Towns were not a novelty to Susan, but the very size of Chillicothe piqued her. "Good morning," said Susan as she joined Abigail at the fireside.

"You slept late," said the woman. "Your husband has been gone for over an hour."

Susan thought she detected a touch of contempt in the woman's voice, but she wasn't sure.

Wawega appeared, carrying some copper pots and pans.

"These are Joseph Patterson's cooking pots," she told Susan, with Abigail interpreting. "I am sure he would not mind if his daughter-in-law made good use of them."

Susan thanked her and asked that she stay and visit. Wawega politely refused, saying that she must see to her own fireside so that breakfast would be ready when Black Fish and Patterson returned from the morning hunt.

Susan was relieved to hear that Patterson had gone hunting, and she felt foolish for not thinking of that.

When the sun was an hour high, the woodsman and Black Fish returned. They both carried turkeys, squirrels, and pigeon. They parted company at the edge of the village.

Susan smiled as he approached. "A good morning's hunt?"

"Aye. Still a lot of game hereabout."

He passed the turkey and squirrels to Abigail but made no offer to hand over the pigeons.

"What are they for?" Susan indicated the birds.

"For a widow whose husband was killed by a bear." He looked at Susan to see if she understood. She did.

He walked away without further comment, leaving her and Abigail the chore of cleaning and preparing the fresh meat.

He returned a while later and squatted beside the fire, taking the food Susan offered, eating it quickly and silently.

He cleaned his rifle and stood it in a corner of the cabin. It was the first time Susan had seen him leave his weapon unattended.

Patterson emerged from the cabin and started toward the village.

"Are you leaving?" she inquired from the doorwell.

261

Patterson continued on as if he hadn't heard.

Susan bit her lip and watched until he was out of sight.

Abigail excused herself, saying she must see to her husband's needs. Susan watched her go, feeling alone and lost.

At noon, she went in search of Ivy and Judith. She saw Ivy working in the fields along with the other captives. Judith, however, was not present.

She made no attempt to talk with Ivy; she still did not know what her boundaries were even though she was supposed to be the wife of Patterson, daughter-in-law of Black Fish.

She made her way back to the cabin and found Abigail with a tall, graying Shawnee, whom she introduced as her husband. Susan recognized the man and forced herself to smile pleasantly. Inside, however, she seethed, for he was the Indian who had savagely slaughtered Sarah and her child, and driven Judith insane.

The Indian studied Susan for a long moment. She was sure his searching black eyes could probe into her very thoughts and it upset her.

The Indian spoke softly to his wife, who said to Susan: "My husband apologizes for harming your captive—the one you call Judith. He says to tell you that he has chastened himself with the black drink that purges the body, and he has prayed to the Maker for forgiveness, so that she might come back to the living."

Susan was astounded by the Indian's penitence, and it showed plainly on her face.

"Tell him," she said after regaining her composure, "that it is over and done and that I hope the Maker hears his prayers."

The Indian nodded, and after a few short words with his wife, took his leave.

"You think he is savage," said Abigail after he was gone. "But you are wrong. He is a fine and decent man."

"I...I did not mean to imply that...that your husband was..." stammered Susan, confused as to what she should say.

"Your face is easy to read," said Abigail stonily. "You must learn to conceal such thoughts you wish others not to see."

"I am sorry," said Susan. "I have much to learn."

"You may never overcome your white teachings," said the woman flatly.

"I will!" promised Susan.

Fontaine found himself standing at the edge of a vast brush-covered field. Ivy worked industriously, chopping out roots and vines that would be burned in the spring when the field was cultivated. The Frenchman studied her as the hoe she wielded rose and fell.

A good woman, he thought. She will make a fine wife for someone. Then he winced as he envisioned her lying in the arms of a savage.

With an aching in his chest, he moved into the field and walked toward Ivy, who had failed, as yet, to notice his presence. The Indian women working with Ivy straightened from their toil and eyed the Frenchman curiously.

Several smiled invitingly as he moved toward them, but he was blind to their enticements. A withered old woman leaned heavily on the hickory stick she used as a cane and eyed Fontaine as he approached. "What is it you want, Frenchman?" she demanded, her voice like ancient parchment.

"Why, old one," cried Fontaine, caught off guard, "I have come to see the nigger!"

"Nigger," said the woman, a new crease forming on her wrinkled brow.

"Oui, mam'selle. The black woman."

The old woman's hand flew to her mouth in a gesture of surprise. "Black woman?"

"Oui," returned Fontaine, pointing to Ivy, who had stopped hoeing when she heard the Frenchman's voice.

"Black woman?" repeated the crone, studying Ivy with a new light in her faded brown eyes. She screeched loudly to the women working the fields. They dropped their implements and ran toward her.

Fontaine realized his mistake too late, for like him, the Shawnee women had never seen a Negro. He could gladly have bitten off his tongue.

The old woman spoke swiftly, gesturing toward Ivy who stood perplexed, not understanding what was taking place.

Fontaine was mortified. It was indeed his fault when the women gathered around Ivy and demanded that she take off her dress.

"I'll not!" cried the horrified girl when Fontaine translated.

263

"Please do as they say, Ivy," pleaded the Frenchman. "They will not harm you unless you refuse."

"Why do they want me to . . . to do this?" asked the girl, close to tears.

"They wish to see if your body is black," returned Fontaine.

"Oh, Fontaine!" The girl was deeply hurt. "Why did you tell them I am a nigger?" It was almost a whisper.

"I am most sorry, Ivy," replied a contrite Fontaine. "I spoke before I thought."

Without a word, Ivy slipped her tattered dress off her shoulders and let it fall to the ground.

The Indian women surged close and scrutinized her body from head to toe. In spite of himself, Fontaine could not take his eyes off the girl. She was truly beautiful. She saw him staring at her, and tried to cover her nakedness with her hands.

"Please, sir," begged the girl as Fontaine's eyes flowed over her. "Please, do not look at me so—I am forever shamed." Then she wept great, uncontrollable tears.

The old woman raised her stave and struck Ivy savagely, knocking the unsuspecting girl to the ground. She made a cutting motion with her hand, then pointed to her eyes. She did it several times before Ivy realized she was being told to stop crying.

Fontaine attempted to intervene, but the woman struck him a vicious blow to the head that caused him to stumble and very nearly drop his musket.

Then, to Ivy's amazement, all the women converged on the Frenchman, pelting him with stones and clods of hard earth, and one reached for the small ax that she wore in her belt.

"Liar!" they screamed. "Her skin is not black. Liar! Liar!"

Fontaine beat a hasty retreat from the field. He had no illusions as to what his fate would be should the women become overly excited—they would kill him, and nothing on earth could stop them.

Ivy took advantage of the excitement, and by the time it was over, she was fully dressed and hard at work with her hoe.

The old woman eyed the girl, hate dancing in her faded, bloodshot eyes. She was from the old school; the school that hated all white people. It would have been far better for Ivy had her skin been as black as night, because the only thing Fontaine managed to accomplish by his thoughtless words was to draw attention to Ivy and to kindle the old woman's wrath for the inoffensive servant girl.

The crone worked Ivy mercilessly throughout the day, not once allowing the girl to stop long enough to catch her breath or get a drink of water. The sun relentlessly beamed fire that left the girl reeling in her tracks as she sank the stone head of her primitive hoe into the hard, sunbaked earth. Sweat poured from her body, staining her dress black.

The girl was staggering when the old Indian called the work force to a halt at sundown; and it was all she could do to pry her blistered fingers from around the rough wooden handle of the crude cultivator she had used without a break since sunup.

The old woman watched the weary girl with satisfaction, noting her toil-worn droop as she joined the other captives and staggered toward the village. A toothless grin of triumph lighted the crone's wizened face as Ivy teetered, then collapsed, sprawling headlong into the dust of the worn path they followed.

The captive behind Ivy kneeled beside the fallen girl, but before she could assist Ivy, the old hag struck the woman with such brutal savagery that the sound of the bone breaking in her upper arm echoed in the village.

The old woman moved murderously toward Ivy, who had regained her footing and stood staring at the injured woman who had fainted from shock, and raised her stave threateningly.

Ivy moved fearfully into the line of captives and, without a glance at the prostrate woman who had tried to assist her, walked steadily toward the longhouses. Once inside the building, however, she collapsed on the filthy pile of straw that was her bed and cried.

"Dear God," she prayed, when the tears finally subsided, "I'm not strong enough to survive such treatment—I'm not! I'm just a servant girl, Lord...I'm not an animal...I want my mistress, please send me my mistress." Then she sobbed, lost and alone—and frightened.

But the Lord wasn't responding to servant girls that day—nor was he helpful the next, for the treatment Ivy endured the following morning was even more barbaric than the day before.

Finally, driven almost insane for want of a sip of water, Ivy cast aside her fear of pain, of cruelty, of even death itself, and staggered to the gourd container that held the life-giving liquid and drank deeply.

The old woman, enchanted by Ivy's disobedience, fell upon the girl with her stave and smashed her to the ground. Ivy was up before the surprised crone could raise her stave a second time. The harridan, having never been faced by a human gone mad with the will to live, was unprepared for the onslaught of a young woman who had every intention of killing her with her bare hands—and would have, had it not been for the Shawnee women who oversaw the fields.

They converged on Ivy like a pack of wild dogs, snarling, howling, screaming for blood. And Ivy, gentle Ivy, was just as wild as they—kicking, punching, biting, pulling hair, and screaming insults; using every curse word she had ever heard Judith utter—right up to the moment they knocked her unconscious.

Patterson was aware that Black Fish was troubled. They had been hunting together since daylight, and it was now late afternoon. His foster father hadn't said three words throughout the day.

The woodsman moved to Black Fish's side. "My father," he said respectfully, "is your heart heavy because of something I have done?"

The old Indian studied Patterson for several minutes, then said: "I have always been proud to call you my son. Even when you were twelve years old, you were a man—a warrior."

Patterson looked deep into Black Fish's dark eyes. "Has my father changed his opinion?"

His gaze was as steady and unblinking as the Indian's as he awaited the answer. Inwardly, however, his heart ached with the sadness of a man who is aware that he has lost the respect of a loved one, for he was certain that Black Fish had discovered that he, Patterson, was nothing but a weak excuse for a human; that he was nothing but a white man after all.

Black Fish laid his hand on Patterson's shoulder. "My son," he said, his voice grave with sorrow, "would you sit with me beneath yon oak tree?" He nodded his head toward the tree he desired.

Black Fish took a clay pipe from his shot pouch and filled it with tobacco. He selected an age-old dry oak leaf and expertly struck flint to steel. A tiny spark appeared in the center of the leaf, which Black Fish fanned until it grew into a smoldering circle of red-hot ash. He laid the leaf on the bowl of the pipe and sucked, exhaling smoke with each new draw. Then he passed the pipe to Patterson.

"My son," he said as Patterson sucked long on the pipe stem, "my heart is heavy with things I do not understand. I am grieved by the words that I have been hearing...."

Patterson held the pipe tightly.

"What are the words my father hears?"

"Why do you not lie with your wife?" said Black Fish, catching Patterson completely off guard.

The woodsman sprang from his squatting position to stare angrily at the Indian.

"It is common knowledge, my son," continued Black Fish, ignoring his adopted son's rage. "All of Chillicothe is laughing about it... they speak of nothing else."

Patterson gripped hard on the pipe stem.

"Have you not noticed that the young men shun you? That the old men turn their backs on you? They are ashamed for you... because they think you have no shame."

Patterson stared hard at the forest around him. The silence stretched thin as Black Fish waited for Patterson to answer. But there was no answer, for the Shawnee were correct in all but one point— Patterson did have shame. But there was no answer he could give his father.

The old Indian's face fell when it became evident that Patterson had no intention of defending his manhood.

"There is more, my son," he said sadly. "The children have heard the gossip about your wife, for the women's tongues have fluttered like leaves in a breeze—and the children, being blessed with the simple honesty of youth, have done a most shameful thing...."

Patterson crossed his arms, Indian fashion, and stared straight ahead. He was not interested in what a passel of children might have done. Nothing would surpass the damage already done by Susan and her precious virtue.

"I apologize, my son, for the children's behavior."

"Just what in hell have they done?" said Patterson, forgetting momentarily the dignity and respect with which he always addressed his stepfather.

Black Fish blanched, but he spoke calmly: "They have snatched up your wife's dress to see if she is truly a woman."

Patterson's face flamed.

"And what did they find?"

"My son is filled with anger," said the Indian, rising. "We will talk at another time."

"Did they find that I have taken a man to wife?" demanded Patterson, ignoring Black Fish's desire to end the conversation.

"No, my son," said the Indian, avoiding the young man's eyes. "She is a woman."

Patterson seethed. "Tell Chillicothe this, my father," he said softly. "Tell them that what my wife and I do is damn well none of their business—tell them that!"

Black Fish's eyes flashed wide: "I will tell them nothing, my son. It is you who is disgraced, not I."

"I am sorry, my father," said Patterson, dropping his eyes. "I have spoken in anger. I ask your forgiveness."

The old Indian's face softened. He studied Patterson with indecision, then said softly: "There is a woman. She is not a maiden, though she is barely sixteen summers old. She has approached me and asked that I send you to her. She will welcome you at her fireside, my son."

"I have a fireside, Father," said Patterson flatly.

"Your fireside is cold, my son." He gripped Patterson's shoulder. "The embers of your Mohawk wife do not burn for you— but Lilies of the Still Waters, the woman you have been taking food to, will open her heart to you."

"I have a woman," replied Patterson as he stalked into the evening shadows beneath the dense timber.

He made his way toward the cabin, skirting the village as best he could to keep from being hailed by those who would still speak to him. Upon reaching the cabin, he plunged angrily through the door.

"Leave us," he snapped at Abigail.

She glanced up from her sewing; then she looked at Susan to see if she endorsed his command.

Patterson caught the woman by the arm and jerked her to her feet. "I said get the hell out!"

The woman started for the door, her movements slow and uncertain.

Patterson's foot caught her squarely in the buttocks and propelled her into the darkness.

Susan stood in a corner of the room wide-eyed. "Have you been drinking?"

"No, I haven't been drinking! I am fed up with chaperones. I am fed up with virgins, and I am fed up with you!" He snatched at the buckle of his belt and dropped his breechcloth to the floor.

Susan's eyes became large pools of darkness in the dimly lighted room, but she remained silent.

Patterson worked his leggin's down over his ankles and kicked them away.

"I am a man!' he said, turning toward her. "I will be treated as such!"

Susan moved slowly into the flickering light of the small fire that burned before the doorwell. Without a word, she eased the hunting frock over her head and dropped it silently to the floor.

Patterson's breath caught. She was more lovely than any woman he had ever seen.

She stared at him, her face a mask, her hands hanging rigidly at her sides, making no effort to cover her nakedness.

Her breasts rose and fell rapidly, the only sign that she was not calm at all. But as he stepped toward her, she shuddered.

Patterson halted. This was the woman for whom he had fought, lied, and killed, to protect—the woman who trusted and believed in him. He moved closer, hating her, blaming her for his ruined reputation. He would take her—take the young woman who stood before him trembling violently.

But the anger that had fired Patterson beyond anything he had ever known suddenly drained away. In its wake was a tenderness that left him shaken and ashamed of what he had intended to do.

Without a word, he scooped up his leggin's and breechcloth and stalked out the door.

The young woman, a girl actually, raised to a sitting position, the blanket that covered her falling to her waist.

She studied Patterson carefully in the dim light of the glowing

269

embers, her eyes searching his naked body. "Welcome to my home," she said as she laid the blanket aside and rose to stand by the firepit. "Would you care to eat?" She gestured toward a bowl sitting at the edge of the embers.

"I did not come for a social evening," he said harshly as he moved toward her.

She did not resist when he lifted her roughly into his arms and carried her to the blanket she had just vacated.

Susan was up before daylight. In fact, she had slept none at all that night. She kindled the fire and set breakfast on to cook. Her eyes constantly searched the shadows for Patterson.

Dawn broke. Women slipped out of the longhouses and kindled their fires. Men carrying bows and arrows, or occasionally a firearm, disappeared into the dark forest.

Susan finished cooking the meal and set it off the fire. When an hour had passed and Patterson still had not come, she fed the breakfast to a dog.

Women walked past on their way to the fields. They spoke to one another, their mouths hidden by their hands; they giggled like schoolgirls as they watched Susan go about her morning chores.

She wondered at their attitude. It was obvious they were gossiping about her. Abigail showed up at noon, looking fearfully in all directions to be sure Patterson wasn't near.

"He has not been here all night," admitted Susan.

Abigail looked at the girl but said nothing.

"He...did not stay," continued Susan, dropping her eyes.

"Why did he leave?" asked the woman. "He was much a man when he entered the cabin. Ah, what a man!"

"I—don't really know," sighed Susan as she toyed idly with the fire. "I suppose he did not want me...after he saw me."

"Are you so bad under the robes that a strong man such as yours does not desire you?"

"I...do not wish to discuss it!" cried the girl. "I have no idea why he did not take me."

Abigail moved to the firepit. "May I speak freely?"

"Please do," said Susan.

"Well," said Abigail, not knowing how to begin, "if it was me, I would go to the river and bathe and wash my hair and rebraid it.

270

Then I would return here and cook a good meal and have it hot and waiting. I would fluff up the robes till they were soft and inviting—and I would lay my dress in the corner—"

"I couldn't do that!" interrupted Susan. "Why, that would be like a seduction. It would be obvious that I awaited him."

"If you want your husband back, you must act the part of a woman. You can be sure that Lilies of the Still Waters will do all those things I have said, and more."

"Lilies of the Still Waters?"

"Yes," said Abigail. "She is a young widow. Your husband has been taking food to her wigwam since he has come."

"Was her husband killed by a bear?"

"Yes. It is said he was pursuing you when it happened."

"He was! But it was not my fault!" Susan hung her head in anguish, thinking of the young Indian who had run headlong into the she-bear.

"No one blames you, mistress," said the woman. "But all the women of Chillicothe wonder why you are not...a real wife to Patterson. They whisper behind their hands that you are made of ice—like a white woman. And they also say that Lilies of the Still Waters will take Patterson from you without a fight."

"I will not fight her!" cried Susan aghast. "I am a lady."

"There are many ways to fight, mistress. The best way is under the robes in the moonlight. Still Waters fought you all night long, so I have heard."

"Is she beautiful?"

"Very beautiful, but not as beautiful as you."

Susan blushed. "Is her body lovely to look upon?"

"Men seem to think so. But you can see for yourself; she has gone to the river to wash away last night's stains, and to make herself clean and beautiful for your husband."

Susan's face flamed as she envisioned Morgan in the arms of the Indian girl.

"I...I would like to see her."

She made her way to the river using the path Abigail had pointed out. She moved cautiously in and out of the tall trees until she had an open view of the Little Miami River.

An Indian girl stood waist-deep in the swirling waters, rinsing her bronze body with cupped hands. Her head was thrown back so

271

that her pointed breasts were thrust high. And although the girl's eyes were closed, Susan could read deep contentment on her full, upturned lips.

The girl must have sensed that she was not alone, for her eyes suddenly opened and the smile vanished. She sank immediately under the water and swam toward shore. When she surfaced, she studied the river carefully, her eyes just above the water line, and spotted Susan standing quietly on the bank.

Lilies of the Still Waters studied Susan for a long while before wading boldly to the bank where the white girl waited. Envy flooded through Susan as the girl stepped out of the water, for she was everything Abigail had said: very young, perhaps fifteen, yet fully developed. Her golden red skin shone with the luster of youth. Her hips were flared and her legs were long and supple. Hanging well below her small waist was lustrous black hair. She was beautiful—and she knew it.

Lilies smiled as she drew near, and Susan flinched at the triumphant victory in the girl's eyes. They studied each other for a long moment.

Susan looked into the girl's eyes and saw the amused contempt that lay deep within. She bit her lip, blushed, and without a word, drew the frock over her head and cast it aside.

"Now look at me," she said through her teeth. "I'm as pretty as you are." And she was. In fact, she was even more exciting. Her breasts were a bit fuller and more rounded, and their nipples larger and more pronounced. Her hips, although no wider, had a more gentle curve. And her legs were even longer and more shapely than the Indian girl's.

The girl studied Susan closely, examining her with new respect.

This is ridiculous, thought Susan, the two of us appraising each other's charms to see who has the most to offer. Then she did a most unexpected thing—a terrible thing. She laughed. The girl quickly wrapped her skirt around her and disappeared into the forest.

Susan stopped laughing and stared after her. She reached for her frock, but Abigail's words of wisdom drummed loud in her ears. She dropped the dress and waded into the water.

Having been "touched by the hand of God," Judith was at liberty to wander about with aimless, irresponsible privilege; something none of the other captives could do.

272

She ate from any pot that was available when she felt hungry—with the blessings of the owner. She slept where she pleased, no matter whose robes she used, or whose longhouse; for she was welcomed by the entire tribe, and watched over like a child. Yet there were times when she was alone, times when she wandered beyond watchful eyes.

During one such period, while sitting on a fallen log at the edge of the forest, her glazed eyes far and distant, she was approached by the French officer DeBeaujue.

"Ah, mademoiselle," he began, "you have wandered far from town. May I sit beside you?" He seated himself, turning so he could see her face.

The scar above her eye had nearly healed, leaving a thin red line that would eventually turn white and be less noticeable. But even so, he found it quite appealing, for it added a mysterious and sinister touch to her otherwise classic features.

"You are quite lovely, mam'selle," he said as he moved closer and took her unresisting hand. "Even without your fine long hair you are beautiful. Do you understand what I am saying?"

Her clouded eyes held no hint of understanding, nor did her childlike face show any emotion.

His fingers played across her hand and caressed her forearm. She did not move. He quickly scoured the countryside to be certain they were alone, then he boldly took her hand and pulled her to her feet.

"We will walk in the woods, eh?"

She did not resist as he led her into the darkness beneath the majestic trees. He found a glade of tall ferns that satisfied his purpose.

"It is a lovely spot," he said, watching her closely.

She gazed vacantly. Again he glanced at the terrain, to be sure they were alone. Not a sound was heard, not even the scamper of a small animal. He laughed lightly at his good fortune.

He touched her cheek, turning her face toward him.

"You shall be mine, to do with as I please. Do you know that? To do whatever I wish!" His eyes ravished her body, taking in the swell of her small breast above her tiny waist.

"The daughter of an English nobleman at my mercy...and I am not a merciful man."

He laughed then, a wild outburst in the quiet wilderness. He began unbuttoning his white tunic, eyeing her with satisfaction.

"But what difference does it make?" he asked, dropping the coat into the ferns. "You are crazy—whom could you tell? And after I am finished with you, my dear, you shall have no desire to tell anyone."

He cast his ruffled shirt next to the coat.

"I have watched you these past few days," he continued. "I knew that you would come to the log to meditate, or whatever you mad people do when you are alone." His sword and scabbard clattered to the ground.

Judith watched him; her eyes began to dilate, and her lips moved as if she were trying hard to remember something she had forgotten—something urgent.

"Ah!" he said as he kicked off his boots and stepped out of his trousers. "Does this remind you of another time? Eh?"

He snickered again.

Something in Judith was alarmed. It was evident in the black pools of her eyes. But even then, even as grief or fear flickered momentarily on her face, the mist slowly overshadowed her, and once again she stood alone, lost, utterly innocent.

He wasted no time trying to remove her dress, he simply laid her in the ferns and raised the ragged cloth above her waist. He took her without prelude, yet even then she showed no feeling; not fear, nor pain, nor pleasure. Instead, her face became almost angelic, so pure was her expression, and as he thrust again and again into her, she closed her eyes tightly and whispered the only intelligible words that had passed her lips since that terrible day the baby was killed: "I love you, Morgan."

DeBeaujue did not spend himself inside her. Instead, he cast his seed upon the ground. He would not chance impregnating an insane woman; indeed, not one drop of his blood would run through the veins of a child begot of a crazy woman, no matter her bloodline.

She lay there humming softly, making no move to cover her nakedness. Her fingers toyed with a fern that grew next to her head, its tall, wide leaves casting delicate shadows across her passive face.

It angered him that she had called Patterson's name; had not responded to him; had in truth acted as though he had done

274

nothing. "You will feel something, mam'selle, I promise you. You will scream with pain!" He retrieved his swordcase, eyed it with satisfaction, and knelt between Judith's widespread legs.

"If you touch her, I will kill you, m'sieur." The soft words caused the gentleman to jerk violently.

"Cover her nakedness and stand up, monsieur, or I will shoot you where you kneel."

DeBeaujue tugged Judith's dress down over her hips and climbed to his feet.

"You have me at a disadvantage, Monsieur Fontaine," he said casually, indicating his own nudity.

Fontaine's eyes narrowed, yet his words were so softly spoken that the officer had to listen hard to hear them. "You are not a man, capitaine; you need no clothing to cover the scales that grow on your body."

"Monsieur," huffed DeBeaujue, "you are addressing an officer of His Majesty's Royal Army, or must I remind you?"

"I should have killed you the day you did that same vile thing to that small girl and her mother—I knew then that you were a beast."

"You killed the woman yourself!" interrupted the officer. "Slashed her wrist so she would not have to suffer the perils of war—we are at war with the English, Fontaine, or have you forgotten?"

Fontaine was aware that war was a license to rape, yet this was different.

"M'sieur," he said, "you seem to prefer crazy women to those that have their wits about them. Is it that you cannot satisfy a normal lady? The young girl at the clearing? You drove her mad! Was that your purpose?"

"Monsieur," said the captain, nonplussed, "I used the naked blade of my sword on her, not my swordcase. Now, either kill me, or get out of my sight. I am growing bored with your conversation."

"I will do better than that, capitaine," said Fontaine. "I will tell Black Fish what has taken place here. The Indians, my friend, will cut your cod off and feed it to you a piece at a time."

The captain blanched.

"Monsieur," he said, taking a deep breath to steady himself, "do as you will, but deliver me from your noble speeches. Your talk sickens me. You are like an old woman. You have no place with the French army."

In any other man, Fontaine would have found a measure of respect for his courage, but in the captain it revolted him.

"M'sieur," he said dangerously, "don your uniform and leave these woods before I forget that you are my superior and my countryman.

"But remember, capitaine, do not come near this woman again, or you will die like the dog you are."

DeBeaujue smiled triumphantly as he drew on his trousers.

"She is not worth the effort, monsieur."

Then he laughed, sure of his position, and of Fontaine's hesitation to expose an officer and a countryman.

"To tell the truth, Fontaine," he chortled, "the young girl in the clearing was much better to lie with—even after she was dead!"

He dropped his head back, and his cackling echoed throughout the silent forest.

It was the last sound he ever made. Fontaine's hand flicked out and the razor edge of Patterson's Damascus blade sliced deeply across the captain's throat. He was dead before he hit the ground.

Fontaine sheathed the knife, glancing in all directions to be sure no one had seen the killing. Then he gently lifted Judith to her feet. She stepped over the body of the captain and followed Fontaine out of the forest—humming softly to herself.

Patterson was reluctant to return to the cabin. He and Black Fish had wasted the day hunting and talking, but night was fast approaching and he knew it was time to make a decision.

He stood at the edge of the woods and surveyed the town. Smoke from a hundred campfires trailed lazily toward the heavens in the breezeless evening stillness.

"Peaceful," said Patterson with a sigh. "But they are all waiting—waiting and watching. The whole damn town is waiting to see whose blanket I crawl under tonight."

He thought about the previous night. He was not sorry for what he had done with Lilies but he was mortified by what he had almost

276

done to Susan, and, although he longed to return to the cabin, he could not bring himself to face the girl; not yet anyway.

He shouldered his rifle and moved toward the wigwam of Lilies of the Still Waters.

Susan let the fire die down. She moved the supper she had prepared to the coals to keep it warm and then surveyed the room. Everything was neat and clean; the earthen floor had been swept and the robes had been beaten with a stick until they were fluffy.

She was happy with her nest, and happy about herself. She had bathed again just before sundown. Her hair hung straight down her back to just above her hips. Abigail had combed it until it shone a silky blue-black. Her skin frock had been laid neatly in a corner, replaced by a kilt supplied by Abigail. She was aware of her bare breasts, but Abigail had assured her she was the envy of all the maidens in town.

"He will not be able to resist you, princess," the woman had said with a wide smile. "He will tear your skirt away!"

Susan blushed prettily. "I am not at all sure I can go through with this, Abby. It goes against all my Christian teachings."

"I am Blue Bird," corrected the woman. "Do you want your husband back? Or do you want him rutting with Still Waters?"

"I want my . . . husband."

Abigail collected her belongings and prepared to leave. "You are a beautiful woman, princess," she said from the doorway, "and I believe your husband thinks that also."

Susan wished that it were true. She wanted to be beautiful for Patterson, especially now that she had made her mind up to be his woman, with or without marriage. She felt wanton because of the urgency of her desire, but she felt serene also.

She heard him coming; soft steps in the darkness. She smiled shyly toward the open doorwell, her hands playing nervously at the skirt draped loosely around her middle. Her eyes fell to her breasts. They were tingling with anticipation. Then her heart stopped.

"Fontaine!" she cried, covering her breasts as best she could with her small hands.

The Frenchman stepped through the door and whistled softly, his eyes alight with admiration. "Ah! ma chérie, you are most beautiful."

"Get out of here!" She dropped her hands, forgetting that she was unclothed and reached for an iron pot.

Fontaine moved like a cat and caught her wrist.

"Listen to me!" he whispered, as he drew her close. "I am most sorry to spoil your...ah, shall I say...wedding night? But I must talk to you. Please, mam'selle, stop fighting me... *Will you not listen?*"

She stopped struggling then, for something in his voice pierced her.

"Is it Morgan? Is he...has something happened?"

Fontaine dropped his eyes, and she tensed, for she had never seen him when he wasn't carefree.

"Please, Mr. Fontaine, what is it?"

"I was wishing Patterson would be here," he said gently, "but, alas, he is much the fool."

Susan blushed and reached for the buckskin frock she normally wore.

"I have not seen him since yesterday evening." She slipped the garment over her head.

"He made the bad choice, mistress, by not coming home this night," said Fontaine dryly.

"Is that what you came to tell me?"

"No, Susan. It has not a thing to do with why I am here. I came to get you, to take you to Lily's wigwam to get Patterson."

"Get out of here, Fontaine," she said icily. "Get out of here before I kill you!"

The Frenchman raised his hand to still her anger, his face breaking into the boyish grin she so well remembered. "Mam'selle, I do not mean it the way she sounds. We must get Patterson out of her blankets—out of her wigwam. *It must be done so no one will suspect anything.*"

"What do you mean?"

"Come," he said taking her hand. "I will explain on the way."

As they neared the Indian girl's lodge Susan drew back. "I can't go in there, Fontaine. I feel like a fool for the way I've acted tonight...to think what I almost did."

"Mademoiselle," protested the Frenchman, "you were a woman tonight. It is a shame Patterson cannot see that...or perhaps—"

"Perhaps what?" blurted Susan.

278

"Perhaps he did see," said Fontaine, putting his hand on her shoulder and gripping gently. "Perhaps he respected you too much."

"He didn't have to go to her!"

"Susan," returned Fontaine patiently, "there is only one way for a man momentarily to forget a woman, and that is to be with another woman."

"I am not going in there, Fontaine."

"All right," shrugged the Frenchman, handing Susan his musket and shot pouch.

"Why are you giving me these?"

"Because, mam'selle, when he comes out of there, he is going to be the mad one. I wish to be free to protect myself." Then he laughed.

Susan watched Fontaine's silhouette as he stepped to the door of the wigwam. He hesitated, listening.

She could faintly hear the sound of heavy breathing and soft moans of pleasure from within. Her face flamed and she clenched her teeth.

Damn him! Damn him! Damn him! she cried inwardly.

Then Fontaine was talking; loud, drunken talk, in the Shawnee language.

"Patterson! You fornicating bastard, are you in there?"

Patterson froze, then his head snapped toward the open door of the wigwam.

Lily's arms tightened around him. "Do not answer," she whispered, rotating her hips to renew their lovemaking. "Finish what you have started."

"Patterson!" came the drunken cry. "Drag your arse out from between her legs and come out here!"

"Fontaine is crazy drunk!" laughed Patterson, as he snuggled against the girl and drew her to him.

Fontaine listened but could hear no movement save the muffled moans of the girl in the wigwam.

"Patterson!" he shouted angrily, forgetting to appear drunk. "I have your wife out here, and I came to tell you that I am going to perform your manly duties this night. She is an overripe berry that has waited all evening to be plucked. I, Fontaine, intend to taste her fruit!"

279

He glanced quickly at Susan to be sure she understood nothing of what was said, then he steeled himself to meet Patterson when he emerged from the building.

And emerge he did. Naked except for the large hunting knife that he held low, cutting edge up. He collided with Fontaine and both men went down in a cloud of dust.

Fontaine had not expected such an onslaught, and he had his hands full just to keep Patterson from killing him instantly.

Susan cried out for them to stop, but her words were wasted—in fact they seemed to infuriate Patterson all the more, and he slashed at Fontaine wickedly as they rolled and tumbled.

"Monsieur," gasped the Frenchman as they thrashed about in the dust, "I must talk to you—away from here."

"You've already talked too much," grated the woodsman through his teeth as he tried again to get his blade into Fontaine.

"It is Ivy, and Judith, you whoring son-of-a-bitch; they need help!" rasped the Frenchman painfully.

Patterson rolled atop Fontaine and looked dangerously into his eyes.

"What are you saying?"

"Not here, Patterson. We must talk—but not here. There are too many ears, eh?"

Patterson climbed to his feet and reentered the wigwam.

Lilies of the Still Waters raised to one elbow and smiled at him. "Did you kill the Frenchman? Come back to my robes, we have not finished . . . we will celebrate his death."

"I did not kill him," said Patterson as he pulled on his leggin's.

"I will kill him for you." She sprang to her feet, taking up a small ax.

"No," said Patterson, buckling his wide belt around him. "I must go—but I will return. Go back to your blankets and wait for me."

She hesitated, studying him carefully.

"You are my man," she said angrily. "You came to me instead of her. Why do you leave?"

He hit her then, a backhanded blow that laid her flat on her back on the blankets she had just vacated. She raised to a sitting position and smiled up at him, a pleased expression on her lovely face.

"I will wait, Patterson."

He joined Fontaine and Susan. The three of them marched toward Patterson's cabin. Indians peered from the doorways of the longhouses. Some even spoke as they passed, but not one inquired into the business just finished. It was none of their affair.

When they were well away from the longhouses, Fontaine stopped Patterson, letting Susan go on to the cabin. He explained to the woodsman what had taken place in the forest that afternoon. He left out nothing.

Patterson nodded. "I am in your debt, Fontaine. You saved me a killing."

"You owe me nothing, my friend," returned the Frenchman softly. "I but wish it ended there." He went on to explain that he had just learned that Ivy had nearly beaten an elderly Shawnee woman to death; and that if Patterson had not been so busy with Lilies of the Still Waters, he would have known that half the tribe was up in arms about it.

"They will burn her, Patterson," the Frenchman said flatly, without emotion. "They will torture her beyond anything you or I have ever seen."

Patterson's face was white in the moonlight.

"Fontaine," he said through his teeth, "Ivy's not going to burn at the stake as long as I draw a breath."

"Nor, I, m'sieur," said the Frenchman softly. "They shall have to kill us both first."

Patterson spun on his heel and started in the direction of Black Fish's wigwam.

"If you think Black Fish can help, you are wrong, m'sieur." said Fontaine. "The women of the turtle clan—*your clan*—are screaming for Ivy's blood."

Fontaine dropped his head, sadly. "Even Wawega, your mother, wishes to see Ivy die. I am sorry to have to tell you that, m'sieur."

Patterson's hand shook as he wearily ran it through his coarse hair. "I'm going in there, Fontaine," he said, gazing at the wigwam that housed the captives, "and I'm bringing her out if I have to kill half this goddamned tribe to do it."

Fontaine grinned widely, looking like his usual jovial self.

Patterson eyed him angrily. "'Tis no laughing matter, Fontaine."

"Ah, m'sieur," said the Frenchman, sobering, "you have no imagination—you are always running off half-cocked."

"Goddamn you, Fontaine—"

"But, m'sieur," said Fontaine, shrugging eloquently, "the great Fontaine has already done that."

Patterson peered into the Frenchman's face, straining to see his eyes in the darkness.

"You did what?"

"I slipped into the longhouse and slit the throat of the Shawnee woman who slept with the captives. I took Ivy and Judith to the river and hid them. I stole a canoe—and I got you away from Lily, and Mam'selle Susan awaits. She has even brought sleeping robes for the cold. Everything is fine, eh?"

Patterson was stark white with shock.

"In the morning," Fontaine continued, "they will miss you and the women. They will find the captain and the woman, and will believe that you killed them during your escape. It is perfect, eh?"

Patterson clasped Fontaine's shoulder. "Fontaine . . . " he said softly, but that was the only word that would come.

"I am very wise, m'sieur," replied Fontaine happily.

True to his word, Ivy and Judith were at the river when Fontaine led Patterson and Susan out of the pitch black forest.

"We were worried that something had happened to you," Ivy whispered as she hugged Susan close. "It seems as if we have been waiting here forever . . . I was afraid you could not slip away."

Patterson moved immediately to the canoe and laid his rifle in the bottom. Not only was Susan's musket there, but bundles of food had been lashed to the thwarts. Patterson smiled, wondering how the Frenchman had managed it—the canoe, Ivy and Judith, and the supplies. Fontaine was, indeed, amazing.

Ivy moved to Fontaine, who was leaning heavily against a tree, and extended her hand.

"Thank you, Mr. Fontaine," she said, her voice soft. "I shall miss you, and you are forgiven for your blunder the other day." She eyed him curiously. "Will you never get over the fact that I am a nigger?"

"Ivy," he said seriously, taking the hand she offered, "I have grown very fond of you...are you ready to listen, to hear my words?"

Fontaine's hand was warm and sticky.

"Mr. Fontaine!" cried the girl in a hushed voice. "You are bleeding; let me see to your wound." Before he could protest, she had drawn his camus aside and was peering at the slash across his stomach. Her gasp was heard by those at the canoe.

"Oh, God!" she whispered, "your intestines are showing—oh, my God!"

"Hush, little one," he said softly, "would you shame the great Fontaine?"

"Oh, no! Mr. Fontaine, I would never knowingly shame you!"

"Then say nothing of my wound," he said, "else Monsieur Patterson will know that he is quicker than the Fontaine, and it would shame me greatly. He is a mean bastard, Ivy, but I love him like a brother."

He put his hand over her lips to still her protests. "Please, ma chérie, say nothing."

She nodded, her eyes wide with pain for him.

He released her and stepped back, again leaning against the tree. But Ivy knew it was for support, and not his normal slouch.

"Goodbye, Mr. Fontaine," she whispered emotionally. "Someday...someday I will listen!" Then she was gone, joining Judith and Susan at the water's edge.

Patterson approached Fontaine and laid his hand on the Frenchman's shoulder.

"Again, you have given us a way out, Fontaine. Perhaps someday I can repay the favor."

Fontaine smiled roguishly. "Keep the mesdemoiselles safe, mon ami; it is enough."

Patterson turned to leave but Fontaine's voice stopped him. "You are lost, Patterson. You can never return to your people...you have no people...not red, or white. I do not envy you, m'sieur."

"It is my choice, Fontaine," replied Patterson quietly. "I knew it would come sooner or later. I just always hoped I would stay Indian."

Fontaine smiled sadly. "No, mon ami, you have not been Indian—since you met the women. It is a shame, for you were once a good one. Now, you are just a good frontiersman, and your hair is up for grabs.

"Patterson," he said, a sudden somberness in his voice, "if we meet again, I will not be able to help you . . . do not let them take you; even Black Fish will turn his back. From this day on, I am your enemy."

"I know, Fontaine," answered Patterson sadly. "If we meet again, one of us will die. I have accepted that—and will honor it when the time comes."

"Be gone, mon ami," said Fontaine roughly. "I hope I never see you again."

16

Patterson peered through the mass of cattails. Five war canoes, thirty feet in length, skimmed silently past, eerie in the early morning light.

The Shawnees, their roached heads and painted cheeks glistening in the sun, had stayed their paddles and were drifting against the current.

The bronzed faces and black eyes probed the banks and sloughs on both sides of the river. It was so quiet Patterson could hear the waves bump lightly against the sides of the birchbark crafts.

He had expected to see them long before now, but, then again, he and the girls had made good time since leaving Chillicothe.

He glanced at their sleeping forms. They were exhausted, especially Susan and Ivy, who had helped paddle the canoe over three hundred and fifty long miles in less than three weeks.

A word was uttered and the war canoes picked up speed as the Indians dipped their paddles and moved upstream, continuing their search for Patterson and the missing women—especially for Patterson, who they felt had betrayed them.

He had seen no French or Hurons in the convoy, nor had he seen Black Fish. He wondered about that. Perhaps they had passed while he slept. He shrugged, dismissing the thought.

Susan stirred in her sleep. He was not certain, but he thought she called his name. He paid no attention, for she had been icy toward him since the night they had left Fontaine standing on the riverbank at Chillicothe. He idly wondered what Susan thought about his bedding Lily. Then he put it out of his mind: it was none of her business. He thought about Lilies of the Still Waters, and he experienced a moment of guilt. He had realized the first time he bedded her that it wasn't the same as when he had made love with Judith.

He was a white man. He had known it then, but refused to admit it. But now he had no choice.

He eased his rifle to a more comfortable position and closed his eyes. It had been a long hard night, and he needed rest. At first, they had found it hard to sleep by day, but after several nights of backbreaking paddling, they looked forward to daybreak like a weary man does sundown.

They had paddled into the reservoir of cattails at false dawn, and hidden the canoe.

The girls had merely balled up in the bottom of the craft and gone to sleep. Patterson had watched the river until fatigue had closed his eyes also, only to be jerked awake moments later by the passing of the Shawnee war party as they raked the shoreline for signs of the stolen canoe.

By the position of the sun, he had slept only an hour when he came wide awake a second time. He eased his rifle to the ready position and waited. An eighteen-foot canoe carrying three men was nosing past the slough, almost touching the cattails that hid Patterson and the women.

Patterson held his breath as the canoe slipped abreast of the hiding place only a stone's throw away.

Susan stirred again, and the canoe tipped and bobbed in the still water, sending tiny rings of waves toward the edge of the cattails and the long canoe that was silently gliding by.

Patterson clenched his teeth as the rings grew wider and bumped against the side of the enemy craft, causing it to sway ever so slightly.

The Shawnee in the bow slowly swung his painted face toward Patterson and their eyes met. The hole in the man's forehead appeared at the same instant. The Indian pitched headfirst into the water, turning the canoe upside down in the process. The remaining two warriors surfaced immediately, then sank almost as quickly.

Patterson dropped his empty rifle and snatched up Susan's musket. He scanned the water, watching for the Indians to surface again.

He saw cattails, not ten feet distant, sway as if touched by a gentle breeze; he leveled the gun on the spot.

The Indian's head flashed out of the water like a huge fish, then it was gone. Patterson fired. He watched the growing ring of waves where the ball had struck and was rewarded by a host of bubbles and a darkening stain in the silty water.

His elation was short-lived. The end of the canoe, in which he stood, erupted like an explosion and flipped sideways, throwing Patterson and the women headlong into the murky pool.

Patterson floundered in the waist-deep water, trying to regain his footing. He lost his balance in the deep mud and plunged under a second time. He burst above the water like a madman, his hair hugging his head and his body glinting in the sunlight.

He cast aside Susan's musket, and drew his knife. He felt wild and free as he stormed through the water to meet the foe.

The Indian waded toward him, slowed by the pressure of the water and the thickness of the cattails; he too was grinning wickedly, the savage in him screaming for release, to kill or be killed.

They clashed with such ferocity, their bodies slamming together with such impact, that it sounded like the discharge of an overloaded musket.

Muddy water boiled up around them as they thrashed and twisted; each man trying in desperation to get his knife into the other.

Susan and Ivy were not idle. They had been too long in the forest, through too many hardships, to stand with their hands over their mouths awaiting the outcome. Ivy had already moved the bewildered Judith to a clump of water willows and hidden her beneath their leafy branches.

She had quickly rejoined Suan who was groping frantically in the shallow water in search of her musket and Patterson's rifle.

"Even if we find the guns," cried Ivy above the splashing and thrashing of the two men, "our powder is wet."

"The minute we find the guns," shouted Susan, "we're running for it!"

"And leave Morgan?"

"Have you learned nothing over the past weeks?" said Susan angrily as she found Patterson's gun and quickly brushed away the mud and slime, and poured water from the barrel.

"We're going to save ourselves, or die trying. If we don't, all he's done for us will go for nothing."

Ivy ripped frantically through the cattails searching for the musket Patterson had thrown aside. She knew that Susan was correct, yet it did not seem right to run out on Patterson when he needed help. But what could she do? The fight had carried the two men into water that was over her head—and she couldn't swim.

She found the musket. The stock was above the water, the barrel forced deep into the slimy mud bottom.

"Let's go!" she called as she pulled the weapon free and waded toward the willows where Judith waited.

Patterson and the warrior fought like animals, rolling over and over in the murky water, at times submerging, only to bob up again, locked together like two huge snakes each trying to bite the other. Patterson, taller, had the advantage over the shorter, more stoutly built man.

The woodsman's feet still touched bottom, but the Indian had lost his balance and was using Patterson for leverage. Both men sank below the surface. The cuts and slashes from their razor-sharp knives turned the boiling water red.

They emerged again, but Patterson had his feet firmly planted in the muddy bottom. The Indian was attempting to tread water. Patterson caught the man's knife wrist in one hand and struck hard with his own blade.

The Indian caught Patterson's hand in a grip that stopped the thrust just inches before it plunged into his chest. Patterson's muscles strained to the point of bursting as he slowly forced the man deeper into the water until, at last, his head was submerged. The man thrashed violently but Patterson continued to put more weight on him, pushing him deeper beneath the surface. The Indian's hand released Patterson's wrist and groped blindly for his throat. Patterson raised the knife and plunged it into the water. Again and again the slapping sound of Patterson's knife breaking the surface could be heard along the quiet rippling river.

Patterson released the man, almost losing his balance and

going under himself when the weight of the dead body abruptly broke free and disappeared somewhere in the muddy depths of the Ohio River.

He waded sluggishly toward the shore, dragged himself out of the water, and collapsed—to lie there watching the clouds change shape high overhead; and listen to the birds sing; and smell the scent of the nearby forest; and thank the Lord he was still alive.

He bled from a dozen minor cuts and one or two that would have required stitches if needle and thread had been available.

He breathed long and deep, and sighed tiredly, totally exhausted.

Susan, with Ivy and Judith at her heels, ran as if the devil pursued, due east and away from the river. They ran like terrified animals, oblivious to noise or obstacles or the threat of ambush. All that mattered was to put distance between them and the Indian, should he emerge the victor.

They ran until they collapsed. They lay there coughing and crying until they were able to control their heaving breasts, and speak in short gasping sentences. Then they clambered to their feet and ran again. They had panicked just as surely as Braddock's army had panicked, and for exactly the same reason—self-preservation.

When they fell to the earth a second time, too spent to run another step, they were three miles from the broad expanse of the Ohio River. They gathered their wits as they lay there waiting for the pounding of their hearts to subside. It was still long before noon, and an eternity until nightfall.

"If we make it till dark," thought Susan, "we will have a chance." She prodded Ivy and Judith to their feet and struck off in a fast walk. No more running through the forest like fools, she decided.

Patterson pulled himself to a sitting position and surveyed the slough. Cattails were bent and broken, the canoe he and the women had used was partially sunk in the shallows. The Indians' canoe was gone—floating upside down somewhere on the Ohio.

"Damn!" he muttered. "A five-year-old could see what took place here from a mile and a half upriver."

He painfully waded back into the water, kicked holes in the

canoe's side, then sank it. He cut the bent and broken cattails off below the water line and carried the stalks to the shore. He looked at the slough again. All that remained out of place was the muddy water he had just stirred up—and that would settle.

When he reached the woods, he hid the cattails, then searched out moss to pack his cuts and slashes. That done, he set out after the women. It was no trouble to tell that they were running with wild abandon, making no pretense to cover their trail. He cursed mightily as he followed the scuffed leaves and broken branches through the damp silence of the menacing giant trees, whose high interlacing branches shut out the sunlight. The trail was so plain he could have followed it by the light of the moon—and that is just what he did, except that it wasn't nearly as easy as he thought it would be. In fact, as the night progressed, he had to give up and wait for dawn.

He found them as the sun was breaking the horizon. They were settled in a small glade beneath a long, rolling hill—and they were still asleep, pressed together against the late night chill.

He had already pulled the ball and wiped the wet powder from his rifle barrel when Susan came awake. She did not seem surprised to see him, nor did she speak, except to say that she had cleaned her gun the night before, and would have cleaned his, except that she knew how sensitive he was about anyone touching his rifle.

He spoke without looking at her. "Whose idea was it to run off and leave me?"

"It was mine," she said, offering no apology.

He smiled, that crooked boyish grin that, regardless of how angry Susan was, made her heart skip a beat. "First sensible thing you've done since I've met you."

She blanched, and the smile that had been forming died before it reached her lips.

"I'm not very smart, Morgan," she said after a long moment. "I told you that weeks ago." If I were smart, she thought, I would not give you a moment's notice. But I'm not smart: I'm even less than that—I'm stupid!

"Quit feeling sorry for yourself," he said sharply. "I just paid you a compliment."

She jumped to her feet and stood facing him, anger flushing her cheeks.

"I don't need your compliments, Morgan. I don't need anything from you. Nothing!"

He laid the rifle aside and studied her face.

"And I don't need anything from you," he retorted. "I almost made a mistake one night. I'm glad now that I didn't."

"And I almost made a mistake one night," she cried, "but you didn't want me!"

"Morgan!" said Ivy in sleepy repose, as she struggled to her feet. "You found us. Are you hurt? You look so pale."

" 'Tis nice of you to ask, Ivy," he said, not taking his eyes off Susan.

Susan was shamed. "I'm sorry, Morgan. I guess I have been feeling sorry for myself lately." She smiled and joined Ivy, who was inspecting the knife slashes on Patterson's arms and hands.

"These need sewing up," said Ivy, as she gently removed the moss from the cuts.

"So did Judith's face," returned Patterson, flinching as a piece of moss was pulled free of the dried blood. "But it's healing pretty good without it. So will these."

"I used to think the Boar's Head was a rough place, but it is child's play compared to the frontier," observed Susan. "Morgan," she said seriously, "you could have killed Kemp so easily that day . . . I know that now. Why did you let him hurt you? Why didn't you . . . get it over with?"

Patterson looked up in surprise. "I had no desire to kill Kemp. In truth, Susan, I have never killed an Englishman."

Susan dropped her eyes. There are some that love you, Morgan, she thought sadly. And it seems, at times, that you rejoice in hurting them. I wish I knew you—understood you. Oh, Morgan! Why do you not want me?

"I asked you a question, Susan."

"I'm sorry," stammered the girl. "I . . . I did not hear you."

"I said, did you think I was so vicious as to sin against the Almighty without just cause?"

"No, Morgan," she replied. "It's just that human lives and feelings have little meaning to you . . . especially white women."

The moment she said it, she wished she hadn't. He pushed Ivy aside and stood up.

" 'Tis time we were moving. Wake Judith, Ivy."

Ivy raised to her full height. "I too think you are vicious, Mr. Patterson!"

"Oh, do you now?"

"Why did you hurt Mr. Fontaine? He was your friend...he loves you like a brother—he said so!"

Patterson looked at Susan; she stared back at him, awaiting his answer also. The realization struck him like a kick in the stomach: *She doesn't even know why Fontaine and I fought. She never understood a word that he said; never knew that I thought her virtue was at stake!*

He ran his hand wearily across his forehead, feeling defeated and alone. The irony struck him as funny; when he did fight for Susan, she was unaware of it, did not even suspect it; and, in truth, believed he had attacked Fontaine because the man had interrupted his bedding. He shook his head, laughing sadly at the mess he and Susan were caught up in.

"Do you laugh, sir?" cried Ivy. "You leave a friend's intestines hanging in his hands, and all you can do...is laugh?"

Patterson's heart sank. "Was he hurt that bad, Ivy? Did I gut him?"

"Aye, it was that bad, Mr. Patterson. You should pray, sir, to the Almighty you spoke of, for forgiveness—for you were wrong, Mr. Patterson...you were wrong."

"At the time, Ivy," said Patterson, earnestly, "I thought I had just cause—to kill him."

17

One hundred and twenty miles below Fort Duquesne, they left the banks of the Ohio and again found themselves faced with the rugged Allegheny Mountains.

They moved faster, if not easier, the second time across, because they knew what to expect.

They grew thinner as the days passed, for game that had been abundant in early summer had moved to the lowlands. They made do, eating nuts and berries and what few squirrels and rabbits the snares could provide.

In spite of the hardships, or perhaps because of them, Judith began to show a change. At times her clouded eyes would almost clear and Susan and Ivy would swear that the blonde girl understood what was being said, was even interested in her surroundings. Patterson was unsure about it and feared that Susan and Ivy were too hopeful. But he had to admit that Judith did appear to be almost sane at times.

It was a tired, hungry troop that topped the rise and looked down on a cluster of cabins snuggled close in a long rolling valley. The girls were jubilant. Patterson "hello'd" the house and started down the hill. A white puff of smoke belched from the door of a cabin, and a boom echoed across the valley. Patterson heard the whistle of the ball as it whizzed by his ear. He lurched backward, hanging his ankle in a vine, and sat down hard. Before he could move, Susan rushed past him. "Stay down, you fool!" she hissed. "Don't you know you look just like an Indian?" She raised her arm and waved.

Another puff of smoke and dirt flew up a few feet in front of her. She involuntarily stepped backward and fell over Patterson. He looked amused. "Stay down, you fool!" he mocked. "Don't you know you look just like an Indian, too?"

Ivy ran past them and waved both arms at the cabin. "Hold your fire," she screamed. "We are English people. We are as white as you are." She raised her eyes to the heavens and whispered, "Forgive me, Lord." But she had gained the attention of the sharpshooters, for someone called, "Lay down your arms and come in slowly."

Patterson picked himself up, then tried to help Susan, who promptly slapped his hand away. "I can manage very well without you, Mr. Patterson," she said, pulling her hunting frock down, it having ridden up over her knees.

He shrugged and looked toward the cabin. "If it be the same to you," he called, raising his rifle over his head, "this rifle gun was made by Joel Ferree, of Findley Township, and I lay her down for no man."

Immediately a voice called back, "Spoken like a true Englishman. Come on down and be welcome."

As the bedraggled party approached the cabins, Patterson's slitted eyes were evaluating the situation. There were five one-room log cabins in a row. The one on the farther end had not been chinked, nor had a chimney been built. But the roof had been shaked and looked as though it would shed water. Without chinking, however, the cabin would afford very little protection should it have to be defended, and defense was always his uppermost thought when he surveyed a settlement. The other cabins were in good repair, well chinked, and dotted here and there with shooting loops and good tight chimneys of stone.

Another log building, a full two stories high, with shooting slots all the way to the rooftree, stood some twenty feet behind the cabin Patterson was approaching. He was familiar with such buildings. They served as a smokehouse or a blockhouse should the need arise. He silently complimented the builders on their foresight and industry, for the building was a fine piece of workmanship. Two necessary buildings stood well off to one side, and someone had even dug a well behind the third dwelling. Patterson was satisfied with the layout, so he let his eyes travel to the people standing in front of the first cabin.

The man standing by the doorwell was short and sturdy of build. His iron gray hair was pulled back in a queue, and he wore a long homespun shirt that hung almost to his knees. His deerskin knee breeches had the slick and polished appearance of hard usage, and he boasted no hose or shoes, which had caused the exposed skin of his legs and feet to be deeply tanned. If he was surprised to see Patterson and the women, he concealed it well. Patterson paid close attention to the musket lying easily across the crook of the man's arm, not actually pointing at anyone, but ready.

A woman came out of the cabin to stand beside the man. She leaned her musket against the doorjamb and openly surveyed Patterson's group, making no attempt to conceal her astonishment. She was dressed in a plain homespun dress, apron, and small mobcap. She, like the man, was elderly, so Patterson assumed she was his wife.

His eyes passed over her and moved to a woman standing in the doorway of the second cabin. He could see two children peeping shyly from around her dresstails. His eyes moved to the third cabin, where a middle-aged woman began walking toward them with several children trailing close behind. She carried a baby, perhaps six months old, in her arms. The fourth cabin appeared to be empty, but the fifth had several people standing quietly before it; a solemn group that, even as Patterson raised his hand in greeting, turned back into the building. He dropped his hand self-consciously and turned his attention to the elderly couple, for they appeared to be the leaders of the small community. "I am Morgan Patterson," he said, watching the old man's eyes. "I am escorting these ladies to Fort Cumberland."

The old man casually viewed the women, taking in their frightful appearance, then returned his attention to Patterson. "We were taking of the noonday meal," he said, clasping Patterson's extended hand and shaking it firmly.

His wife interrupted. "Land sakes, Mr. Pettigrew, you need not be so formal. These folk look nigh on half-starved to death." She stepped to the side of the open door and beckoned the women to enter.

Ivy led Judith inside, out of view of the gaping children. Susan, however, dropped the butt of her musket to the ground and leaned on the barrel, hip shot, totally relaxed.

"Come in, come in," said Mrs. Pettigrew, eyeing Judith with concern as she and Ivy filed into the small cabin. "And the both of you," she said pleasantly, motioning to Patterson and Susan. "Come on now, while the victuals are hot. We can talk later." She hurried into the cabin without awaiting an answer.

Patterson turned to Susan and frowned. "Is something wrong, mistress?"

"No, I just thought I would wait for you," she replied with evident embarrassment. She had gotten so used to being with Patterson that it had not occurred to her simply to walk off and leave him just because they had found a haven of security and refreshment. Patterson stared at her, then stepped toward the door. She quickly lifted her musket and followed, avoiding the twinkling eyes of Mr. Pettigrew.

The cabin was sparsely furnished. A table, with a chair at one end and benches at the sides, served for all meals. A churn sat at the edge of the hearth, accenting the oversized fireplace where the cooking was done. A cornshuck mattress lay in one corner, covered neatly with a brightly colored quilt. A ladder disappeared through an opening in the ceiling to the loft above. Herbs and spices hung on strings from the exposed beams. Rough-hewn shelves held a variety of earthenware jugs and bottles and a small cask of gunpowder could been seen in the shadows of the upper reaches of one shelf. The floor was hard-packed earth that had been swept clean and smooth. Two hunting pouches with powderhorns attached hung from a peg by the door. Patterson leaned his rifle against the wall beside them, as did Susan.

It was then that he noticed Pettigrew's gun. It was an ancient wheellock musket, an antique.

"Is this what you shot at us with?" He lifted the gun and inspected it, incredulity playing across his face.

"Surprised, ain't ye?" grinned the old man. "Bet you ain't never seen a gun like that."

"No, I haven't. Not one this fine, anyway."

"She is a beauty. I traded it off'n a trapper out Albany way when me and the missus raised our first cabin. The boys was just young'uns then. I wouldn't take a pretty for that gun. It was built in fifteen and seventy-eight."

Patterson looked at the top plane of the barrel. The letters were worn smooth but he could barely make out "W. Pat——son, 1578."

"It sure shoots straight," said Patterson, standing the wheellock in the corner. "Darned near took my head off, and that was, what? Couple hundred yards?"

"Well," said the old man grinning sheepishly. "She shoots straight as a string, but I'll admit, that was mostly luck."

Mrs. Pettigrew was bent over the hearth dishing food from a large copper pot. She turned, carrying two wooden plates heaped with steaming fresh vegetables and the eyes of the girls followed the food hungrily.

"Sit down, sit down," she said pleasantly as she set the plates on the table. "And you, Mr. Patterson, can wait a moment till I fetch you a shirt. There will be no naked bodies at my table."

Patterson blushed, realizing for the first time that he was all but naked. He stepped outside to await the shirt that Mrs. Pettigrew had mentioned. The woman with the baby, having just reached the cabin, stepped aside and modestly averted her eyes, embarrassing Patterson all the more. White women are foolish, he thought, as he looked at his torso. His breechcloth and leggin's covered most of his lower half. He was barefoot, but then, so was the old man. With the child astride her hip, the woman sidled past him and entered the house. Patterson paid them no attention. Three small children stood observing him shyly. He made a face at them and they scurried after their mother. Patterson laughed silently. He glanced down the line of buildings. The other settlers had disappeared into their cabins, so he assumed they also were taking the noonday meal. Mrs. Pettigrew appeared with the shirt. Patterson thanked her as he slipped it on and returned to the table. He was seated next to Susan and she smiled self-consciously as he eased down beside her. The last time they were in a cabin together she was his wife. She wondered if the thought occurred to him too, but when she glanced out of the corner of her eye, his face disclosed nothing.

They bowed their heads, and Mr. Pettigrew asked the blessing. Patterson raised his head at the last amen and noticed the three small children staring at him again. He was uncomfortable under their scrutiny and began eating quickly. Mrs. Pettigrew sensed his discomfort and scolded the children, shooing them out of the house as quickly as she could. She answered the unasked question of the woman with the baby; she would let her know if there was any word. The woman silently nodded and left. Mrs. Pettigrew smiled and told Patterson that the woman was her daughter-in-law. No other explanation was forthcoming, so Patterson devoted his attention to the food, thankful that the prying eyes of the children had been removed to the outdoors. Mrs. Pettigrew had heaped their plates with potatoes, beans, and a piece of pungent smoked ham. It was accompanied by a generous slice of dark bread. They ate ravenously, washing the food down with large pewter cups of strong black tea.

They ate silently, trying not to appear famished but not succeeding. Mrs. Pettigrew was everywhere, filling this, replenishing that. She reminded him of a mother hen the way she took the girls under her wing. She marveled at how thin they were. "Eat up; put some flesh on those bones." They finally had to refuse, for their stomachs had shrunk from poor usage and even though they eyed the food wistfully, they could not hold another bite. Susan offered to wash the dishes, but Mrs. Pettigrew wouldn't hear of it. Frequently her eyes rested on silent Judith, but she asked no questions.

Mr. Pettigrew lighted his pipe and offered it to Patterson. They smoked in silence. A flock of children gathered at the door, peering at the strange assortment of guests. Mrs. Pettigrew sent them packing. She apologized with one word: "Grandchildren."

Ivy had been unusually quiet throughout the meal. In fact, she hadn't spoken one word since arriving at the clearing, and though no one else seemed to notice, Patterson was bothered by her silence. He glanced at her, and her eyes sidled toward the door. He frowned as she repeated the motion. Patterson handed the pipe to Mr. Pettigrew and stood up.

"Ivy," he said, "would you help me fetch Mrs. Pettigrew an armload of wood?"

She sprang to her feet and started for the door.

"Don't worry yourself about firewood," insisted Mrs. Pettigrew. "Mr. Pettigrew will get it."

Patterson stopped at the door. "'Tis no bother, ma'am; we will be more than glad to fetch a load."

He stepped out before she could protest further and walked with Ivy to the woodpile. "You wished to speak with me?" he asked.

"Morgan," she said, dropping her eyes miserably, "the man, the one in the forest that Judith found?" She looked at Patterson and her eyes were pathetic. "She said his name was John Pettigrew."

Patterson nodded slowly while watching her torn expression.

"What should I say to them, Morgan?" she asked softly. "I do not want to hurt them."

"I will break the news to the Pettigrews. There is no need to involve you, or Judith."

Ivy took his hand and squeezed it gently. "Thank you, Morgan." She smiled sadly. "I just feel so sorry for those folks. They are goodly people."

Patterson nodded and turned to the woodpile. "We'd best take in a load of wood or they will know something is wrong."

They returned to the cabin and laid the wood in the box. The Pettigrews were listening to Susan, who was relating the perils the four had faced.

She looked up as Ivy and Patterson entered; her face was a mask that Patterson couldn't read. She immediately turned her attention to her narrative. Mrs. Pettigrew was exclaiming with every breath. Mr. Pettigrew was listening with calm attention, but he had laid his pipe aside.

Patterson walked to the oaken water bucket and drank deeply. He watched Ivy over the gourd dipper as she seated herself on the bench beside Judith, and he was proud of her for her thoughtful decision not to blurt out her knowledge of John Pettigrew's death. Susan finished her story and everyone stood up.

Mr. Pettigrew insisted he had to finish plowing the new ground he was breaking and wondered if Morgan would accompany him? Yes, Morgan would. Mrs. Pettigrew said that would work well, for she would heat water so these poor girls could take a real bath, with soap, and she did not want to be bothered having a bunch of menfolk around. She told them she expected her three sons home any minute, so they had better hurry and bathe while they still had a little privacy. Mr. Pettigrew winked good-humoredly at the girls and escorted Patterson through the door.

The old man's oxen were yoked and standing in the shade at the edge of a large meadow, where he had already turned eight or nine acres of the black sweet-smelling earth.

"My boys been helping me," Pettigrew said apologetically, "but they went hunting several weeks back and haven't come in yet." He looked at Patterson; the question was plainly visible on his face.

Patterson squatted in the shade and idly rubbed the nose of the nearest ox. He spoke softly as he told Pettigrew about the three hunters who had run the gantlet.

From the description Patterson gave, Pettigrew was sure the three captives were his boys. He said they were probably taken to Fort Le Boeuf. Patterson shook his head. "They were headed toward Canada, Mr. Pettigrew."

"Them boys know their way around," said the old man thoughtfully. "They will be back."

It was a flat statement, but Patterson had the feeling the man knew what he was talking about, at least for two of the boys. Patterson looked at Pettigrew and said simply: "Mr. Pettigrew, John won't be coming in, sir."

Moments passed. Then Pettigrew asked, "Was it bad?"

"Aye, it was bad," said Patterson, still holding the man's eyes. "He was suffering—I killed him."

Pettigrew looked away. He studied the line of cabins on the far side of the field. "I thank you for your honesty, Mr. Patterson. John was my wife's favorite young'un, him being the youngest . . . I do not know how to break the news to her." He sighed and bowed his head.

Patterson remained silent. The old man sighed again and moved slowly to the oxen. He untied the lead line that secured the pair to the tree and hooked the yoke to the plow. He made a clicking sound and told them to "git up." The oxen plodded slowly into the field.

Mrs. Pettigrew and the girls drew bucket after bucket of water. They had built a fire behind the cabin and were heating water in a large black iron kettle. Nearby stood a wooden rainbarrel half full of cold water, and as the water in the kettle began to boil, the old woman began pouring it into the barrel, testing it with her finger.

They decided Judith should go first. They slipped her out of her ragged dress and helped her climb into the barrel. Even to Judith's addled mind the hot water was voluptuous. Mrs. Pettigrew handed Ivy a ball of lye soap, and Ivy scrubbed her mistress vigorously. Several children wandered up, gawking at Judith until Mrs. Pettigrew threatened them with a stick, and they scattered like a covey of quail, laughing and hooting.

The old lady picked up Judith's dress and examined it critically. "We can wash this thing, and I can make you a loan of needle and thread, but it's not going to do much good." Mrs. Pettigrew left, to return shortly carrying a crock jug. "Now, girls," she said sternly, "do not take offense, but you could use a dose of this sorrels and vinegar."

The girls blushed.

"Now, now," chided Mrs. Pettigrew. "Don't look so down in the mouth." She smiled good-naturedly and prattled on. "Never seen a woman yet who could go without preparations for days and days and still smell like a lily." She laughed and the girls finally joined in.

Susan asked timidly, "Mrs. Pettigrew, do you think Mr. Patterson smelled me?"

The woman gave her a stern look. "Can you smell yourself?"

Susan replied faintly, "Yes, I can."

"Well, if you can," nodded the old lady, "other folks have been smellin' you for a week! And as for Morgan Patterson, why, he can smell a bobcat forty feet up a tree. I suppose he didn't have no trouble smellin' you."

Susan was mortified. Mrs. Pettigrew continued. "Ladies, Mr. Patterson is a woodsie and 'tain't like he was delicate. When you live out here, they's lots of things you get used to or ignore. Women problems is one of 'em."

The two girls blushed miserably and avoided each other's eyes. Mrs. Pettigrew laughed again and went off to wash Judith's dress. Susan joined the old woman as she gingerly sudsed the ragged, once elegant finery.

"Not much here to work with. You girls been through a lot more than you told if these skirts is any indication." The old woman shook her head in sad appreciation. "I reckon this was a beautiful dress."

"We have been through quite a bit, Mrs. Pettigrew," Susan said quietly.

"Tell me," said Mrs. Pettigrew, frowning up at the girl from the washboard. "Has Judith always been like she is? Is she dangerous?"

"Oh, no! She's as gentle as a lamb." Then Susan told her about their captivity, the baby, and Judith's madness. "But she's doing better," Susan said excitedly. "She has days when she almost comes out of it. I believe she even understands what is said to her. But she never talks."

"Well, it breaks my heart," said the woman, "to see such a pretty girl in the shape she's in—but the good Lord knows what he's about. They's a reason for what's happened."

"I used to believe that, Mrs. Pettigrew, but I'm not so sure anymore. It seems as though God has turned his back on us . . . so much needless suffering and death . . . I just don't know what to think anymore."

"Child," said Mrs. Pettigrew sternly, "faith in the Lord comes hard at times. Even the Saviour questioned the Almighty when he was nailed to the cross, so it can't be a sin for us mortals to have doubts once in a while—but don't lose faith; the Lord knows what he's doin'."

When the men returned that evening, it was three scrubbed and shining young ladies who met them at the door. The old man laughed appreciatively as Susan and Ivy curtsied. Even Patterson smiled at the bloom upon them. Their beauty caught his eyes and stirred him. Judith's and Ivy's dresses had been mended and, except for being too short for modesty's sake, the garments looked serviceable again. Susan was still wearing Patterson's leather hunting frock, but she had brushed it clean, and it looked elegant on her. Then Susan and Ivy announced to Patterson that he would take a bath. He argued. They heckled him. He took a bath in the same barrel they had used. Yes—he felt better. No—he didn't want his hair cut.

When he sat down to eat the evening meal, he looked like a different man. His black hair fairly shone. They had pulled it back into a queue and tied it with a piece of ribbon that Mrs. Pettigrew had supplied. He wore the same white shirt she had loaned him earlier, along with his newly washed breechcloth and well-brushed leggin's. And he had shaved.

After supper, Mr. Pettigrew took his wife by the hand and told

302

Patterson they would return shortly. Patterson knew the old man's intent. He did not envy Mr. Pettigrew his task.

After they had gone, Patterson moved to the yard and eased his tired frame down beside the chopping block. The sun was going down. A whippoorwill called low and mournful. Patterson could hear a woman crying in one of the cabins. He did not look in that direction; he had heard that sound too many times. Getting taken by the Indians was fairly common on the frontier, yet one never seemed to grow accustomed to it. The girls finished washing the dishes and came out to sit quietly beside him.

Two men emerged from the fifth cabin and sauntered toward them. They were young men, about Patterson's age, maybe a little older, and they were big, weighing over two hundred pounds each. Both wore homespun shirts, knee breeches and moccasins, but they were not woodsmen. Patterson could tell by the way they moved. They had the gait of a man who followed the plow, instead of the agile movements of a hunter. Neither carried his weapon, which a woodsman was never without. Patterson watched them approach through narrowed eyes.

They moved closer, candidly appraising the three girls while ignoring Patterson completely.

"Evenin', ladies," said one while the other grinned openly. "Me and Jake seen you come in and thought we'd make your acquaintance." He let that sink in, then continued. "Looked like you was about done in, so we waited till you rested a mite 'fore we come down."

"That was nice of you," said Susan with unaccustomed sarcasm. She did not like the men, or the way their eyes denuded her and Ivy and Judith.

"I weren't talking to you," he said politely. "I was talking to that pretty little copperheaded wench." He motioned toward Ivy.

Ivy smiled at the young man. He told her his name was Jack Baylor and his brother was Jake. They were twins. Ivy introduced herself, then each of the others, including Patterson.

The men dipped their heads to the women but continued to ignore Patterson, who found the insult amusing. Jack and Jake eased their weights to the ground. "What's wrong with her?" Jack nodded toward Judith. "She looks loony."

Patterson didn't hear Ivy's answer: his mind was on the Pettigrew family meeting. He felt a great sadness for the Pettigrews: losing three sons had to be a savage blow for the old couple, and equally hard on their daughters-in-law and grandchildren. He wished he could do something to lessen their pain, for they were good, humble, God-fearing people, but he knew there was nothing he or anyone could say. The family had to work it out among themselves.

He turned his attention to the girls and surprised Susan, who was staring at him with unfeigned curiosity etched lightly on her finely honed face. She immediately turned her attention to the story Jack was telling Ivy and laughed lightly at whatever it was he said. Patterson climbed lazily to his feet and ambled toward the old man's cabin. The sun was down, but there was still enough daylight to see by, so he had little trouble locating the milkpail.

His pace increased as he stepped over the split-rail fence and headed directly for the pole building that served as the barn, chicken house, and stables. The cow standing by the barn was restless, so Patterson figured it was well past her milking hour. He squatted and gently brushed the dust from her udders. She turned her head and looked at Patterson with large quizzical eyes, causing the bell about her neck to clang. Susan moved to his side, kneeling down also. Patterson glanced at her wonderingly.

"Let me do that," she said, taking the bucket from him. " 'Tis woman's work and judging by the way the cow looked at you, she's probably not used to a man's touch." Her eyes held a touch of mockery as she glanced at Patterson.

"I just got tired of hearing her bawl," he countered.

"I heard her too," said Susan, "but I just could not be impolite and leave our company in the middle of a sentence."

"No, I guess not."

Susan expertly stroked the cow's teats and the pail filled quickly. The cow stood contentedly chewing her cud as the girl worked.

"I appreciate your helping Mrs. Pettigrew with the supper," Patterson said abruptly, not used to making small talk. " 'Twas a goodly thing to do."

Susan smiled and laid her forehead against the cow's flank. She hoped Patterson couldn't see the joy that a few kind words from him could kindle.

"So! Here is where you ran off to," Jack said. "I've been looking everywhere for you."

Susan glanced at the hulking man standing over her, then immediately beyond him to Patterson's retreating form. She felt like slapping Jack's face for his bad timing.

"The truth is," he drawled, grinning widely, "I got the feelin' you didn't like me much, but that don't make no difference. You'll like me in time."

A cold rage caused her to pull hard on the cow's teats, and the animal grunted and stamped its foot. Susan patted the cow's flank soothingly and apologized to the animal. Mister, she said to herself, you are in a for a big surprise.

When Patterson reached the cabin, a beargrease candle had been lighted and the old man was silhouetted against the flickering light. "Sit down, Morgan," he said kindly, indicating a spot beside him. "Them's good women my boys took to wife."

Patterson nodded but remained quiet, knowing the old man expected no answer. Pettigrew began to reminisce. He told Patterson about his sons and their wives; about how the family had migrated from New York to settle in the valley two years ago. Two of the boys had brought their wives and children, but John, the youngest, had left his girl in Albany. The fourth cabin down, the empty one, was to have been John's. It was almost finished, and they had been looking forward to the girl's arrival this fall. The old man looked off into the night. "I will get someone to write a letter and tell her of John's death."

Susan stepped into the faint light. "Mr. Pettigrew," she said gently, "I would be most happy to write your letter."

The old man raised his head and searched her face for a long moment. Neither he nor his wife could read or write, so he experienced a moment of hesitation before deciding her offer was genuine. "Thank you, lass," he said slowly. " 'Twould mean a lot to me and the missus."

Jack, standing in the shadows, said good night to Susan and disappeared into the darkness. She watched until he was out of sight, then stepped past Pettigrew and entered the cabin. Judith and Ivy had evidently been inside for some time, because Patterson could hear Ivy talking while Susan strained the milk and dipped off the cream to make butter. He wondered if Jake were in the cabin too, but he resisted the impulse to look inside. The old man's eyes narrowed as he looked at Patterson through his bushy brows. "You don't like them boys much, do you, that Jack and Jake?"

Patterson didn't answer; he just smiled at Pettigrew and changed the subject. "How much livestock have you got here, Mr. Pettigrew?"

The old man smiled silently at Patterson's tact. "Well, let me see," he said, looking into the darkness, "we got us two oxen, one sow and seven piglets, two cows and one man cow." He hesitated, searching his memory. "Aye, and a passel of chickens. We make out right proper." He wasn't bragging; he was stating fact.

Patterson looked down at his bare feet and spread his dusty toes. Mr. Pettigrew observed Patterson's controlled anxiety. "Something bothering you, son?"

"Might not hurt nothing," said Patterson, still looking at his feet, "if you put your stock up for a few days."

The old man's expression remained unchanged. "You think them Indians might hit here?"

"Aye," said Patterson quietly. "They will be here."

Patterson and the old man quietly discussed building pens for the stock, and a lean-to off the side of the barn for the hogs. They would start splitting rails come sunup.

As the moon rose directly overhead, they stood up and shook hands. "It has been a long day, Morgan," said the old man with a sigh. "Believe I will turn in." He stepped into the cabin with Patterson following. Patterson made a pretense of drinking a dipper of water, using it as an excuse to look over the cabin. The girls had gone to the loft, and he could hear their low voices from above. Mrs. Pettigrew had already gone to bed, and Patterson discreetly avoided looking in her direction. He slipped the borrowed shirt over his head, hung it on a peg, and slid into the crisp night.

Ivy undressed and lay down on the cornshuck mattress. "Lord, this feels good," she sighed. "I had forgotten anything could be so soft."

Susan agreed. The three girls nestled into the mattress and

relaxed. It had cooled down considerably since the sun had set, and although the cabin still retained a good deal of the day's heat, the loft was cool.

"Susan," whispered Ivy.

"Yes," came the sleepy reply.

"I do believe Jack and Jake like us."

"Those two would like anything that wore a dress," retorted Susan sleepily.

"You did not appear to like them overmuch," said Ivy. "Why?"

"I've seen their kind before, at the Boar's Head. And I have no doubts as to how they would act if they knew you were a handmaiden, and I was an indentured girl fresh from a taproom."

"Do you think it would make a difference? Most of the people we meet are very nice to us. I think you are wrong, Susan."

"I probably am," said the sleepy girl. "Now go to sleep before you awaken Mr. and Mrs. Pettigrew."

But Mr. Pettigrew was awake and had heard the whispered conversation. He stared into the darkness, troubled by Susan's remark. Although he thought highly of Ivy and felt sorry for Judith, it was Susan that had won a place in his heart and it bothered him that she was a tavern wench. She didn't appear to be that kind of woman. Well, it wasn't any of his business. The old man drifted off to a troubled sleep and dreamed about his three lost sons.

Patterson left the cabin and walked toward the barn to bed down. Jake and Jack were waiting at the rail fence. "A word with you, Patterson," said Jack, moving away from the fence, making it difficult for Patterson to watch both men at once.

Patterson cradled his rifle, raising the muzzle until it was pointed at Jack's breastbone. It was done very nonchalantly but Jack knew it was no accident. He moved back to the fence and stood beside Jake.

"We been wonderin' about those women," he said nervously, eyeing Patterson's gun in the moonlight.

"What about them?"

"Why, we was wonderin' what they are to you?" Jake snickered suggestively. "You've probably laid with all three of them, ain't you?" Patterson eased the hammer to full cock. The click was loud in the darkness.

"Now, now, Patterson," said Jack. "Jake meant no disrespect, did you, Jake?" Jake's eyes flashed defiance in the pale light and Patterson knew that if trouble was inevitable, he would kill Jake first. Jack began fidgeting as Jake and Patterson continued to stare at one another.

Jake finally turned his head and spat a stream of tobacco juice over the rail fence. "If them women decide to stay here when you leave, they stay." He looked hard at Patterson and there was no fear in his eyes.

Patterson's voice was so soft they had to strain their ears to hear him. "Only if it is their decision. Now get out of my way."

Jake stood his ground for the briefest moment before pushing Jack ahead of him toward the cabin they shared with their family.

Patterson let the hammer down to half-cock as he watched the two men fade into the darkness. He had the feeling he had made a grave error by not touching the trigger on Jake.

Daybreak was shattered by the sound of Patterson's ax. The old man joined him, embarrassed that the woodsman had commenced work while he lay abed. They worked in silence, splitting out a sizable stack of rails by the time Mrs. Pettigrew called them to breakfast. Patterson washed his face in the spring below the barn and walked toward the cabin. Mr. Pettigrew had gone ahead, so Patterson was alone as he rounded the barn and started up the path leading to the house.

"Wait...I would be pleased to walk with you," called Susan from the open doorway of the pole structure. She was carrying a pail of milk, spilling some over the side as she hurried toward him. "Did you sleep in the barn last night?" she asked breathlessly as she joined him.

He nodded.

"I wondered," she said, then caught herself, for a lady was not supposed to think about a man's sleeping habits, much less inquire about them. "I mean, sir," she stammered, "I hoped you did not have to sleep outdoors."

Patterson smiled openly at her. "Thank you for your concern." It amused him, her discomfort, and he took a perverse pleasure in her vexation, especially since they had shared a cabin as man and wife not a month earlier.

They crossed the fence in silence and moved up the path toward the buildings. As they came abreast of the Baylor cabin, Jake and Jack stepped through the door. Patterson knew it was no coincidence.

"Mornin', Miss Susan," said Jack. "You look bloody well purty this morning."

Susan forced a smile. "Thank you, sir."

Jack fell in beside her and offered to carry the pail. She declined, but he insisted, so she passed the bucket to him. As he took the pail he let his fingers linger on her hand. Morgan stalked ahead, leaving her to the Baylors—deliberately, she thought, as Jake moved to her other side.

She raised her hand, intending to ask Patterson to wait . . . and then let it fall. Impulsively, Susan slipped her hand through Jake's arm, and Jake grinned, patting her fingers possessively.

She realized her mistake, but it was too late to undo the damage, for they had reached the cabin. She had no intention of leading Jake on, and she was afraid he had gotten the wrong impression from her impulsive gesture, so without any preliminaries she disengaged his hand and curtly thanked them both for their assistance. Jake whispered that he would see her later, but she didn't even hear him. Her mind was on Morgan Patterson.

Mr. Pettigrew watched with mixed feelings as the Baylors passed out of sight. Although he didn't care for Jake or Jack, the rest of the Baylors seemed decent enough folk. But he didn't want them hanging around his cabin or his sons' cabins. They hadn't made trouble while his boys were at home, having kept pretty much to themselves since showing up at the clearing six months before. But now that the boys were gone . . . well, he just didn't know. True, the Baylors had done little work on their cabin, and their garden hadn't produced well, and their stock roamed at will, occasionally becoming a nuisance; but all said and done, they had minded their own business and he couldn't fault them on that account. Still, to see Susan arm in arm with Jake didn't set well with him; but, again, it was none of his business. Besides, if she were a tavern wench, she probably knew what she was doing. He threw a sidelong glance at Patterson, who was busy with his breakfast and didn't appear to have noticed. The old man's mouth turned down at the corners in disappointment.

Patterson and Pettigrew split rails the rest of the morning. The woodsman could feel his strength returning and worked hard to build his weakened body back to its former endurance. At noon they laid their axes aside and started for the house. Everyone except the very young had a job to do. The older children were hoeing and pulling weeds; the women were picking vegetables. Susan and Ivy were boiling water in the big black kettle, doing the laundry. Susan was wielding a pole, punching and stirring the clothes as they boiled, and Ivy was fetching another bucket of water to pour into the kettle. Patterson looked for Judith but didn't see her anywhere; he figured she must be in the cabin with Mrs. Pettigrew.

Jack and Jake weren't present, but the rest of the Baylor clan were lazing in the shade of their cabin. They were all lazy, he decided, as he headed for the Pettigrews.

Mrs. Pettigrew was baking bread. Her hair was pulled into a bun at the nape of her neck and perspiration dampened her forehead. She smiled at Patterson. "Getting a lot of work done, you and the mister?"

"It's coming," said Patterson, looking about the room.

"If you are looking for Judith," said the old woman, pushing a lock of damp hair off her forehead and leaving a smudge of flour in its place, "she's asleep. That girl sure is a pretty thing, even with that scar on her face. Makes one feel plumb sorry for her."

Susan and Ivy came in, smelling of lye soap and perspiration. Ivy told Patterson what she had learned about boiling clothes. He smiled. Things that frontier folk took for granted impressed the British girl.

When the evening meal was finished and the chores were done, Patterson and the old man sat in the yard and smoked. The girls came out and were immediately joined by Jake and Jack. Pettigrew watched prudently as the Baylors and the girls talked and laughed. Jake tried to put his arm around Susan, but she whispered something in his ear and he removed it. The old man's eyes twinkled.

Night was slipping softly from the darkened forest, inching its way across the open valley, and Patterson listened contentedly to the sounds of its approach. An owl hooted; another answered from afar. A whippoorwill called.

310

The bell clanged with a distant echo in the fading twilight as the milk cow plodded back to the pasture to feed. Patterson took a long pull at the pipe. He was enjoying this brief spell of tranquility, knowing it would end soon enough for they were still a far piece from Fort Cumberland.

Mrs. Pettigrew came out to join her husband. She told him the hawk had been in the chickens again and had got off with two little ones. Pettigrew said he would kill the hawk first chance he got. She said they may not have any chicks left by then. The old man said he'd see to it when he could. He turned to Patterson.

"We'd best start layin' fence tomorrow, Morgan. Them hogs is going to take awhile to drive in."

Patterson nodded.

Jack asked abruptly, "What for are ye building them pens, Mr. Pettigrew?"

The old man looked at Jack for a long moment before answering, then said slowly, "Well, Morgan here thinks we might be bothered by Indians afore too long."

Jake snorted. "Why, ain't no Indians foolish enough to hit here. We got too many guns." He snickered. "That's just plumb tomfoolery talk."

Patterson remained silent.

Susan spoke up. "You had best pay attention to what Mr. Patterson says, Mr. Baylor. He knows Indians."

Patterson looked hard at Susan, and she dropped her eyes. The look he had given her hurt worse than words. She wished she could retract her statement.

Pettigrew's grandchildren were throwing rocks into the air, watching the bats dive at the objects. It appeared to be great fun the way the children whooped and laughed. Susan edged closer to Patterson, almost touching him.

"'Twould be nice to have no cares, would it not, Mr. Patterson?" she asked, watching the children tease the bats.

Patterson smiled at her. "Your cares will be over upon reaching Fort Cumberland, mistress."

She studied the happy children. "Perhaps, Mr. Patterson, perhaps."

Jake leaned down and whispered something in Susan's ear. She smiled and shook her head no. Ivy laughed at something Jack said and Patterson involuntarily looked at her. He couldn't understand the change that had come over him. Seeing Susan and Ivy so obviously happy and contented had a depressing effect on him. He wasn't angry; he was sad. He wasn't needed here at this outpost, this semblance of civilization. Nor would he be needed once they reached Fort Cumberland. But wasn't that what he wanted? To reach Fort Cumberland and dispose of the women as quickly as he could? It was all he had thought about for mile after weary mile, day after weary day. Yet here, now, he was melancholy because the girls were neglecting him. He almost wished they were back in the wilderness. Self-pity washed over him like a wave. He stood up and walked off into the night.

Had he glanced back, he would have seen two lovely young women staring after him with concern marking their faces. And, had he looked harder, he might have seen the anger and dislike on the features of the two young men. But all this went unnoticed, for Patterson didn't look back. Instead, it was Mr. Pettigrew who observed each face with rapt attention. Then he settled back with a satisfied grunt and continued to smoke his clay pipe.

The Baylor boys are wasting their time, the old man thoughtfully reflected as he swung his attention to Patterson, who had just stepped over the split-rail fence. Pettigrew was familiar with woodsmen. He had known a few who absolutely refused to take wives, but Patterson wasn't cut from the same bolt of cloth as they. That type usually was more animal than human, preferring the solitude of the forest and the company of wild beasts to the companionship of humans, white or red. But Patterson, though a loner, plainly liked people. Patterson was a hard lad, anyone could sense that, but he wasn't as uncaring as he tried to pretend, nor was he as oblivious to the young ladies as he strived to appear.

The old man shook his head in disgust. Youth—he would never understand them. The days and nights laid to waste, while they battled, to prove ... what? That they can make it through life alone without needing or depending on anyone, afraid to give themselves, be vulnerable, accept rejection. He drew absently on his pipe, his mind preoccupied.

He decided the Lord must be a juvenile himself to have wasted the seedtime of life on those wonderful sidesteppers of reality. Only the aged, he thought, appear to have sense enough to desire others openly and honestly and to rejoice in the simple pleasures of companionship that the opposite sex was wont to offer, the delightful intimacies shared by those who are not suspicious of life or frightened by it.

Having made the mental circle from young to old, he found himself thinking again of youth. Patterson is a bit backward, he reasoned, so, 'tis foolish as hell for the girls to beat around the bush where he is concerned. The lass that wins his affection will be the one who leaves him no alternative.

The Baylors continued to sit there after Patterson had walked away. They wished the Pettigrews would leave also, but the old man smoked his pipe and didn't appear to be the least bit inclined to move one way or the other. Their repeated attempts to entice Susan and Ivy away fell on deaf ears. The boys were becoming angry, frustrated, and dangerous. They had been too long without a woman and Susan and Ivy reminded them of it. They had coveted the Pettigrew women for months, but were not so foolish as to make advances in that direction, for although the Pettigrew boys were an easy lot, Jack and Jake were afraid of them. Their eyes were too steady and their trigger fingers too light for the twins to attempt an unwanted gesture toward their wives. But these three strangers (or rather two strangers, for they had excluded Judith as being completely mad, and therefore dangerous) were a different proposition entirely. After all, according to a thoughtless slip of the tongue by Ivy, one was a servant, the other a tavern wench, and everyone knew that servants and tavern wenches were loose women.

It infuriated the Baylors that Susan and Ivy, with their indecent clothing and open acknowledgment that they were alone for weeks with a stranger, still pretended to be of gentle breeding. They were sick of their airs, sick of being treated like fools by a pair of common sluts. Their minds were made up. They would have the favor of the women—with or without their permission.

But what fantasies they had dreamed up for that night went unfulfilled, because when the old man and woman finally retired, the two girls followed their footsteps through the dewy grass.

They climbed the ladder to the loft and undressed immediately, for the loft was still warm from the heat of the day. Ivy turned to Susan in the darkness.

"You are quite correct in your opinion of Jack and Jake. They are becoming overbold; 'tis a little scary."

Susan smiled. "Aye, they are trash, but the rest of the people here are very nice, don't you think?"

Ivy looked toward Judith's sleeping silhouette. "Susan, I have decided to stay in America. I—I feel that I can find a place for me here." She faltered, then continued. "I believe America is a place where you can start over and be whatever you wish to be, if you are willing to sacrifice." She reached out and touched Judith. "I wish she understood what I am saying, for I love her very much, but—but, I want a home and a husband and babies, lots of babies. I would be happy to live in a log cottage, such as this, and work a garden and milk bullocks..."

Susan burst out giggling, then immediately sobered and apologized to Ivy. Indignantly, Ivy demanded an explanation, which brought more giggles from Susan.

"Ivy, darling," she said affectionately, "you do not milk a bullock." She laughed again, then resumed. "You milk a cow; a bullock is a male cow."

Ivy laughed, putting her hand over her mouth, then persisted. "I know I'm ignorant, but I can cook and sew and mend—and I'll learn to do all the things a woman should be able to do for her husband."

The girls lay back, each engulfed with her own thoughts. Neither Ivy nor Susan saw the tears that streamed down Judith's cheeks. She wanted to take Ivy in her arms and tell her that she would die of loneliness if Ivy should be separated from her. She wanted to tell Ivy of the long-ago conversation she had overheard, and that she was proud, yes, *proud* that Ivy was her sister. She wanted to tell Ivy that she loved her... but even as her deranged mind sought the words, her lips would not speak them. Judith turned her face away and her clouded eyes filled with silent tears.

Mrs. Pettigrew turned to her husband in the darkness. "The Lord don't take kindly to old men what eavesdrops on young girls' conversation," she whispered.

Mr. Pettigrew chuckled and patted his wife's buttocks affectionately. "Go to sleep, old lady," he whispered. "If the Lord hadn't wanted me to hear what them girls said, he wouldn't have given me ears."

And after his wife was asleep, and after the house settled in for the night, he thought about Ivy, and wondered if perhaps he had been a little harsh on youth.

18

Mrs. Pettigrew shut the privy door and started toward the cabin. She could hear the ring of axes, as the men felled trees in the woods beyond the barn.

Humming happily to herself, she rounded the corner of the cabin and stopped short; Judith was clinging to the wall for support. Perspiration streamed down the girl's ashen face.

"You've been throwing up again," cried the old lady, moving quickly to Judith's side and putting an arm around her.

"My Lord, child, what is it?"

Judith clutched her abdomen and vomited again. Mrs. Pettigrew looked into the girl's tear-filled eyes. "You've been sleeping a lot of late, and now you are sick at your stomach come mornings." Mrs. Pettigrew's faded eyes softened. "Child," she whispered, brushing tears from her eyes, "you are going to have a baby." She took the sick girl into her arms and held her close. "You poor, baby," she sighed, "you can't even take care of yourself, and now you're going to have a child of your own."

The old woman felt the girl become rigid in her embrace. She held Judith at arm's length and peered into her clouded eyes. "You understand what I said, don't you?" Her voice rose with excitement. "You understood when I said you are expectin'?"

"I . . . cannot have children." Judith's voice sounded as if she were dreaming.

"Why can you not have children? Tell me, child, tell me!"

"I was kicked in the stomach," said the girl, her eyes squinched shut, her face ashen. "I...I can't have babies...," the girl's voice trailed off.

"Don't go back!" cried Mrs. Pettigrew, shaking Judith, fearing that she had lost the girl. "Talk to me...talk to me!"

Judith's eyes slowly opened, and they were almost clear.

"You are going to have a baby, Judith—your very own baby. Do you understand?"

Tears welled up in Judith's eyes, and her lips trembled. "I...I don't believe you. You are trying to hurt me, like all the rest...please don't hurt me anymore." Then she cried. And Mrs. Pettigrew cried with her, and talked soothingly in her ear about how beautiful her baby would be and how much pleasure it would bring to her, and on and on until the girl quieted.

"Child," said Mrs. Pettigrew thumbing a tear off Judith's cheek, "you and I have some serious talking to do. Will you walk with me to the woods so we can be in private?"

Judith nodded that she would.

They talked in the shade of a giant oak. Slowly at first, then with a passion as Judith's mind cleared and she, indeed, accepted the fact that she was with child.

The old woman laid a calloused hand on Judith's arm. "Need I ask who the father is?"

"It wasn't his fault," said the girl softly. "It—I wanted him."

Mrs. Pettigrew patted Judith's arm affectionately. "Under the circumstances, I'm mighty glad it happened—but I will have a word with him. You're goin' to need a husband."

"Mrs. Pettigrew...please don't say anything to Morgan. I don't want him like that..."

"Whatever you say," agreed the old woman, "but you better think on it. He'd be a good man."

"He does not even like me."

"Well, how do you feel about him?"

"I'm...I'm in love with him. I don't know whether I love him or not...but I'm 'in' love with him."

"Well, I don't rightly know what you mean by that, but 'tain't none of my business." She took the girl's hand and caressed it gently. "Can you remember anything of the past month?"

Judith put her hand to her forehead and massaged her temple. "It gives me such a headache to try and think."

"Well then, don't you try too hard. They's plenty of time for that."

"I remember getting captured by Indians—Shawnees...friends of Morgan's. I...I remember bits and pieces of...things. It seems like a dream...I can't tell what's real and what's not."

"It's all right," said Mrs. Pettigrew. "Don't try to remember, it's not important."

She stood up and smoothed her long dress and apron, eyeing Judith with pride.

"Will you wait here and not move till I come back?"

"Where are you going?" asked the girl alarmed, rising to her feet.

"To the house; I'll be right back," assured Mrs. Pettigrew.

"Can't I go with you? I want to see Ivy, and Susan, and...Morgan." She blushed and the scar on her forehead stood stark white against the tint of her heated face.

"I'll bring them to you, child. I promise."

Mrs. Pettigrew assembled them all in the cabin. Morgan wondered at the expression in her eyes when she looked in his direction; it was a combination, a mixture of tenderness and anger. It bothered him.

She closed and barred the door, then leaned against the facing. Mr. Pettigrew frowned but remained silent. He knew his wife well. She had a reason for everything she did, but for the life of him, he couldn't figure out why she closed the door on such a warm day.

She told them abruptly that Judith had regained her senses, omitting, of course, the fact that the girl was pregnant. She informed them to be careful what they said or did, explaining that Judith remembered nothing of her life after being captured by the Indians.

"She's just barely herself," cautioned the old woman. "We can push her back to wherever she came from if'n we ain't careful. You understand?"

"Where is she?" asked Ivy, fidgeting with excitement. "I must go to her—please, Mrs. Pettigrew."

"She's at the edge of the woods, behind the house," said the old woman as she removed the bar. "Now, go to her. She's waiting for you." Ivy and Susan were out the door before Mrs. Pettigrew stopped speaking.

Patterson took the old woman by the shoulders. "I don't know

318

what you did, or how you did it, but...you have my thanks, Mrs. Pettigrew." Then he, too, was out the door and running.

Mrs. Pettigrew watched him go and her face became grave. I don't approve of what you and Judith did, Morgan, she thought, but I'm mighty glad you did it...otherwise that girl might never have come back.

"Old woman," said Mr. Pettigrew, pulling her to him. "Have I told you lately that I love you?"

She pursed her thin lips and blushed; beautiful, young, and happy. "Ten year ago, Mr. Pettigrew. Ten year ago on March eighteen." Then she threw her arms around him and they laughed joyfully.

Judith rose gracefully to her feet and watched Ivy and Susan come. She took a step toward them, then another.

They stood there facing each other, Ivy a few feet ahead of Susan. She's my mistress, thought Ivy, I cannot run to her and hug her; it isn't proper. Oh, God! I want to so very much!

Judith saw the hesitation and it sobered her, for she too wanted to take Ivy in her arms and hold her, and kiss her. She stood there, not knowing what to do, afraid to make the first move.

"How do you feel, mistress?" asked Ivy, trying hard to hide an anguish that was threatening to send her flying to Judith in spite of her lot in life. But she stood there waiting for a sign—anything— that would be enough to send her running blindly into Judith's arms.

Susan watched the two girls face each other. With all her heart she longed to intrude, to push them into each other's embrace. Patterson moved up beside her, and he too waited.

Judith very possibly might have thrown tradition aside and run to Ivy—it was in her mind to do that very thing—before Patterson arrived. She turned deathly pale as she gazed into the eyes of the maker of the new life forming in her womb.

She wanted to call joyfully to him—to tell him he was going to be a father, but she couldn't. She felt it coming and she tried to stop it, but she couldn't do that either, and she bent from the waist and vomited—again and again.

Patterson was awake before dawn. He lay on his pallet, watching the gray light filter through the barn, and he listened to the sounds of a world coming awake. A quail called; a rooster crowed; birds began to sing. He could hear the clang of the cowbell as she came in for her morning milking. He wondered briefly what it would be like to settle down and live in peace and tranquility. He shook his head. He would always be the wanderer, for the long hunt was as much a part of him as eating and breathing. He knew he could never be a settlement man even if he tried. His thoughts were interrupted by Susan with her milkpail. He heard her speak quietly to the cow and a moment later he could hear the milk splashing against the bottom of the oaken bucket.

"Morning, Susan," he said, as he stepped through the barn door.

She smiled up at him. "Sleeping late this morning?"

He grinned, then squatted beside her. She continued milking, but the silence was not oppressive. Both were aware of each other and conversation did not seem necessary.

"Morgan," she said finally, "how long do you propose to stay here?"

"Why do you ask?"

She wanted to tell him of the feeling she had—that something bad was about to happen, but it seemed so childish that she said instead, "I suppose I am homesick. I would like to see my family." Which was indeed true. She had been thinking about her mother, stepfather, and the children a great deal lately. She missed them terribly, but, in truth, it was the feeling of foreboding that bothered her so. She shuddered, but then smiled at him. "A rabbit jumped over my grave." She wished she hadn't said it.

"We will leave here soon."

She nodded and looked long at him. "Morgan, the other day, when I defended you against the Baylor boys—about the Indians—I did not mean to anger you by what I said." He dropped his eyes and arose to his full height, then looked off at the distant hills. She continued hesitantly. "I just could not sit there and let trash like the Baylors belittle you." She blushed. "I spoke before I thought. I am sorry."

He looked at her several moments, then said slowly, "A man must speak for himself, Susan. He cannot let his woman speak for him or he will be less than a man."

She looked at him wide-eyed, a smile playing across her lips.

"Am I your woman then, or are we still play-acting that I am your wife?" He realized what he had implied and fled clumsily.

She watched him intently, laying her head over and pursing her lips. Her eyes were alive with wonder. Then she smiled to herself and resumed milking.

Ivy caught him just as he was donning his shirt for the morning meal. She was bubbling with joy. Taking his hand, she told him of her decision to stay in America. She was as excited as a child and her happiness was contagious. Patterson laughed with her, congratulating her.

"Ivy, 'tis a fine choice you have made," he said. "The colonies will be a better place with ladies like you."

She brushed his cheek with her lips. "Thank you, Morgan. I feel so grand, so American—Judith is doing so well. Oh, Morgan, I'm happier than I've ever been in my whole life!"

It humbled him, the inner strength of the lovely young woman whose decision it was to face a world completely alien to her.

Patterson and the old man worked hard throughout the morning, building pens and fences. They would have to split more rails, however, if they were to complete the job, so they agreed to do that after the dinner meal. Patterson shielded the October sun with his hand as he looked toward the cabins.

Susan was running toward him, with Judith stumbling along behind. They were waving their arms. He had been through too much with the girls to take them lightly when they became excited, so he picked up his rifle. The old man frowned.

"What is it, son?"

"I know not," frowned Patterson, "but the women indicate something amiss."

Pettigrew buried his ax in a stump and reached for his wheellock. "We'd best see what ails 'em." But Patterson was gone, running hard toward the two girls.

They were both talking at once and gesturing wildly. Patterson waited for them to quiet down. Judith told him that Ivy had gone

321

into the forest with the Baylor twins and had not returned. The children said they had gone into the woods to hunt wild grapes. The girls were worried sick. Patterson asked where the youngsters had seen Ivy enter the woods. Susan pointed toward a big beech tree behind the cabins. The old man, having arrived in time to hear the last of the conversation, said quickly, "Them boys ain't so damn foolish as to try anything with the lass." But even as he spoke the words, he knew that he didn't even believe them himself.

Patterson was halfway to the woods before the man had finished speaking. He passed the beech tree, hesitating just long enough to pick up the trail. He cursed Ivy for being so foolish, cursed Susan and Judith for not keeping an eye on her, and he cursed himself for not seeing this coming. Ivy had been too absorbed with her hopes and plans to think straight about the Baylors.

Fear for Ivy hastened Patterson's footsteps as he darted through the woods, and even though the sun shone brightly on the fields, it was gloomy under the dense canopy of foliage. Patterson stopped . . . listening . . . allowing his eyes to adjust to the change in lighting, but the forest was quiet. Not even a bird called.

He cocked his head to one side in an effort to hear better, but heard nothing. He moved deeper into the gloom, stopping often to listen. He could hear people entering the forest from the direction of the cabins, but he paid them no heed; Ivy was somewhere ahead. He gritted his teeth and pushed on.

He stopped again, straining . . . listening . . . Then he heard it: a muffled cry. He ran faster than he had in his life, knocking branches aside, indifferent to the scratches and tears of the greenbriars and grapevines. Then he saw them. Ivy was trying to raise herself from the ground, but the effort was taxing what little strength she could muster. She made it to her knees before convulsions overwhelmed her, causing her to clutch her naked belly and vomit. She hung her head and coughed, shuddering from nausea—and then she cried: soft, heartbroken tears of one who has lost all reason to live. Jake was tucking his shirttail into his breeches while Jack worked with the belt of his trousers.

The sound of a lock coming to full cock can be terrifying, especially if the gun is pointed straight at one. And this was exactly what Jake faced as his startled eyes looked down the bore of Patterson's rifle. He was even more terrified with what he saw in

Patterson's eyes, for if Jake Baylor had never before looked death in the face, no one had to tell him that it stood not ten paces away.

The ball caught him squarely between the eyes. He didn't even hear the thundering boom that shook the stillness of the forest. Jack looked at his brother's body as it jerked spasmodically in the dry fall leaves. He turned toward Patterson and recoiled a step. He too saw what Jake had seen and it turned his knees to water. His heart raced. He swallowed twice before he could speak.

"Patterson," he pleaded, sweating, "I did nothing—I swear." He was screaming. "She's just a nigger—no better than a slave. She's just a nigger."

Patterson moved toward him. "She might be a nigger, but she's whiter than either one of you sons-o'-bitches."

Jack stepped back, then back again, retreating before the advancing woodsman. He turned to flee, but Patterson was on him, and Jack felt a white hot pain run the length of his body as Patterson kicked him in the groin. He doubled over, to grab his testicles, but another pain, equally intense, exploded in his face and bounced off the back of his head as the butt of Patterson's rifle crushed his nose and mouth. He screamed, but blood had filled his mouth, and the sound was no more than a gargle.

Patterson would have beaten Jack to death had it not been for the old man and Susan throwing themselves on him, taking several bone-crushing licks to their own bodies, before Patterson's maddened eyes flickered any knowledge of recognition.

"Let him live, boy, let him live," pleaded the old man, as he tried to halt Patterson's murderous punches to Jack's face and body. "He's all them Baylor folks got. He's the only boy they got left . . . "

Susan was crying and hugging Patterson close. "Oh, Morgan, please, please stop it."

Patterson could feel her tears on his face where her cheek lay against his and it had a calming effect. He looked at Jack. The man was beaten beyond recognition, but he still breathed. The old man and Susan slowly lifted Patterson off Jack and moved him away, afraid he might go berserk again and finish beating the man to death. They ignored Jake altogether, not even bothering to brush away the blowflies that had gathered on the gaping hole between his open, sightless eyes.

Judith had already gotten Ivy away and Susan was glad, for if

Patterson had seen her again, the way the Baylors had used her, she knew without a doubt that nothing on God's green earth could have stopped him from killing Jack. She gently guided him toward the cabins, taking great sucking breaths, trying hard to stop crying.

The old man stooped and picked up Patterson's rifle, then bent again and lifted a small pearl-handled dagger out of the leaves. He wondered where it had come from. Had he thought to open the dead man's shirt, he would have seen a bloody line cut from Jake's collar bone to his pap; that's how close Ivy had come to saving Patterson the trouble of killing him. But the twins had overpowered her, throwing her to the ground with such force that she had lost her grip on the knife—and what followed was a descent into hell.

The old man shoved the dagger through his belt and turned toward the cabins. He didn't give Jack or Jake a second glance.

When Patterson and Susan reached the cabin, the women had already laid Ivy on the Pettigrew's pallet and stretched a quilt across the room for privacy. The children stood outside in mute silence, too young to understand what had happened, but old enough to know it was something terrible. The children's mothers were rushing about carrying buckets of hot water and what clean linen they could find. Judith was behind the curtain with the old woman.

Susan stepped inside to see if she could assist, but Mrs. Pettigrew instructed her to see to the men and their dinner meal. She protested, but Mrs. Pettigrew was firm, so she did as she was told. Reluctantly, she filled wooden trenchers with food, but they were left untouched, as she knew they would be.

Although they had sat there for only two hours, it seemed to Susan more like a week before Mrs. Pettigrew emerged from the cabin, wiping her hands on her bloody apron. All three jumped to their feet, eyeing her anxiously.

"The way they hurt that poor child would fairly turn a woman plumb against men," she said angrily. "She be sleeping now, and if'n the good Lord's willing, she'll be all right."

Susan stepped toward the cabin. "I'm going to Judith. She'll need someone."

"You might try an' get her to eat a bite," suggested the old woman. "That Judith is made from tougher stuff than she appears."

324

Susan approached the cabin quietly so she wouldn't waken Ivy. She could hear Judith's soft voice through the open door. She started to call softly, to let Judith know she was there, but the girl's earnest words stopped her dead in her tracks.

"Ivy," said Judith, touching the sleeping girl's cheek with the tips of her fingers, "oh, Ivy...it should not have been like this...not dirty and degrading. It should have been beautiful like it was for me. I'm going to have a baby, Ivy...it's true! I—I wish I could talk to you about it...I feel so wonderful...Oh, Ivy...I'm so sorry for you, so very sorry."

Susan stood there in shocked silence. She wanted to scream that it wasn't true, what Judith had said; she wanted to run and hide, to get away from the cabin, the clearing, from life itself. Her shoulders sagged and her whole being slumped—but not one soul who inhabited the Pettigrew clearing was aware that Susan Spencer's world had just fallen apart.

Late that evening, when the shadows were long and the candles had been lighted, an old woman, thin and worn, stepped into the cabin. All eyes turned toward her. No one needed to tell Patterson that she was the twins' mother; the resemblance was unmistakable. She stood there, straight and proud, her gaze steady, as she surveyed the room. Patterson wondered how a woman with such courage and dignity could have whelped two sons like Jake and Jack. Tension fairly danced across the room.

"Will the girl live?" she asked abruptly.

Mrs. Pettigrew nodded slowly. "She'll live."

Mrs. Baylor returned the nod, her head held high. "I want you to know this—them boys come by their meanness honestlike. They was the get of such a trick as was pulled today." She looked hard at Mrs. Pettigrew. "I be thirty-six years old and look seventy, so I know what it can do to a lass." The faces in the cabin softened, and the woman saw it. "I did not come here for pity," she said evenly. "I come to tell you," she hesitated, looking at Patterson, "I come to ask you to let me bring my boy in an' bury him decentlike. Then we'll be leavin' here." She held Patterson's eyes without wavering.

Patterson inclined his head ever so briefly, but it was enough. The woman's eyes misted and she nodded her thanks.

"Where will you go?" asked Susan softly.

The woman looked at her a long moment, trying to be brave, then her body sagged. They had to listen closely to hear her answer. "To another settlement, another place, where no one knows us. But, mayhap, it will be different, this time . . ." Her voice trailed off and she turned toward the door, but Mr. Pettigrew stopped her.

"Mrs. Baylor," he said gently, "you show us where you want the bury-hole." She nodded and stepped through the door.

Patterson did some quick mental calculating and was appalled to find that Mrs. or Miss Baylor, as it might be, could not have been over twelve or thirteen years old when she was raped. He had known of girls marrying and bearing children at that age, but it was a rare occurrence, and likely as not, they would die in childbirth. This one had twins.

The next morning Patterson and the old man dug the grave in the hillside back of the barn. The woodsman whittled a crude cross from a piece of cherrywood and left it beside the freshly opened pit. But the only folks who attended the funeral were the Baylors. True to the woman's word, directly afterward, the family packed its meager belongings and struck off in a ragged line toward Fort Cumberland. Jack had to struggle to keep pace with his family, but not one of the observing people had a minute's worth of pity tó waste on him.

Ivy would have been perfectly happy to lie abed for the rest of her life, hiding her face in shame, but Mrs. Pettigrew would have no part of it; so Ivy was up and about on the second day after the incident. Except for a multitude of superficial cuts and bruises and the inability to look anyone in the eye, she appeared to be her old self. But Judith told the woodsman that the girl moaned and cried in her sleep, and all Patterson could do was shake his head sympathetically and hope the scars on her mind would heal as quickly as those on her body.

Patterson and the old man finished the pens on the first of November and spent two days herding in the pigs. The sow didn't like being hemmed in and ran the perimeter of the pen endlessly. "For domestic hogs," Patterson told Pettigrew, "they surely have a wild mean streak in them—even the piglets."

That evening Ivy joined the folks as they relaxed in the yard on a rare warm day. It was the first time she had ventured from the cabin and it lifted the spirits of them all.

Mr. Pettigrew produced the pearl-handled knife and asked if it was hers. She accepted it gratefully and caressed the blade lovingly with her fingertips, explaining that the knife had been her mother's and her mother's before that. What she didn't say was that she had promised to pass the knife on to her child, but should she be pregnant by Jake or Jack, she would use it instead to end her life. She would bear no children conceived from force and born in shame.

She studied Patterson from the corner of her eye and wondered if he would understand. She wanted desperately to talk with him, to see how he felt about her now, after she had been violated. Oh, Morgan, she thought, can you not see that my soul is still pure, no matter what has happened to my body? But she was afraid to say it; afraid of the answer. So she sat there, locking it inside a broken heart, unable to do anything about it.

"What are you so down in the mouth about?" snapped Mrs. Pettigrew. "You ain't said three words in . . . I don't know when. What's botherin' you, girl?"

"It's nothing, Mrs. Pettigrew," said Susan as she churned the morning cream into butter.

"Now, child, somethin's wrong. If you don't want to talk about it, that's all right . . . but, well, I don't mean to pry into your affairs, but they's a question I'd like to ask."

"What is it, Mrs. Pettigrew?" Susan's brows wrinkled as she gazed steadily at the old woman, wondering what she had on her mind.

"Well . . ." The old lady fingered her apron nervously.

"Well, what? Please, Mrs. Pettigrew!"

"Susan, I don't know how to ask, except to come right out with it. Are you all right?"

"Of course I'm all right. Do I not look all right?"

"Don't get flippant; it ain't like you!"

"I'm sorry, ma'am," said the girl. "I feel fine, really I do."

"Well, that ain't what I mean. What I mean is . . . you were with Morgan so long in the wilderness . . . and that frock does very little to hide your . . . charms . . ." She hesitated.

The astonishment on Susan's face was almost comical. Then she laughed joyfully.

"Mrs. Pettigrew, you certainly know how to shock a person." She sobered then and resumed her churning. "I haven't slept with Morgan, Mrs. Pettigrew. I'm not with child, if that's what you're asking."

The old woman bobbed her head. "That's what I was asking, but not about being with child, but whether you are still a maiden."

"Well," said the girl as she raised and lowered the long handle of the churn, "I am still a virgin, but to tell the truth...it's not my fault. At the Indian village, I was his make-believe wife...I wanted it to be real."

"What happened?"

"Nothing happened. I know now it was the best thing that could have happened—the *nothing* part of it."

"Why is that?" coached the old woman, attempting to draw the story out of Susan, for she felt sure that she was close to reaching the roots of Susan's gloom.

"Wouldn't it be nice if I had slept with Morgan, and come up pregnant? He wouldn't know which way to turn, with Judith's and my bellies swelling a little more each day!" The girl's bitterness alarmed the old lady.

"Do you hate Judith because she is with child—his child—Morgan's child?"

"Yes, I hate her!" cried the girl, "I hate her because I envy her. I have always been jealous of her, even when she was crazy! He always treated me like a lady—always! Yet Judith is a real lady and he...he gets her with child...I do not understand it."

"I think I'm beginnin' to figure it out. How do you feel about him, child?"

"It is ironic, Mrs. Pettigrew, but he saved my virtue the first time I met him...and he's been saving it ever since...and I don't want it to be saved."

Mrs. Pettigrew cackled loudly, and patted Susan's hand. "I've never seen a girl more upset because she's still intact!" She shook her head in disbelief. "Usually, 'tis the other way around."

Susan grinned. "I sound like a real slut, don't I? But—but it's not right, Mrs. Pettigrew!"

"What's not right, child?"

"I love Morgan with all my heart, yet he treats me like a little girl...like a fragile child...I hate it!" She dropped her head, her face flaming. "I tried to trick him into kissing me...it didn't work. Judith just walked right up and put her lips against his and kissed him. I hated her forwardness...I hated her self-confidence...and I hated her. But in truth, I...I envied her. I still do."

"And you've never even kissed Morgan?" The old woman's eyes were sympathetic.

"Well, yes...I did." Susan turned her head to avoid the old woman's gaze. "I waited for a dark night...and I kissed him. He never knew which of us it was. It almost drove him mad with wonder."

"Well done!" shouted the old lady, clapping her hands gleefully. "I haven't heard the like of it since I was a lass—go on, go on!"

Susan laughed and hugged Mrs. Pettigrew close. She was caught up in the telling of it and felt better because of it.

"I have been taught from childhood that virtue is to be prized above all else," she explained, "and under normal circumstances, that would be true...but we are not living in normal times; war and the threat of death change one's way."

The old woman's eyes widened with respect and perhaps a touch of awe. "You're so learned for a mere slip of a girl, I'm not sure I understand everything you say...but it sounds fine...go on!"

"Nothing is the same, Mrs. Pettigrew. I'm not the person that climbed up on that wagon seat in Williamsburg to follow Braddock's army into the wilderness...The manners and conventions I learned as a girl have no meaning out here. Neither does class or position. All that counts is character: you lie or you tell the truth; you fight or you run; you live or you die. Weak, or mean, or devious people don't survive long out here."

"But Judith. Be she not a lord's lady?"

"Judith has become another kind of lady here. In her own fashion she's as open and straightforward as this vast wilderness... Patterson is like that too. Even you and Mr. Pettigrew are that way...able to take life as it is—on its own terms. Perhaps all frontier folk are so turned. Perhaps one has to be to survive here."

329

"I never reckoned it like that," said the woman, "but I guess we do reach out and pluck what we want from the tree of life, and not worry about the consequences till later. Yes, I suppose we do."

"I didn't have that courage," said Susan. "All those nights we camped together, I lay there wanting him, longing for him to touch me, afraid that he would, knowing I would refuse him should he try."

"You are a fine and decent lass," sighed the old woman. "There be nothing wrong with such feelings. All girls fetch up such humors."

"But, Mrs. Pettigrew, I feel like a harlot, for I have seduced Morgan Patterson so many times in my dreams that only my body is virginal."

The old woman laughed aloud, finding the girl truly refreshing.

The woman's laughter unsettled Susan. "You think I'm awful, don't you?"

"No, child," said Mrs. Pettigrew, taking Susan in her arms, feeling the girl's wet cheek against her own, "I think you are a beautiful young lass who is stronger than most. Ye'll have your reward some day, some day."

"I've waited too long," wailed the girl. "I've lost him."

"What makes you think so?"

"He doesn't want me, Mrs. Pettigrew. He's made it plain!"

The old woman held the girl at arm's length. "I was wrong about you. I thought you were a fighter—not a quitter!"

"But Judith is going to have his baby—"

"How'd you find out about Judith?" interrupted Mrs. Pettigrew. "She swore me to secrecy."

"It was . . . by accident," said Susan. Then she explained what she had overheard the day Ivy was raped.

"Well, all I can say is this," said the old lady. "When I set my cap for Mr. Pettigrew, it weren't no easy task—he was a handsome devil in them days—had several girls' fathers searching for him with fowlin' guns. I knowed all that. The whole colony knowed it. But I loved him and set my mind to have him. He tried his dangest to get me in the bushes with him...." The old woman cackled, remembering those long-forgotten days and Susan smiled with her. "But I kept saying no, till one day he showed up with a man of the

330

cloth. He was mad as a wet hen, 'cause he knowed that was the only way he could get me...but he married me all proper and legal...that was almost forty wonderful years ago."

She looked deep into the girl's eyes. "It weren't easy, gettin' the man I wanted...but I never stopped trying!" She cackled again. "Tell the truth, I wouldn't have wanted him if I hadn't knowed how lusty he were!"

Susan laughed joyously and clapped her hands. "Mrs. Pettigrew, you should be ashamed!"

"Well, I ain't."

"Well then, I ain't either. And, Mrs. Pettigrew?" said the girl, her face shining.

"Yes, child?"

"Thank you."

19

Patterson could hear Susan's brisk step, the milkpail brushing softly against her dress. It was still an hour before sunup. He stepped through the opening that served as the barn door. "Mornin'," he said as she joined him. He could see her teeth flash in the darkness as she smiled.

"The cow has not come in yet?"

"Appears to be late this morning, probably fed on the other side of the ridge last night." He looked toward the hill. "The stock is having to range farther every day to find grazing, and judging from the way the leaves are falling, we will have a mean winter."

Susan nodded, looking toward the hill also, and they stood like that, lost for words, and embarrassed by it.

She finally broke the silence. "What will you do when we reach the settlement, Morgan? What are your plans?"

He stood ill at ease, shifting his feet, still looking at the hill, black in the predawn darkness. "I know not," he said honestly. "I do not know if we even have an army left, but you can be sure the crown will not let Braddock's defeat go unchallenged. It will mean war and—I will fight. But when that will be, I have no notion."

She looked up at him. He could see the whites of her eyes plainly in the obscure light. "Do you not want a wife and children?" she inquired softly. "A home to return to after the war?" He remained silent.

"I am eighteen now, Morgan," she said, smiling shyly at him. "Did you know that?"

Patterson studied her, trying to see the expression on her face, for he could not help but wonder what difference another year made. "I am as old as Judith," she said in answer to his unasked question. "I am a woman, fully grown."

"I always thought you were," he said softly. She took a hesitant step toward him, her eyes anxious and excited.

"Do you mean that, Morgan?"

"Why, yes," he said nervously, more than a little aware of her nearness, remembering how beautiful she had been that night in the cabin, when she had stood nakedly before him. "But when was your birthday? You never mentioned it."

Even in the dark, he sensed the hurt in her eyes. He nervously looked away, pretending to study the treeline where the sky was but a shade lighter than the black forest. "You should have said something about it," he continued, awkwardly. "We would have celebrated."

"It was the day...Ivy was hurt."

"I believe we all aged a little that day."

"'Twas certainly not a happy birthday." Sorrow laced her words.

"Anyway," he said lightly, "celebrating birthdays was invented by white women to appease the chil—"

"Oh, Morgan," she blurted. "What is this thing you have about white women—you must know I—"

Patterson quickly put his hand over her mouth, cutting off the statement before she could finish. He was looking intently toward the hillside, and Susan could hear the sound of the cowbell moving slowly across the ridge toward the cabins. She slapped his hand away and anger touched her voice: "'Tis only the cow, Morgan."

He listened a moment longer, then turned quickly to her. "'Tis no cow carrying that bell, lessin' old Bessie's just got two legs." He heard Susan's intake of breath. "Get back to the cabin. Tell Mr. Pettigrew to get everyone into the smokehouse." He looked toward the ridge again, then added, "And fill that pail with water when you pass the well."

"What will you do?"

"Get a closer look," he said hurriedly, as he attempted to check the priming of his rifle in the bad lighting. "Now, get moving. There's little time left."

She ran with wings on her feet, her legs flashing white as the buckskin skirt rode high above her knees. For a split second Patterson watched her retreating form. Then he was gone.

The Pettigrews were building the morning fire when Susan burst into the cabin. She hastily set the bucket of water on the floor and took her musket off the wall. "Indians," she said softly as she poured a charge of powder down the barrel.

Mr. Pettigrew ran to the door and looked out at the false dawn. "We have to hurry," he said over his shoulder. "Get Judith and Ivy down here."

The old woman began gathering foodstuffs and cramming them into a linen sack. Susan called up the ladder, and Judith answered that she and Ivy had heard and were preparing.

The old man ran from cabin to cabin, spreading the news. Swiftly and silently they carried all manner of provisions to the smokehouse. A child whimpered from being awakened so abruptly, but was hushed immediately. Each family knew exactly what was expected of it, and because of the old man's foresight, they quickly and quietly prepared for the attack.

Patterson slipped into the woodline and glided quietly toward the high ground. He peered into the darkness, trying to silhouette the Indians against the skyline, but the forest was black, and he could see nothing. He slipped like a shadow from tree to tree, keeping abreast of the clanging bell. Then a break in the tall timber briefly skylined the Indians as they moved in single file off the crest of the ridge. Patterson counted forty-one, but figured there were maybe ten more acting as runners and scouts.

Satisfied, he eased out of the woods and struck off in a long lope for the smokehouse. As he slipped through the door and dropped the locking bar in place, dawn was breaking.

"We're as ready as we'll ever be," said the old man, holding a candle high. Its flame barely illuminated the shadowy interior.

Patterson nodded and moved to the makeshift ladder leading to the upper reaches of the building. The smokehouse was perhaps twenty feet square and eighteen feet high at the rooftree. The old man and his sons had inserted two tiers of log beams across the building, the first being seven feet off the ground and the second five feet above that. They were spaced about four feet apart, with flat two-inch-thick slabs laid crosswise to be used as boardwalks.

Susan was perched on the lower boardwalk, peering intently through an opening in the outside wall. Such openings appeared frequently, to be used as shooting slots or loops, as they were normally referred to. Most of the loops had large wooden pegs driven into them that could be removed as needed. Judith was on her knees beside Susan working with the girl's shot pouch and powderhorn. She had laid the lead balls in a neat row for quick access and was measuring out powder charges into cane measuring sticks that held exactly the right amount for Susan's musket. Ivy was up there also, waiting for Patterson. He flashed her a grin, and she smiled back, then grinned openly, showing her pleasure at having been elected to load for him.

The old woman and her daughters-in-law were sorting out food while the old man was busy with the children, instructing them to lie flat on the hard-packed earthen floor below the first line of beams. They would be safe there should a ball penetrate the chinking.

Patterson quickly climbed the ladder to the top tier and pried out a plug. At first he saw nothing, but as his eyes adjusted to the early morning light, he could barely distinguish the faint shadows of the war party as it filtered soundlessly toward the smokehouse. He eased his rifle barrel through the loop and took careful aim at one of the silhouettes. Before he touched the trigger, Susan called to him.

"A wager, Mr. Patterson?"

"Done!" he said as his rifle roared.

The shadow flopped to the ground, kicked, then lay still. Patterson grinned down at Susan. Eerie screeches and yells ripped from the darkness of the forest, but no movement was visible. He handed the rifle to Ivy and moved to the far end of the building. From that vantage he could see the barn clearly and even as he watched, a small glow appeared at the far side of the structure. It grew steadily until it was a sizable flame. By the light of the fire, Patterson could see naked savages in turkey-feather headdresses jumping wildly about, looking, in effect, like painted demons fresh from the pits of perdition. Ivy handed Patterson the loaded rifle. He took a long steady aim, resting the gun lightly on the bottom of the loop. He fired. One of the Indians pitched headlong into the fire. The embers spiraled skyward like miniature Roman candles. His body was quickly pulled from the flames and carried around the corner of the barn. Patterson laughed silently.

"A hit, Mr. Patterson?" asked Ivy.

"I don't know, Ivy, but I sure burned his arse." Patterson sobered as the flames leaped high and the barn began to burn in earnest. The warriors began their assault on the smokehouse then, their muzzle flashes bright orange in the predawn darkness. Patterson handed the empty rifle to Ivy and dropped down the ladder. "They have fired the barn, Mr. Pettigrew," he said. "Shall I try to free the oxen?"

The old man went to that side of the smokehouse and removed a peg. Bullets were thudding into the building like exploding corn, causing the old man to whang the peg back into place. He shook his head sadly. "No, Morgan. They'd kill you before you got out the door."

Even through the heavily timbered walls of the smokehouse they could plainly hear the popping and crackling of the barn as it burned, and above that, the terrorized bellowing of the oxen. The bawling turned frenzied as the flames engulfed the structure. It was a horrible sound, so dreadful that it set the children crying. The old man spoke sharply to them, and they hushed. Patterson felt a moment's pity for the Pettigrews. He knew the oxen were the old man's pride, for very few people on the frontier possessed such a fine pair of beasts. Patterson didn't dwell on it long, however, because Susan's musket roared, and he moved quickly to the wall she was defending. Judith was reloading as Patterson peered down from the top tier. Susan looked up and grimaced.

"Missed, did you?"

"Aye," said Susan sourly, putting her eye back to the slot. "Hurry, Judith," she cried. "He is still there; mayhap I can get him yet."

Judith flipped the frizzen closed and rapped the buttplate of the musket soundly against the boardwalk, thus priming the gun. She quickly extended the loaded weapon to Susan.

The whole valley echoed with the thunder of muskets and a heavy acrid smoke hung low in the trees. Visibility was getting better

336

by the minute as dawn approached, and Patterson could see the Indians darting from tree to tree, shouting, their gunbarrels glinting in the early sun.

Pettigrew's gun roared, and he cackled loudly. "My old eyes are damn near as good as they ever was," he said as his daughter-in-law reloaded. "I got that'un right in the mouth." The other daughter-in-law fired from another side of the smokehouse, then called for him to move over there.

Smoke in the log building choked them, especially in the upper reaches where Patterson and the girls were. The old woman climbed the ladder and passed Susan and Judith the water bucket. They drank sparingly. Patterson refused the offer, and Ivy followed his example. The old woman shook her head in mock disgust and climbed down the ladder.

Patterson used his tomahawk to knock loose some roofing shingles, creating a hole through which the smoke could escape. They sniped at anything that moved throughout the morning.

Mrs. Pettigrew carried food to them at noon. They took turns eating, afraid to leave a wall undefended even for a moment. Susan eased her aching body to a sitting position and began wolfing her food from a wooden trencher, stuffing her mouth full and swallowing without chewing. Judith sat beside her and ate with what dignity she could muster. Susan finished and got wearily to her feet.

"Morgan," she called, "you can eat now. I will take the watch."

Patterson hung his head over the crosswalk and thanked her; and when she turned her face up and smiled, he burst out laughing. She looked at Judith in bewilderment. "What *is* he laughing at?" Susan's face was black with burnt powder and the front of her hair singed off from pan flash. Her deep brown eyes, with the lashes gone, looked large as saucers.

Judith glanced up from her trencher and swallowed. "Your hair looks worse than mine, Susan. 'Tis a good thing we do not have a looking glass; you would just die."

Susan put her hand to her face, feeling her singed eyelashes and hair. She looked again at Patterson, raising her scorched brows in nervous laughter. "If I do not improve my shooting, my looks may well be the least of our worries." She turned back to the slot and peered out, then immediately shoved her gun barrel through the hole and pulled the trigger. The gun bellowed and she stamped her foot in exasperation.

"Go slow, Susan," the woodsman said. Susan nodded, taking her time, sighting long, finally pulling the trigger. The hammer fell, creating a shower of sparks. The musket, however, remained silent with not so much as a flash in the pan. She looked critically at the weapon. Patterson hung his head over the walkway and whispered around a mouthful of food that the gun would shoot better if it were loaded. Judith told him to mind his own damned business.

Ivy laughed and Patterson continued munching. While Susan reloaded, an Indian darted to the smokehouse, plastering himself against the wall, making it impossible for anyone within to get a shot at him. Using his tomahawk handle, he drove a peg out of a shooting slot, took a quick look inside, and fired through the opening. His ball smashed into a side of venison hanging from the crossbeam and spun it around. Before the warrior could withdraw the weapon, the old man seized the barrel and yanked with all his strength, drawing the musket into the building. Then he threw his weight against it, splintering the stock and bending the barrel. After the initial shock of having his gun snatched from him, the Indian yanked back. The old man released the weapon and the surprised Indian staggered backward. Susan quickly sighted on him and pulled the trigger. When the smoke cleared, the Indian lay sprawled in the dirt, an ugly blue hole in the top of his shaved head. The useless musket was still clutched in his fists.

"I got him," cried Susan. "I got him, Morgan, I got one. He is right down there." She pointed triumphantly through the log wall.

Patterson spoke with his mouth full. "Will he be there when I get done eating?"

Susan's elation vanished. "Go to hell, Mr. Patterson," she snapped, as she turned again to look at the dead Indian.

"Don't do that, Susan," said Judith.

"Don't do what?"

"Don't curse. It's unbecoming in you."

"Well!" returned Susan in surprise. "'Tis quite a statement, coming from you!"

338

"I know," said Judith, peering through the loop. "But who says I'm a lady?"

"Judith," laughed Susan in admiration. "If I could be like anybody I wished, I would choose you."

"And if I could be like anybody I wished," returned the blonde girl with a smile, "it certainly wouldn't be you!"

They laughed then, but Judith's eyes held a strange glint, for she had not been totally candid. She saw in Susan qualities that she did not possess, qualities that she envied, and at times even tried to cultivate.

Patterson finished his meal, then moved back to his shooting loop. Ivy moved up beside him.

"How long do you think the Indians can hold out, Morgan?"

"Probably longer than we can," he said. "But Indians don't like siege-type warfare, so I don't look for them to hang around overlong."

"But we have killed so many," she argued. "One would think they would have had enough."

Patterson spoke from over his shoulder. "We might have killed two or three. No more than that. Indians are bad to play possum. They will fall when you shoot and lie still until they deem it be safe to move, then they jump up and run when you least expect it. That has likely happened several times today."

"The one Susan shot will not be running anywhere," she said firmly. "I peeped through the loop and saw him, and he is good and dead."

"Aye," answered Patterson. " 'Twas a fine shot." He poked his rifle through the slot and fired, immediately passing the gun to Ivy.

"Then why didn't you tell her?" asked Ivy as she took the gun.

Musket fire from the woodline toward the smokehouse dwindled to only an occasional wasted round.

"What do you think, Morgan?" called the old man. "Have they quit?"

"We will know soon enough, but likely as not, they be up to no good," said Patterson, his eye pressed against a loop in an effort to gauge the enemy's actions.

As if in answer to his statement, an arrow buried itself deep in the side of the building. Patterson peered through the loop as far as the angle of his vision would allow, but was unable to see the shaft. He could, however, see wisps of smoke rising past the opening; he called for a dipper of water. Mrs. Pettigrew rushed up the ladder and handed Patterson the bucket. Carefully, he eased the gourd through the loop and poured the water down the side of the building. The fire sizzled out. The next arrow hit on the roof and rolled off, but two more followed in unison. In a matter of minutes the wooden shingles began to burn. Patterson snatched up the water bucket and ran to the hole he had poked in the ceiling. He quickly knocked more shingles loose and climbed to the roof. Bullets snapped like tiny thunderclaps, so close he was sure he could feel the heat of their passing.

The Indians were in a frenzy: Patterson, plainly visible on the rooftop, had drawn the fire of every enemy musket in the woodline. Yet, miraculously, he remained untouched. He doused the flames and crawled back toward the hole. The Indians howled angrily, aware that their quarry was regaining the safety of the building. Several of the younger, less wise warriors rushed, heedless of the danger, toward the waiting guns of the enemy. Susan kept her sights on one young Indian until he was no more than twenty paces from the building.

She watched down her gunbarrel as he pulled his bowstring taut; then she touched the trigger. The gun bucked and she began fanning the smoke to see if she had hit her target. She had. The Indian was in a sitting position, clutching his chest. A moment later he toppled over into the dust. Judith snatched the musket from Susan, and with hands that trembled so badly that she spilled the charge, she began reloading it. Both weapons on the lower level bellowed as one and another savage stumbled and fell. The remainder broke for the forest. Patterson swung through the opening and set the empty bucket on the slab crosswalk. An arrow was driven through the side of the container. He looked hard at Susan.

"Damn it, woman, shoot a little faster next time."

She tilted her head up and smiled sweetly. "You told me to take my time and make each shot count, remember?"

Patterson snatched his rifle from Ivy and moved to a loop. The firing from the woods stopped. A tormented quiet threatened to burst the eardrums of the powder-burnt people in the smokehouse. Every eye was glued to a shooting loop, looking this way and that. Nothing moved. The old man packed his clay pipe, struck a spark from flint and steel, and settled back to smoke.

The old woman snatched the pipe from him and flung it across the room. "We've enough smoke in here, and you'll not be adding to it." She eyed him with a vengeance. The old man looked at her, startled. Then he grinned sheepishly and produced his twist of tobacco.

"Mind if I chew?"

The old woman retrieved the pipe. "Go ahead and smoke," she snapped. "I'd rather put up with that than have to watch where I step."

Susan asked Patterson to change the flint in the musket lock, but he knapped it instead, using the top edge of his hunting knife to flake off the dull edge of the glasslike stone. Satisfied, he passed the gun down to Judith. One of the women on the ground floor informed the group that the heathen were burning the empty Baylor cabin. Patterson saw smoke billowing from that direction but could see no human movement.

The quiet grew nerve-racking. Susan wiped perspiration from her brow, streaking the burnt powder across her face. She absently dried her sweaty palms on her buckskin dress and resumed her vigilance at the loop. Judith put Susan's shooting gear in order, laying out more balls and charges of powder. She called down, asking Mrs. Pettigrew to send up a wet cloth. She wiped her face and hands, then wiped Susan's face, removing a large portion of the grime. Susan thanked her gratefully. Judith passed the cloth to Ivy, who wrung it out, then gingerly wiped Patterson's face and her own. Patterson grinned his thanks. Nothing moved at the woodline.

The children became restless and began milling about. A five-year-old girl climbed the ladder to the first tier and crawled on hands and knees across the plank to where Susan was peering through a loop toward the woodline. The child pulled herself to a standing position by gripping Susan's buckskins. The young woman glanced down, startled, then smiled at the young upturned face.

"Are you not scared up this high?" asked the child maturely.

Susan kneeled and instinctively held the girl close. "Aye, darling," she said, "I am nigh scared to death, but it makes me feel better knowing you are down below to catch me should I fall."

The little girl smiled and returned Susan's embrace. "I will go down now," she said contentedly.

Feeling the child in her arms had upset Susan, reminding her of home and the children she missed so much. Tears ran down her cheeks. Judith moved to her and drew Susan's head against her breast. The well-concealed strain that had been building in the young woman for so many days finally burst. But only Judith was aware of the torrent.

The old man's raspy voice broke the silence. "Morgan, can you tell from up there what in bloody hell is going on up behind the barn?"

Patterson moved to the far side of the smokehouse and put his eye to the loop. He could see several warriors digging furiously in the earth. Tomahawks flashed in the sunlight as they hacked the soil away. Their excited chatter could be heard in the distance. Patterson watched them, puzzled. When the realization of their intentions became evident, he swore.

The Indians had found Jake's grave and were digging furiously at it. Patterson wasn't surprised: every frontiersman knew that Indians were notorious for digging up white corpses and mutilating them. Yet should a white man desecrate an Indian grave, it could very easily spark a war.

The old man climbed to Patterson's side and surveyed the scene. He spoke low so the women couldn't hear. "I was afraid the stinking fiends had found the grave. Can we put a ball among them?"

Patterson shook his head. "The range is too great. 'Twould be a futile effort."

The whooping increased, causing Pettigrew to put his eye back to the loop. The Indians had flung the body out of the grave and were hacking it to pieces. The old man cursed under his breath.

Evening came and the savages resumed a halfhearted assault on the smokehouse, but it was evident they were tiring of the game. As night approached, campfires could be seen casting eerie flickering shadows throughout the dark woods. Drums began their monotonous rhythm, adding to the dread among the defenders in the smokehouse.

The old woman served cold food to everyone; no one complained. They settled back and ate in silence, glad for a moment of relaxation. It had been a long day. They cleaned their weapons and reloaded them, taking stock of how low powder and ball were becoming. They could not stand a prolonged siege, but Patterson felt sure this was a hit-and-run attack.

By losing the element of surprise, the Indians had lost an easy victory, for the smokehouse was as sturdy as a blockhouse, and (as had been proven throughout the day) could be defended quite easily. The Indians had suffered several casualties and Patterson figured they were about fed up with the whole affair. The only trouble was, with Indians one never knew exactly what they might decide; they could hang around for days or be gone come morning.

The drums thumped all night, keeping the weary settlers from getting any rest. So it was a worn-out bunch that met the attack at daybreak. With red-rimmed eyes and frayed nerves, the defenders fired, reloaded, and fired again, and again. Heat waves from their gunbarrels distorted their vision, and smoke fumes made it difficult to breathe in the confined area. The children cried from fatigue and fear. Powder and ball were consumed alarmingly.

Still the Indians kept up their relentless volleys against the small building. The defenders began wiping their gunbarrels with wet cloths to cool them, but even then, heat waves shimmered off the front sight. Patterson knew that something would have to give—and soon—if they were to survive. The first casualty inside the building was the old man. He staggered from his shooting slot and fell heavily. Mrs. Pettigrew was beside him instantly, wiping his bloody face. A chance shot had sent a ball crashing into the wood at the edge of the loop, gouging a long sliver which had embedded itself in the old man's forehead. The old woman removed the splinter, but could not stanch the blood that was quickly covering his face and chest. Judith scrambled down the ladder and, taking up his Wheellock, moved to Mr. Pettigrew's firing position. Mrs. Pettigrew barked at one of her daughters-in-law to load for Judith while she tended to Mr. Pettigrew.

"How is he?" asked Patterson during a lull.

Mrs. Pettigrew answered that the cut was deep but not fatal. "It could have been one of his old eyes that he says are damn near as good as they ever was." Everyone laughed and breathed a sigh of relief.

Several minutes passed before the people in the smokehouse realized it was quiet outside. Neither shot nor sound was heard. Susan looked up at Patterson, a question in her eyes. He shook his head. They would wait. Then the stillness was shattered by a "hello" from the woods.

Everyone rushed to a loop and peered at the woodline. The old man tried to rise, but Mrs. Pettigrew pushed him back firmly. "You lie still now and let me finish cleaning this cut. You want to get blood poison?" The old man lay back, not liking it one bit, but his wife was right; he felt weak as a newborn.

The "hello" came again and Patterson answered.

"Is that you, Monsieur Patterson?"

"Aye. Fontaine?"

"Oui, m'sieur."

"What do you want, Fontaine?"

A moment of silence ensued. Then the Frenchman stepped from the forest, bravely exposed to the guns of the whites. Patterson admired his courage.

"I wish to parlez vous, Monsieur Patterson," he called, holding his hands high to indicate he was unarmed. "If you would but join me . . ." The Frenchman gestured toward the open area between the smokehouse and the woodline. "We would talk, no?"

"Do not go, Morgan," said Ivy quietly. "It could be a trap."

The thought had already crossed Patterson's mind. He surveyed the interior of the building, placing things and people in their proper perspective. The people were courageous, but weariness was taking its toll. Although food was in abundance, there was almost no water and there were no facilities for a fire. Lead balls were running low. And now, Mr. Pettigrew was down. He decided to talk with the Frenchman.

Fontaine, accompanied by two Indians, moved to the center of the clearing and waited. Patterson threw back the crossbar and stepped into the bright sunlight. Susan and Ivy followed, with Judith close on their heels. Patterson objected, but they argued that the Frenchman was not alone, so neither would Patterson go alone.

Their decision was final. The old woman caught Judith by the arm.

"You ain't goin' nowhere, Judith. You got no business taking a chance of harming yourself out there—think of your baby."

Judith jerked her arm free, and moved back angrily to a shooting slot. "I would rather be out there with him," she said, peering through the hole.

Patterson walked to within thirty feet of the Frenchman before handing his rifle to Ivy, insisting that she and Susan remain there, and, if trouble should arise, to waste no time in returning to the smokehouse. They assured him they would. He doubted it.

Patterson advanced to where Fontaine, flanked by the two braves, stood waiting. The Frenchman offered his hand, but Patterson ignored it. Color rose in Fontaine's face. He bowed toward Susan and Ivy, but they too remained staunch, preferring not to recognize his attempt at friendliness. His ruddy face inflamed even more. He visibly collected his composure and addressed Patterson.

"It is good to see you again, my friend."

Patterson nodded briefly, acknowledging Fontaine's words but not committing himself. An unseasonably warm November sun beat down on the small party in the clearing. Patterson could feel perspiration forming on his brow and trickling into his eyes, and he knew that his sweat had little to do with the warmth. But he refused to brush it away for fear the Indians might take his discomfort as a sign of weakness. If that were to occur, the savages would never give up their siege. So he stood there, with an outward show of calm that he wished were real. The Indians stood as statues, arms folded, and black eyes burning into the woodsman's. Patterson returned the stare.

"Much has happened since the last time we talked," ventured Fontaine. "Black Fish grieved, and then went after you. He sent many canoes, but they returned emptyhanded. You are a much sought-after prize, m'sieur. Taking your hair is all that they talk about in Chillicothe."

Patterson remained silent, his face cold and hard. He had no reason to doubt the Frenchman, but it was hard to accept that his people would turn against him so totally and with such vengeance.

Fontaine walked in a small circle, contemplating, then turned again to Patterson.

"M'sieur, things are going badly. I have been losing control of these Indians since the day you escaped. They blame me for losing the ransom the women would have brought. I showed them the wound—"

"What wound?" interrupted Patterson, feigning ignorance of the near fatal knife slash; for Ivy had told him of her promise to Fontaine not to mention the incident.

Fontaine grinned broadly, eyeing Ivy proudly. "Mam'selle, you are—how you say—magnifique."

Ivy blanched.

"Just how damn bad did I cut you, Fontaine?" demanded Patterson quickly, drawing the Frenchman's attention away from the shamefaced girl.

"Not bad, monsieur," said Fontaine, opening his camus to reveal a wide-puckered freshly knitted wound that ran half the length of his abdomen.

Patterson's eyes narrowed. "Mister, you're lucky to be alive."

"I told you before, m'sieur," laughed Fontaine, "I will be killed by a beautiful mam'selle, not by an ugly Englishman such as you!"

Patterson smiled. "Perhaps you are right."

"Anyway," continued Fontaine, "the Huron did not like it that you escaped with the women and killed Capitaine DeBeaujue!" He winked humorously at Patterson. "So they have become a quarrelsome lot, threatening to return to Canada and forget this war between England and France . . . In truth, m'sieur, that is where we were bound when our spies told us you were here—I am sorry that you are."

One of the Indians at the Frenchman's side spoke irritably in Huron. Fontaine translated: "He says to tell you, you must surrender the houses and you can leave here in peace." He looked apologetic.

"You know I don't believe a damn word of it," snapped Patterson, his voice as harsh as the Indian's. The Frenchman merely shrugged.

"Tell them this," continued Patterson. "We have much powder and ball, and twenty rifle guns aimed at them this minute." Patterson stopped to let Fontaine translate, then continued. "Tell them we will surrender nothing, and, if these savages continue to wage war upon the English, we will mash their guts out through their teeth like piss-ants under a moccasin. Tell the sons-o'-bitches what I said, word for word, Fontaine."

The Frenchman didn't like it, but he translated exactly as Patterson instructed. The Indian spat contemptuously at Patterson's feet. Fontaine spoke softly as his eyes moved toward the women.

"I cannot control these Indians, m'sieur. They have lost confidence in me, so do not provoke them unnecessarily." He studied Ivy solemnly for several moments. "I will try my best to persuade them to leave here, my friend—but I can promise you nothing for certain." Having said that, he pushed through the Indians and walked toward the forest.

The next events happened so fast that no one knew exactly what happened. The Indians, glancing quickly at the back of the retreating Frenchman, took one quick step, seized Patterson by the arms, and began dragging him toward the woods. Fontaine, thinking Patterson had stooped to treachery, spun around, knife in hand. It was then that Ivy shot him.

Susan ran to the Indian nearest her, pushed her musket against his body, and pulled the trigger. The Indian sagged down, his side a sheet of powder-burnt flesh that smoldered like charcloth.

The second Indian released Patterson and sprinted for the security of the woodline but was brought down by shots from the smokehouse. Shot and ball poured from the treeline and several Indians dashed into view, but well-placed balls from the smokehouse sent them scurrying for cover.

The girls bolted for the smokehouse. Lead peppered the earth, creating small geysers of dust around the terrified women as they raced madly toward safety. Patterson heard the soft plop and sucking sound made by a ball entering live flesh. He sickened as he saw Ivy stumble, regain her footing for a few steps, and then collapse in a cloud of dust. Her eyes were wild as she attempted to rise. Susan veered toward the stricken girl, but Patterson motioned her on as he snatched Ivy into his arms and raced for the smokehouse. Bullets snarled past them, angry sounds.

Judith held the door open and he lunged for it, hearing it slam as he passed through. The women were hastily creating a pallet for Ivy, and Patterson carried her toward it. Her eyes were closed; her face was deathly pale; a smile hovered at the corners of her bloodless lips. He gently eased her down and smoothed back a lock of stray hair that had fallen across her forehead. His forearm was covered with her blood as were his chest and abdomen. Ivy opened her eyes. They were clear and bright. Patterson continued to kneel beside her, supporting her head and shoulders, refusing to release her.

The shooting stopped, and the hush that preludes death filled the building. Patterson attempted to stanch Ivy's wound, but she stopped him.

" 'Tis no use, Morgan," she whispered. "Lean closely, for it is difficult to speak."

Patterson held her close, his face only inches from hers. Her eyes were large and wide as she looked up at him. "I love you, Morgan," she whispered softly. "I love you." His eyes misted as he listened, her small voice fading with each spoken word, and he wanted to scream at her not to die.

"I have never been kissed, Morgan, never in my whole life," she whispered softly.

A rage began building in him and for a moment the smokehouse was empty. Only he and Ivy were there, and he kissed her, long and hard, then tenderly, ever so tenderly, and he prayed that somehow the strength to live would pass from his body to hers, through the physical contact of their lips.

Judith was on her knees, beside the girl, weeping openly, with Ivy's cold hand pressed tightly against her cheek. "Ivy . . . Ivy, I love you. Please don't die, please." Judith's eyes were pitiful, imploring. "I love you."

Ivy smiled at her gratefully and her fingers brushed away the tears on Judith's cheek. She touched her lips lightly to Patterson's and for a moment he felt the warmth of her faint breath against his cheek—then it was gone. For a long while Patterson held her close. Then he gently laid her to rest, crossing her hands upon her breast. Not a sound could be heard in the smokehouse. The children stood wide-eyed, wondering about death. The adults hung their heads, and there were tears streaking their cheeks.

Judith buried her face in her hands and moved to Susan, who had dropped to her knees, head bowed in silent, grief-stricken prayer. She would cry later, alone, when she could break down. If she did so now, she knew she would not be able to stop, for during the past weeks she had learned to love the happy unassuming servant girl. She would talk of Ivy a great deal in the days to come, remembering her courage, kindness, and loyalty. Ivy possessed all those qualities, and more.

It became apparent as the day drew long that the Indians had withdrawn. None had been seen and not a sound heard since Ivy had died. Patterson cautiously slipped from the smokehouse to scout the area. Actually, the sight of Ivy lying there greatly disturbed him. He no longer felt the dread and rage he had previously harbored toward white women. Judith, Susan, and Ivy, each with her own outlook toward life, love, and happiness had changed him. But Ivy's death had gone even deeper, piercing his soul, leaving an emptiness—a loneliness he had never before experienced. He needed to be alone in the solitude of the forest to sort it all out. As he rounded the corner of the smokehouse, a flicker of movement froze his actions. Fontaine was trying to sit up. He called Patterson's name; it was a feeble sound. Patterson ignored the Frenchman, looking instead toward the dark, threatening treeline, where slowly and methodically he searched for the hidden enemy. The woodsman in him would not allow him the pleasure of relaxing, even now, when he so wanted just to sit down and think...but not forget. No, he would never forget.

Fontaine called again and rolled onto his side, clutching his chest. Patterson moved to the wounded man and knelt beside him, cradling the man's head, much the same as he had Ivy's. Blood trickled from Fontaine's nose and mouth, and he made a rasping noise as he tried to breathe. Shot through the lungs, thought Patterson sadly as he supported Fontaine's shoulders.

"The mademoiselle, how is she?" asked Fontaine weakly.

Patterson gazed at the dying man. "She is dead."

The Frenchman closed his eyes and crossed himself. "She thought I had betrayed you, no?" he asked, searching Patterson's face.

Patterson stared into Fontaine's glazed eyes. "It happened so fast, I know not what she thought."

Fontaine grimaced and his body shuddered with pain. His hand moved involuntarily to the bullet hole in his chest. "Forgive me, Patterson, but I must ask a favor." He coughed and bloody bubbles frothed at his mouth. He closed his eyes and Patterson thought the man had died; but he spoke again, his voice so weak that Patterson had to strain to hear it. "I would be greatly pleased," he said as he laboriously fished the gold locket from his hunting shirt, "if you would accept this." He handed the locket to Patterson. "It is my wife."

"I know," said Patterson softly as he took the locket and turned it over, to reveal the face of a lovely young woman. The lower half of the locket was gone, shot away by Ivy's bullet, but Patterson didn't mention it, and Fontaine appeared not to notice.

"Wear it, Patterson," said Fontaine. "It will bring you luck."

"I will wear it," said Patterson. "In memory of you."

Fontaine gripped Patterson's hand with surprising strength. "One more thing, my friend," he whispered. Patterson nodded. Fontaine's hand fell limply to the ground; his strength was waning. "Bury me beside the mam'selle. I . . ." He faltered, breathing shallowly. "I would rest peacefully, knowing I lay next to the most beautiful woman in the world." Fontaine tried to smile, but it was a grimace that followed him to his grave.

Patterson looked into the open lifeless eyes of the Frenchman. "You said you would be killed by a beautiful woman," he whispered softly. "'Tis the way you wanted to die. Rest well, Fontaine—you were a fine man."

20

They buried Fontaine next to Ivy. Somehow Patterson felt that Ivy would like that too. They hid the grave, covering it with leaves and brush, and vowed to put a marker there when the threat of discovery by savages was no longer a problem.

Although the Indians had disappeared as quickly as they had come, Patterson kept a watchful eye on the forest while they worked. As they finished obliterating all signs of the freshly covered grave, Mrs. Pettigrew handed Patterson Ivy's small pearl-handled knife.

"I took it from her dress when we prepared her," she said. "Thought maybe you would want it."

Judith spoke from Patterson's side. "Please, Morgan, Ivy...was my sister." She looked Patterson defiantly in the eye. "Had she lived, she would have passed that knife on to her child." She raised her chin determinedly. Her words came slow and precise. "I will continue the tradition."

Susan ran to Judith and clutched the girl's arm tightly. "You knew all along?" she asked bitterly.

Judith nodded, dropping her eyes. "I knew, but I hated her for it because I loved her so much. Oh, Susan, why was I such a fool?" A tear trickled down her cheek. "All those wasted years." The girl was crying openly now. "Do you think she forgave me, the awful way I treated her?"

Susan softened. "Aye, Judith, she loved you as a sister and a friend. She never stopped loving you." Then bitterness surged through her again, for Judith had never treated Ivy as a sister in life; never returned Ivy's love until too late. But as Susan glared into Judith's grief-stricken face, she was suddenly ashamed of herself.

Judith saw it all in Susan's eyes: the anger, the resentment, the forgiveness. And she was overwhelmed by the realization of how very deeply she needed Susan to believe in her; to understand the loss she was experiencing; to know that her love for Ivy was real, and always had been, no matter how haughtily she had once behaved. Her unsteady hand gently touched Susan's cheek. It was a gesture as completely alien to her as the mixed emotions churning within her breast, but it was a beginning.

They moved back into the cabins that night, but it was a solemn group that found sleep a long time coming.

Patterson was gone when they waked the next morning. No one questioned his disappearance; they knew he was checking the forest to be sure none of the Hurons was still hiding near the settlement in hopes of catching one of them alone or unprotected.

He slipped silently beneath the giant trees, like a shadow among shadows, his eyes and ears alert. He found a hollow burial log and pulled the body from it.

Then he cut the man's head off and cast it down the hillside, watching it roll and tumble until it vanished in a mass of ferns. He felt better after that, and even managed a tight smile as he ghosted through the silent forest.

It was near noon when he broke from timber to stand in the bright sunlight and survey the surrounding countryside. There was motion in the skies: specks, perhaps fifty of them, corkscrewing closer and closer to the tops of the endless trees.

He studied the country around him as he worked his way down the hill, aware that any searching black eyes would also see the buzzards and know that something or someone was dead.

He smelled the carrion long before he saw it, and when he did approach, the foul air was fanned by the flapping of a hundred wings, six feet from tip to tip, as the ugly scavengers burst into flight.

The bodies were vile: the flesh-eaters had been at them for some time, ripping, tearing, and pecking at the bloated, maggot-infested torsos of what had once been people.

Patterson took a deep breath and moved quickly to the carcass nearest him, then on to the others. He ran from there, for the smell of death and rotted flesh was overpowering, and he was sure he was going to be sick.

When the color had partially returned to his cheeks, he took stock of what he saw. The entire Baylor clan had fallen under the hatchet and scalping knife—all except Jack, whose body was nowhere to be seen. Anger surged through him as he thought of Mrs. Baylor, and her innate dignity; a woman who had never known peace or happiness. He was sorry for her—and the others.

When he thought of Jack, however, he felt nothing; not even curiosity about his fate.

At that very moment, the Pettigrews and the girls sat down to dinner. It was a solemn meal, eaten in silence. Ivy and her happy chatter were like a hollow space at the table.

"I wonder where Morgan is?" blurted Susan in an attempt to brighten the desolate atmosphere, or at least give them something else to talk about.

"There is no telling," murmured Judith. "One never knows what Morgan thinks or does."

Mrs. Pettigrew studied Judith and Susan for several minutes before reaching a decision. "Would you girls like to know about Morgan Patterson?"

It was spoken quietly; not at all like the old lady's hearty talk.

The old man looked up from his trencher. "Mrs. Pettigrew," he warned, "'tis none of our affair about the lad's past. 'Tis better left unsaid."

"I thought so, too!" snapped the lady. "But I'm of a different mind now. They's things need to be said. These girls has a right to know!"

The old man chewed his food thoughtfully, his eyes on his wife. "Maybe so...maybe so."

Susan sucked in her breath. "Do you know about Morgan's past? Please tell us, Mrs. Pettigrew."

"We know," sighed Mrs. Pettigrew. "'Twas the talk of the

countryside up Albany way. But the actual happening was in the hamlet of Schenectady, some sixteen miles from where we lived.

"But we was there the night it happened. We had come in our cart to look at a piece of land we was thinking of tradin' for..."

Judith and Susan instantly leaned forward, their faces animated.

"We never bought no property there," interrupted the old man. "You couldn't have given us a million acres there... not after what happened."

"Why does he hate white women?" asked Susan directly.

"Well, like I said," continued the old woman, her face twisted in concentration, "'twas in the township of Schenectady some fifteen, eighteen years ago, maybe more, I cannot recollect, but I remember that night like 'twas only yesterday." She sighed and looked down at her hands. They were clenched tightly, white across the knuckles. "'Tis a hard tale to tell, girls, for I was there, and I am ashamed of them folks that lived there. For they was sure enough guilty."

"Guilty of what?" interrupted Judith.

"Well," snapped the old woman, "when Joseph Patterson—that's his father—brought his new bride to Schenectady, 'twas the talk of the town, of Albany, too, far as that goes. He was proud of her, he was, and had a right to be. She was one of the most beautiful of women, elegant, like a queen or something. Joseph built her a fine house on a hill and gave her servants. Wasn't many in such a small village as had servants, but she did."

"Never did know where Joseph found her," Mr. Pettigrew interrupted. "Some folks thought she was part Indian, others said French, and I still think she had a touch of Spanish in her, but whatever she was, she sure was purty." Mrs. Pettigrew gave her husband a long hard look.

"Aye," she said finally, "and that was one of the reasons for the trouble that came later. You see, she was friendly, but she never mingled, and the good women of the town began to resent her aloofness and not a few, the way I heard it, was jealous of her beauty. And the men, married and single, did not help matters any, always bowing and scraping they was, and tipping their wide brims. Anyway... " she paused again and took a deep breath, "Joseph was gone much of the time. He was in the land and fur business, you

354

know, and he traveled often, leaving his wife in full charge of the mansion, and that started tongues to waggin'."

Mrs. Pettigrew's eyes snapped as she thought about the lies and gossip that young Mrs. Patterson had endured.

Judith cried out in exasperation. "Please go on, ma'am!"

The old woman leaned forward. "She was alone so much of the time in her fine house with servants and all, yet she never entertained, had parties or teas. Indeed, she mostly minded her own business—then she got with child and Morgan was born. The good women of the town figured she'd be fat and ugly after the baby come, but she was not. Truthfully, she was even more beautiful and mysterious. Joseph stayed home for a year after the baby come. They even began attending church. The ladies tried to play up to Mrs. Patterson, inviting her to afternoon socials and such, but never once did she accept an invitation. Then Joseph commenced his travels again and his wife promptly stopped attending church. The good reverend, I never knowed his name, paid a call on her and reported to the congregation that he thought he could save her soul. They encouraged him to try. Ah, they was so righteous..."

"What happened, ma'am?" demanded Judith.

"Well, young lady," said Mrs. Pettigrew irritably, "the reverend began paying social calls on Mrs. Patterson. His horse would be at her house all hours of the day, but still she didn't return to church. They questioned him about her. He said that it would take time to win her soul to God, but he was determined to sacrifice his time and energy to bring her under the wing of the Lord. He was such a fine dedicated man, that preacher was."

Susan wondered if the old woman were being sarcastic.

Much to the agitation of everyone present, she stopped her narrative and moved to the water bucket and drank a full dipper. Then she raised her apron and delicately wiped her chin.

"Well, sir," she said finally, "little Morgan was four or five years old and a prettier boy you never did see—when the good reverend started preaching long and hard that Mrs. Patterson was a lost soul. He quit calling on her and turned his attention to his congregation, which had begun to stray. He began to visit with all the better families and, very discreetly, he would bring up the subject of Mrs. Patterson—of her wicked ways, and her rejection of God Almighty and the church. He called her beauty 'the creation of the devil to lure the menfolk of the town into the shadow of sin' and he insisted the poor wretched menfolk were not to be blamed for their adulterous thoughts. ''Tis the woman,' he would say. 'She is evil; not of our kind; and she should be ignored as if she did not exist.'

"That suited them pious folk just fine and they believed every word the preacher said, just like it was gospel." Mrs. Pettigrew looked at the people gathered around her. "Mayhap," she said, watching their faces, "the folk should not be blamed too much. The lady would not accept their faith, their town, or them. They hated her for it."

Susan wanted to cover her ears, not to hear the terrible story, afraid to hear the finish, yet afraid not to. Judith slipped her hand over Susan's, gripping hard.

The old lady went on. "The town began to shun the woman—and the little boy too. At first Mrs. Patterson was bewildered; then she was hurt. You could tell by her eyes. But she was proud and that made them hate her all the more. The good reverend kept preaching how wicked she was and how the town would be better off without the like of her. 'Satan's daughter,' he called her.

"So finally, it happened. After prayer meeting one night, the congregation, led by the reverend, paid a visit. He knew that Joseph was away, so he marched right up to her door, bold as you please, and called her out. She opened the door unafraid, and I believe to this day that her courage was what set them wild. They screamed at her and called her names that good Christians shouldn't even know, but she just stood there like a statue—or . . . a saint.

"Then the reverend shouted, 'Jesus ran the devil from the temple, so we shall run the temptress from our town.' He dragged her into the crowd and, I swear, all that happened thereafter is unclear to me.

"It was like the Salem witch-hunts of sixteen and ninety-two. I was a wee one then, but from the stories that was told, it was mighty near the same thing—the torches bobbing and weaving as they half-drug, half-carried her through the streets. With every step they took, the congregation turned more vicious. Shouting—cursing—saying awful things. People were wild; folks I had known for years were suddenly strangers. We was afraid, me and Mr. Pettigrew . . . but what could we do? We was outsiders and we dared not interfere.

"They reached the square and flung the poor woman upon the podium and...and her clothes were ripped from her body.

"She tried to cover herself, but they wouldn't let her. I dare say that there was not a woman among 'em but what secretly envied her...her charms, and...she looked so—so pure and virginal standing there. Then somebody, I know not who...yes, yes I do...it was the reverend, he was hollering for someone to bring a pot of hot pitch."

Susan, who had been listening with rapt attention, suddenly buried her face in her hands. She could see in vivid detail the young woman Mrs. Pettigrew had described standing naked and alone before the eyes of the entire town, and she could feel what Victoria Patterson must have felt, knowing she was at the mercy of the crowd—a crowd without compassion.

Yes, thought the girl, I can feel your shame and your disgrace, Mrs. Patterson, for I too have seen a woman, standing alone, stripped of her pride and dignity while a crowd of sailors humiliated her until she felt cheap and tarnished and...wished she were dead. I know what you were feeling, Mrs. Patterson, because I endured my mother's shame and disgrace right along with her.

Mr. Pettigrew put his hand gently on her shoulder. "Are you all right, Susan?"

She raised her face quickly and smiled feebly. "Yes," she whispered, "I am fine."

"You're sure?" he asked, eyeing her carefully.

"Yes—yes, I'm sure. Please, Mrs. Pettigrew," she said, turning quickly to the old woman. "Please continue with your story."

The old lady nodded. "Well, by the time the hot pitch was produced, they had worked their selves into such a state that they was worse than savages. They covered her from head to foot with the stuff. Then they beat her with pillows till she was covered with feathers. Still, she just stood there, not trying to defend herself. I was ashamed to the very marrow of my bones and I ran back to the cart and got down on my knees and prayed to God to stop the awful thing that was happening."

Mrs. Pettigrew took a corner of her apron and dabbed at her eyes. "I am still ashamed of what happened that night, and it shall follow me to my grave." Mr. Pettigrew put his hand on his wife's shoulder and patted her gently.

"There is more to the story that should be told," he said. He gently caressed his wife's shoulder as he talked. " 'Tis hard to believe that a whole town could go crazy, but the awful proof was there...right before our eyes. The terrible part of it was...every man there knew that Mrs. Patterson was innocent; the only thing she was guilty of was loving her husband and her son totally, without the need or desire for prominence or outside friends. And those men who stood in the crowd and did nothing will have to stand before God and explain why they let a fine decent woman, a girl really, be disgraced beyond endurance.

"I called them cowards then, and I call them cowards now, because they damn well knew there was no truth to the stories the preacher told about the Patterson woman's virtue.

"She was a strange person, withdrawn and shy, but she was a lady."

"Morgan is like that," said Judith quietly, looking at Susan for confirmation.

Mr. Pettigrew went on. "I was disgusted with the whole God-awful town. But it was done and I couldn't change it.

"Mayhap nobody could have done nothing 'cause there was a lot of decent men stood in the crowd that night and they didn't lift a finger to stop it. They said later they didn't know what was happening until it was too late." The old man spat contemptuously into the fireplace, then said softly, "Mayhap they didn't." He paused. "The boy, Morgan, was there, too.

"He had somehow followed the crowd to the town square and had climbed up on our cart seat and witnessed the whole sordid mess. When I realized who he was, I was even more ashamed of what had taken place, for the lad just stood there, high on that seat, and I tell ye," said the old man, shaking his head, "he was dry-eyed. He watched the town tar and feather his mother, but he never uttered a sound, just stood there, dry-eyed."

Susan almost cried out. She felt closer to Patterson than ever.

Judith stared at Mrs. Pettigrew in unblinking stoniness. "Did you not see him, ma'am, on the seat?"

"I never saw him till it was too late," sighed Mrs. Pettigrew, "or I would have taken him down from there."

Judith dropped her eyes. "Forgive me, Mrs. Pettigrew. I'm upset."

"His mother saw him finally and she cried out to him," continued Mr. Pettigrew. "It was a terrible sound. The crowd fell back and an awful hush there was, 'cept for the agonizing sobs of the lad's mother. I believe she could have withstood the ordeal had the boy not witnessed the whole thing."

Mr. Pettigrew walked the length of the room before moving once again to stand beside his seated wife. He continued. "The preacher must have realized he was losing his hold on the crowd 'cause he ran to Mrs. Patterson and screamed, 'Repent, Jezebel, in the name of the Father, the Son, and the Holy Ghost.' And bless her proud heart, she slapped the son-of-a——, slapped him hard across the mouth and he just stood there, hate in his eyes. It was the last straw and, like a dog with its tail 'twixt its legs, everybody slinked home.

"I wish it had ended that night, but it didn't." He took another turn around the room, plainly bothered. Each of the listeners, except for Mrs. Pettigrew, waited.

"Please go on," whispered Susan. "I must know the outcome."

He looked at Susan for a long moment. "Aye, my dear, you have a right to know, though 'tis not a pretty finish."

"I will tell it," interrupted his wife. "'Tis only hearsay, mind you, because when Victoria Patterson returned to the mansion, she gave the servants a year's salary and quietly dismissed them. So none but Joseph and the lad knows for sure what actually did take place late that night. We do know, however, that Joseph returned home three days later to a dark and seemingly empty house.

"He knew something terrible had happened for he took the front steps in one great leap and burst the door clean off its hinges. He ran through the great hall calling her name. His voice echoed throughout the empty rooms. Then he found her and his cry was awful...almost inhuman in its anguish." Mrs. Pettigrew began weeping and Judith and Susan cried too.

"She had hanged herself from the great chandelier in the parlor, and little Morgan was sitting on the floor...hugging her dangling feet to his bosom and nigh starved to death." The old woman raised her apron and dabbed at her eyes. "Some said that Mrs. Patterson left a note, but if she did, no one ever seen it. But I do know this: after Joseph bathed his wife's body, removing as much of the tar and feathers as he could, he dressed her in her finest gown and buried her on the hill behind the house. He dug her grave, carried her body, and laid her to rest, alone, 'ceptin' for little Morgan—and I truly believe he would have killed anybody that offered to help."

"They was guilty of her death jest as sure as if they had put that rope over her head," added Mr. Pettigrew, bitterly.

"After Joseph and Morgan filled the grave," he continued in a low voice,"they went back to the house. They took a few belongings and, riding double on Joseph's horse, reined in at the reverend's house. The reverend came to the door, and upon seeing who his caller was, tried to run back inside. Joseph shot him through the back of the head with a dueling pistol. Then he calmly reloaded the gun and rode out of town. It was so shocking, the easy manner in which he killed the preacher, that nobody never even noticed he had torched the mansion. He must have fired every room in it, for it burnt to the ground in minutes. 'Twas a shame, for it was a grand house. Neither Joseph nor Morgan ever set foot in Schenectady again, far as I know."

"Where did they go when they rode away from there, Mr. Pettigrew?" asked Judith.

"Miss Susan can tell you that, Judith," the old man said, looking at Susan to see if she felt that Judith was ready to be enlightened about Chillicothe—and the lost days she spent there.

Susan took Judith's hand. "I can tell you what I know later . . . is that all right?"

"Yes," said Judith slowly. "Did he go to the Indians?"

"Yes," said Susan. "His father took him to the Indians."

Patterson trotted into the clearing, weary, limping slightly from the knife wound that still bothered him occasionally. When he entered the cabin he wondered at the strange expression on Judith's and Susan's faces. They've been crying, he decided. He moved to the water bucket and drank thirstily.

The old man told Patterson that he had taken note of the damage wreaked by the savages. The barn was gone, as was the Baylors' cabin. The oxen, of course, had burned, but the hogs had survived.

Patterson reluctantly told Pettigrew of finding the milk cow dead, shot full of arrows. (He avoided mentioning his finding the Baylor family dead and mutilated.) The old man sighed and gingerly fingered the bloody bandage above his eye. "The other cattle may still be alive," he said absently, doubting the words even as he spoke them. Patterson nodded and said he would look for them the first chance he got. The old man nodded, but he was sure that it would be a waste of time.

For a week they worked hard to set the clearing in order: they buried the bodies of the dead Indians in a shallow grave, after Patterson painstakingly removed their entire scalps with the ears attached and tacked the bloody trophies to the side of the smokehouse nearest the woods—a silent reminder to any prying black eyes that death waited for those who wished harm on the settlement.

They repaired the roof of the smokehouse and cut logs for a new barn. The bull and a cow finally came out of hiding and were herded into the fenced pasture. Except for the ashes and charred wood of the burned buildings, it would have been difficult to tell there had ever been a battle fought there.

It was time to go. At supper that night, Patterson reluctantly told the Pettigrews that he and the women would leave come midnight. The old man nodded, telling Patterson that he had expected it for several days. Mrs. Pettigrew silently began preparing food for the journey as the girls gathered their few possessions and laid them out to be checked and mended. Susan wrote a beautiful letter to John's fiancée in New York Province and Patterson volunteered to deliver the letter personally so they could rest assured it got there. The Pettigrews were touched.

Judith found Patterson beside Ivy's grave, his head bowed. She moved silently to his side and took his hand. They stood there a long while, thinking separate thoughts, yet drawn together by the memory of the young woman who had unselfishly loved them both, and changed each of their lives.

Patterson self-consciously broke the silence: "I want to say something to her, but I don't know how to put it into words."

Judith's hand tightened on his. "I know, Morgan—I know."

"I feel empty inside. I can't explain it—just a great emptiness."

"She would understand, Morgan."

"I want her to know..." He paused, and looked through the earth to the beautiful girl that lay in eternal sleep. "I want her to know that she did not die in vain; that her life did not pass without meaning." His voice was almost inaudible. "I would shout it to the heavens if I but thought she would hear."

"I think she has already heard you, Morgan," whispered Judith. "The voice of one's heart can reach to far and distant shores."

Patterson raised his eyes to the starry skies. "I hope so, Judith— I hope so."

Ivy's death had an even greater impact on Patterson's life than he realized. Years of hatred and mistrust—not to mention insecurity, and a loathing of white women—had deteriorated and finally crumbled, leaving the man empty, vulnerable to the pains and passions of the heart, yet filled with the inner strength to face a world he had previously been afraid to approach. He understood none of this as he stood in the moonlight holding tightly to Judith's hand.

Judith's thoughts were just as intricate as Patterson's. The inborn distrust, and contempt, for persons of lower condition than herself had vanished, leaving in its wake a confidence in herself as an independent person; she knew now that she could endure danger and hardship and emerge the stronger for it, and perhaps even a little humble.

She regretted that Ivy would not be with her to share the new pleasures and excitement she was finding in life itself. Then it dawned on her that she was finally experiencing, for the first time, what Ivy had been aware of throughout her entire life. She hugged her abdomen lovingly, swaying gently, as if she were rocking her unborn child. "Ivy, darling," she whispered, "a new life is coming, growing stronger every day. If it is a girl, I will name her after you. I love you, Ivy."

She moved against Patterson, laying her head against his chest. Patterson instinctively put his arm around her, drawing her close. Susan, approaching in the darkness, halted midstride at the sight of the embracing couple silhouetted against the lighter skyline. She turned quietly and slipped back to the cabin. She felt alone and bewildered and, for the first time in her life, unsure of herself.

Patterson and Judith found the whole Pettigrew clan in the cabin when they returned from the grave.

The children watched the woodsman through shy, scared eyes.

362

Their feelings had not changed toward the tall, soft-spoken man. They were awed by him and had been since that first day he had brought the women down off the hill. And they knew that he had killed Jake Baylor and almost killed Jack, and they had been deathly afraid of the Baylors.

They had watched in scared silence when Patterson scalped the dead Indians and tacked their hair and ears to the smokehouse wall.

And, being children, the boys had gone off to play games of "scalp the Indian," arguing over who was to be the Indian, while the girls had gone to the necessary house and cried because they were afraid of the woodsman, afraid he would cut off their long hair with his razor-sharp hunter's knife.

Understandably, then, they viewed Patterson as somewhat of a threat to their secure little world. It would be years later, when they were old enough to understand, that they would brag of knowing him. However, on that November night, in 1755, Patterson was naught but a tall stranger, a woodsman, whom their mothers spoke highly of, and whom their grandparents adored.

"Morgan," said the old man, taking Patterson's hand and shaking it firmly, "I wish you and the lasses would change your minds and stay here with us. My boys will come in one of these days . . . they'll be wantin' to thank you for all you've done."

Patterson smiled. "You tell your sons to be a mite more careful about the company they keep. The French and Hurons aren't our kind of people."

"Aw, they'll turn them French and Hurons aloose one of these days, when they're tired of playin' with 'em," said Mrs. Pettigrew, laughing. "But we would be pleased to have you and the girls stay on for the winter, if'n you was so minded."

Patterson shook his head. He had never felt as close to having a white mother as he had with Mrs. Pettigrew, and he did not know how to respond. He longed to reach out and take her in his arms and hug her close—but he didn't.

"Mrs. Pettigrew," he said, "I shall remember your kindness as long as I live . . . it has meant a lot to me, ma'am."

"Well, my, my," said the old woman. "Ain't we the formal one tonight!" She threw her arms around Patterson and hugged him. "You are a fine man, Morgan Patterson," she whispered, close to tears. Then she turned to Judith and drew her near. "You must be careful, child. You have a long way to travel—and there be more than just yourself to think of. I love you, child."

She kissed Judith lightly on the cheek. Judith stared at the woman, her lower lip trembling.

She embraced Mrs. Pettigrew tightly. "I love you too, Mrs. Pettigrew. You are as fine a woman as I ever knew." She could not understand the change in herself. Six months ago she would not have touched a woman of Mrs. Pettigrew's class; yet, here, now, she was sorry to be leaving her, and she would have died had she not had a chance to kiss the old lady goodbye. She astounded herself even more when she ran to the old man and hugged him. "You take care of them 'damn old eyes' that are as good as they ever were," she said, clinging to him tightly.

"Missy," he said softly, "when you get back to civilization, don't you forget us, just 'cause you'll be sportin' around in fine carriages and such."

"I'll never forget you! None of you!" she cried as she turned to the folk assembled in the one-room cabin. They moved on her then, kissing her and hugging her until her heart fairly swelled with natural affection, a feeling so new to her she burst into tears.

"Well," said Mrs. Pettigrew to Susan, as the girl lifted her musket from the corner where it had stood since the battle of Pettigrew station, as they had started referring to it, "I suppose we'll never see you again?"

"I suppose not," replied the girl, checking the priming.

"You mad at me...or the world?" snapped the old woman. "Land sakes, child! We may never see one another again..."

Susan pressed the old woman close and laid her soft cheek against Mrs. Pettigrew's wrinkled brow.

"That's why I can't say anything, ma'am. I don't like goodbyes—they're so final."

"Susan," said Mrs. Pettigrew, hugging the girl affectionately, "I ain't got many years left on this old earth, but you'll be with me till they lay me out! And that's the only thing that's final."

Susan kissed the old lady's brow. "Then someday I'll see you in heaven, Mrs. Pettigrew."

"I'll be waitin' on you, child."

Susan moved to the old man and looked deep into his eyes. "I don't suppose you would let a tavern wench kiss you, would you?"

"No," said Mr. Pettigrew slowly, "but I would be right perturbed if as fine a lass as I ever knowed didn't kiss me 'bye."

Susan kissed the old man softly and hugged him close. "You was my favorite, you know," he whispered as he squeezed her hand.

"I know," she smiled, "and you are my second favorite."

He laughed silently and nodded his head. "I figured that when you come off the hill . . . Take care, girl, and keep your head about you. He's a family man; he just don't know it yet."

Susan smiled sadly, her eyes resting on Judith. "Yes, Mr. Pettigrew, he is a family man."

21

"Sir," said the orderly, standing at attention just inside the log-walled office of field-commissioned Major James Southhampton.

"This gentleman says he must have a word with you . . . says it's important, sir."

Southhampton looked up from the letters he was writing and scowled at the man. "What in bloody hell do you want? I'm a busy man!"

Jack Baylor swallowed hard, cowed by Southhampton's arrogance.

"Speak up, damn you, I haven't got all day!" snarled Southhampton.

"Yes, sir," said Baylor quickly. "It's about your fiancée, Miss Judith Cornwallace, sir."

"She's dead."

"No, sir, she ain't."

A distinct quiet settled over the room, causing the man even more discomfort.

"Perhaps you'd better explain yourself."

"Well, sir," stammered Baylor, "she's alive, or was the last time I seen her . . . but she's crazy, sir."

"What do you mean, she's crazy?" Southhampton raised up in his chair, threateningly. "Speak up, you bloody bastard. What do you mean, she's crazy?"

"Yes, sir!" cried Baylor, wringing his hands and wishing that he had kept his mouth shut, had not even come to Fort Cumberland. "She's crazy as a loon...and has a scar from here to here—awful scar, sir." He ran his finger from his hairline to his eyebrow.

Southhampton visualized a hideous scar marring Judith's beautiful face and he cringed. God! What she must look like! And to think, he was still engaged to her; betrothed to a woman he would be ashamed of in public. Southhampton's face paled at the thought.

"You said she was alive the last time you saw her? That sounds as if you think something might have happened to her since then—speak up man—tell me what you know, or I'll have the hide off your arse!"

"They was expected to be hit by Indians, sir. Patterson said—"

"Patterson!" Southhampton rose out of the chair and stared at the man.

"Why, yes, sir," said Baylor. "Patterson brought the women in...three of them, sir."

"Three of them?" Southhampton's eyes widened even more. He couldn't believe that Patterson had even located Judith and Ivy, much less kept them alive all these past months, and had saved another woman too! Incredible!

And then it hit him: they would know. All of them would know how he had fled under fire. For months he had dreaded the pointed finger of some survivor of the Battle of the Wilderness. But nothing had happened, and gradually his fear had eased, and he had even begun dreaming up noble reasons for all that he had done in those terrible hours, until his craven cowering had been transformed in his mind to leadership.

Damn that Patterson, he thought. He knows I was going to organize the retreat; knows I was out hunting Judith...but he'll twist it all and make me look dishonorable!

"What about the Indians?" he demanded so curtly that Baylor flinched.

"He said they would attack—he was sure of it. Him and old man Pettigrew built pens for the stock...some of it was my stock," he lied, "and they was preparin' to defend the place." He shifted nervously and cleared his throat. "Me and Jake didn't much believe him though."

"Who is Jake?" Southhampton was angry. He pounded the

desktop with his clenched fist, causing the inkwell and quill to rattle.

Baylor was scared out of his wits. He had intended to inform the major that Judith was alive and to beg a halfpenny for a cup of ale. He had not expected an interrogation; was not prepared for the endless questions that Southhampton shouted at him. He was so rattled that he blurted out the story of Ivy's rape and Patterson's part in the killing of Jake.

Southhampton smiled and eyed the man with fresh interest. "So you lay with Ivy. Well, well." He laughed and leaned across the desk. "Was she good? Did you make her beg? Tell me, man! I've waited months for her to get what she deserved... months!"

Baylor shifted his feet, and smiled fearfully at the glaring officer.

"Well, sir," he mumbled uneasily, "we brought a lot of blood out of her. We never thought a nigger serving maid would... be unbroken... but she was. She was a fighter, she was. She damn near killed my brother with a little pearl-handled knife, but that never stopped us none. She begged and begged, but that never stopped us neither!"

Southhampton gripped the edge of his desk, his knuckles white with strain. "I would like to have seen it! Ivy dragged down, to grovel in the dirt with scum! Lord, how I would like to have been there to hear her scream."

Baylor flinched at the word *scum*, but he forced a grin as Southhampton eyed him with a thin smile.

"What happened next? Tell me all of it... every detail."

Baylor cleared his throat, and shifted his bare feet. "Well, sir, Patterson slipped up on us afore we knowed it... he killed Jake without a by-your-leave... just killed him dead."

"He did, did he?" Southhampton's eyes danced.

"Yes, sir." Baylor breathed easier, encouraged by the major's obvious joy in the fact that he and his brother had raped the servant girl. He started the story from the beginning and told it to its sordid finish, including the massacre of his family. Southhampton sat back in his wingchair and listened with interest up to the point where Baylor and his family left the clearing. He was bored by the rest of the story, but his face showed nothing as he watched Baylor through half-closed eyes.

When Baylor had finished, Southhampton remained still for several moments. His expressionless eyes so fiercely bore into the man that Baylor again cursed himself for a fool.

"You said Judith was insane. Do you know what made her that way?"

"We never was told . . . but my ma'am said she was getting some better. Me and Jake weren't round her none . . . we ain't never been around crazy folk afore . . . we didn't go near her!"

"What do you mean she was getting some better?"

"My ma'am said she was about to get over the crazies—said she was actin' right natural. That was just 'fore me and Jake took Ivy to the woods."

"Did she see what you did to Ivy? Was she there?"

"I don't rightly remember, sir . . . I believe she were."

Southhampton smiled with satisfaction. He hoped that Judith had witnessed Ivy's rape and ruin with her own eyes—it was time she learned that life is something more than a beautiful woman's whim. Yes, she needed a lesson, such as the devastation of her noble sister's virtue.

Of course, he decided, if she were insane as Baylor said, then she had probably seen the real world and couldn't handle it. Yes, he thought, she had very likely been deprived of a meal or two, or some such foolishness, and had gone berserk. But the scar? That part of the story bothered him. He had already lost interest in Judith before Braddock had evacuated Alexandria. She had been beautiful then. God! If she were scarred and ugly, he wouldn't want her to touch him—couldn't bear her disfigured face near him. He scowled. Damn Patterson for saving her! Judith should never have come back . . . she should be dead . . . and he should be free of her.

Now everything was changed. Southhampton sprang to his feet and paced the room, lost in thought. His whole future was teetering on the brink of disaster, and Patterson was the force that could bring it plummeting down.

"Ames!" he said gruffly to the aide still at attention. "Take this man to the sutler's and buy him a round or two of grog."

"Yes, sir." Ames caught Baylor by the shoulder and turned him toward the door.

"Baylor," said Southhampton, "it would be unwise on your

part if you mouthed a word of what was said here. Do you understand?"

"I'll keep my mouth shut, major," assured Baylor.

Southhampton nodded and resumed his pacing.

By the time the sun burned away the frost on November 16, 1755, Patterson and the women were several miles beyond the clearing, having traveled quickly, making the most of the predawn light when movement is most difficult to distinguish. Patterson felt good; the forest affected him like that. He glanced at the women. They were holding up well under the pace he had set. He signaled for a rest stop and the two girls sank to the ground, grateful for the chance to catch their breath.

They ate sparingly of the parched corn and drank even more carefully from the gourd canteen Mr. Pettigrew had thoughtfully supplied. Patterson thought about the Pettigrew family and smiled to himself. The old man had drawn him aside just before their leavetaking and had quietly, but earnestly, tried to persuade him to stay.

"Morgan," he had said, "the family would be pleased if you would settle here with us. You could move into John's cabin and we would all pitch in and help you make it into a home."

Patterson had remained silent, so the old man continued, knowing even as he spoke the words that he was fighting a losing proposition.

"We will bring in another brace of oxen, and in a few years have real farms running from one end of the valley to the other." Pettigrew had extended his arm in a sweeping motion that encompassed the glen, and his eyes had taken on a distant gleam as he shared with the woodsman his lifelong ambition.

Patterson could visualize the old man's dreams, could see the valley himself: homes, church, school, animals grazing peacefully on the hillside, children swinging on grapevines, wives ringing the dinner bell to call their men in from the field. Aye, he could see it plainly—but he knew that such a dream was a long way from reality. And should it become reality, even in his lifetime, it would be after the Indians were annihilated and the French were pushed off the North American continent. Of this he was sure.

The old man's shoulders had sagged. He was reluctant to admit defeat, but he had exhausted his argument. He looked at Patterson through bushy brows and said simply, "The girl loves you, son. Make a home for her here with us." Patterson knew it could be that simple. Just declare a marriage and set up housekeeping. It was done every day on the frontier.

Patterson had quietly declined. "Mr. Pettigrew, your offer overwhelms me, sir, but I have no desire to take a wife." He was thankful for the morning darkness that hid his flaming face. Much as his thinking had changed toward women, he still had a shyness about him that would remain with him all his life.

"Mr. Pettigrew," he had said, changing the subject, "why don't you folks pack up and come to Fort Cumberland with us? The frontier won't be safe until the French are beaten."

The old man had shaken his head. "No, Morgan. I reckon we'll wait on the boys. Why, they wouldn't know how to act if'n they was to come home and find the hearth cold." He held a quilt out. "Take this with you. It's been frostin' for nigh on a week now. You'll be needin' something to keep them girls warm."

"Mr. Pettigrew, that's a kind offer. Judith will be needing it, I suppose. Susan, she's tougher and can get along. But you keep it. You need it more than we..."

"Not with a son gone," Pettigrew had finished quietly.

The memory caused Patterson to study the girls as he munched his handful of corn. They were entirely different people, not only in looks but in thought and belief as well. Patterson frowned, recalling the exact words of the old man: "The girl loves you, son. Make a home for her here with us." Which did he mean? And why was the old man so sure one would consent to marry him? His eyes narrowed as he considered the two young women. Perhaps the old man had taken a worse lick in the head than was first thought.

"Are you all right, Morgan?" Judith asked.

Caught by surprise, Patterson's face flushed. "'Tis nothing," he said. "Just a memory."

Judith nodded with uncertain understanding and resumed eating.

Susan finished her corn and wiped her hands with a hank of dried grass. She lay back, watching the shadows play in and out of the last bronze foliage of the oaks, as the morning sun rose above the hills. She had a great desire just to close her eyes and sleep forever.

She had slept none at all the night before and very little the one before that. Insensibly, she drifted into a troubled slumber filled with visions of Ivy, savage Indians, and burning buildings. She was relieved when Patterson gently shook her awake.

"Bad dream?" he asked. She nodded and wearily got to her feet, feeling worse than before.

They traveled without incident the remainder of the day, camping that night in a densely wooded area where a small well-concealed fire could be laid with a minimum of risk. They sat by the flames, eating cold cornbread and roasted venison supplied by the Pettigrews. They ate little but savored every bite, still remembering the hungry days before they had accidentally stumbled onto the Pettigrew settlement. Taking stock of their provisions, Patterson estimated that, barring delays or unnecessary overeating, they carried enough food for a week, perhaps enough to take them to Fort Cumberland.

Susan stared into the fire even though Patterson had many times cautioned her against such foolishness. But at that particular moment night blindness was the least of her worries, for as she gazed into the flames, she was questioning God's reasons for sparing her life instead of Ivy's. Why, Ivy had never knowingly hurt anyone, or anything in her entire life. She did not deserve to die. Yet Ivy was dead. And Susan was alive. Why? Ivy had taken Fontaine's life, true, but only because Patterson was in danger. Yet Ivy was gone, lying cold and alone beneath the hard earth. No, not alone—Fontaine was there.

"Why, Lord?" she whispered. "Why could it not have been me? I have broken thy commandments; I have sinned; I have lusted heatedly and wantonly for a man not my husband; indeed, who never will be. I have caused the death of a fine young lad, whose only mistake in life was to fall in love with me—I am terrible." Guilt cloaked her like a shroud as her eyes reflected the dancing light of the flames.

She thought of Bobby Green and the others who had died in the wilderness...died trying to protect her—and other women who were camp followers.

She remembered Sir Peter Halket, who was Bobby Green's commander. He was magnificent, brandishing his sword toward the enemy while ordering his men to stand firm even though they were dropping like flies under the effective fire of the French and Indians. Halket and his four hundred soldiers had been ordered to guard the baggage, wagons, and teamsters, as well as the women. So Susan, along with a score of other women, had witnessed the fall of Halket's command. She remembered it plainly. Always would.

William Shirley and Halket sat their mounts in conversation. It appeared that Halket had ordered Shirley to take a detachment to aid Braddock's withering defenses. But even while they talked, Shirley was knocked from the saddle, shot through the head, and as Halket leaned from his horse extending a hand toward his fallen comrade, several bullets tore into his body, killing him instantly. Young Lieutenant Halket rushed to his father's side, but a ball caught him squarely in the back of the head, and he fell lifeless across the body of his father. Then it was absolute pandemonium, with Indians darting in and out of the stranded wagons, screeching, screaming, killing . . . Susan blinked her eyes to rid herself of the memory, but Bobby Green kept slipping into her thoughts, smiling and laughing, full of love for life. She buried her face in her hands and wept silently for Bobby Green—for the young life he had wasted on her, for the love she had been unable to return. She cried for the both of them, Bobby and herself. Him, because he had loved her enough to die for her—knowing she only regarded him as a friend; herself, because she understood that devotion—that unselfish willingness to give one's life to protect a beloved. She understood.

The next morning, not a mile from where they had bivouacked, they discovered the remains of a large campsite. Patterson gingerly kicked the coals with his bare foot. Still hot. His eyes automatically penetrated the deep gloom about them, searching, prying, overlooking nothing—he hoped. He turned to the campsite, letting his gaze travel in a slow circle around the warm ashes. Judging by the indented depressions in the leaves, he estimated that fifteen Indians had lain like the spokes of a wheel with the fire as the hub. With that in mind, that the enemy was quite near, they drifted soundlessly back into the underbrush, slowed their pace, and became more watchful.

Southhampton came to a decision. He sent the orderly to fetch Baylor.

"Master Baylor," he said, after dismissing Ames, "I take it, sir, that you are not overly fond of Patterson."

"I never said that, major." Baylor's eyes widened with apprehension.

"Come, come, my man." said Southhampton, "he killed your brother...do not play coy with me, I'm in no humor for games."

"I ain't got no use for Patterson, sir. I hope the Indians killed him."

Southhampton pursed his lips, then smiled to himself.

"I can understand your feelings, Baylor. I know Patterson to be a scoundrel and cutthroat."

"Well," said Baylor sheepishly, "I ain't heard nobody ever say nothin' like that about him, sir. Truth is, most folk here at Cumberland talks kindly of him."

"Have you been running your bloody mouth?" shouted Southhampton.

"No, sir, I sure ain't," said Baylor quickly. "But afore I talked to you, I said somethin' in the pub about Patterson and them women he was bringin' in—'twas afore I talked to you, sir."

Southhampton took a deep breath and exhaled through his teeth.

"All right, there's no harm done. Do you have any notion when he will arrive?"

"Why I ain't for sure he will arrive, sir!"

"If he does, damn it, when will it be?"

"I don't rightly know, major."

Southhampton glared at the man. He would have enjoyed having Baylor flogged.

"Baylor," he said, "I have a proposition for you because I believe what you said about your brother and your family—that Patterson is responsible for their deaths. I believe you should have justice."

"How's that, major? How can I get justice? Patterson will kill me sure, if he ever sees me again."

Southhampton was disgusted. Baylor was a coward—and cowards were dangerous—especially if you had to depend on them—they would leave you in a clutch. His face reddened as the truth struck home.

"Sir," he said thinly to Baylor, "I would protect a man that had courage enough to kill his brother's murderer. I would make certain that no harm befell him—and . . . that he might profit by the deed."

Baylor stared at Southhampton, unable to speak.

Southhampton drew a heavy pistol from his desk drawer. "This would probably work very well, don't you think?"

"They would hang me, major. These folks here at Cumberland think a lot o' Morgan Patterson."

"They won't hang you," assured Southhampton. "I will see to it that nothing happens to you—you have my word."

They talked and schemed the evening away, and when Baylor left, carrying the pistol and a small purse of gold, Southhampton settled himself in his wingchair and smiled smugly.

Everything was working out just fine. Patterson would be dead, thereby eliminating any public misunderstanding of Southhampton's courage in battle.

As for Judith, he would have to marry her, no matter how ugly she was. But once she became his wife, she would be honor-bound to protect his good name and reputation for her family's sake.

He cursed loudly then, thinking of a marriage with Judith. But he had no other choice, if he wished to protect his reputation.

For the next two days, Patterson and the women worked their way steadily toward Fort Cumberland, elated to be making such good progress. Still, they avoided the known trails, and although time was lost, and traveling more difficult, Patterson felt that they were doing the right thing. The Baylors had used the warrior's path; the easy traveling had cost them their lives.

He did not dwell on the Baylors' misfortune, however, for he knew well that the frontier dealt a swift and deadly vengeance on those who ventured unprepared into its midst. Only the strongest survived and perhaps that was as it should be. Patterson moved the girls steadily in a roundabout way toward Fort Cumberland, crossing creeks, climbing hills, picking his way through thorns and briars.

They camped in late afternoon, for the days were short and winter was in the air.

A small fire would be kindled in a secluded spot and kept burning all night. The three would huddle close together, entwining arms and legs, pressing their bodies close to absorb as much heat as possible from their companions. Even so, they would awaken from a restless night, shivering, numb, and swollen from cold.

Their thin clothing did little to turn the penetrating wind that had sprung up the past week, so they kept moving in hopes that their blood would circulate more freely and fight against the chilling in their bones.

It was by far the most miserable existence the girls had yet suffered, but they knew that each step was carrying them nearer their destination, so they endured.

A week elapsed before he noticed the change in Susan. She had become withdrawn, preferring her own solitude when they camped. She appeared to be combating a problem known only to herself. She still conversed occasionally with Judith, but was distant and quiet when approached by Patterson. He had no notion why.

Judith, of course, was delighted to have Patterson more or less to herself, and wasted no time in letting him know it. He found himself enjoying her obvious pleasure as they lay huddled together under the cold starlit sky while waiting for the weariness of a grueling day to close their tired eyes. And, when he awoke to find her clutching his hand in the night, her body pressed against his, he was pleased.

At the same time, however, Susan troubled him. He had awakened to find her staring at him with unfathomable despair in her dark eyes. Yet when she realized he was awake, she had quickly feigned sleep. He had pondered the problem for a long while before putting it from his mind. Tomorrow they should reach Fort Cumberland. From there, each would go his separate way; their paths would probably never cross again. But even as he angrily pushed Susan's strange actions aside, he knew that she would never be completely out of his thoughts.

22

The Indian's intense, black eyes gauged the movements of the three white people as they struggled through the maze of giant timbers in the hollow some three hundred yards below. He could tell by their movements that the man and two women were exhausted.They would be easy prey. He turned to his companions and grinned slyly, his teeth starkly white in his black and green-painted face. He watched the whites a moment longer, howled a bloodcurdling scream, and dashed down the slope.

"Run for it," shouted Patterson as he dropped to one knee and steadied his rifle on the lead Indian.

"I said get the hell out of here!" he shouted angrily as the women hesitated.

"Run to where?" cried Susan. "We don't even know which way to go!"

"Straight ahead!" snapped the woodsman, taking a finer bead on the Indian, still two hundred yards away.

Patterson held his breath and squeezed the trigger. The Indian pitched headlong into a shallow ravine and lay still.

"Goddamn you!" shouted Patterson when the women didn't move. "I don't want to have to watch over you two; I don't want you here. Now do as I say!"

Susan and Judith burst into headlong flight down the wooded hillside. When they were a hundred yards beyond Patterson, Susan pulled up abruptly and flipped the frizzen forward on the lock. She scowled: the flash pan was empty.

"Are you going back?" said Judith, who had run a bit farther before stopping and was making her way to where Susan stood fumbling with her powderhorn.

"Yes, I'm going back," said the girl, not taking her eyes off the pan as she filled it with fresh powder.

"Then I'm going with you," said Judith flatly.

Susan snapped the frizzen closed. "No, you're not," she said calmly. "The fort cannot be very far ahead—you're going to the fort."

Judith shook her head. "I'm going back with you, Susan—I love him, too."

"If you love him," snapped the girl, "then save his child. You owe him that much; it should be first and uppermost in your mind, Judith!"

"You know about the baby?"

Susan nodded.

"You hate me, don't you?" said Judith. "You must! For you have loved him from the very first..."

Susan stared at Judith. "I hated you and Morgan both...until a few minutes ago. But knowing that he could be killed...changes things."

She touched Judith's arm. "The only thing that I hate at this particular moment is the fact that you are carrying his child and not I." She smiled into Judith's pale eyes.

The report of Patterson's rifle as it echoed through the forest cut the girl's words short.

"I will send help as quickly as I can, Susan," promised Judith, hugging Susan close. "Be careful."

Susan pushed the girl into a stumbling run, and watched as she disappeared in the direction of the fort. Then, she too was running, her buckskin dress riding high above her knees. This time, however, she was running to defend the man she loved; the man she had loved since that first day she had seen him leaning on his long rifle at Fort Cumberland, not a mile from where he stood now, months later, fighting for her life.

She scrambled over the deadfall where he had taken his stand and slid in beside him.

"I told you to get the goddamned hell out of here!"

Susan wiped the sweat out of her eyes, took a deep breath, and raised her musket.

"I'll leave when you leave," she said, letting her pent-up breath slip through her teeth as she squeezed the trigger.

"Damn it, you missed!" he exploded.

"Well, damn it, I tried!" she returned, with equal vexation as she commenced reloading.

"Stop that cussing!" He raised his rifle and fired again.

"I'll curse if I damn well please!" she retorted, dropping a ball down the barrel and pounding the buttplate of the musket against the ground to seat the bullet.

He too ran a ball down the barrel of his rifle. Then he drove the ramrod into the ground by his foot for easy access should he need it in a hurry.

"What's come over you, Susan, to make you talk like that?" he said, firing again.

"What difference does it make, Morgan?" She sighted on a naked savage who was bounding toward her with his tomahawk raised. "You never cared a damn how I talked or acted . . . you made that plain"—she fired and the Indian hit the earth and skidded several feet on the hard ground before coming to a halt against the roots of a great oak tree—"every chance you got!" She eyed the Indian with satisfaction.

She jerked the stopper out of her powderhorn and calmly poured a charge into the palm of her hand.

"I've always cared how you talked and acted," retorted Patterson as his rifle bucked against his shoulder.

"And I hate you for it!" she cried as she brought her musket up again. But she could not find a target anywhere; the Indians had disappeared.

"Where are they?" She searched the hillside frantically.

"They'll break again shortly," replied Patterson as he too scrutinized the empty forest.

Nothing moved.

"Do you hate me for treating you like a lady?" he asked.

"You know I'm no lady!" she said stonily. "I'm an indentured serving girl . . . no better than a slave—you said so yourself. You—you mock me with your false respect."

"'Tis not false respect that I feel for you, Susan. And you are so a lady—you were born that way." He looked hard at her. "Now get the hell out of here while you've still got the chance."

"I'll leave when you leave."

"Damn it, Susan, I didn't bring you all this distance just so you could die here, within hollerin' distance of the fort."

"If you have chosen to die here, Morgan," she said firmly, "then I shall die with you."

"Are you crazy? That don't make any sense at all."

"I'm not crazy, Morgan!"

She was in such a passionate rage that he withdrew his attention from the forest, where sure death awaited his slightest mistake, and stared into her furious face. "And it would make sense," she continued, almost in tears, "if you weren't so damn hardheaded and stupid. I love you, Morgan...I always have!"

Patterson stared at her dumbstruck. "You don't know what you are saying," he said at last. "How could you care for me after...all that has gone before?"

"Because I am crazy, I guess. But I love you—no matter what went before...or will go after."

She looked away then, embarrassed, and made pretense of studying the surrounding forest.

"You've got to get out of here, Susan!" said Patterson angrily, through his tightly clenched teeth. "I want you out of harm's way. I don't want to lose you—not now...not now, damn it...*I love you too!* I just did not have sense enough to know it."

She turned to him, stunned, never believing she would hear such words; loving them, and loving him with all her heart.

She would have kissed him then, so gloriously happy was she. But then her face fell, and with it the most beautiful moment of her life.

"Morgan," she said, dropping her gaze, "before you say anything more, there's something you should have been told days ago..."

The sentries of Fort Cumberland rushed the frantic woman into Southhampton's quarters.

The major raised his head and studied the disheveled, dirty ragamuffin who stood before him.

"My God!"

She could hardly speak. And the sentries on either side of her were obliged to lend a shoulder to keep her knees from buckling.

"James," she gasped, fighting for control, barely succeeding, "send a detachment of troops...Susan and Morgan need help...immediately! They can't hold out much longer!"

"Calm down," said Southhampton. "I cannot understand what you are saying."

Judith took a deep breath and attempted to relax.

"Susan and Patterson need help," she said raggedly. "Indians have attacked...send a detachment of soldiers...please!"

She began to reel, then steadied herself.

"Really, Judith," replied Southhampton after a pause, while the girl regained her strength. "You surely do not expect me to send my regulars into the wilderness...after what happened to Braddock?"

"I don't give a damn what happened to Braddock!" cried the girl. "Susan and Morgan are out there alone...fighting for their lives—that's what I give a damn about—and only that!"

Southhampton blanched under Judith's onslaught, but he was not about to give aid to the one man in the world who could ruin him.

"'Tis out of the question to send half my troops into the forest to fight Indians. Why, if they were defeated, who would protect the fort? Who would keep the savages from coming here?"

He eyed Judith irritably. "I cannot do it, Judith. I'm sorry."

"Can't do it?" said the girl almost calmly. "Or won't do it?"

Southhampton rose to his feet and leaned on the desk.

"Really, Judith," he said, smiling "'tis plain you are overwrought. Can I offer you a brandy?"

Judith shook free of the sentries and bolted through the door. A crowd had gathered in front of the small office, curious about the sudden appearance of the haggard woman they had seen race into the fort.

Judith looked out over the crowd. "Are there any Williamsburg men here?"

"Aye," came the reply, "they's a bunch of us still here."

Judith took a deep breath. "Susan Spencer and Morgan Patterson are fighting Indians about a mile from here." She pointed

381

toward the forest. "They are going to die if someone doesn't help them."

Tears filled her eyes then, for the men were gone—running for their weapons, pouring through the gate, heading toward the dark and forbidding forest without a thought for their own safety.

"Judith is going to have a baby," said Susan in a cool voice. Patterson sucked in his breath. "A baby?"

Susan nodded, afraid to speak; afraid to trust her self-control, for she knew that she would fall to pieces should she even so much as whisper a single syllable. She stood there staring at the gray pallor beneath the wind-burned tan of his face; and she both loved and hated him at that moment.

Patterson, knowing what he did about DeBeaujue and Judith, made a hasty presumption. "Forgive me, Susan, for speaking of such an intimate subject to a lady, but there is something that needs telling, here and now."

"Say it, Morgan." She hoped it would somehow release Morgan from the responsibility of being a gentleman and therefore honor-bound to make Judith an "honest woman."

Patterson looked steadily at her. "DeBeaujue raped Judith the day Fontaine killed him."

Susan's face turned deathly white. "Oh, God!"

Patterson went on. "We have no way of knowing how many times he . . . was with her. We'll never know, but we do know she was gone all day long, the day Fontaine . . . found them."

That DeBeaujue had been with Judith only for a short while, minutes actually, was unknown to Patterson. And that the Frenchman had avoided pregnancy no one would have guessed or believed.

"I feel just awful for Judith, Morgan, because she doesn't even suspect that DeBeaujue came near her, much less that he actually . . . did it to her."

Susan paused, then blushed with embarrassment. "This will sound terrible, Morgan," she said, avoiding his eyes, "but I'm glad that Judith is not going to have your baby. I want to boast that privilege—me, and only me!"

"Susan," said Patterson quickly as he lined up his sights on a savage crawling through the brush toward them, "if God should grant me another chance to love you, to have you, it will be forever. Will you marry me, Susan?" He pulled the trigger. The Indian flattened out on the ground and lay there quivering in death.

Susan coolly raised her musket and fired as a dozen more painted savages broke from concealment and bounded toward the breastworks where the man and woman worked furiously to reload their empty weapons.

Susan's eyes were bright with wonder as she hastily poured a powder charge down the barrel. The woodsman was hers! She, Susan Spencer, the girl who thought she didn't stand a chance, was the woman he cast aside his years of hatred, fear, and prejudice, to love; to want to marry.

Susan's smile was so unbelievably beautiful that Patterson's breath caught in his throat as he awaited her answer.

"Oh, Morgan!" she cried, "with all my heart, yes!"

But God had apparently granted Patterson his last favor, for Susan never finished her statement. He heard the sickening sound of lead tearing into live flesh; and he heard Susan's intake of breath, but he was not allowed even the small consolation of catching her when she fell.

He spun, firing point-blank at the howling savage who had jumped the deadfall where Susan lay and was drawing his scalping knife to take the prize he had earned. The Indian was slammed backward against the logs of the breastwork before pitching headlong over Susan's still form. His face was shot away.

Then other bronze bodies were vaulting the deadfall, firing their muskets, screaming with victory—and Patterson, standing astride the body of the girl, clubbed viciously with his Joel Ferree rifle—his most cherished possession—until the stock splintered and the gun came apart in his hands. He used the barrel then, wielding it with the strength of a man gone berserk—smashing, destroying, and laying waste all that came near.

He heard the roar of muskets, but the sound meant nothing. That painted bodies fell around him; that the victory chants of the Indians had ceased—they meant nothing. Nor did the Indian, trying valiantly to withdraw while carrying a wounded comrade— Patterson burst the roached head without thought, then killed the man's wounded comrade with equal vengeance.

Then it was over. White men were streaming past, screaming

like savages; using their muskets, hatchets, and knives as deftly as any Indian who ever drew breath.

But Patterson didn't see them; didn't hear them; didn't smell the smoke from their guns—he was beyond feeling.

He cast his bloody rifle barrel aside and dropped to his knees beside Susan's body. He gently gathered her to him and rocked silently back and forth.

A hush fell over the wilderness. The Indians had vanished into the darkness of the virgin timber.

The men that Judith had sent from the fort stopped their grisly task of scalping their victims to stand in silence, gaping in awe at the woodsman and the girl he held so tenderly.

They were hardened to the ways of the frontier, those men in buckskins, homespun, and leggin's, yet they were a caring people, an understanding people, perhaps even a romantic people. They removed their tricorns, widebrims, and, yes, even a coonskin here and there, for they were also a respecting people—when respect was due.

23

Every eye in Fort Cumberland was turned toward the forest. They watched as Patterson stepped through the dense foliage into the sunlight of the open terrain. He stood there a moment, gazing at the wooden palisades, the safe blockhouses, the threatening gun ports, the Union Jack fluttering magnificently in the breeze.

He held Susan Spencer's limp form in his arms. Her slender hands dangled toward the earth, her head was dropped back, the colorless lips barely parted in a lovely smile.

"So close," whispered Patterson. "We were so very close, Susan."

They watched his slow, agonizing progress as he carried the girl away from the wilderness. They gathered around him as he made his way through the gate, a hushed crowd of men, women, and children. They gazed in morbid fascination at the beautiful young woman he carried so lovingly. Their eyes moved over her body, to rest on the small, dingy red hole in her deerskin dress just above the swell of her left breast.

"Thank the Lord," someone said, "she died instantly; the pretty young thing did not suffer..."

Suffer! thought Patterson, and he laughed aloud; the sound rang hollow through the haze that made his head light and his steps heavy as he pushed his way through the gaping crowd. She has suffered more than any of you could imagine... could ever imagine!

Southhampton, standing with Judith on the parapet above the milling crowd, watched the scene through narrowed eyes. He was looking for a man, a fellow conspirator, and he was rewarded for his vigilance. Baylor was making his way through the mass of spectators, straight for Patterson.

Southhampton smiled knowingly, engrossed in the drama that was unfolding below him.

"Oh, my God," cried Judith, tears streaming down her cheeks. "Please, Lord, do not let Susan be dead—please, Lord!"

She flung Southhampton's hand aside, and bounded down the wooden steps of the parapet two at a time.

Southhampton let her go—more important events were in the making.

He observed with keen interest as Baylor stood, with legs spread, directly in Patterson's path.

Baylor's belligerent eyes met those of the woodsman for one brief instant before he raised Southhampton's pistol and fired into Patterson's chest.

Time stood still. The assembled folk could not absorb it all as they gazed unbelievingly at Patterson's prone form lying in the dust with the body of the girl clutched to him. Even then he was protecting her.

Then pandemonium erupted. Baylor threw the pistol aside and broke through the crowd, to race maniacally toward the elevated walkway where the major—and safety—awaited.

Judith had already leaped from the steps and was racing toward the crowd that surrounded Patterson and Susan when she heard the shot. Ice crept into her. She knew that something ghastly had happened, and she quickened her pace.

Baylor broke through the mass of petrified people, and barged straight at her. His eyes were wide with fear, yet Judith knew the man did not see her, was unaware of her presence. He would have run her down had she not spun aside.

Then the screaming crowd surged around her, jamming her backward in their stampede toward the murderer. She shoved, pushed, and fought her way through the berserk tide until, finally, they let her through.

Her breath caught as she kneeled beside Susan's body. She

smoothed the girl's tangled hair from across her face; a face that even in death retained a measure of living beauty.

She bent and kissed Susan's pale lips.

Fearfully, she laid her ear against Patterson's bloody chest. Her face turned even more ashen, and tears sprang to her eyes.

"Surgeon!" she cried as tears welled in stricken eyes and slid down her cheeks. "Somebody get the surgeon...for God's sake, somebody find the doctor!"

"I am here, miss!" said the physician as he knelt beside her and grasped Patterson's wrist.

"Well, damn!" he exclaimed. "He has a pulse. Incredible!"

The doctor motioned toward a squad of redcoated soldiers who were running to join the crowd that had captured Baylor.

"Here! You men, over here on the double. Take this man to my quarters, and you two"—he pointed at two soldiers trying to slip into the crowd—"you might as well take the body of this poor child there also."

Four men lifted Patterson and carried him toward a row of log buildings that were erected against the palisade that ringed the fort.

Two others, those attempting to slip away, begrudgingly caught Susan's wrists and began dragging her toward the cabin.

"Damn you!" cried Judith, falling upon them with flailing arms and fists. "Be gentle with her—damn you to hell! She is a lady!"

Her eyes blazed with fury as the soldiers gathered Susan gently into their arms.

"A thousand pardons, ma'am," said one, frightened almost witless, for he knew Judith to be the major's betrothed, and he did not want to have to answer to Southhampton.

They carried Susan with gentle reverence even after they had moved inside the log house, away from Judith's scathing eyes.

The howling mob had captured Baylor at the steps. Heavy hands dragged him off the rough, wooden stairway and spun him into the crowd.

Thumbs gouged at his eyes; fingernails ripped at his flesh; fists smashed into his face—every person there seemed bent on delivering a blow in one form or another.

Strong arms hefted him above the heads of the mob, and he was carried to the entrance way of the fort, where a rope had already been cast over the crosspole of the main gate.

The crowd, still holding the man high, turned toward the parapet.

Southhampton stood tall and straight, arms folded across his chest, and stared at the spectacle below him.

They waited.

Southhampton's eyes narrowed. "Hang him."

Shouts from a mob gone mad with righteous lust—or perhaps justice—drowned out the cries for mercy that the terrified man screamed at Southhampton.

They slid the noose around his neck and, without further ado, hoisted his kicking, quivering body aloft.

Judith and the surgeon rushed into the cabin as the soldiers laid the two bloody bodies on a rough oak table.

"Get the lass's body off of there!" shouted the doctor as he hastily fumbled in a trunk for his instruments.

The soldiers, angered because they were missing the excitement outside, dropped the girl roughly to the hard-packed earthen floor.

"This man's shot all to pieces," murmured the doctor as he eyed Patterson's ravaged body. "Waste of time to try and save him."

Her face white with fear, Judith caught the man's arm and spun him toward her. "Your job is to get the bullets out of him! Now, damn you, go to work!"

"I'm moving as fast as I can, madam!"

Judith spun to the table and clutched Patterson's cold hand. "He can't die! I won't let him die, and damn you, you'll not let him die!"

"Man's shot to bloody hell, mistress," the doctor said, bending over Patterson's chest, "and cursing me is not likely to change that!"

"I'm sorry," bristled Judith, striving to control a desperation that was fast giving way to panic, "but he's all I have left. Ivy's gone, Susan's gone...Oh, God!"

"You men!" shouted the surgeon at the soldiers idling near the door."Get this woman out of here! Christ almighty, she's in my goddamned way!"

"I'm staying!" warned Judith, angrily. "You'll need a helper..." She eyed him hotly. "I'm not leaving!"

"Can you stand the sight of blood?" he demanded as he pushed the probe into Patterson's body.

"Yes!" she lied, remembering she had fainted the first time she had seen Patterson's blood.

"All right, get over here and hold this box of instruments. When I ask for something, give it to me in a hurry!"

Judith sprang to the doctor's side and grabbed the wooden case.

The front of Judith's dress was soaked in blood when the surgeon raised his head and smiled into her pale face.

"That's the last one." He dropped a fragment of lead to the floor. "Now, if we can stanch the bleeding, he may have a chance."

He moved around the table and stumbled over Susan's lifeless form.

"Damn!" he shouted, clutching the table for support. "Damn soldiers can't do anything right."

He flashed an angry glance at the door. The soldiers had slipped away.

"Damn!" he said again. "Give me a hand, will you . . . Judith, you said you name was?"

Judith nodded and stepped slowly around the table. She did not want to look into Susan's dead face, afraid she would not be strong enough to endure the pain of it.

"Help me move her close to the wall," he instructed, lifting Susan's feet. Together they eased the girl aside.

Tears welled in Judith's eyes as she took Susan's bloodless hands. "I had grown so fond of you," she whispered. "And I lied that day at the clearing. I would be proud to be like you—just like you."

Judith's head sagged to Susan's breast and she held the girl for a long moment.

The doctor glanced up as she joined him at the table where he was applying compresses to Patterson's wounds.

"What's the matter with your face?"

"Why, nothing!" she said defensively.

"Have you cut yourself? There's blood all over your cheek."

Judith drew her fingers across her face and stared at the bright-red blood.

"'Tis Susan's blood. I laid my cheek against her chest—"

"Dead people don't bleed!" muttered the doctor as he stormed past Judith and dropped to Susan's side. He put his ear against her chest.

Judith rustled toward him.

"Goddamn it!" he bellowed, "stay still. I've got to hear!"

Judith watched with mounting excitement as he pressed his ear harder against Susan's breast. "Dear Lord," she prayed, but the surgeon cut the prayer short.

"Fetch that lamp to me...Now!"

She sprinted around the table and scooped up the lamp.

"Careful!" he cried, eyeing her savagely. "I've got to use that flame!"

He snatched the lamp from her and cast the globe aside, shattering it into a thousand tinkling pieces as it exploded against the wall

Quickly, he held the flame to Susan's pale lips.

Judith held her breath, afraid to breathe as her eyes fastened on the flickering light.

The doctor's shoulders slumped. "She's dead," he said wearily.

Then the room burst into incandescence, almost bedlam, as the ecstatic young woman sprang for the case of instruments while the doctor began cutting away Susan's hunting frock. The flame had swayed.

"You sound disappointed, James." Judith frowned wearily at her fiancé, studying his face while she sat on his office cot. "He may die any moment—would that please you?"

Southhampton was uncomfortable under Judith's direct gaze. He fingered the collar of his tunic, a collar that had suddenly become too tight.

"Nay, my dear," he said uneasily, "I am merely surprised. I cannot understand how a man could take a blast at point-blank range and survive..."

"Morgan is strong-willed. Otherwise he would have died instantly from the shock of it."

Southhampton studied the young woman before him. She was a stranger, not at all like the elegant, sophisticated, spoiled young lady who had followed him halfway around the world.

Her dress was bloodsoaked from the hours she had spent with the doctor. Her legs were cut and scratched, bleeding in places. The exposed portion of her body, weathered from long days in the wilderness, still bore a deep-tinted bronze burnt in by the hot summer sun.

But her face was the part most changed: she was no longer beautiful in a young and petulant way—her face was fine-chiseled, the eyes straightforward and honest, the mouth full and soft with a touch of sadness about it. The provocative pout was gone, replaced by something even more appealing—sensuality.

But that scar! It spoiled the whole effect—or did it? In a way, it was fascinating. It spoke of mystery and adventure; it caused a man to fantasize about how it got there, and to wonder what other terrible things she had endured.

She would be the darling of society in London with such a disfigurement; the men would be unable to keep their eyes off her!

As he watched her his blood raced. She had such a wanton, commanding allure about her.

"My dear," he said, shaken, "I do believe you are showing pity for a man we detest. Have you forgotten that he is nothing but an American woods hunter—a serf, really?"

Judith laughed hollowly. "A serf? He has never been, nor will he ever be a serf."

"Whatever he is," said Southhampton pointedly, "must I remind you—"

"There is no need to remind me of anything, James," she retorted.

He studied her, not knowing how to interpret that. She made him nervous, the way she searched him. Did she know? Was she aware that he had left her and Ivy...surely not!

But he wasn't sure—she had been with Patterson for a number of weeks—months, actually. Perhaps he had told her the truth. The thought caused Southhampton to sweat profusely, even though the room was chilly.

"You look as though you could use a spot of sherry, my dear," he said, changing the subject. "Yes, I think a drink is just what we need."

He fished two glasses and a bottle from a cupboard.

"This should perk you right up—you've probably not tasted anything this good since..."

Judith smiled. "Since leaving here in June?"

"Has it been that long?"

"Yes, James. It has been that long."

He fingered his collar and eyed her defensively. "I intended to come for you, you know? But I had to warn the column...I sent Patterson for you. He was to bring you to me."

Judith's eyes met his. "Patterson did not come from the direction of the column." She smiled then. "But he did fulfill his obligation, didn't he? For I am here."

"He took his own bloody good time in doing it!" snarled Southhampton.

"Yes, he did, didn't he?" She sipped her drink.

She knows! The thought staggered him. She's making sport of me because she knows.

"Well, really Judith," he blustered, "I do have more obligation to the army than to a—"

"A camp follower?"

"That is not what I intended to say!"

"But that's exactly what I was, is it not?"

"What in bloody hell are you speaking of? You know you were my fiancée!"

"Were, James?"

"I mean...you confuse me, my dear; of course you are my fiancée."

He edged close and embraced her, but it was without feeling. Her whole appearance appalled him—her filthy clothing and dirty skin, her cropped hair—and that thin blue scar on her face.

She felt him stiffen as he touched her. She turned away in embarrassment, for she could read the loathing that filled his face. She had not seen that look in Patterson's eyes, or Susan's, or Ivy's—or in any of the folk at Pettigrew station. For the first time she felt disfigured and undesirable.

Southhampton saw it. He smiled thinly. He had discovered a vulnerability that could be used to his advantage. He pressed that advantage testingly. "Have you seen yourself in a looking glass, my dear?"

Her eyes became guarded.

"No...I haven't. Only in clear pools of water." She laughed shakily. "I really have no great desire to see myself...I know I look horrible."

"Well, regardless of your appearance, you are still my betrothed. I shall do right by you."

He patted her hand patronizingly. "You must bathe and change into something more suitable. I'll make the arrangements."

She sat there after he was gone and slowly traced the indent of the scar with her fingertips. She wanted to see it, to know how dreadful the ridged flesh was, but she was afraid.

Still, Southhampton would favor her with marriage. He had said so. For that she was grateful. But he hated to look at her, or touch her. He had made that plain.

She wondered how he would react when he found that she was with child. She sighed, refusing to consider the eventuality. She would cross that bridge later.

"A great improvement!" He took her hand as she entered his quarters and led her to a couch in front of the open hearth, where a bright cheerful fire burned. "A bath, a new dress, my, my. What a difference!"

She smiled absently and curtsied.

"It is nice of you to say so, James."

Her hair had been brushed until it shone, but it was still ragged, with small unkempt curls clinging tightly to her scalp.

He handed her a glass of sherry.

"You look... very healthy, Judith. The wilderness must have agreed with you."

She smiled, thinking of the starvation days; of the nights she had cried herself to sleep because her stomach ached from hunger.

"If it weren't for that scar, you would be ravishingly beautiful—how did you get it?"

She set her untouched glass on the arm of the couch.

"I... really can't remember, James. Must we talk about it?"

"Well, my dear, I think explanations are in order. After all, you have been gone for a long while."

He faced her on the couch, eyeing her closely.

"You have changed, Judith."

"Yes," she said, "I have changed." More than he would ever know, she thought.

She told him the whole story, then, omitting nothing except the fact that she had slept with Patterson, and that portion of her life that was blocked from her memory.

He listened with feigned interest after it became clear that she knew nothing of his conduct in the Battle of the Wilderness. He was relieved. His thoughts drifted to the frigate that was to carry him to England. It was to sail within the month. Patterson would probably be dead by then, but even if he lived, Southhampton would be gone before the woodsman would be well enought to start spreading lies.

He took a long pull on his drink. Things were working out very well—very well indeed. He would take Judith and embark before Patterson was even aware that they were no longer here. Then Patterson could say what he would, but without Judith to corroborate his story, not one soul with authority would listen.

"We sail for England in less than a month," he said abruptly. "I've been recalled to give eyewitness account of Braddock's blundering stupidity. A most unworthy general, Braddock!"

Judith was stunned. "Less than a month? We sail in less than a month!"

"Aye, but we evacuate this God-forsaken place in two weeks!"

He took her hand, and discovered it was rough. A scowl twisted his handsome face.

Judith blushed and withdrew her hand. There is nothing about me that pleases him, she thought, and nothing about him that pleases me! The last portion of her reflection came as a shock.

She realized then that in spite of all that had happened, all the cruelty and death and destruction, she had grown to love the colonies and their freedom. She admired the people who struggled to civilize a wilderness. She also discovered, much to her amazement, that she had no desire to return to England or live her former life as a simpering lady, with afternoon teas, extravagant parties, and finely embroidered flattery intended to entice one, married or not, to the lover's couch. She knew that she could never live with such hypocrisy. Yet such a life was what Southhampton was offering should she become his wife. No! she thought, I will not go!

Southhampton slipped his arm around her and drew her close. It was not a tender gesture that expressed caring; it was the weak protocol of an English dandy, and she found herself despising him for it.

Then she thought of Patterson, of the strength of his arms when he carried her from the awful sight of John Pettigrew. She blushed as she remembered, in detail, that same night when he had taken her virginity. His arms had been tender and caressing then.

"James," she said without emotion, "there is something I must tell you. I am expecting a child."

His face flamed into rage and he bounded up from the couch, pacing wildly.

"You are nothing but a whore, Judith! An unfaithful whore!" he shouted. "And to think! I have lived for the day when we could be together again!"

"I am sorry, James."

"Sorry! You don't know the meaning of the word! You lie with the scum of the earth—wallow with filth—and say you're sorry?"

Her eyes flashed angrily. "I wanted him to."

"No doubt you did, Judith," he sneered. "It was probably all he ever wanted from you in the first place."

"No, James," she said, "you're wrong. All he ever wanted was to get Susan, Ivy, and me safely back here, to you. He would have given his life for that, and almost did, several times."

"And you gave youself to him!" He clenched his teeth, his face thunderous. "You're my betrothed, yet never would you give me aught but a kiss—and you were stingy with those!"

She hid her face, for he had spoken the truth. She had never given herself to James, not totally, body and soul, as she had to Patterson.

"I love him, James," she said quietly, praying for him to understand, sure that he would not. "I did not intend to fall in love with him—I hated him at first. I fought him every step of the way because I thought he was beneath me . . . of lower class. I could feel myself changing . . . but I did not want to change. I kept watching him, looking for a weakness, for a sign that would prove that he was less than he appeared to be."

Southhampton glared at her sarcastically. "And what did he appear to be?"

"He was courageous," she answered softly. "He was kind, in his own fashion; he was thoughtful, and even considerate—"

"The perfect man!"

"No, James," she said wearily. "He's mean, dangerous, and sometimes without feeling. But he was always there when I needed him—no matter the cost."

She took Southhampton's hand and held it tenderly, her eyes begging him to understand. "I tried to be faithful to you . . . I prayed for you to come for me . . . even after I knew I would give myself to him. I prayed that you would come and take me away before that happened."

"Don't try and lay the blame for your infidelity on me! If you had been true in your desire to remain chaste, nothing could have persuaded you otherwise."

"I suppose that is true." She sighed wearily and dropped his hand.

"I tried hard to hate him, James, but I ended up loving him instead."

Southhampton was outraged by Judith's unadorned, plain-spoken confession. Worse, he could barely look into her honest, guileless eyes. He hated her for what she had told him, for unburdening her soul. He hated her for being pregnant—not because she was with child, but because another man had carnal knowledge of her, and he had not. He hated her because she had not surrendered to his passionate advances months ago—before coming to America. And he hated her most of all for betraying him.

On further reflection he hated her also because she was the key to whatever future might be awaiting him, a future that depended on her position and dowry.

As he mentally reviewed the account of her life in the wilderness, fear gnawed at his insides. He had lost her as surely as Braddock had lost his battle in the wilderness.

"Do I perceive," he said at last, "that you intend to break your pledge to me?"

"I am asking to be released from that pledge, James." She said it with a certain amount of shame, for she held her word in high regard. Yet her love for Patterson was the strongest emotion she had ever experienced, surpassing even her reluctance to break a promise given a thousand years ago, when she was a child.

"Someday," she said with a faraway light in her eyes, "if he will have me, I will marry him, James."

"And if he won't marry you?"

"Then I will go to him without marriage."

Southhampton laughed without mirth, his face twisted with the bitter realization that he was not, nor had he ever been, man enough to stoke the fire of passion that burned beyond control in Judith's breast for Patterson.

His cunning mind began to race. He watched Judith closely, studying her every move, her every gesture, as she spoke of her love for Patterson. He realized that he could use it. She had a weakness after all. He felt elated. His fear of her vanished and he pushed his face close to hers.

"I respected you, your virginity," he complained. "I respected your position, your family . . . your pleas to wait until we were wed. Yet you would follow trash like Morgan Patterson wherever he would lead; allow yourself to be disgraced, shamed, and despised by society."

"I no longer care what society says about me, James. I will go where he goes . . . if he will allow it."

"Allow it!" he cried. "Of course he would allow it—his own personal whore!"

She slapped him then, an openhanded blow that left his eyes watering.

He grasped her shoulders and shook her violently.

"You will not marry him," he whined. "I promise you, you will not marry him!"

"And what will you do to stop it? What can you do! I am not afraid of you." She laughed lightly, then moved to the hearth.

Southhampton strode to her side, and his voice was almost a purr. "I will do nothing to you, my dear . . . but if Patterson lives, it will be for the hangman's rope."

He laughed as Judith's eyes widened.

"He has done nothing that would possibly warrant a hanging—nothing!" Then she laughed also, at the ridiculousness of his threat.

"You are mistaken, my love," said Southhampton, enjoying his power. He noted with satisfaction that she was afraid, not for her own well-being, but for that of a loved one. He laughed wickedly as he eyed her.

"He has done nothing to be hanged for," Judith replied quietly, "so proceed with whatever you intend."

"You are so silly, my dear. I shall bring charges against him...and I shall hang him."

"What charges? You speak like an idiot, James. Whatever it is you are planning, 'tis folly. You cannot be serious."

"I am serious, and well you know it!" He massaged her shoulder.

She cringed under his touch, her eyes big.

"He deserted the army on the field of battle," said Southhampton as he traced the outline of her sensual lips with his forefinger.

"You sent him to look for Ivy and me."

"I know that and you know that—but it would be your word against mine." He smiled knowingly. "Whom would they believe? An officer of His Majesty's Royal Army—or a woman carrying the bastard child of the man she would defend?"

Judith's face turned ashen, but she remained silent.

"He abducted two young ladies of quality to hold for ransom. You said so yourself when you told of being captured by the Shawnee."

"But he did that to keep the French from taking us to Canada!" Her voice broke.

"He will have to prove that in court, my dear."

"You vile bastard!" she hissed. The fear that turned her knees to water suddenly became an all-consuming anger.

Southhampton laughed at her outburst. He was delighted that her only defense was to ridicule him. "He murdered a white man, in cold blood, for raping a nigger, and everyone knows that raping niggers is not a killing offense. It happens every day here in the colonies."

"He killed Baylor for raping my sister!" spat Judith. "You *know* that Ivy was my sister."

Southhampton chuckled. "You have made sure that that particular knowledge was never made public, Judith—who would believe you?"

"You son-of-a-bitch!" said the girl, but the fight had gone out of her and the words carried no conviction.

Southhampton shrugged. "He will hang, Judith, unless..."

"Unless what?"

"Unless you do exactly as I say. Unless you agree to become my wife. Unless you forget Patterson completely and return to England with me."

Judith's shoulders sagged. She looked old, old and tired. "Damn you, James!" Hot tears flowed down her cheeks. She wiped them with the back of her hand. "I will do as you wish...anything...I have no choice. But hear me well, James, I'll hate you till the day I die!"

"Not if you want the father of your bastard child to live, my dear."

He drew Judith to him. He would test his newly acquired control of her, for like most weaklings who suddenly find themselves in a position of power, he would not be satisfied until he had brought those of stronger character to their knees.

He kissed her hard, then cruelly, angered that she did not respond, that her lips were unyielding and cold. His anger turned to rage as he pictured her in Patterson's arms, giving herself with wild abandon.

He caught the fabric of her borrowed dress and ripped it to her waist. She attempted to cover her nakedness but he slapped her hands aside and gazed at her exposed breasts.

"Pregnancy has improved your bust, my dear."

Judith's face flushed but she made no further move to cover herself.

Southhampton clawed at the remainder of the dress until it lay in shreds about her ankles. He eyed her exquisite contours with fascination, his eyes resting on the slight bulge of her abdomen.

"You are quite beautiful, Judith, except for your face. I suppose one can overlook that flaw if one tries hard enough."

Judith trembled. Then she mustered dignity: "James, I...would prefer that you did not subject me to such immodesty. I have agreed to become your wife. I implore you as an officer and a gentleman not to do this shameful act until we are wed."

"You are hardly a virgin, Judith. So my conduct as an officer and a gentleman does not apply." The last was muffled as he pulled his shirt over his head and flung it carelessly across the couch. "I shall feel no remorse whatsoever for having soiled you. Patterson can boast that conquest, madam."

Judith felt trapped.

She loved Patterson, truly loved him. She had no desire for

another man; not Southhampton, not anyone. She was Patterson's woman; she would be faithful to him. She buried her face in her hands. Faithfulness was beyond her control. Her life was beyond her control. Only Patterson's life remained in her grasp. She could submit to Southhampton and save Patterson, or she could—could do what? She dropped her hands and moved to the couch.

"Then fuck me, James."

Tears of hopeless resignation streamed down her face. "Go on, damn you—do it!"

"My dear," he said as he bore her back onto the couch, "I am offering you a way out of disgrace—the only way that is open to you."

Then, without preliminaries, and without the slightest care about her, or her condition, he took her.

24

Patterson opened his eyes, but the sunlight streaming through the open door of the log room caused him to squinch them shut again in pain. He reopened them slowly. It was not the first time he had wakened, nor the second. As in those previous moments of awareness, she was there. Sometimes she had been asleep, worn-looking even in slumber; other times she had gazed upon him with anxious worry. But he had been conscious only briefly then.

This time, however, she was observing him through wide, clear eyes—there were no tears as before. She had even cried in her sleep. He wondered if she knew that.

She moved to his cot and knelt beside it.

"How do you feel?"

He remained silent so long that she became distraught, afraid that he would not answer at all.

"I'm alive."

"It was a silly question," she said quickly.

He shifted on the cot.

"No! Don't move! The surgeon says you are to lie still." She eyed him with concern, fearful that he would insist on sitting up, or attempt to stand. If he did that, it could be fatal. But he lay back without protest and closed his eyes.

"How long have I been here?"

"For a while."

"How long?"

"Almost two weeks, Morgan." She absently pushed her short, ragged curls off her forehead, then immediately regretted the impulse, for he was studying her. She looked away to hide the scar.

Southhampton had taught her that trick in the past two weeks, having convinced her that she was so hideous that men found her appalling to look upon.

"Have they come . . . for Susan?"

"Yes, Morgan." She said after a long pause. "They came a week ago."

She wished he would cry out, or scream, or curse, instead of just lying there staring at the wall.

She wanted to hold him, to cry with him. But she knew his code of manhood would never permit tears.

"I tried to get her to leave," he was saying. "But she just laughed at me . . . I begged her to save herself . . . " He closed his eyes. "I tried to protect her . . . after she fell."

"You did all you could, Morgan." Judith's eyes were brimming. "Do you not know that you were shot three times before our men got to you?"

"I never felt it." His voice was so hollow and lost that it cut Judith to the marrow.

Oh, Morgan, she pleaded silently, her heart breaking for him, for the agony he was enduring because of Susan. Let me come into you . . . to suffer with you. Need me, Morgan. Just this once, reach out to me . . . *please, Morgan.*

But Patterson, who could read the invisible signs of the forest. missed the desperate longing, need, and love that filled Judith's face.

"Was it Baylor that I saw just before . . . did he shoot me?"

"Yes, Morgan," she said brokenly, "he shot you. They hanged him from the crosspole."

"I can't, in truth, say I'm sorry."

Judith said nothing. Instead, she dipped her hand into the pocket she wore outside her petticoats and withdrew a painted porcelain miniature of a lovely Canadian girl.

"Fontaine gave this to you. Do you remember?"

Patterson eyed the ruined locket. "He said it would bring me luck."

"It did more than that, Morgan," she said, caressing the locket lovingly. "It saved your life. It deflected the ball...caused it to flatten out...so that it only went a little way into your chest."

He reached for the pendant but a searing pain ran the length of his body and his hand dropped heavily. Judith was ashen as she raised the hem of her dress and blotted his perspiring forehead.

"You must lie still, Morgan. The wounds are barely closed...please."

"I shall try and bear that in mind."

Judith gently raised his head and placed the gold chain of the locket around his neck.

"The locket is almost all shot away, Morgan. But the memory is still beautiful."

She bowed her head. I'm like that locket, she thought, damaged beyond repair. My beauty is gone, my pride is gone, my body feels unclean since Southhampton has touched it, my—my whole life has fallen to pieces, shattered like this beautiful porcelain locket.

A tear forced its way between her long lashes. Then her face softened and she gently wrapped her arms about her abdomen: the new life growing there had kicked. She hugged her stomach tightly, as if to rock the unborn child and savor the great surge of love it brought her. It was the only thing she had left to live for—the only thing Southhampton could not destroy—the only thing she would not let him destroy.

Almost as if Patterson had been reading her mind he spoke. "You, Ivy, and Susan remind me of this locket, Judith. Two precious pieces have been shot away—gone forever. The one remaining fragment..." he took her hand and held it tightly, "although it is marred, it is still lovely beyond compare."

Judith looked deep into his eyes. He was surprised by the open, honest tears of gratitude that brimmed in hers and it embarrassed him that she should be grateful to him. He did not understand that those scant syllables, uttered with no underlying intention, had quickened her pulse and prompted a catch in her breath. Those few words, spoken earnestly, had, for the first time in days, made her feel like a woman, a wonderfully beautiful woman.

She took a deep breath.

"Go to sleep, Morgan. You must rest.'

He squeezed her hand and closed his eyes. In moments, his breathing was regular; he was asleep.

She watched him for several minutes, her face an avenue to her soul. Then she gently kissed his lips and laid her wet cheek against his dry, feverish one.

Perhaps, somewhere deep in the chambers of his heart, he heard her soft-spoken words, for he stirred restlessly as she whispered into his ear: "I shall be gone when you awaken, my darling. They will tell you that I have left with my husband to return to England. For you see, Morgan . . . Southhampton and I were married over a week ago. You are safe, my love. In a few minutes we shall be gone . . . and his need to kill you shall leave with us."

Judith laid her head in the hollow of his shoulder and wept.

"I lied to you, my darling," she said finally, the words muffled against his shoulder. "I lied to you about Susan—because I . . . wanted to be alone with you . . . to have you to myself—but . . . she was still there. Even though you thought she was dead—she still came between us."

Her tears trickled down his chest as she forced herself to go on. "She lies in the adjoining cabin, Morgan. So close to death that it is frightening. But . . . she . . . " Judith cried openly then, her body convulsed with quiet sobs. "She cries out to you, saying over and over, 'Yes! Oh, yes, Morgan! I'll gladly marry you.'"

Judith tenderly pressed her lips against his.

"I love you too, Morgan," she whispered. "I'll love you forever . . . and some day, some way, I will see you again . . . I promise you."

Epilogue

Morgan Patterson and Susan Marie Spencer were married in the Bruton Parish Church in Williamsburg, Virginia. Five months had passed since the day they were shot.

The small chapel could not accommodate all the people who gathered there to wish the young couple well.

As Susan marched slowly down the aisle, leaning heavily on the arm of her stepfather, her eyes met Patterson's. She faltered, ever so briefly, as her heart filled with wild, abandoned joy. For she had seen that hard, brittle gaze that had hounded him since childhood change to soft glowing pride that only love could achieve.

And, indeed, Morgan Patterson was proud as he watched her approach on Rothchild's firm arm. For, frail as she was, she had found the love and courage and strength she needed to make that short walk to the altar.

His heart pounded wildly as he gazed into her luminous dark eyes, for she was stunningly beautiful—and she was his. She always had been.

On May 11, 1756, Judith Ann Cornwallace Southhampton gave birth to an eight-pound boy.

She christened the child Richard Morgan in honor of her father and, with Southhampton being the only one knowing the truth, the baby's real father.

If Ivy had been present, her soft gray eyes would have misted as Judith held the newborn to her exposed breast—and if someone had inquired about the strange expression in Judith's eyes as the child's tiny lips sought and found her nipple, they would have wondered at

405

her slow answer as she recalled Ivy saying, so many hundreds of years before: "Ladies of quality do not breast-feed their babies. But you just may be the exception to the rule, Judith."

And not a few would have wondered at the tears shed by Ivy's mother as her fingers caressed the strange little pearl-handled dagger that Judith insisted upon placing in the child's cradle.

Brevet Major James Southhampton received a hero's welcome in London. With much pomp and ceremony, he accepted as his just due, for valor on the field of battle at Braddock's defeat, the permanent rank of major of His Majesty's Royal British Regular Army.

His elation over his undeserved promotion collapsed, however, as he lay in the arms of his redheaded London mistress, and cried on her freckled shoulder. For again he thought of the strong little blackhaired boy, that constant reminder of the one man who knew the truth about Southhampton; who knew his promotion was nothing but a farce, with the English ministry being the butt-end of the joke. And it almost drove Southhampton mad knowing that Patterson had won out in the end. For as the ship that returned Southhampton and Judith to England moved out of the Alexandria harbor, Judith had cast aside the submissive cloak she had worn at Fort Cumberland, and told Southhampton in a dulcet voice that if he ever touched her again, she would kill him.

He showed his London mistress the tiny scar below his chin where Judith had cut him with a dagger when he had laughed in her face and started to strike her. The woman patted him on his white cheek and told him what a fine officer and gentleman he was.

He snuggled his head into the cleft between her overlarge breasts and pitied himself—over his mistreatment by a wife who hated him, a wife so absorbed with her child that the rest of the world didn't exist. Then he consoled himself with the thought that Patterson, having known Judith intimately—possessing even this day her undying love—would never see the child of that love.

But in that, too, Southhampton was mistaken, for Patterson would see his son, after the boy was a man full-grown. He would see him over the sights of his rifle when two mighty nations came to blows.